Return To The Heartland

JUNE MASTERS BACHER

HARVEST HOUSE PUBLISHERS
Eugene, Oregon 97402

Scripture quotations are taken from the King James Version of the Bible.

RETURN TO THE HEARTLAND

Copyright © 1993 by Harvest House Publishers
Eugene, Oregon 97402

Bacher, June Masters.
    Return to the heartland / by June Masters Bacher.
       p.   cm. — (The Heartland heritage series ; bk. 4)
    ISBN 1-56507-094-1
    I. Title.   II. Series: Bacher, June Masters. Heartland
heritage series ; bk. 4.
PS3552.A257R48   1993   93-10101
813'.54—dc20   CIP

Printed in the United States of America.

Contents

My candle burns at both ends;
It will not last the night;
But, oh, my foes, and, oh, my friends—
It gives a lovely light.

—Edna St. Vincent Millay

I must have the hands of Martha:
  Hands that scrub and cook and sew—
I can have the heart of Mary
  While I do these things, you know;
Though my hands are in the dishpan,
  This soul of mine can soar
And in thoughts sublime and lofty
  Go right up to heaven's door.

I must cook, oh endless dinners,
  For dear ones have to eat;
But my soul need not be cooking—
  It can sit at Jesus's feet!
Help me, God, while doing duties
  Against which my soul rebels,
Meekly still to peel potatoes,
  But not to grovel in the shells.

Grant me, God, 'mid things prosaic,
  Ere to choose the better part;
Grant that while I must be a "Martha,"
  I can have a "Mary" heart.

—Author Unknown

(Clipped and contributed by Marvel Harrington to her "Auntie Rae's" cookbook, *Stretching to Survive*, post-World War II.)

The steps of faith fall on the seeming void, but find the rock beneath.

—Whittier

Ye have not chosen me, but I have chosen you, and ordained you, that ye should go and bring forth fruit . . . that whatsoever ye shall ask of the Father in my name, he may give it you. These things I command you, that ye love one another.

—John 15:16,17

*This story is dedicated
to our extended family of
all creeds, codes, and colors
as we march together
in search of
God's eternal* truth*!*

I love you all,

Shalom!

Now faith is the substance of things hoped for, the evidence of things not seen.

—Hebrews 11:1

1

Uses of Adversity

"Sweet are the uses of adversity..."

Marvel Harrington tried to recall the rest of the Shakespearean quote, the phrase seeming important somehow. She had suffered too much during her 20 years to allow another layer of pain. And, since words were her craft, they rose to serve now against hurt like a shield. *Another loss... another loss... it could not be. It simply could not be.* A shadow fell across her desk. Someone at her window, some very distant part of her reminded her of the surroundings. Oh yes: Office of Price Administration. Trying to smile, she moved woodenly to greet the man.

The applicant for a gasoline rationing book looked at her appreciatively, a wry grin playing around his eyes and mouth. "We've met. And I must say you look beautiful—even more so than before."

Marvel blushed. "Beautiful" was not a word she would select in describing herself. Such adjectives distressed rather than pleased her. "Thank you," she said primly without meeting his gaze. Then, from force of habit, she concentrated on the papers spread before her.

How good that Americans were, according to foreign analysts, consumed by the work ethic. Certainly it was therapeutic on this particular day, Marvel realized during the challenging process of transferring ownership of the recently acquired automobile, preparing the standard "A" coupon book for gasoline, witnessing the signature of this giant by the name of Carl Atkins for "B" coupons for transportation to work, and explaining that the

10

Board would decide on the B's. Throughout the efficient procedure, she had felt both exhilarated—and dead. Behind it all lay the morals instilled within her by the parents to whom she was committed (and morals included no familiarities with strangers), along with a sense of guilt at the news delivered by her coworker. Both feelings ran deep. And yet, God was setting her universe back in orbit—through work.

Carl Atkins, whom Marvel would not see again, did not press his point—if he had one, which was improbable. Certainly this young lady gave no indication of interest. He thanked her and walked into the late-afternoon sunshine, now seeping with golden promise of a colorful sunset. She would miss the ocean when they went home to the heartland....

As the door closed behind him, the red-haired Marie cut off the hopes of the next applicant in line. "Let one of the volunteers replace you—and follow me to the ladies' room, hear?"

Marvel heard. Feeling her heartbeat ripple beneath the light lavender of her blouse, she followed—needing to hear details her usually bouncy but now frighteningly sober friend had to tell, while dreading it with all her being. But she could handle it. God would see to that.

"He's right, y'know—man at the window yonderways. You've got it all—high cheekbones, generous mouth—and you stay so slim and still look feminine. Yep! And if ever you need that confirmed, all you gotta do is look into any man's eyes. They'll tell you you're beautiful. Forgot already how he—uh, the *captain* looked at you? *Marvel!* You haven't heard a word, have you?"

Marie's voice broke as her freckled hand fished in the oversize purse for a handkerchief. Automatically, Marvel handed the other girl her own. The smile she managed was prompted by Marie's foolish question. How could she respond to someone who talked nonstop as if in a one-woman show? In spite of her own shock, Marvel's heart went out to Marie. After all, Captain Philip Prinz had been the pilot from whom her "Johnny" was tailgunner.

Philip!

"Tell me more," Marvel said softly, daring add nothing else.

"It was awful— Oh, how can God let these things happen? *How?*"

Marvel inhaled deeply, remembering Marie's fledgling faith. "I can't answer that. Just—just know He took no joy in it. But for now," she exhaled raggedly, "tell me about Philip. *Please* do."

In a quick flashback, she recalled warm, sun-filled, near-carefree mornings and balmy evenings spent with Philip on the beach. He was filling the void within her empty heart in an almost frightening way. The officer was undeniably attractive, and she was becoming more vulnerable with each day that Titus Smith, her first love, was missing in action. Correction: "Presumed *dead*!"

An emotionally shaken Marie was now fishing for words as she had fished for her kerchief. This time Marvel was unable to help.

If only it had happened some other way, Marie said haltingly. But to be killed right here in maneuvers the men had practiced so many times that they had thrown their rule books away? And by one's *own men*—the same men to whom he had entrusted his life thousands of times up there in those lonely skies? Just one of those crazy nightmarish things that couldn't happen but did—like this whole senseless war! Intelligence—*hah*! Some word for it. What intelligent member of the Air Force would confuse the photography button with the guns to set off fire in case of aerial enemy attack—dogfight, you know? No similarity, except that both the cameras and the guns were located on the wings. The culprit had to be another of those 90-day wonders: You know, go to college a short spell, learn to act *superior*, so he could *be* a "superior office"! Well, there'd be an investigation, you could bet your life. But that wouldn't bring back the captain . . . or stop her Johnny's nightmares. Oh, why did he have to witness the horror with his own eyes? Why, *why*, WHY?

Again Marvel had no answer. She could only repeat the still-elusive Shakespearean quote: "Sweet are the uses of adversity. . . ."

"Bible, I betcha," the plump young war-bride said a little sadly. "I wish I knew more about it. But I promise to learn—"

There was no time to correct the guess. Nothing to be gained by it at this point. Marie, seeming to sense Marvel's own emotional needs for the first time, turned toward her in the confines of the dark little box serving as their "powder room."

"I'm so sorry, honey—*so* sorry. I was afraid you'd think I was buttin' in, so I never asked just what he meant to you—your captain."

How could she explain what she herself did not understand? The entire relationship was confusing, upsetting—and now heartbreaking. If she had said yes to Philip Prinz's proposal, one day she would have been his "dream wife," and now she would be his widow. It was that simple—and that complicated. For by what must have been Mother Nature's idea of a joke, two men were identical twins. As it was, she was twice grieved. She had learned to appreciate Philip for himself: the young man with a promising future who so obviously adored her. He had endeared himself to her for opening his heart and allowing her to glimpse the inner self the rest of the world would never see. But other than feeling the deep sorrow of another person's demise, a someone she could have loved totally perhaps had there been no other man in her life, she only felt a little emptier (or as her cousin Mary Ann would phrase it, "more dead"). Otherwise, the real grief sprang from the unbearable thought: "I have lost Titus again."

Marie's heavy perfume said she had moved closer. "Quick— we hafta go. Why—what kept you from marryin'? *Oh*, he loved you!"

Marvel nodded. "I know—and Philip was wonderful, Marie. Let's say I loved him too much to marry him. I know that sounds strange. But it would have been wrong for us both. We both would have been marrying a dream. And life is real. The war has taught us that cruel lesson. Try to explain to Johnny that his captain had created an image—almost a *graven* image of his 'dream girl' and tried to fit me inside. While I—I—you are right, it *is* late—but I'll try to make *you* understand someday that I still love the man back home. And now—" her voice broke and the lump in her throat made breathing almost impossible, "I—I have lost them both—along with so many others I love."

"I don't get it—I just don't. Let's run for it. I played a part in this. I introduced y'all then up and gave you a *death* notice. I feel awful," she whispered, closing the door behind them. "Adversity's *sweet*?"

"Its uses. God will find a way to use this in His plan."

* * *

The remainder of William Shakespeare's words came back when Marvel attempted a partial explanation to Mary Ann. Mary Ann (who was running as scared as the Southern redhead with whom she, too, worked before marrying Jake, her childhood sweetheart) had as much difficulty in understanding as did the other girl.

"There are countless other references to adversity, I know that. It's just that this felt like *physical* pain, as if I were afflicted by some incurable disease—all boxed in, desperate. The English writer's words kept drumming away at my heart. It all comes back to me now. Oh, this is it, Mary Ann. Want to hear?"

Mary Ann shrugged her shoulders, causing the cascade of raven curls to swirl about her almost sensuously, of which she was so sweetly unaware. "I have a feeling I'm about to, so fire away. That man Shakespeare talked a lot!"

Marvel's blue eyes closed in concentration as she recited the illusive words. "Sweet are the uses of adversity, which, like a toad, though ugly and venomous, wears yet a precious jewel in its head."

"Ugh. Who likes those warty creatures? And *venomous*, I doubt. But comes the dawn! Like in the fairy tales, you had to kiss one of the critters to awaken the prince in case he'd been *bewitched*. So you were taken in by that name: Prinz! You, my sweet cousin (and Mary Ann was laughing—oh, how could she? But her next words would tell)—why, *you* are the one who was bewitched! Now get this straight, once and for all: Titus Smith is alive—*alive*, I tell you!"

Oh how cruel! "Mary Ann, please, we know better. You have only a dried clover to go by—nothing concrete. There's no hope."

No hope. But hope was what Christ gave: the jewel of hope!

2

This One Day

The year was young—younger than springtime. But in California, seasons tend to ignore calendars. The fruit trees, Marvel noted, were decked with rose-pink blossoms. Mother and Auntie Rae would need to apply for their five pounds each of canning sugar early. The yard was ablaze with flowers, and already the family was enjoying every known variety of green vegetables from the joint venture of the victory garden. "Victory garden" it was preordained to be, Daddy said, for this was indeed the year the war would end!

Others tended to agree. At the very moment, a commentator was suggesting national prayer and setting a good example:

> God bless our men and women in uniform in the four corners of the earth...where Old Glory stripes the sky in red-white-and-blue...knowing that where the flag does not yet fly, it is destined to fly soon! And let us not forget those patriotic Americans who serve here on the home front...in the defense plants, in the civilian tracking stations...Red Cross...our president, the commander-in-chief of the armed forces and his aides...our ministers who serve to comfort the bereaved...our lawmakers and our law enforcement officers. And Lord, let us not forget out law-abiding citizens...those who serve by obedience to restrictions without complaint...who do not cheat or hoard. Add to these those who have served in all previous

wars and are now confined to veterans' hospitals. And that group which gave its all: the sons, daughters, fathers, mothers, life-mates—gave them and lost, but won the ultimate. For we beg another chance to prove our worth...to make this our *last* war of aggression.... Give us the courage to face this, our year of victory, a day at a time—and wait upon You....

Yes, a day at a time. "That is what I must do," Marvel whispered. "I will make a list and try, Lord, but first I must, yes, I must honor my father and my mother by sharing myself."

Dale and Snow Harrington were weeding the garden. Looking at the two of them, Marvel felt her throat thicken with affection. Her father's face was so open, so honest, and now (with the aid of California's healing sun rays) he had acquired a becoming tan and looked downright handsome. The added color represented a return of good health—just what dear Dr. Porter had hoped. How ironic that in the awfulness of war Kate Lynn's father himself should be among those who sacrificed his life.

Marvel winced and forced her thoughts back to her parents. Her mother was equally appealing. Her heart-shaped face (of which Marvel's was a "spittin' image," Grandmother always said—not that she could convince the child!) showed absolute trust and adoration each time she looked at the man squatting beside her. The couple had been married a quarter of a century, yet she looked at him now as if she had never seen her husband before. The glowing eyes sang a wedding march, renewed a love so strong it would endure against all odds. And it had!

"Oh hello, pet!" Daddy hauled himself to his feet. "Watch out for this mother of yours—she'll put you to work. Take a look at her. Doesn't she look for all the world like a recruiting officer?"

"More like a farmer." Mother's smile said she did not mind the work-roughened hands whose talented fingers held a bouquet of tender new lettuce, green onions, and crisp orange carrots. "Wilted lettuce tonight for supper—you always liked it, honey," she reminded Marvel."

"Whew!" Daddy mopped his brow. "No preparation—wilted already. It's high time we got going, darling," he added, helping Mother up. "'Heigh ho, heigh ho—it's off to work we go....' But wait. Marvel, I have a feeling you had something you wanted to say—maybe?"

He was right. But she would have preferred to make no issue of Philip's brief entry into and exit out of her life. Yet what alternative remained to plunging in and explaining? She inhaled and began.

"Mother—Daddy—remember the young man I saw several times?"

"Let's see," Mother said, surveying the flowers, "wouldn't the delphinium be nice for the supper table?"

"I thought we were having wilted lettuce," Daddy said with a characteristic twinkle in the Harrington eyes, whose blue caused the delphinium to look faded. "Now your daughter deserves a hearing!"

Snow Harrington pushed a stray butter-colored curl from her damp forehead. "Oh, I'm listening," she said with little-girl innocence. "I can look and listen at the same time. Let's see, honey— which one of the young men?"

"There was only one who called, Mother."

"Oh, the—uh, officer—whose pants were creased just so? I know he was tall," she said thoughtfully, then brightening, "and oh, something else: How nice the top of his head looked when he stooped over to pick up the purse you dropped. It was parted so straight. Of course, I just saw him in the dim light. I haven't met him yet."

And you never will, Mother, Marvel's numbed heart reminded. The conversation was more painful than she had expected. Best get it over.

There had been no time for a proper introduction, Marvel tried to explain in a run-on sentence. A coworker introduced Captain Philip Prinz, but they had not seemed like strangers exactly. At least, they each reminded the other of someone else. War made everything bend laws, violate speed limits. The two of them had to cover a lot of ground in a short time—trying, always trying, to establish a common ground. She learned that there was little. Marvel *loved* music, Philip didn't understand it. Texas was "back home" to her, *rural* life. But Pennsylvania was to Philip what Texas was to her . . . and nix on suburban living. He was "big city"—namely, Philadelphia. She adored her family; he hardly knew his. In fact, his mother was English and lived there. Both thought the war would be over soon—the only real thing they had in common. Philip didn't understand Marvel's conviction that God had a plan for each person He created. Now (she hurried on because of the lump in her throat), Captain Philip Prinz loved travel, adventure, discovering new places, but had no concept of the greatest exploration of all: discovering his place in God's kingdom. He promised to learn... *was* learning...

"It's hard to understand, but in spite of it all, we—well, we came to appreciate each other just for ourselves. It was like we didn't belong, but *did*—like a dream when you're wide awake, not seeing the world around you, just sort of belonging to a new self."

When Marvel stopped for fear of losing control, her father laughed. "Of course, of course!" Then, lifting his arms, he mimed Mother's incomparable manner of playing a violin.

"Dale Harrington, stop that! Stop that this minute, hear? You—why, of all the nerve! You're poking fun at two women who love you—or did once upon a time! We know what you're up to—that you're pretending a wedding march! Let Marvel tell us if he proposed."

Daddy stopped. It was he who saw first that something was wrong. "What is it, baby? Did this—uh, Captain Prinz have no time to propose—things happen too fast, got his orders—"

"All of those," Marvel heard herself saying in a voice she had never heard before, "ex-except—the proposal. He asked me—but—"

Mother sighed in resignation. "Oh Marvel, surely—*surely* you're not clinging to that first love—the boy back home—"

"There will never be another man for me—I know that now. Philip taught me be-before he left." Her pained voice stopped.

"He'll be back, honey," Daddy consoled. And if you change your mind, just give us time to get used to it. Lucky he's in the air—safer than on land or sea, I'd say. Pity the poor Marines, goin' ahead to soften up the enemy. The seas are alive with enemy subs and destroyers." His blue eyes pierced hers. "Did I say something wrong? Wait, Snow!" Daddy called to Mother who had started walking toward the end of the lima-bean row. "I think there's more to the story."

Marvel bit her lip, priming herself to break the news to her parents. It was best that they know. "He's not coming back, Daddy. Phil-Philip is dead." Her voice broke.

"What?" Dale Harrington sprang forward to hold his daughter close in fatherly protection. "Dead? He *can't* be! Didn't he just leave?"

Mother joined them then. "Maybe there's some mistake—"

No mistake, Marvel told them quickly. She had known that less-experienced pilots were undergoing rigorous training at the air base. Philip himself felt the pressure, was often detained, his plans subject to change. Something big. Captain Prinz did not know details and, had he been privy to the nature of what was in progress, he would have been unable to share it.

Something to do with the secret weapon undoubtedly, Daddy guessed, a frown of concern furrowing his brow briefly. The weapon which was designed to end the war. So men at the plant knew, too? Not much—although it was the subject of conjecture. How could anybody know much about it when pieces were assembled at various plants? Here, there, everywhere—nobody knowing what the weapon was or, in the final stages, what its purpose was when it was completed. Marvel shuddered in apprehension, then regained control quickly.

"It was not my intention to upset you," she said quietly. "I only wanted to share as we always have. I will be all right."

"And well you should, baby bear," Daddy said affectionately. Some far part of Marvel noted that his collar was rumpled, his hands soiled, and his eyes tired. And yet, in spite of his concern for his two soft spots, his wife and daughter, there was a look of fulfillment in his face. Dale Harrington loved the feel of soil just as his Snow loved the sight of growing things. Marvel resolved again that nothing—absolutely *nothing* save the will of the Lord—would stand in her way in returning them to the heartland.

Marvel felt her father's work-hardened hands catch in the strands of her hair as he pushed the tawny cloud from her forehead and planted a gentle kiss where the piled-high curls had been. "Have I made mention of how *marvelous* you are—how inspiring—how proud we are?"

"Only one thousand plus one times," she managed to smile, as she reached to touch his hand. "And why shouldn't I be?" Encouraged by her mother's acceptance of the situation and her obvious relief to be getting away from unpleasantries, Marvel ventured farther. "Why wouldn't I be all those things and more, considering that I came of such fine stock?"

Snow Harrington brought her tapering fingers together in soundless applause, her eyes shining. "There, see, Dale? Everything's all right—and this war *will* be over. It's just a matter of *when*."

Again father and daughter locked blue eyes in understanding. But Mother, it seemed, needed one bit more reassurance. Then she could be totally happy—seeing that her loved ones were—and her heart would resume creation of the symphony her violin would one day express.

"And the boy back home . . . you've put him out of your mind, too?"

"Titus? Titus Smith, Mother. We can no longer refer to Titus as a boy. He would be a young man now—22, closer to 23—if—if he were still living. But no, I have not put Titus out of my mind or my heart. I never will. But I have dealt with my loss—dealt with it twice, in fact. When I lost him, and again when I lost Philip. That's what I wanted to share. The two men were identical in appearance. That's what drew me to Philip. But," she inhaled deeply, "there the likeness ended. Both are gone now. And I do believe we voted in favor of a quick meal. So thanks for listening!"

Strangely, it was Mother who hesitated. "But I don't understand how—how you will cope and still go on. Be happy—how?"

As always, it was Mother who must be comforted, although it was Marvel who had experienced the loss. Very well. "How will I cope? A day at a time—that's how. And I'm not alone. I have all of you, and God walks with us."

* * *

The atmosphere was heavy with incongruity at the Office of Price Administration. One moment there was fear of the unknown. The next, there was exhilaration of the known. It was the clouds of war versus freedom. Here, too, conversation centered around the "secret weapon" the president himself had referred to in a fist-shaking threat at the stubborn enemy. Germany was breathing its last breath. But Japan was the wounded animal. And a wounded animal is a dangerous beast.

Marie looked white and drawn when she approached Marvel's desk to say, "Are you doin' okay? I—I feel like a dog about the captain. And now I"m worried sick about my Johnny. They were so close, Johnny and him—workin' on that mission they knew would take them into the thick of things. Philip—I mean, the captain—never made it. And Johnny'll go, he'll *go*. And if he never makes it back—will you—?" Her voice broke in half at that point and she stopped.

"Be there to help you?" Marvel said gently. "You know I will, Marie. And remember, God will be there, too—is *now*. He's faithful, even if we lose heart. But Marie, Johnny most likely will be back!"

Marie squeezed back tears and gulped a "thank-you" before returning to the window where an applicant waited. "Oh," she whispered with a quick turn, "here, take this—somethin' to make you smile. Phil—uh, the captain—and tail-gunner Johnny smiled just the night before." Shoving a folded piece of paper to Marvel, Marie hurried away.

The night before. In the other girl's disjointed manner, she had referred to the dread "friendly fire" of a trainee in Philip's own squadron which took his life. It was all a mistake, a ghastly mistake that accident, Marie said. Shocking, unbelievable, Marvel had nodded—too overcome with sadness and a senseless guilt that somehow, someway her gentle refusal to Philip's proposal contributed to his death. Now that her mind was clear, the burden of guilt was gone. But something else had taken its place: a sudden wondering if there existed the faintest chance that the fiery crash had been no accident at all. Melodramatic as it might seem, there must always be a vigilant watch for spies and counterspies in this deadly game of war. And now with rumors rampant of a secret weapon... *No!* Marvel scolded herself. *I will not let myself get caught up in groundless hysteria.* She would redouble all efforts to bring the war to a close. Brave words—but more easily spoken than abided by, she was to find.

Marvel hurried to the elm-lined street in order to see her family before they went their separate ways—ending one workday and beginning another. Mary Ann threw open the door leading into the inviting hall. She began talking without prelude, her voice lacking its usual banter. Trust Mary Ann to create no undercurrent of something left unsaid—an endearing quality Marvel coveted for herself.

"Marvel, I'm heartsick. I could kill myself! Life's worth nothing without him—just never-ending punishment. Oh, I could *die*. Jake called and it's true—all that secret weapon stuff. He called and said—oh, how can you stand there looking so in control, like you just stepped off the page of some glossy fashion magazine? How *can* you? Can't you see I'm dying? And you don't help."

"How can I help, Mary Ann, when I don't know what you're saying? Come on, let's go to the library." Taking her cousin's arm,

Marvel propelled her to one of the two gray, soft-cushioned chairs. One corner of her mind noted that Mother had gathered enough delphinium to fill the silver urn atop the heavy library table. Then, practically, she commenced drawing the heavy drapes for wartime blackout.

"Go ahead. Talk, honey," she encouraged. "So Jake called?"

Mary Ann dropped heavily into the first chair and burst into tears. "I'm s-sorry—so s-sorry I took it out on you. But I—I couldn't face th' rest of 'em," she gasped. "I—we, Jake and me—I planned—you know what we planned. I need your handkerchief—"

Marvel held a kerchief to her cousin's slightly tilted nose, now swollen and red from weeping. "Blow," she said. "Yes, I know. Jake was to be discharged—and you were going home, sooner or later."

"It'll be later, lots later if—if we ever get home a'tall. Whatever this Frankenstein weapon is c-could de-destroy *us* if we make a mistake, or they do—our enemies, I mean. So even after t-they surrender, if they do— Oh Marvel, they will, won't they?"

The upturned face, framed by its wealth of black curls, begged for reassurance, just as when the two birthday twins were little girls. And Marvel obliged. "Of course they'll surrender. Unconditionally—wasn't that what President Roosevelt promised?"

Mary Ann's sigh turned into a hiccup. "H-he prom-ised our boys w-wouldn't go overseas, too. And now, look—j-just look!"

This was no time to correct the statement. "So?" Marvel said instead.

"So now, there's got to be somethin' called a—an *occupational* deal—even after a truce. Our guys can't be discharged, muster out, be re-replaced, no matter how many missions they've been on. Oh Marvel, those weird sisters are after Jake and me!"

"The Fates? Don't be silly. We'll manage. Haven't we always?"

"But how? This is different. So *how* can we manage?"

"Together—that's how. And Mary Ann, remember it's our duty to help keep up morale—theirs and ours. There are millions of ways, and God will show us some more. Chin up now. Let's make plans!"

Mary Ann's eyes brightened slightly as Marvel outlined a quick plan for survival. There were still vacancies at the Office of Price Administration (OPA), constant turnover of personnel as servicemen-husbands came and went...the need for assistance with reading programs...help in the nursery schools while mothers worked in defense. Both of them should lend a hand at the USO centers...*so* much to do at church (the vital component she herself had neglected, Marvel admitted)...and the *books*.

"Especially the books!" she emphasized, feeling a sudden fire kindle within herself. The books, indeed, and the columns Editor Corey had extracted a promise from Marvel to complete. The clincher had been the man's one-liner: "Titus would have wanted that."

"Yes," something akin to a smile lighted Mary Ann's face. "I remember your poem—so beautiful. I want to memorize it like you did and spring it on Jake. How did it go: 'One leaf is for hope'?"

Managing to nod, Marvel inhaled raggedly. "That's it."

Sitting up straight, Mary Ann said, "Okay, hope we've got. Now where do we start? How do we get through the hardest time?"

"A day at a time. Oh, I have a super idea. Ready?"

"*I* am!" Mary Ann's high-school brother said from the door.

"Billy Joe Harrington!" Mary Ann chided gently. "Who asked *you*?"

"B.J.'s the name, Mrs. Brotherton. *Marvel* asked. Th' guys at school named me captain of the baseball team, I'll have you know. And I got the green light from every teacher. I'm on the honor roll!"

"Wonderful, B.J. We're proud of you!" Marvel applauded.

"Me, too," Mary Ann said, "but I don't know what—"

"The honor has to do with writing, big sis? Because I have to do a write-up for the sports column. That's what! S'pose Uncle Dale'll help us—help me with the rules, the history. *I* might do a book!"

"Dream on." Mary Ann was *laughing*. Oh, what a welcome sound! To Marvel's ear it was like the tinkle of Grandmother's silver spoons.

"Check with him, B.J., but I'm sure Daddy will welcome the opportunity to help you. He's quite a baseball fan—had a chance at the big league one time. Let's reserve that for him to share," Marvel reassured one of her two remaining boy-cousins, since war took Duke. The thought brought back the pain, so she resumed talking to Mary Ann. "Now, about you and me. Remember *Stretching to Survive*, the cookbook put together by the Pleasant Knoll ladies? Of course you remember. Auntie Rae was in charge. You know, it occurs to me that she could do a real service by adding wartime recipes."

Mary Ann's curls bobbed up and down in agreement. "Yep—but now *our* survival? A "how to" that one of us could contribute?"

"Exactly! Incorporating ideas in one of our own collections—or yours, Billy Joe. I'm sorry: B.J. I'll tell you what. Let's turn this into a family project. You know, we three start and the others follow—a sort of credo we'll call 'One Day at a Time,' beginning with the words of Paul: 'I press toward the mark for the prize of the high calling of God in Christ Jesus.' Paul knew pain but pressed on."

B.J. was concentrating. "I get it. That credo will work in whatever we're up to. Me—I may not hit a homer, but I can make it to first base. Pastor Jim says we all can do *somethin'*."

Mary Ann nodded again. "Teamwork. It'll take that to win the war. All right," she said in resignation, "I know when I'm licked. Two against one here—make it *three*. God'll give me no peace either."

Coming from another, that would sound like a sacrilege. But the words were Mary Ann's way of what Grandmother would call "truckling." Understanding, Marvel said, "Not until you find your ministry—same thing with us all. Now let's set short-term goals—"

"And let the trouncing come later!" B.J. added eagerly.

The three agreed then that a day was easier to get through than worrying about a year. Anybody could tolerate one meal's dirty dishes. But a day? And a *lifetime*—forget it! So tackle the job that can't be done, and *do* it happily. Ideas flew past like B.J.'s baseballs then. Marvel's fingers had trouble jotting them all down. But from the brainstorming was to come invaluable resource material for her column and B.J.'s, and for articles, stories—and eventually, books:

> *This one day I can:* make others happy even if I am sad... bind up others' wounds when I, too, am bleeding... bask in the brightness if the sun shines (or know, if it is cloudy, I will make no shadow)... rejoice

in my victories, shrug off defeats—knowing I did my very best, gave life my best shot...work on my weaknesses instead of letting them work on me...learn something new—a revised rule, another way of preparing a food I do not like, a quote from literature, or a new meaning of a Bible verse ("I shall not loaf mentally!")...do mental and physical push-ups to prevent fatness or flatness, one push-up this day, two tomorrow...finish a job I have hidden from myself—a letter, an assignment, a hem or cuff to be shortened or lengthened...practice my skills ("Practice makes perfect"), then on to master new ones...keep my mind and my body clean, speak softly when I am angry, smile when I am blue, be patient with others on my "team" and help them improve, knowing that I am improving with them...stand for what is right even when I stand alone, but not alienate others in my self-righteousness...devote more time to my faults than to those of others...think before speaking, listen without interrupting, and refuse to repeat privileged information or rumors. Can I achieve my goal? *This one day I can.*

3

Credo for the Country

All proceeded according to plan for the Harringtons. Parents added to the ever-growing list of *this-one-day* living with enthusiasm. It was a fast-paced, tense time in which they were living. Who knew what tomorrow held? Hopefully, please; but, as in God's kingdom, workers must help achieve that blissful state. Neither world problems nor personal ones could be overcome with one blow.

"Rome wasn't built in a day," Mother quoted Grandmother Riley, relieved that the burden of thinking beyond that 24-hour period was removed. Uncle Worth remarked that it would keep him awake the few precious hours he allowed for sleep if he thought he would continue the defense work for a lifetime. But getting through a day was downright rewarding—"like climbing a stairway to the stars." Auntie Rae was enchanted with her husband's words. She *loved* the phrase, she said. One had to *stretch* to reach the top. *Stretch to Survive* fit so many occasions. "I must get on with recipes," she said dreamily. And Daddy—oh, the glow on his face at his nephew's idea. "Make that All-Star B.J.," he said with a twinkle, when invited to assist with baseball. He would find time, Daddy said.

"We'll wait upon the Lord, as told, but not be sitting around on our hands until His peace comes to the world. Remember how our father quoted Honest Abe, Worth? 'I am convinced that most folks are about as happy as they set their minds to be.' Even that's easier to accomplish on a daily basis. We have a plan—a far-reaching one—like your son's home run. But first base'll do for starters."

Without discussion, the family's led-by-the-Spirit prayers somehow tacked on the Lord's Prayer, spoken in unison. *"Give us this day our daily bread,"* carried the ring of italics. *This day...*

It all happened so naturally. What began between the three younger members spread through the immediate family and then, by means of letters, to the extended family of Harringtons. That was understandable. Understandable, too, was the I *can for one day* message traveling on to encourage a newspaper audience in need of a straw of hope to clutch. Little did Marvel, Mary Ann, and Billy Joe know, of course, that their words would become their *country's* credo when the war-torn world found the taste of victory bittersweet....

The Office of Price Administration welcomed Mary Ann's return. Yes, there was a growing need for her services in reading instruction as well—and if she could spare just a few hours at the nursery school? Pastor Jim asked no questions, required no commitments. Anything would help—*anything*. And maybe the young ladies would consider giving him a hand in formation of a beginners' Bible class.... The USO had reported requests from young servicemen and women—the chaplain was *so* busy....

Mary Ann moaned. "Oh, how could I be so zany? I got what I deserve, letting you lead me into this."

"Maybe," Marvel said slowly. "*I* didn't lead. God led us both."

"Well," Mary Ann fumed, "I wish He'd led me somewhere besides into *tires*. I know absolutely nothing about tires."

"You know they're rationed," B.J., who seemed to be everywhere at once, pointed out. "And you *said* you wanted to help—I heard you. You're a mugwump. Know what a mugwump is, big sis?"

Mary Ann stiffened. "I know it's slang for an independent in politics. And I know that you're no longer a little pest—you're a *big* one. Get lost!"

"Like I did in the dunes—and *you* came to the rescue? You don't want rid of me. Just proves my point that you're a mugwump! You see, a mugwump—as I heard it defined on th' radio today—is a bird with its mug on one side of th' fence and its *wump* on th' other!"

He ducked from the room before "big sis" could answer. Mary Ann and Marvel shared a needed laugh and relaxed. Even as she laughed, Marvel was looking ahead to listening for news. B.J.'s mention of the radio had served as a reminder. How long had it been?

* * *

"Now and then, it's wise to traverse roads of the past," a commentator, whose voice Marvel was unable to identify, suggested when she turned on the small white radio on her writing desk. "Such trips require no gasoline, wear and tear on tires, and no time off adding to the critical manpower shortage. And these travels offer a view—a *point* of view, that is, an understanding of our todays."

With that leadoff came the promised review and then the news:

The nation *will* return to normal one of these days. There's a promise in the air. Once more citizens will be ready to progress into a future—so remember what those days were like? Are you old enough to recall "The Merry Days at Mad Meadow"? That magnificent spectacle of a luminous world, apparently suspended in space as you and fellow fair-goers trudged on numbed feet with dazed eyes? Ah yes—'twas the New York World's Fair, the biggest, giddiest, costliest, and most ambitious international exposition ever attempted. Even before it opened on April 30, 1939, 'mid a blaze of fireworks and a blast of publicity, it had cost over $150 million. The vast acreage, 1216 to be exact, in Flushing Meadow, Queens, was landscaped by planting some 10,000 trees and a million tulip bulbs from Holland. Centering this, 300 massive futuristic buildings were planted. These housed the fair's wares from 1500 exhibitors from 33 states, 58 foreign countries and 1300 business firms, ranging from the Ford Motor Company—remember when we could buy new models?—to Dr. Scholl's Footease. Ah yes, the wise Doc maintained an emergency clinic to treat fair-goers whose arches had sagged along the exposition's 65 miles of paved street and footpaths....

Marvel wished for such a climit to care for aching other-part arches! Her hand were so busy taking notes that she had no choice but to overwork her fingers. This recap was invaluable! Her mind was equally occupied in mental review of the year 1939. A depression-weary world scarcely noted the far-distant World's Fair. New York? Wasn't that where Wall Street was—site of Black Friday which marked the crash of the stock market? Those devoted to news—and caring as Marvel Harrington, and yes (she thought with the never-ending pain), *Titus Smith* cared—thought more about the possibility of war than the "privileged" who recklessly parachuted from the high point of an amusement center. Innocent? More like *shallow*. Maybe the writer—she struggled only for a moment with the name—oh yes, Sid Shallett, was right when he summed up the age in much the same manner of Charles Dickens and later quoted by Somerset Maugham: "...the best of times...the worst of times." "It was the paradox of all paradoxes," Shallett paraphrased in 1940. "It was good, it was bad; it was the acme of all crazy vulgarity, it was the pinnacle of all inspiration." Holding onto the thought, Marvel turned full attention to the radio:

The fair's president, gardenia-wearing Grover A. Whalen, christened the gigantic conglomeration "The World of Tomorrow," dedicating it to the blessings of democracy and the wonders a technology. What marvels to come: nylon hose, a robot named Elektro that could talk while puffing a cigarette, naked statues with questionable titles like Freedom of Assembly (and assemble they did—spectators, that is!), surrounding the fair's Theme Centre—that 700-foot-tall needlelike Trylon and the 200-foot globe called the Perisphere. Suppose there was such an extravaganza and nobody came? Oh, they came all right. A bewildering assortment of promotional gimmicks, sideshows, and downright corn attracted some 45-million gawkers with fat purses to dial-direct long-distance telephones (for the future, *our* future which, like all else, is on *hold* for that "someday,") and television, allowing Americans to *see* as well as *hear* the news and their "Guiding Light" soap! Small wonder *The New York Times* columnist, Meyer Berger, would refer to that fair as "*Mad* Meadow." Example: "See me get milked on a merry-go-round!" shouted Elsie, the Borden Milk cow.

And sure enough, at the canned milk exhibit you could see 150 of Elsie's sisters being spun on a revolving milking platform. Now if you were lucky, you just might hit Elsie on her birthday and hear a squad of Western Union boys deliver a singing telegram: "Mooey Birthday to You." At Ford there was a floor show called "A Thousand Life Times *Neigh*," a horse's-eye view of the automobile. And wow! You could even take in a "skin show" and ogle at an innocent (near-nude) maiden as she wrestled with Oscar the Obscene Octopus in "Twenty Thousand *Legs* Under the Sea."

Well, folks, draw your own conclusions, but that two-year fair did indeed provide everything for everybody... giving us a something to cling to in an older and wiser world... and what to throw overboard. For little did the blind foresee that in just two short years the vulgarly inspiring fair would close for the duration of World War II. What began with a blaze of fireworks, slammed shut with an explosion of live ammunition on Pearl Harbor! We are wide awake now and God help us to *stay* awake, profiting from history!

America hopefully knew the allies from the enemies now in 1945, the announcer went on to say, making mention of such exhibitors as Italy's modernistic pavilion, atop of which stood the golden goddess Roma holding court... American 80-foot ships' prows flanking entrance to Marine transportation (in warning?)... Poland's 141-foot tower beneath which was the restaurant boasting Polish vodka and 40 exotic hors d'oeuvres ... symbols of socialism at the Soviet pavilion, including "Big Joe" (No, not Joseph Stalin), the 30-ton statue of a worker brandishing a red star....

Ah yes, 1939! The year of shifting ideologies and political bedfellows. Capitalism had collapsed, so the world had thought (only to be proven wrong!).... Odd people with odd ideas had failed: the engineer of technocracy... the nostrum of the Louisiana "Kingfish" Huey P. Long who, sad to say, had drowned in his own blood—shot down by a sadistic assassinator's gun... the Townsend plan to care for the aging had died as had its anticipated recipients... and the self-proclaimed "Messiah" Charles Cloughlin gradually slid so far to the political right that his speeches smacked more with Jew-baiting than economics. Alas, many decided that Adolf Hitler was the real Messiah and closed ranks with the Berlin-directed German-American Bund, aping the Nazis' salute and dubbed our Depression-wresting president "the first Fascist." And the Communists made the fatal mistake of signing the 1939 alliance with Hitler ("I know how much the German nation owes its führer," Joseph Stalin said in a toast to the executioner's health!). But that so shocked our misguided, well-meaning would-be Nazi party, it did a doublethink and crawled away. Panaceas? There were none. Furthermore, the American economy was alive and progressing....And so it was that Americans returned to traditional values and put politics back into the hands of the two-party system.

The commentator broke for a commercial, his timing perfect where Mary Ann was concerned. "Marvel!" she called from downstairs, "Mar-*vel*! Yoo-hoo! I can't compete. Is that the news? Are you *listening*?" She sounded both urgent and impatient.

"It *was*—and *I* was." Marvel sighed and went to the door.

"Well, turn that thing off. The outlook's bad—"

"Then don't look *out*—look *up*!" B.J. called from his room. He had joined his sister by the time Marvel reached the last stair.

"Says who?" Mary Ann asked, her impatience gone, replaced by a grin.

"Says Pastor Jim, that's who. 'If you don't like the outlook, try the *up*look.' Pretty good, huh? I'm a good listener."

"Eavesdropper's more like it," Mary Ann said suspiciously.

"So big sis is happy again. Jake called, so she's looking *up*!"

"You *were* listening. Then *you* tell it, little brother."

B.J. pulled himself to full height and jutted out his chin. "*Big* brother—remember you called me a big pest. Well, I'm taller than *you*!" He waved a hand between them to prove it. "So *big* fits."

Mary Ann ignored the gesture. "Big ears anyway—you proved that, too. Well, you've spilled the beans to Marvel, so go ahead—tell her what your brother-in-law *said*!"

"Silly—I couldn't hear *him*, just you gigglin' and moonin' like what Gran'mere used to call billin' and cooin', Marvel—"

Mary Ann had every reason for those silly words, she burst out, unable to restrain her excitement any longer. Jake *had* called and talk about looking *up*—wow! Oh, his squadron had to go—no idea where, of course. But the way things looked (so *up*, you know?) he'd not be in the occupation deal after the unconditional surrender. And that surrender was close—that much Jake knew. Oh Marvel, they'd all be going home—have that double wedding. She and Jake had it all planned. They would renew their vows when Marvel married Titus.

"You're right—you're absolutely right. Right as rain, Marvel. Just put it all in God's hands, and everything will turn out right. I gave Him back my trust, my heart—I gave that to God, too."

"*Gave*, Mary Ann? Your heart was His already—bought and paid for."

Mary Ann bit her lip. "B-but my doubt—the sins. I wondered—"

"He paid for those, too. It sounds too good to be true, but—"

"It works! Why, I—I didn't think I could handle those silly tires—even after you said I could. But you told me to pray, and I did. So now I'm the expert in tire rationing, honest to goodness."

On and on the bright-eyed bride talked about Jake's finishing school, possibly going into banking, after all. Oh, to go home. And it would happen to Marvel, too. It *would*! That clover *was* real.

"Don't!" Marvel wanted to cry out. Buy why prick Mary Ann's shimmering bubble? She said instead, "So now we can concentrate on the books—some articles, anyway, if we can find the time. We did promise to give help at the USO. Someone from there called to say we're scheduled for Wednesday evening—the earlier, the better."

"Not without a man along. I'm it!" B.J. volunteered.

It was at the USO that Marvel met a young soldier whose brief appearance on the stage of her life stirred up a myriad of emotions. Private Samuel York could have served as a prewar recruiting poster: so young, golden, and fresh-faced . . . so clear of eye and skin. The crew-cut hair served to make him look all the more youthful, emphasizing the perfection of the face below it. Undoubtedly his morals were as impeccable as the regulation press of the olive-drab G.I. trousers. Why then did Marvel hesitate just a fraction of a second before speaking? The young man was so obviously in need of hospitality, a word of welcome. Standing apart from the other servicemen who were laughing and talking among themselves, he appeared to be searching for something—something to remind him of home, which could be anywhere in this world of displaced persons.

"I guess one of us ought to speak," Mary Ann said through the corner of her mouth. "It's not his fault he's pretty. *You* do it! Here come the doughnuts. I really should get one for our noble escort. Would you believe he's makin' the rounds to announce Bible class?"

As if timed, Private York's searching eyes met Marvel's. Touched by the puzzled, faraway expression on his face, she felt a nudge to approach him. His needs outweighed her uncertainties.

Shy though he appeared, the lad from Michigan spoke first. "Have we met? I'm Private Sam York and I—I'm trying to recall where it was. But I know you from somewhere and it bothers me."

An old line—so typical of boys away from home the first time. But Marvel understood and was neither flattered nor irritated.

"We have not met, private. Perhaps I remind you of someone— a young lady from back home, perhaps?" She introduced herself.

Flushing slightly, he looked down at his shoes. "There's a girl, yes. But—Miss Harrington, was it?—I wasn't making a pass—"

The source of his embarrassment was not due to mention of his "girl" then, but to fear that Marvel would get a wrong impression of his behavior. Suddenly, it was she who felt embarrassed.

In a rush to make things right, she suggested that, in case he was alone, perhaps he would wish to attend a beginners' Bible class? There would be doughnuts afterward. All very informal, just sharing—

But he was shaking his head. "I'm not a beginner—not a quitter either. Sue—she's the girl waiting—studies with me. Actually, this is a one-night stand, just passing through and dropped by here to be with a few civilians." The way his head kept shaking bothered her. Was he still puzzling over her identity?

"I'm glad you came, Private York. I understand loneliness," Marvel said a little uneasily. "I must leave you now—make my services available to others. But maybe you would like some home cooking, too. The food's brought in by women to let you know you're not forgotten and is about as bountiful as wartime restrictions allow."

"Not forgotten—that's good to know. But *I* seem to be the one who forgot. Where was it? I *know* I know you—saw you—"

The blood seemed to drain from her heart. *Don't tell me something I can't absorb, build hopes on—just don't!* Tears welled up behind her eyes but did not fall as this wayfaring stranger might have expected. Instead, with her usual discipline, Marvel Harrington's soft mouth set in a firm, resolute line. "We have not met."

There was no indication that he heard. Still unconvinced, he studied her face with penetrating concern. "A model maybe—an extra for Hollywood, a stand-in—" Samuel York mumbled to himself. Then, in address to Marvel, "Do you sing—professionally, I mean?"

"No," she said somewhat stiffly. Here was good soldier material, not easily won over. But enough was enough in her case. On the verge of saying a good-night and hurrying on, she turned to go.

"Oh, I have it—sort of. *Please* wait! On a magazine cover—no, a newspaper. I know it was a picture, and it has a special meaning."

A picture. "No meaning for me, private. I'm sorry," she denied.

And then, even as she tried to avoid what would force her to exhume buried memories after all searching had led to nowhere (except the self-destruct words "Missing in Action"), this minstrel had sung out, "A photograph, a photograph!" Marvel's legs shook, forcing her to sit.

A series of *who, what, where, whens* led to another dead end, for each was interrogating the other. "That settles it," Marvel said quietly, knowing better. They parted in confusion.

She would not go through this again. Repeat: *would not!* "This one day," the credo required. Believe it. Lean on it. And Marvel prayed that her internal gyro would set her back on course. Meantime, she would think of other people, other matters, and get on with life.

✷ ✷ ✷

The folded sheet of paper Marie had given her, heretofore unread, helped. Some joker had come up with a clever takeoff on another supposedly written by a G.I. Joe. B.J., having declared himself a "Texas Doughboy" in faint recall of The Lightcrust Flour singers after stuffing himself on doughnuts, had gone to his room. She and Mary Ann could be alone and share the satire, but not the upsetting incident. Together they could smile. And smile they did as Marvel read aloud:

Dear Ma, Pa, Brothers, Sisters, and Draft Dodgers:

I am making your world safe. We have to fight, and I did! I fought but had to go anyway, being first-class (Class A, you know). Next time, I'll volunteer to be Class B—like coupon books. I had all the right answers for the draft board, I'm proud to say. One guy wanted to know my birthday but quick-like changed the subject: "When did you first see the light of day?" I told him I'd seen it twice: "First time was when I left L.A. and the second was when I learned what being Class A meant." Next guy wanted my name and I said, "John Hancock—August" (meaning my birthday), and the dummy put it down as my name. "You'll be shipping out, John Hancock and that'll be the last of *August*." My life would be short then? No wonder they put me with the *Air Corps*. They asked what brought me into the service. I told them the draft board.

You should see my uniform. Uniforms come in two sizes: too tight or too loose. I took the little outfit and was ready to fight the minute I shrunk to fit it. Decided on the big-size shoes so I'd be able to turn around without lifting the heavy weapons of war. Look like I kicked a cow from the rear like I planned to do the enemy. First one I met was a big shot with all kinds of bars and medals. I was squatting like always because the tight pants won't let me stand when this guy roared: "Atten-SHUN! Stand up straight! Didn't you see my uniform?" I roared back: "You got nothing to gripe about. Look at mine!" He gave me time off so I could rest up—in the brig.

We sailed after my rest. Worst luck! The sergeant stuttered and the "H-h-h-halt!" took so long, the whole platoon marched overboard. The water shrunk my pants some more. When some guy fished us out and yelled, "Fall in!" I knew he didn't mean me for I'd done that already. That gave me some more time off—this time down in the galley where I could peel onions. I cried for joy. I was on board two weeks and seasick for three of them. I leaned over the rail all the time. The captain asked where my company was and I told him I was all by myself. He said, "Sonny, we'll fix that as soon as the brigadier comes up." I told him it was up already if I'd swallowed it. He was pretty dumb anyway. Kept saying things would be fixed, anchor was about to drop. I told him it was probably gone already. (I knew it was loose.)

We went straight from the ship to the trenches. Some of the guys didn't like that, but I did because bombs were exploding up top and somebody was apt to be hit. I shook with patriotism. When we had to change shifts, I decided to shoot from behind a tree. Good planning except for no vacancies. Officers occupied them all. I asked one for a furlough and he said, "Don't you have any red blood in you?" I said, "Yeah, but the sight of blood makes me sick like the sea." I didn't apply soon enough. By the time my furlough could be processed, they sent us out to greet 10,000 Japs. But they weren't friendly—kept looking at me like I started this war. The captain knew I was brave so chose me to do his job. "Fire at Will!" That was a wrong name for a Jap, so I knew the guy behind me must be a traitor. I missed him but he shot back—*my* back. When I came to, I was riding in a hearse (shortage on transportation out here, too). I asked the driver where we were headed. He said, "To the morgue." I knew he was shell-shocked and needed help, so I said, "I'm not dead!" Poor guy. He said, "Shut up before you make a fool out of the doctor. That could be dangerous. He's an officer!" I'll be home soon. Kind of a secret, but I overheard them saying, "This thing's ready to be boxed up." I *told* you I'd win this war!

—So light the candles for:
Your G.I. Joe

The two were giddy from laughter. Then very suddenly, Mary Ann sobered. Her usual rush of youth and energy was gone, as was her laughter. The dark eyes gazed deeply into Marvel's.

"You know now. I can feel it. You know Titus is alive."

Marvel drew back, steeling herself against the hurt. "Because of the clover or this note?"

"Both! Jake knows him. And he didn't say anything—Titus, I mean. Didn't *have* to. He knew you'd understand the message about one leaf of that clover being for hope. And the note? I know it came from Marie, but you couldn't have laughed like that without hope!"

Marvel had a sudden vision of Titus in uniform, ordered to the front . . . saw buildings collapse around him, brick after brick, as wave after wave of bombers showered fire from the heavens. She came out of the trance with her heart pounding, her palms wet. "Mary Ann, *please* don't tempt me to go back. Help me live by our credo. I know Titus won't be back, just as I know Philip won't be. Both are *dead.*"

Mary Ann sounded angry. "There's a difference. Marie's husband witnessed Captain Prinz's crash, said that note came the night before. All right, if it upsets you, I'll shut up. But I'll still *know*!"

Yes, she knew, too. Knew that Titus was more than MIA, but declared dead. It was official. *Sleep*, she willed when she lay alone. Did she sleep? She felt wide awake, breathless with wonder, delirious with joy. Somewhere high in the stratosphere she floated out to meet Titus, to snuggle into his outstretched arms. Nobody in this world had felt like this ever before. Everything was exactly as it always had been. The fine, gossamer-thin but stronger-than-death cord between them had commanded time to stand still. And time had obeyed. The contours of the only man Marvel Harrington could ever love were the same. She had memorized them well, traced them in her dreams, and now they were *real.* They were together, without words, just a smile that refused to come off her face even when she awoke. "Let it last, Lord . . . *this one day.*

4

Death of a President

Dr. James Murphy hesitated slightly after his Sunday service. The Harringtons were making their way toward him. Such a dedicated, hardworking family—dare he ask more of them? Reading his look of hesitancy, Marvel did some introspective thinking. How could she and Mary Ann manage to give him a hand with the day nursery? The service did free young mothers to work in defense while awaiting their husbands' return. One hour before or after work?

In a whispered exchange of words with Mary Ann, they reached a quick decision. Books—they had collected stacks of children's books most of their lives...had a regular library...the little ones loved the read-alouds...and classroom management was a pushover.

Mary Ann, in her enthusiasm, pushed ahead in line. Fine, that afforded Marvel an opportunity to recall the exciting times spent with Titus beneath their sprawling oak tree on the high-school lawn. Textbook-type readers held little charm, little challenge for young minds. These books were lukewarm—as colorless as a Charlie Chaplin, Fatty Arbuckle, Buster Keaton, or Harold Lloyd silent movies after the talkies came in. Children's minds should stretch like prewar elastic, she thought now, just as the two of them had thought then: talking animals...dialogue, living color. Fiction, yes, but with fact tucked in. Let little readers discover *truth*. "So we'll write them ourselves, darling," Titus promised.

"Praise the Lord for you two!" Pastor Jim was saying. "I just don't see how you do it. How on earth—"

"On earth as it is in heaven!" Mary Ann sang out. Then, sobering, she added, "God manages for us. And there's Marvel, who just keeps reminding me that faith without works is dead. Otherwise, to be honest, me—I'd be like some wounded soldier who knows he's done for if he lies down. Soooo, we just keep marchin'."

And marching became a way of life to suppress my inner sadness. Marvel hoped the smile she attempted looked genuine. Work *did* help.

B.J. had decided the same for himself. "Pastor Jim, we're all helping at the USO. They," he tilted his head to include his sister and cousin, "have the Bible study going. They listen better than they used to. Guess they forgot some answers, or were bluffin' all along. But the beginners like it, keep coming back for more."

The minister smiled tiredly. "It's a hard lesson, learning that skill. But we have to listen before knowing how to hep. Listening *is* helping. It's a gift. Nobody knows all the answers, so we pray."

Here was a great guy, Billy Joe's eyes were saying—knew how to talk man-to-man and treat everybody like a *somebody*! Somebody with a gift to offer. Well, he would offer one now. "I'm makin' some posters—sort of funny ones for the baseball team I'll be managing. You know, attention-grabbers—I let the *posters* talk instead of me blabbing. My Uncle Dale's helpin'. He's major league stuff, you know. I have to do a term paper and (gee-whillikins!) some sports write-ups for the school newspaper. So I'll kill a dozen birds with one shot—"

"Stone," Mary Ann corrected.

"Stone. Illustrate, write, make posters—use 'em for the USO bulletin board to snag in more for Bible study. An' someday I'll write a book—me and Uncle Dale—get rich. I'll tithe, of course."

"Of course," Dr. James Murphy replied soberly.

The conversation led Marvel and Mary Ann back into the world of books. Oh, it was good to go exploring again! Unpacking the children's books, they chose the ones most likely to please (and were right, as time would tell). Mary Ann said outright that she had "feelings" about these things—just *knew* when they would be right. Call it *intuition*, Marvel suggested, and felt a warm rush of thanksgiving that ever so gradually her beloved cousin was now groping toward fulfillment. God would use Mary Ann just as He would use her in His plan. Just how remained uncertain. But life had taught them already that it was made up of moments in time, small matters which, woven together, eventually became powerful fabric. Imagination made that fact no less real.

"Oh Marvel, look!" Mary Ann said holding up a book without straightening. "Here's the book we intended reading—never did—"

Marvel took it from her hand. *"The Grapes of Wrath*—I'd forgotten Steinbeck's book. It's so real."

"Too real! Even the title sets my teeth on edge. You know what I'm remembering: those terrible times when we killed ourselves in the vineyards, tryin' to get hold of enough money t-to help our parents make it here. *Migrants*, they called us, spitting in our faces. Then that one *awful* man—*two* awful ones—who tried t-to steal our honor! Oh, I still have nightmares, and I never told Mother and Daddy."

"All the more reason we should try to read it, Mary Ann. We've put it all behind us, and he—John Steinbeck—did exactly what we'll end up doing. We didn't plan to do it this way, but neither did he."

Mary Ann did not understand, so Marvel explained how the writer gathered material as he gathered grapes . . . moving among clusters of desperate people who had fled the Dust Bowl. His intentions were to do a series of articles for some magazine, just as Marvel had done for newspapers (and *must* continue doing, she reminded herself, gathering a few articles scattered here and there among the dusty books).

Mary Ann straightened, sneezed, said "Bless me!" and blew her nose. "Dust—guest we brought it from Texas. Then *that's* why everybody says this book sounds so real. Only it's fiction?"

Marvel nodded. "Both, I guess. Some said the *facts* didn't sell. Nobody knows for sure. But somehow the writer trashed his idea but kept the notes. What he'd sold made less than he would have earned harvesting grapes. He harvested far more when he fabricated names and created some fictitious characters and let *them* think. But, you see, it was backed up by exhaustive research, gained through reading and living. I remember two stripes against it: Friends told him it wouldn't sell, and then when he proved them wrong and found a publisher, it was 'Banned in Boston'—remember that label?"

"I do—and something else you told me, that this grapes book won the Pulitzer prize for fiction, even though it was based on history, recent history. Your eyes are shining! Okay, Marvel, we read!"

They tried, but the memories were too painful for Mary Ann. Why punish herself? she asked, throwing her hands up in despair. Marvel, fascinated by the merging of fact and fiction, read on and on, almost to the point of obsession—until at some point, she could bear no more. The form which the writer intended became too great for its intended audience, yes, and she could understand why he chose a novel instead. Fact-finding was intoxicating. But need it be so graphic? She was stunned by the idea that people, no matter how desperate, would toss the body of a stillborn baby into the stream leading into town to prove a point. Shuddering, she laid the book aside.

And then came the terrible truth. Small wonder the idea was so revolting, Marvel thought, feeling the churn of her stomach warning that she was about to be sick. She had witnessed worse.

"Oh, dear God," she whispered, "this part is only fiction, and what we saw was real. It happened! Oh, forgive them for shooting the man. They couldn't have known what they were doing. Forgive—"

Dropping her head onto the library table that night, Marvel Harrington wept against the cool smoothness of the wood. But even through her suffering, she knew the story must be told. People must know, but in a more palatable form. Yes, and God would help her, through research, to make it more beautiful, to see the good He saw in mankind. She, too, would use both secondary and primary research—and add something more. What was it? Oh yes, the quote from Montaigne, that French essayist of sixteenth-century literature: "I have gathered a bouquet of other men's flowers," she murmured, "and only the ribbon that binds them is my own."

* * *

Schedules stretched and stretched some more, but the Harringtons managed to meet the demands of each day. Only one item remained—one. And yet, it was among the most important. She must get back to her writing, Marvel told herself, feeling a sort of panic at having neglected it too long already. Tonight— yes, tonight for sure she must listen to the news and clip it to her brain as she had clipped the shamefully postponed newspaper items, only to allow them to go unread.

The click of her heels on the pavement quickened at the thought as she neared home that evening. Her father stood behind the gate, glancing speculatively toward the roof. His face showed strain, but his smile was brave. He took a deep breath, started to say something, and seemed to change his mind. What came out was "Another busy day, my little tycoon?"

The tension in his blue, blue eyes caused her throat to ache with sorrow. Daddy did not like life in the big city. He wanted and needed to be a part of his land. Well, he would be when this hateful war ended. Putting away the disappointment she felt at being unable to get on with her evening, she forced a laugh.

"Oh, not bad—just a killer!"

Marvel saw him wince. "That bad—huh?" There was hurt in his voice.

"Oh, not really," she said lightly. "Just the usual chaos. Everything looks lovely, doesn't it, Daddy—the place, I mean?"

It was true. The rays of late-afternoon sun enlarged the blossoms on the lemon trees whose branches hung heavy with last year's crop of yellow fruit. The glossy-leafed trees were as faithful as the California sunshine, which they seemed to have captured in the fruit. The old bricks used in the fireplace and repeated in the walks curling through the orchards, gardens, and yard gave back a warm sheen. Small wonder the geraniums Auntie Rae had planted in sawed-off barrels and Mother's pansies and petunias bloomed in defiance of the calendar. But Daddy's mind seemed focused elsewhere.

"You keep looking up," Marvel said gently. "A good direction!"

"I was thinking," Dale Harrington said slowly, as if speaking to himself, "that we were pretty farsighted—buying at yesterday's prices. We can turn this property at a good profit—*real* good. It was so overgrown, so neglected. But we fixed it, didn't we, baby?"

"That we did, Daddy," Marvel said, surveying the great house with its look of stability. The structure had aged gracefully. The family had worked long and hard to refurbish it, and nature had taken care of the rest. The vines, shrubs, and trees had grown beyond all predictions—seeming to yawn and stretch luxuriously in the warmth of the sun. That same warmth had matured the brick to a rich patina. "It all has a look of belonging in England."

Why had she said *that?* Daddy must have wondered, too. He was searching her face, communicating as they always did without words...remembering Captain Philip Prinz. But neither of them spoke the name.

Marvel hurried to speak of the property instead. "The house has character—something contributed by us all: Auntie Rae's ruffled cottage-like curtains, yours and Uncle Worth's old-fashioned shutters, Mother's flowers, and so much else. The house that love built!"

"That's what concerns me. I mean, it's just the way your mother envisioned. And well, frankly, I wonder if Snow will consent—"

"To a sale? Oh Daddy, you *know* Mother would follow you to the ends of the earth. And you remember what Grandmother Riley said, that her daughter would rise to meet the occasion. Hasn't she always? And we're wrestling with the future. The war's not over—"

The sun was sinking, and a mist of fog added silver to the rose glow of the sky. Still her father lingered, although it was mealtime. "But going back—I know the place has memories," he said softly. "Can you take up where you left off? With the family, yes, but—"

"Titus? Yes, Daddy. He would want that. Oh, I wish you had met."

Dale Harrington leaned over to brush a kiss on the forehead of his marvelous daughter. "I feel I know him. It will all work out."

"When the time is right," Marvel managed. "And now, chow time!"

* * *

The news reports filled up with reviews of events leading up to the war, moved on to recap the most recent developments, and stopped short of saying the war was all but over. Oh, there would be "mopping up" to do, reporters agreed, and there would be occupational forces at strategic points. But all were banking on this powerful new weapon, *the* weapon (which must be "mighty powerful") designed to end the atrocities in short order. "Or," one newscaster jested, "as we civilians say, 'It's all over but the shouting.' One Johnny Doughboy corrected us to say, 'Sir, it's all over but the *shooting*!'"

Marvel listened to the reports, read through the stack of newspaper clippings, and digested the information into what she hoped covered the situation. Taking up where the recap of the European front ended, she proceeded to do the same with the Asian theater.

The war in the Pacific followed somewhat the pattern of that in Europe: early defeat, a holding action, then an irresistible Allied advance. But in the days immediately following Pearl Harbor, there was no glimmer of hope in any news releases. Although General Douglas MacArthur's command had received notification of the assault, Japanese pilots sweeping over Manila's Clark Field nine hours afterward found row after row of Flying Fortresses and P-40's parked in the sun almost unprotected, so later stories claimed. In a single raid the Japanese wiped out half of MacArthur's bombing force and a large percentage of fighters.

Disasters mounted. Guam fell December 11, 1941 ... Wake Island, December 23, and Hong Kong on Christmas Day. . . . "Impregnable" Singapore fell February 15. Enemy forces conquered the East Indies . . . overran Burma . . . moved into New Britain . . . the Solomons . . . and gained control of the Indian Ocean and Bay of Bengal. Frighteningly, five months after Pearl Harbor the Japanese held an empire extending south to Australia and west to British India. No conquest in modern history had been so quick, so far-reaching. MacArthur fought vainly to stem the tide . . . abandoned Manila, withdrew to the Bataan peninsula for a desperate last stand. Painfully, Americans recall those dark days when medical supplies ran out and food became so scarce the Army was fed mule meat. The general left, vowing to return. . . .

What could be worse? Yes—the death march on Bataan when American and Filipino forces, abandoned, were compelled to capitulate . . . 78,000 weakened and weary men . . . forced by bayonets to march to prison camps. Thousands died . . . those who stumbled, slaughtered. A month later Corregidor had fallen and the last American flag in the Far East was run down. The date? May 6, 1942!

In the determined days that followed, American and British forces stemmed the Japanese tide. In May a Japanese armada headed toward the Coral Sea. A now-wiser

American fleet cut enemy plans short in a history-making battle in which battleships exchanged no shots and never saw one another! On Midway, Admiral Chester Nimitz outfoxed the enemy and regained the island at a high cost. Or, as one foreign correspondent wrote: "The empty chairs stood in silent question and on a night of victory voices were hushed."

Tired of typing material from hastily scribbled notes, Marvel opened her window one late-March Sunday afternoon, thinking with a smile that the love songs of the mockingbirds in the lime trees outdid the hum of the light traffic. She inhaled deeply and smiled again. Downstairs, Daddy, Uncle Worth, and B.J. were warming up for the first baseball match of the season, the men as excited as the boy. The high-school coach was in charge at school, but Daddy served as coach, teacher, umpire, consultant, and co-owner in their yard—Uncle Worth being his business partner! The two deacons had volunteered to combine need with pleasure, train a youth group from the church of their affiliation, and challenge similar organizations from other churches in a "World Series." All three of the Harringtons were as exuberant as the birds. And they were not alone in their pleasure. Mother and Auntie Rae stood applauding from the sidelines. Marvel felt her own heart leap with joy at the sights and sounds of it all. What darlings!

Mary Ann agreed a short time later. Her cousin had come for something. Marvel wondered just what. It was unlike the other girl to show restraint. This was an ideal time for seeking her opinion.

"How are chances of your proofreading this for me?" Marvel asked, holding out the completed papers. "It's a review of the Asian war."

As she read, a frown of concentration creased the unblemished area of Mary Ann's forehead between the dark eyes. "So far, so good—excellent, of course, like all your other work. You're such a polished writer, but—"

"It lacks something? Don't hesitate to say. It's for a column."

Mary Ann's black curls fanned out in her headshake of denial. "The only thing it lacks is—is completion. I mean, bringing things up to date. And of course you know that. But Marvel, don't you think you should pay tribute to our president—our commander-in-chief?"

"Absolutely. But in another column, maybe?"

"I don't know," Mary Ann said slowly. "Sometimes, well, it's best not to wait. *Words* can die, too. They lose their meaning—"

"What's troubling you, Mary Ann?" Marvel asked gently.

The words of explanation tumbled out with a rush. Marvel hadn't heard? There was a hint—just a hint, mind you, because reporters dare not alert the enemy, even if the whisper meant something. But there was a reason why President Roosevelt canceled his usual "fireside chat" and why the White House refused to answer questions. He—he just might be worse— even— Oh no, he couldn't be close to the end!

"They don't know. Nobody would know that. You are right, so let's not repeat the rumor. I'll tell you what: Let's lay the rumor to rest, without a tribute!" Marvel made her voice as light as possible, partly to console her cousin and partly to allay her own fear. There could be no denying that Franklin Delano Roosevelt, always fragile of stature since his long battle with polio, was weakening. Commentators had pointed out the dark circles beneath his eyes, the increasing lines of pain in his otherwise smile-creased face. He was weary.

Mary Ann stood on first one leg and then the other. "I should go—let you get back to your writing, and see if I can settle down to my own. I *am* working on our heritage in language, but this is so serious. We know it could happen. We *could* lose our leader. And, oh Marvel, if—if that happened, we'd lose this war—couldn't we?"

"I can't answer that. Our president has a vice president—"

Mary Ann nodded. "Truman. What does he know? I love our FDR!"

"We both love him. He's the only president you and I have ever known. The only one we remember clearly, anyway." Marvel felt her mind sweep backward. It was true. One of her earliest memories was—

But Mary Ann interrupted her thinking. "I'm hearing from Jake from some Army post office—could be here or out there anywhere. So hush-hush. You realize, don't you, that if—if we lost him, the president, this war could go on and on—and Jake wouldn't come home ever?"

That brought Marvel's memory back. Of course! That was the early memory she had tried to recall. She smiled faintly, as faintly as she remembered. Mother, Daddy, and she lived in the big house in town.

"How can you smile after what I've told you? How, Marvel?"

"I'm not smiling at the news, Mary Ann. You know there's nothing amusing about our president's infirmity. I was remembering our first awareness that there *was* a president. Remember when something called 'Black Friday' was the tragedy lying there all coiled to strike? I'm not sure either of us had heard of Herbert Hoover."

Mary Ann squinted in concentration. "I—I ought to remember if you do—us being birthday twins." Her face changed expressions suddenly. "I *do* remember! He—Mr. Hoover—was leaving, admitting defeat. Let's see, in two ways he was defeated. That president had lost the election when our Franklin Delano Roosevelt ran against him. You're right. That's my first memory of—of politics. But," the squint was back, "I don't think it was anything to smile about."

Marvel shook her head. Would she be able to make Mary Ann understand? She would try. "We were too young to think much about it, but Mr. Hoover's words came to mean more later: 'We are finished.' But you must have understood better than I did. You were concerning yourself with Jake's welfare *then*, and you're doing it again."

To her surprise, Mary Ann nodded. But then she sighed. "I am right now, too. I mean, I'm understanding better than you. Oh, a day at a time, we decided, didn't we? So I'll stop stewin'. But Marvel, you *will* do a big article a-about President Roosevelt?"

"I will," Marvel said.

Jake. It had always been Jake Brotherton with Mary Ann. Just as it had been Titus for her. There was room for none else. Marvel let her mind retrace another avenue she had unintentionally opened then closed off quickly during the conversation. But with Mary Ann gone, she returned to political plans Titus had shared with her. Churches should involve themselves, he had said. People simply did not understand that it was their duty. Religion carried a powerful wallop. And someday he would prove it. And he would have—had he lived. . . .

The thought chafed, causing Mary Ann's suggestion that the president's condition could have worsened to enlarge. The lump where her heart belonged gathered circumference like a rolling stone. Her hand reached for the radio dial. Maybe Mary Ann's rumor was true!

Is it true. Dare we hope (the announcer parried, as if shielding himself against further disappointment) that victory *is* nearing? That "unconditional surrender" demanded by our president is close enough that Americans should prepare themselves for the shape of a postwar world? Mr. Roosevelt was always one to give others hope when his own hope must be faltering for our nation—and yes, for himself. One gets the feeling—the *thinkers* among us—that even before the United States entered World War II, President Roosevelt concerned himself with its inevitability...spelled out in his incomparable mind postwar aims...attributing a jazz-crazed country with more judgment that it appeared to possess. How much more clearly could the man make it than the precious four freedoms he enunciated in January '41, before the "day that will live in infamy" in December? Freedom of speech and worship...freedom from fear and want... Oh, we have paid the price...are paying it even now.... Blood still flows....Hearts still bleed. And now, in this long blackout on news, we ponder what lies ahead. "There will be no rejoicing when we win, as God has preordained we can, we *will*, we MUST!" our leader often declared. "*No* celebrating, rather a tearful promise to our brave men and women who offered themselves as a living sacrifice, the sacred vow that this will *never* happen again!" And so we know that a long period of adjustment lies ahead.... We will have won the *war*. Can we keep the *peace*?

Oh, I was among the thinkers, Marvel thought now. And the blood seemed to drain from her heart, trembling now as she had trembled then...how many years ago? Radio was new to her in those childhood years. But from those incomplete news reports she had gleaned enough to convince her that the then-new President Franklin Delano Roosevelt sensed that the massacres overseas would entangle the rest of Europe and, eventually, spread like Bermuda grass to cover the world. What was the name applied to the German Nazi party? Oh, yes, *gestapo*—ignored for a time, dismissed as long as the world applied the "live and let live" policy like blind mice. "And blind we were," she whispered in despair now ... "isolationists." Then, with prayers on her lips, she traveled back....

How many nights Marvel Harrington had lain awake staring at the ceiling to imagine overhead rafters dripping with Jewish blood. The vision was so clear and so unbearable that often she would pull the downy covers above her head for protection, dozing to awaken during the spring storms when thunder turned to roaring cannons; lightning, to sharply honed steel bayonets slashing the sky in deadly aim. Running was impossible. There was no hiding place. Bodies of the dead lay everywhere ... victims of executioners!

Daddy would come to awaken her, sitting with her until she slept. And later, there was Titus. Titus, who took her willing heart into captivity ... Titus, who shared with her his dreams, his countless callings. Then came Spain ... and Titus was among the fallen....

And now there was no one left to awaken her. The nightmare was reality. No one? There was God, her ever-faithful refuge in time of trouble. "My mission remains unaccomplished. Help me, Lord," she whispered. "Let me complete the one goal of this day. I'll be back to ask day after day after day, begging Your help. Be patient, bear with me. Strengthen my legs, my heart, my faith. I'll be back—"

With a stifled sob, Marvel hurried down the stairs, walking (she thought triumphantly) on the legs of faith. The mail had come. Without interest, she sorted through it. Then, with a gasp, she groped for the settee nearest the front door. Feeling faint, she tried to focus on the properly addressed envelope. There was no name on the unfamiliar return address. But the letter bore an Austin, Texas, postmark! *Titus*. Titus Smith—impossible.

In numbed silence, she stared foolishly at the white rectangle, afraid to open it—afraid of the words inside. There was hope—ever so faint, but hope all the same—as long as she left it sealed.

Oh, how stupid—asking God to help but not trusting. Although her hands trembled uncontrollably, Marvel tore off one end of the envelope and forced her eyes to the signature.

Kate Lynn. Kate Lynn Porter ... now widowed ...

Shattering disappointment came first, followed by all-consuming fury—a fury so great, so devilish, that she did what must have been the most impetuous act of her life: tore the lengthy pages in half. She would have thrown it, unread, into the trash had there been a wastebasket near. As it was, somehow she managed to climb the stairs to the sanctity of her room.

Marvel checked her watch. How long had she slept, if sleep she did? She must have, because composure had come. *Praise the Lord!* The Austin postmark seemed suddenly to bring the warmth and gentleness of Titus back, and she would have him with her forever in memories designed to strengthen, not drain. Life must go on. "And You knew it all along, didn't You?" she whispered, looking upward. Yes, God knew. So He would understand that resolutions were an "inside job" and took time. As yet, she was unable to absorb the contents of whatever her friend had written, and unable to write, as if in memorial eulogy, a living person. The president was alive—just as Titus, Kate Lynn's husband and father, Duke, and countless others were not.

With characteristic determination, Marvel returned to her review of the war. Prompted by some inner voice, she again turned the radio on—just in case. Thrusting the rumor aside, she listened. And yes, the news was on. Something was in the air—something she was unable to pin down, just hanging there unspoken. The commentator's voice sounded past-tense to Marvel's trained ear:

> History now is the conference of the Big Three who at Yalta, according to reliable sources, seem to have engaged themselves in *postwar* diplomacy. No, it is not over—not by a long shot. But Lloyd's of London have declared the winners, and have we ever known that group to fail?
>
> Not that it has been easy. But the good news is that as recently as March 7, here in 1945, by a great stroke of good fortune, American troops captured the Ludenhendorff Bridge at Rematen before it could be destroyed. Allies poured into the German heartland. German resistance crumbled like stale bread as Montgomery-led British swept the northern plain while Bradley-led Americans trapped some 250,000 Germans in the Ruhr. Within days American forces would be in Berlin, we said. But caution about speculation! Eisenhower sent his troops against a mythical "national redoubt," supposedly readied for a last stand

by Hitler in Bavarian and Austrian mountains. When our troops reached the Elbe, the truth was out...both to bitter, disillusioned forces and those of us waiting on the homefront for the news blackout to lift.

Again we wait...hoping and praying for President Franklin Delano Roosevelt...while remembering his years of warning to lay aside rumors. American troops, meanwhile, are more cautious now. And so we wait for the Russians to take the German capital, just 53 miles away! Churchill's plea that Allies should shake hands with the Russians as far east as possible appears to have been ignored by American commanders who spurn "political decisions." And, if news leaks prove true, the world is faced with a seriously ill president and a poorly briefed successor, neither seeing fit to countermand the generals. Although we pray that history will record this morning's address a false prophecy. But, admittedly, we share concerns. His words, and I quote, were: "In this melancholy void, one president cannot act and the other cannot know...."

* * *

April 11, 1945! The day began as usual for Marvel and Mary Ann. There was the usual push of impatient lines at the OPA office. It seemed normal. *Almost!* With the usual pasted-on smiles, the well-trained girls set to work with a behind-the-scenes meshing of gears. Looking back, Marvel had sensed a sort of restrain in attitude. Or was it her imagination, her own tucked-away misgivings? The name of the president was not mentioned, as if by design. She was glad when the day ended—glad to hurry away.

The same atmosphere repeated at the USO. Mary Ann made one significant observation, a cautiously phrased question. "Did you notice that lots of the men in uniform were missing—that the few guys there were strangers? It seemed—well, different."

"I noticed, yes," Marvel agreed. "But we've watched the faces change all along. Some seem to be stationed close by, others just passing through. I remember one such boy—" She checked herself before it was too late. Wasn't it pointless and upsetting to mention the young soldier who insisted that he had seen her photograph? "In fact, I remember several," she recommenced, "who were one-nighters."

But both girls knew the probable cause of the undue quiet.

It was the latter part of the evening that made April sixth a red-letter day in Marvel's memory. Little did she, other members of the Harrington family, or the nation know that it was a prelude to tragedy. Although, in retrospect, some may have suspected.

Marvel was all too ready to accept as a possible air of denial, if one existed, the festive attitude of the family. Auntie Rae hummed as she put a copper kettle on to boil the coffee water. "Gives off lights, doesn't it? Your mother said I was guardian of this heirloom, so I polished it today."

"Again?" Uncle Worth teased. His whistle of appreciation set Daddy to whistling which, in turn, came out in note by B.J. With more volume than talent the youngest Harrington bolted out: "Whistle while you work!" And suddenly the entire family joined in song while performing swing-shift tasks.

In the breathless pause that followed, Mother said with a hint of regret that she wished they could sing around the piano again.

"Well, my sweet, that thing was a little heavy to carry—uh, slippance!—so shall I say *tote*? Let's settle for calling that stored music maker an *overhaul!*"

"Oh, you—off with your head!" Mother laughed, her tone now light. "There are other music makers. We have time for one song. Oh, please—*pretty* please!" Without waiting for an answer, she was removing her violin from its fleece-lined case.

"Tonight," Snow Harrington said, lifting the bow of the instrument near to but not touching the strings, "I shall play for those I love: my beloved family, those who fight to keep us safe and hold us together, our c-country's commander-in-chief, and to a God whose wisdom will one day lead us to peace. I—I—"

Mother, who had begun so professionally—as if addressing an audience in some great cathedral—now faltered. The gaze which had been so steady now sought support as the expressive eyes locked with each member of the family, one by one.

"And we will listen," her husband half-whispered before dropping his face as if to hide tears (or fears?).

"With all our hearts," Marvel finished for him.

Mother played then. And the sad-sweet notes combined to make what surely must be a part of the unfinished symphony she

52

had pledged to write one day. Surely her talented fingers had never produced such beautiful music. It spoke. It whispered. It promised. What was its message? Hope. Of course: *hope*. All things were made possible.

All sat in awed silence, each interpreting perhaps according to a special need. Surely all felt they could touch God's face....

And then the temp changed to a melody so triumphant that the stringed instrument rivaled the marching brass bands that quickstepped past a lifetime ago when the world was safer... more secure. Could she be the little girl who listened...believing in all things? The coming of a circus...a revival meeting ...an opening of the state fair? And later the few-in-number (but cherished all the more) school assemblies or football rallies? Then, support for the now-weakened president...his promise that our boys would never have to fight overseas? Ah, but that was before Satan and all his dragons moved in to launch war in an effort to overcome the world.

Mother's music clenched determined fists in the fallen angel's face. He would *not* win! Her audience agreed, now clapping with such abandon that the noise almost—but not quite—deafened all ears to the hiss of steam and warning shriek of the hot kettle.

Auntie Rae moved to shush it, set the coffee to perking, and hurried back to join into the jubilate roundelay. Time was forgotten, as were worries and concerns. For this one day...

* * *

April 12, 1945! In Warm Spring, Georgia, Franklin Delano Roosevelt joined the ever-lengthening casualty list of World War II casualties. Americans everywhere were stunned at the quiet announcement that their leader had died of a massive cerebral hemorrhage. It was impossible to believe that the dynamic man who had been president for 12 years was suddenly gone. Women stood in the streets and wept—wept for a loneliness akin to nothing they had known before, for their loved ones "over there" or "right here," if they were among the few unemployed. Men, hurrying home to join them—or men and women rushing home together—heard the news via car radios or newsboys hawking on every hand: "EX-TRA! EX-TRA! SPECIAL EDITION! THE PRESIDENT IS DEAD!" There were no strangers left in once-unfriendly cities. Numbly, they shared their mutual loss, becoming friends in their grief and through their newspapers. Among the latter was the *New York Times*. One writer said: "Men will thank God on their knees tonight—and a hundred years from now) that Franklin D. Roosevelt was in the White House."

Flags lowered to half-mast. Heads lowered in prayer. Inside the OPA office, windows lowered as soundlessly and with the same finality as eyelids closing in death. Any future triumph would be married to tragedy.

Radio programs preempted all scheduled programs, all commercials. Stations switched immediately to soft strains of organ music and would continue to do so for the three-day mourning period in which Franklin Delano Roosevelt, the most controversial president of all national leaders, lay in state. Americans mourned the president's passing...weeping their loss...the loss to his family...and yes, the loss to his beloved pet, the little Scottie, "Fala," who would never hear his master's voice again. For all this, the day would live forever—the day when America wept together....

But someone must be practical, carry on with the same precision as that exhibited by First Lady Eleanor Roosevelt in her simple message to their sons. "Your father has passed away peacefully." The whole world was to know soon. Difference in time zones made it possible for other countries to learn of the American president's death before Americans themselves—to learn, yes, and to respond. Allies and enemies alike sent brief condolences—with one exception: *Japan!*

Sensing the need to lay her own grief aside, Marvel Harrington became that "someone." It was she who alerted the adjutant general at the base where Captain Philip Prinz had been stationed before he, too, met with death. And, as she suspected, no, the general did *not* know then. Next she notified Pastor Jim. Shocked, he promised a prayer service for the evening. Marvel then turned to take a weeping Mary Ann in her arms....

5

The Cutting Edge

In the days, weeks, and months following the president's death, Americans grappled for a vague understanding of their situation. It was a period of confusion and uncertainty for people at home and abroad—as well as for the poorly prepared successor, Harry S. Truman. The new president faced a fateful decision Americans had known little or nothing about, except within the closed ranks of the military. The news media had managed to glean only bits and pieces concerning the "secret weapon," said capable of ending World War II with a bang—to bring peace to the universe or destroy it! This in the hands of a bumbling man who, to the despair of the White House, Secret Service agents were unable to guide through proper entry and exit doors?

"How do you feel about it all?" a white-faced Mary Ann asked of Marvel at one point.

"Like I'm standing on the cutting edge of a knife," Marvel answered frankly. "It will take time for us to adjust, and I'm not sure how much we have."

"Time," Mary Ann tasted the word and nodded. "What was it Benjamin Franklin said: 'Time is the very stuff life is made of, so spend it wisely'?"

"Correct. I'm proud of you." She could have said more—that her cousin had been a brick: no recriminations, no blame-fixing or chest-beating. Not even a mention of Jake, although she was well aware that the world might be facing a graver situation than ever before with the threat of the weapon and knowledge that war still raged in the Pacific where service personnel knew nothing of either its existence or the death of their leader. Who could reach them?

"I keep remembering what Brother Jim said, telling us at the prayer service how brave we'd have to be the day we lost our president. He was right. We *do* have to carry on. Said we had a mission to carry out, and life was like a relay race. Our president had carried the national baton around the racetrack in three four-year laps. He expected us to be ready when he tossed it to us, to carry on un-until our men come home and we can hand it back to *them*. I—I thought about that and, oh Marvel, I prayed—"

"I know you did, darling. And you *did* catch the baton."

Mary Ann lifted her head proudly and, basking in the praise, said: "And I'll *keep* running. But it's hard. I guess," she went on slowly, "that's what God expects. Who threw *that* baton?"

Mary Ann asked *that*? "Try Jesus," she improvised quickly. And then Marvel Harrington was wondering who said what came next. "A relay race could be lost in the shifting of that baton. I guess we dare not fumble or miscalculate when our time comes. Yes, we must keep on with the race until it's finished. And we don't know about time."

The two girls embraced in sudden silence. It was Mary Ann who pulled back eventually. "And you—you all the time standing on that sharp blade, whacking your feet to the bone. Sorry. I had to try to joke be-before I start blubbering."

She had waited too long. Marvel handed Mary Ann a tissue. And both of them laughed through their tears. . . .

The secret weapon. What was it? Marvel pondered after hearing the words spoken from lips of a man who should know—words which jarred the world: "A new era is upon us. Men since the beginning of time have sought peace. Military alliances, balances of power, leagues of nations, all in turn failed, leaving the only path to be by way of the crucible of war. The utter destructiveness of war now blots out this alternative. We have had our last chance. If we do not devise some greater and more equitable system, Armageddon will be at our door."

The words radioed by General Douglas MacArthur from aboard the *Missouri* (in a secret location) underscored an inescapable moral to the American people. Some understood better than others, but all looked to his war record and trusted his judgment.

Marvel, who had listened, read, and kept endless pages of notes, was among the more informed. But she, too, felt an aching need to know more about this "ultimate weapon" of which the general himself was cautious. Talk about standing on the cutting edge! "Help him, dear God," she whispered fervently. "Help us all. Somehow we have lost our way."

Yes, lost their way indeed. Just as—as when? In her overtaxed mind, Marvel saw it clearly then through memories she had thought buried. Certainly they should have been, for she was not among those attending the costly extravaganza in New York, the last World's Fair, back in 1939. But she had traveled vicariously—as she traveled now—and felt as lost in the labyrinth of streets, plazas, and buildings as those fair-goers would have felt when confronted with working their way through the grounds and eventually seeking an exit. Oh, but there had been an indexed map. Maps were bewildering sometimes, without a guide. Mercifully, there had been one standing near to point the way.

Just as there always would be, Marvel realized with clarity. The index was the Bible; the guide was God! Finding solace in that, she felt a surge of strength. Now her research could continue.

With a half-smile playing at the corner of her lips, Marvel remembered displays of science-based industry, both dazzling and spooky. Spookiest was the Westinghouse time capsule to be opened 50 centuries from then. Imagine! Inside would be items of that day in common use for most: alarm clocks, can openers, tooth-cleaning powders, and safety razors with blades. Other inclusions were materials used in construction such as silver in coins. But ranked as most important were names: Jesse Owens, the black athlete who won the 100-meter dash in the 1936 Olympic Games, famous baseball players (oh, those Daddy and Billy Joe must see!), leaders in the war between China and Japan, Margaret Mitchell who wrote *Gone with the Wind* . . . and (Marvel winced) President Franklin Delano Roosevelt. . . .

Quickly turning the page of her thoughts, she recalled—immediately regretting the recollection—the General Electric exhibit: a million volts of manmade lightning, accompanied by the crash of synthetic thunder . . . a display which astounded spectators and astounded her equally even now. The *why* of astonishment was no secret. As if in prophecy, the display foretold the secret weapon!

Never mind other memories. The "ultimate weapon" now foretold the world's future. Its infancy lay in the year of the fair of

1939. There was a connection. History would prove her right, Marvel Harrington felt with all her young heart. And although the future was screened by time, history would bear out her vision. There would come a day when the world would know as she knew back in 1945.

The real threat to Japan (although neither the Japanese nor most Americans were aware of it) was scientific. The services of American scientists had been called to an extent never known before the fateful year of 1939. There were remarkable strikes as one might expect, for even then those at the top felt the threat of war. At first, scientists nodded approval of such newly developed weapons as a rocket-launching "bazooka," with which two infantrymen could destroy a tank, and the proximity fuse which used radio waves to detonate a shell as it neared its target. A beginning, yes, but "show us more."

And so it was that the greatest of the new weapons grew from an acorn of thought abroad to a sprawling oak with roots so firmly imbedded that it shook the very foundations of the earth. On January 25, 1939, a Danish physicist announced that two German scientists had succeeded in achieving atomic fusion in uranium. The discovery made possible construction of a bomb infinitely more deadly than any known to man. Albert Einstein brought the matter to President Roosevelt. Yes, the American president agreed reluctantly, this country dare not fall behind in national defense.

Early in 1940, noting implications of atomic fission, America launched an atomic program at the University of California. Outcome: "the atom smasher," using a mighty cyclotron. Follow-through: "nuclear chain reaction." Date: December 2, 1942. Place: University of Chicago football stadium.

Enormous technical problems remained to be solved and there might be little time.... Various corps of engineers worked around the clock in plants at carefully selected, uninhabited sites to make fissionable material. Overnight, Hanford, Washington, became a tarpaper metropolis...population: 51,000 citizens. Another, Oak Ridge, with a population of 75,000 became the largest city in

Tennessee. Yet so carefully guarded was the dangerous weapon's production that one professor's wife asked: "Why don't you get into something important instead of trotting blindly from place to place?"

And then it happened. In the spring of 1943 at Los Alamos, New Mexico, work began on the mighty bomb, and on July 16, 1945, scientists and military men donned dark glasses and gathered to watch with fear and trembling a predawn detonation of the atomic bomb! The New Mexico desert at Alamogordo might well have announced that the last battle—the battle between good and evil—had begun. A blinding flash, like a great green super-sun, illuminated the desert...rising higher, ever higher into the clouds in a fraction of a second to a height of more than 8000 feet. "The whole earth lighted up with dazzling luminosity," shaken reporters noted in awe as the gigantic column assumed a mushroom shape that symbolized the new age. There came a thunderous roar which shook the earth with more force than the strongest earthquake. One scientist said: "I was sure the end had come—the last millisecond of earth's existence—and am persuaded that the *last man* will see something similar if—"

Implication: *If we use it!* Question: Has man created the monster which will destroy himself and his fellowman?

Given the bits and pieces Marvel had gleaned from news reports, her father's question came as no great surprise. Or was it that she was more conditioned to shock? The Harringtons had faced far too many dragons to find a puff of smoke alarming.

"We've known," Daddy said slowly, "since Eisenhower took it on himself to make the decision on ordering troops to capture Prague that it sealed some postwar fates—and meant we'd have to reach some decisions on *our* own, too. Our family, I mean," he paused for Uncle Worth's nod before finishing the thought. "And the time has come. It's not new and shouldn't be unexpected, so why am I beating around the bush? Here I come, ready or not, as we used to say in hide-and-seek games. Would you fair ladies wish to give some thought to making a move? We gents have an opportunity to double our income—"

Mother gasped. "Move? Move *where*? What's wrong *here*?"

"Nothing's wrong here, Snow, dear. It's just something I want you to talk over. *Where* could be Oak Ridge, down south in

Tennessee—or there's Alamogordo testing grounds for this hush-hush weapon we keep hearing about. Strange thing that parts were made in so many places—shipped here, shipped there. We did some without—"

"Without knowing it? Wow! Maybe I oughta do my paper on *that* subject instead of such a trivial thing as baseball!" B.J. interrupted. "Of course I could do it somewhere else—"

"We aren't going anywhere right now," Auntie Rae said softly.

"We aren't going anywhere later either!" Mother sounded ready to burst into tears. "And baseball is not trivial—it's important. I mean it used to be. And it will be again. The war's over!"

"Not as long as our boys have to keep fighting on so many fronts, Snow," Uncle Worth said. "But we'll not be hasty. We'll vote on the matter, girls. Just think over our postwar plans."

"Oh, we will—we will!" Mother's smile shimmered like morning dew as she rose to clear the table. "We'll talk and plan—even start packing when you're ready. Oh, to be going *home!*"

The clock struck a warning. There would be no more talk....

The clock of time struck its own warning repeatedly, the hands picking up tempo. Yes, Eisenhower's delayed plans worked. American and Russian soldiers met with an embrace (in spite of the Soviet's previous protests) and, as if wound too tight, time rushed on, allowing no time for absorbing historical events. Italian partisans killed Mussolini and strung him up by the heels alongside his mistress in a Milan gas station. Adolph Hitler committed suicide holed up in a Berlin bunker. And the United States Fifth Army cut through a sobered Italy to meet the Seventh Army approaching from Austria. At 2:41 A.M., May 7, at Eisenhower headquarters in Rheims, General Alfred Jodi unconditionally surrendered ragged, misled remnants of the German forces. The long-awaited victory in Europe—V.E. Day—had come at last. Winston Churchill moved through cheering crowds, smiling and holding up two fingers in his famous "V for victory" sign with an aching heart and a mind oppressed by forebodings. Grief for the departed president mingled with anxiety over the Pacific war which continued to rage out of control.

Oh, there was more—much more—Marvel Harrington needed to write. But time was unfriendly with her, too. Service personnel, many maimed and disfigured outwardly and hopelessly scarred inwardly, limped in for comfort at the USO. And bitter—oh, such bitterness! Marvel listened and the sharp blade of pain stabbed deeper into her heart. The only rays of sun peeking in at the OPA office glistened in the eyes of young wives, some leading small children their fathers-at-war had never seen, who rushed in for additional rations.

"I understand," they invariably said, "that we are allowed gas for a permanent change of address? My husband's been away since Pearl Harbor, and he's mustering out. We can go back home!"

Going home! Oh, the sunshiny thought.

But even its brightness dimmed all too frequently. Satan, always waiting in the wings, moved in to tighten the noose of discouragement and depression around the necks of battle-weary veterans. And before the processed-and-ready coupons could be claimed, the telephone (once a threat to wives employed in the dreary office fearing news a husband was shipping out, now became the feared black monster telling of another type disaster) would ring out a death knell.

"Help—we need help. Need it *now*! I'm a neighbor—needing gasoline to get family—a doctor. Oh, they're dead—all *dead*! He came home—nobody knows what happened. Oh, dear Lord! They've all been shot! He—he shot my friend—their children— then blew his brains out. *Help!*" Another serviceman had come home....

Later Marvel would wonder how total responsibility for taking those calls—in fact, to monitor *all* calls—fell on her shoulders. For now, she set that Harrington jaw and performed all soul-shaking duties. The Greatest Physician a war-torn world could hope to meet stood by her side, guiding her step-by-step—and more! He supplied Marvel the strength to clench her fists and shake them in the very face of Satan. Mary Ann saw and caught the baton, taking over the relay at the appropriate moment. The race would be won!

Once she paused to whisper: "Oh Marvel, the president tried to prepare us for postwar adjustment—and these are the same! Let me tell you," her tone grew fierce, "if ever Jake gets back— and he *will*, just like Titus will—let's allow nothing short of natural death to come between us. *Nothing!* Do you vow?"

"I promised that a long time ago, and it was a part of your vow."

The telephone rang again. That night the two of them stopped by for counseling themselves. And Pastor Jim understood....

Marvel was surprised to find her father waiting at the gate again. "Still appraising real estate, Daddy?" she tried teasing.

Daddy smiled back, but his tone was serous. "The nursery's calling, need you both—you and Mary Ann. Some kind of emergency detained the little guys. I guess there are adjustments—"

"When the servicemen return? Yes, Daddy, there are adjustments in coming home We have to prepare in advance. Hard!"

He reached out to touch her hand. "You are so understanding, and I feel inadequate, like I'm putting too much burden on you. Sometimes," he sighed in the shadowy twilight, "I wonder if fathers are important." His grip tightened around her fingers.

Marvel took the hand so dearly remembered and pressed it against her cheek. "Fathers are *very* important. You especially! You are there when I need you, which is all the time, saying what I need to hear."

Something made him laugh. "And telling myself those pearls of wisdom will be forgotten, but pretending they never will be!"

"Stick around, Daddy, so I'll know you were right," she teased again. But all the while a niggling through remained unvoiced. Dale Harrington, head supervisor at the state's highest-producing defense plant, deacon, and in charge of so much his daughter had lost count, had not come for an analysis of his self-worth.

"What's wrong, Daddy?" she asked gently. "Better tell me before the line-up-for-chow call comes. And *then* we'll take time to smell the roses before running our separate ways on this 25-hour shift. Aren't they wonderful—the roses, I mean?"

"Everything your mother does is wonderful. That's why I feel like a heel. My sails are sagging."

"So put, cry, or—if it makes you feel better—strike back!"

"I'd just hit *myself*! Remember when I mentioned about moving? Your uncle and I told about the job offer? It boomeranged."

"You mean, oh Daddy, you teaser! You mean there was no such offer?" Feeling a great wash of relief, Marvel laughed.

"No, that part was real, only—" he hesitated, but his voice was stronger. "I didn't want to go. Neither did Worth."

This time when Marvel laughed, her father laughed with her. It was she who spoke. "Well, you got your answer. Mother *will* go home. You men can sell without fearing a custody battle."

Daddy inhaled deeply. "Oh, the roses *do* smell sweet."

"Sweeter than ham and red-eye gravy?" Mother called from the porch. "Hurry, Marvel—the nursery's calling you, honey."

The telephone rang again, and Marvel rushed in to answer. . . .

"I knew it was bad," Mary Ann said wearily after it was all over. "It wasn't even our evening. But I'm happy they called—let us help—"

"Yes," Marvel said quietly, glad that darkness hid the tears gathering in her eyes, "it is good that we could help—and that you saw it as a privilege. Goodness knows we've had experience."

A passing bus interrupted the brief conversation. The girls were almost home before Mary Ann could answer. "I kept thinking about— Oh Marvel, do you remember that awful, *awful* incident back on—on the trip to California? It was a living nightmare all the way. I'll have grit in my craw forever. But I'm thinking about the time when those helpless little girls, just babies, were abandoned in that migratory laborers' shack. Their daddy was drunk, their mommy dead—"

"I'll never forget either—never. This time it was the mother who skipped out. 'Tired of waiting,' the note she left said, before deserting her two. I was about to say, 'It's the children who always suffer most,' but this time I wonder."

Mary Ann groaned. "I thought about that one, too. That no-good gal had the gall to write a 'Dear John' letter to her husband: 'Dear John, I love you very much but—*blah*, blah!' and her man fighting for her. Oh, I could *kill* her. All she had to fight was boredom—chasin' like she did! And she *did* chase. Don't tell me different-differently! Those babies had a list of 'uncles' a mile long. Maybe sometime it'll be funny, but not now. They thought like those tots thought in the fields that she would be back—kept saying they *knew* Mommy would come back, "'cause her 'n Unkie Don picked out uh baftub big 'nuf fer 'em both'! Good thing Mommy didn't show. I'd have choked her to death!"

Marvel felt equal fury. But it was best not to encourage her impetuous cousin's anger. Instead she said lightly, "'Thou shalt not kill'—and I'm not sure about capital punishment here, either."

"I'd stand my chances! But," Mary Ann's voice grew gentle, "there are better ways. I'm needed. And Marvel, God has to give me a good shaking every so often to remind me—make me see that His little ones have to be cared for. And," she sighed, "much as I want to get on with my own life, there'll always have to be other things—other ways I have to serve. Children need parents—*both* parents. And they need Sunday school and learning the basics of plain old mundane readin', writin', and 'rithmetic. And, I guess, maybe taught-to-the-tune-of-a-hickory-stick has its place. Okay, *now* laugh!"

"I don't feel like laughing—more like crying."

Arm-in-arm, they walked up the steps of home.

* * *

Tossing her wear-it-out, make-it-do purse onto the nearest bedroom chair, Marvel sighed, thankful that another trying day was finished—as finished, she thought with a smile, as the handbag. Well, she could replace it soon, without luxury tax if the war ended as hoped. No, the day was not finished—not quite. A must was listening for news.

Let us not forget Pearl Harbor and the 100 beachheads to Tokyo—when we reach it. And reach it, we can, we *will*, we MUST. Also we must remember . . . for ourselves and for our children—stamp it all indelibly in history, lest we, in blind ignorance, relieve the "death march of Bataan" . . . the slow, grinding American advances from island to island until now cities of Japan lie within range of our newly-created weapon . . . *if it must be used*. Victory spelled out in sweat, blood, tears, and the stench of death, represents countless D-days, H-hours, and V.E. Day in the European theater—and now, with trembling hearts and praying hands, we stand on the brink of V.J. Day—or annihilation which destroys our world! Remember soberly the fury by day and the terror by night . . . through steamy jungles . . . in the air . . . under the water . . . the losses which shocked and sickened us all. They fought—and we fought with them. For victory, yes, but oh, the price to pay for those isles of rubble! One foreign correspondent tells of the wounded Marine, looking back on a useless island of sulfur in which Japanese holed up, refusing to surrender. The American Marine saw an eight-mile stretch of volcanic wasteland covered completely with smashed materials and mangled bodies. Fervently, he cried out: "I hope to God we don't have to take any more such screwy islands" . . . and then mercifully collapsed. But it took two months of vicious fighting— *agonized* fighting . . . use of flame throwers and dynamite

...forgetting that either they or the enemies were human beings—to knock out the dead Marine's "screwy islands" and allow Americans to march on the road to Japan. And now over us all hangs the mysterious mushroom cloud which at the push of a button will bring a hush of history.

Never would Marvel Harrington forget the plea in the voice of that radio reporters. Feeling the weight of early-August heat press down on her, she stretched full-length across her bed—but not to rest. Thoughts were as heavy as the heat, and, driven by the urgency in the announcer's voice, she rose to make notes of all his words and filed them for future reference. Again she lay down—this time to pray. "Dear Lord!" she cried out as fervently as the reported Marine, "Help our president in this fateful decision. Save us—save the world You created, and we misused!"

6

Day Dawns on a More Dangerous World

Hot-breathed August moved on. The Harringtons' victory garden continued to flourish in spite of the heat. Perhaps, Marvel was to think later, it was due to frequent waterings—from sprinklers and from tears. All was still. Leaves hung motionless on the trees as if aware that the world's final countdown had begun. Conversation dwindled. And the earth stood still on its axis.

"I hope and pray that Harry Truman has enough horse sense to listen to experts before ordering use of that bomb," Dale Harrington commented at one point. It—it sounds inhuman."

His brother nodded. "Oh, for *God's sake*, man!" he cried out in a voice overcome with emotion. "Surely he won't use it. After all, the Japs *are* human beings—"

B.J.'s young face flushed. "There's some doubt about that!"

"We're all upset. Who isn't these days?" Rae Harrington said softly. "We must bridle our tongues, except in prayer."

The family talked then, their love for one another shining through every word spoken above distant strains of a radio playing:

> I kneel in my solitude and silently pray
> That heaven will protect you, dear,
> And there'll come a day
> When we'll meet again at the place heaven blest—
> The Shrine of Saint Cecelia.

"Wasn't that the British shrine that escaped the bombs?" Mary Ann whispered to Marvel in a choked voice.

It was Uncle Worth who responded by saying that prayer was all that could save the world. The others were quick to agree. They agreed equally with Daddy's suggestion that they listen even more closely to the radio—pray and listen both to the news and for God's answer. "And there's no time like the present!" he concluded, clenching it with a twist of the radio dial to a local station as Mother and Auntie Rae brought fresh fruit, thinly sliced cheese, and crackers to the table. Marvel and Mary Ann refilled the iced-tea glasses. The around-the-clock news came:

> Scientists are urging the United States to use caution...conduct a public test demonstration as a warning before dropping a bomb that is such a horrendous weapon. Americans should be aware of the possible aftermath. Some military men insist that Japan is on the verge of surrender. A secret survey conducted by the Strategic Bombing Survey Commission may bear this out one day—when it is too late. But most of the president's advisers seem of one mind: "Japan remains a formidable foe, the only remaining alternative to dropping the A-bomb is an invasion which might cost millions of casualties." True? A civilian committee recommends that the bomb be used as soon as possible on a joint military-civilian target—*without prior warning*!

"An eye for an eye!" Mother cried out in despair. "Oh no—"
B.J.'s face flushed again, the angry red staining his boyish cheeks on which pre-shave fuzz showed a private countdown all its own. "I wonder if that prophet was married or had a family. He'd swallow those words, I'm here to tell you. That's a lot of baloney!"

"Let's have that prayer now," Uncle Worth said quickly. His head dropped, but not in time to hide the telltale crinkle around his eyes.

The others followed his example, and amusement gave way to solemnity made sublime by knowing God's Spirit would sustain them, but more warmly human by the freedom to address issues as they saw them. There would be no placid relationship in this family with the likes of one Billy Joe Harrington in their midst. There might be moments of conflict and disagreement, but there would be no boring relationships. And each praised the Lord for that.

"Well," Daddy said softly, "the rest is in the hands of our new president." His blue eyes sought those of his daughter.

Marvel nodded mutely. And then, although it was time to be about duties waiting almost accusingly, Daddy hesitated. Did he need confirmation of his statement? Words? She nodded again. "In President Truman's hands, yes—and in the Lord's pocket for safekeeping."

All rose and, obviously strengthened by the treasured moments, hummed as they cleared the table. "How wonder-ful ...how marvelous..." Daddy sang out. There was no way of knowing that the lovely old hymn tugged at his daughter's heart. Titus, Marvel remembered with the usual ache, had sung those words at one parting.

Mary Ann saw, her look at Marvel said. In their harried rush, several days passed before her cousin mentioned the hymn, however. "I'm sorry Uncle Dale used that song. It had to make you feel just awful. But *I* knew—you'd told me. Oh Marvel, when will it all be over? Don't answer that. It'll never be over for some—"

"Maybe—" Marvel said haltingly, "the war will never be over for any of us. I see so much corruption and indifference—hatred, intolerance—even among our own people And oh, the dreams that fall apart at the seams! Sometimes—sometimes, in moments of weakness, God forgive me—I feel Titus and I are the fortunate ones. It would be more than I could bear to have him come back and have one of those tragedies happen in our dreamed-of life. At least I *know*."

Then, for the first time, Mary Ann offered no argument. "You could be right. Yes, you know—you and Kate Lynn—"

Marvel gasped. "My goodness, my goodness! I had a letter from Kate Lynn so long ago I can't remember. So much has happened, but that's no excuse. That letter came before— Oh Mary Ann, she would have mailed it before— Oh, I can't even remember the date!"

"I know—I know. And me, I didn't even look at Billy Joe's term paper. He wanted me to proofread it, and I failed him."

"I—I didn't even realize he finished," Marvel whispered. "The one on baseball—and Daddy was supposed to help. Oh, this can't go on. We have to put our arms around our own family, and I've used up all my smiles on outsiders. Something has to change!"

"This minute!" Mary Ann cried out, and she rushed to embrace Marvel. Together they stood as the saffron of that days' sunset faded into night. The date, Marvel remembered later, was August 4.

*   *   *

A quick scan of Kate Lynn's letter cried out for more. It was hard for Marvel to concentrate on the lengthy contents, harder still to comprehend portions. The paragraphs capturing her imagination centered around the other girl's change of plans— and the *why* of it all.

> My life has taken a surprising turn, dear Marvel. To you goes the credit... to God, goes the glory... and to Daddy and Bill, my love and eternal gratitude. It is the sum (being greater than the sum of the parts, as Mr. Phillips used to say in math—I understand now!) of you all that led me to go back to college and enter the nursing profession. Daddy would be so proud, and Bill would have wanted me to apply his insurance to making the lives of others more bearable. I've known so many miracles—all involving love, but I just never thought of a miracle springing from death! That is, until I did volunteer work and met Mrs. Sachs. The terminally ill lady was losing weight and I just had to stand by and watch her waste away. "She's old," they told me. "She has cancer—there's nothing to be done." Nothing? I was horrified. There *was* something! Mrs. Sachs could use a whopping dose of love! My fury gave me the strength—like my Bill must have felt when afraid but, facing it, he performed like the hero he was. And I was able to go right in, while others stood back. I just hoped my anger and hurt didn't show. Guess it didn't, for *she* wasn't hostile. She reached out... comforting *me*. And, oh Marvel, the dear lady approached death with dignity. "Just stay with me, child," she whispered over and over... and, holding back tears the way I did when I lost my father (oh, he loved *you*!)... and then my husband (oh, I loved *him*!) and then my heartbroken mother, I promised. The night the end came, Mrs. Sachs asked that I read the Bible to her, and I watched that once-beautiful face turn beautiful again. There was a lantern

burning inside her that set those pain-glazed eyes shining. She knew ... and I knew too. Before the break of day my wonderful friend would have slipped from that ugly hospital gown into the robe of peace God held waiting. And me? I wasn't scared anymore. Like Mrs. Sachs, I knew I could do it. My sweet patient had heard God's clarion call and answered without fear of the grave. Calmly, I stood holding her hand ... not seeing the dark, just knowing that morning would swallow it up. And I remembered that it was you who told me about the real source of light. And I knew then what I had to do. I now work here in Baylor where Daddy always wanted me to work—and, in case you haven't guessed, with the terminally ill. You are right: From suffering comes good.

Tears of sheer joy welled up and overflowed from Marvel's great, blue eyes. "Oh, thank You, Lord, that I could help through You—and for reminding me that there is a reason for human suffering, that somehow Your turn our *dis*appointments to Your *ap*pointments, which in a way I don't understand lead us into the plan You have for us. I still have to learn."

Soon now she must read the other shocking paragraph. It was unavoidable. But first it was better to read Kate Lynn's touching account of finding God's pattern for her lifework. Far better, yes, for Marvel found details omitted in the first scanning.

You must go on with your writing. Your letters are super ... pulled me through when everything else failed and maybe even led me to know my calling when I met Mrs. Sachs. I remembered your gratitude to Daddy when he took care of your dad back when there was no money. And Daddy was so grateful to you for all you did to drag me through that hateful math—so grateful he wanted to pay your way to college just to get my head on straight. And something else! I remember your sharing with me about your uncle—step-uncle, I guess he was—a man you called Uncle Fred. How he chose you to be with him when he passed on. You didn't think you could, but God made you do it! He made me do it, too. Oh, I'd been stubborn.

Yes, you have to keep those columns going, put them together like you planned. And what happened to the plans you and Titus made to write kids' books? You'd be a natural—

like you would be with *any* kind of writing: history...
Christian material.... Oh, God will make you do this, too! I
guess you knew all along. But then, you could do everything! You were so patient with us all. I keep thinking how
you told me about learning your patience from the persimmons...how you watched their bare branches in winter,
knowing spring would come...sweated out the hot East
Texas summers and waited and waited for frost to blush the
cheeks of those lush fruits. "The Patience of the Persimmons" you called one article. And hear this! I told my
supervisor about that piece and she wants you to send it to
me. Says she'll pay for it ...publish it for our patients here
in our little medical journals. You'd be doing us a service
with your persimmons.

Kate Lynn would remember that small subject, and after all
these years—unbelievable. "Great oaks from little acorns" was
true then? God saw to that...another miracle.

And now, she thought (feeling her heart pick up tempo), on to
the rest of the letter. It was short. But the subject was Titus! She
closed her eyes. It did no good. His gentle face centered by the
most expressive gray eyes in the world danced behind her closed
lids. Read—she *must* read:

P.S. The hardest part about losing Bill was reading a
letter from goodness-knows-where (just the usual
APO postmark and stamped CENSORED)...dated
who knows when (clipped off in the censoring). It
came a long time after his effects.... Still hurts talking
about it. But Bill *did* meet up with Titus...in uniform.
No details, but sounds strange. Wasn't he reporting?
It all sounds like a movie: intrigue, danger, secrecy.
But deep down I feel the story hasn't ended for you.
K.L.

The words unleashed a new storm of feelings. The storm had
to end. Storms always do. Clouds break apart like dreams. Broken clouds produce rain and broken dreams produce tears. And
so Marvel wept again. But no rainbow came, just another cloud
of uncertainty. If only others would leave it alone—but no!
Titus is alive. "Here's proof."

Titus is dead. "Here's proof."
Titus is alive. . . .

Why at this agonizing moment would the ancient tale of Sinbad the sailor invade her thoughts? How did it go? Oh yes: Sinbad anchored his rickety craft to a supposedly sturdy atoll in that farfetched story. Sturdy? Perhaps. But safe? No. A fish bigger than the one which swallowed Jonah gulped down sailor, craft, and supplies before returning to the deep. Was there a moral here—a Christian moral to which she could anchor hope? *Yes: God offers solid-ground hope.* The thought came through loud and clear.

"But I have to look beyond this day, Lord, for hope and life are one with You. So forgive this stammering heart. You make use of broken things in Your heavenly workshop."

Yes: bruised grain to make bread, broken bread to remind of His sacrifice. It took the bursting of sunburnt bolls to release the treasure of frothy, marshmallow-white cotton locked within.

It had taken Kate Lynn's thrice-broken heart to produce a dedicated nurse. All right, Marvel thought submissively, I will not let doubt and uncertainty immobilize me. Satan would love that! The Lord created order from chaos, so I will cope a step at a time as our family decided to do, and just give life my best shot!

What was that best? For right now, her writing. So, tucking Kate Lynn's letter from Mary Ann's eyes, she thrust a copy of the persimmon story into an envelope for mailing. In a one-line message she promised, "Letter following soon."

The promised letter followed—but not soon.

* * *

President Harry S. Truman was single-minded in purpose, holding steadfast—if not stubbornly—to his determination to avoid an Okinawa from one end of Japan to the other. Back on July 26, he and Clement Attlee, successor to Prime Minister Winston Churchill of Britain, issued a dire ultimatum to Japan: "Surrender or face utter devastation of the Japanese homeland." The Japanese emperor ignored the warning, refusing it the dignity of a reply.

And then . . .

On the fateful morning of August 6, 1945, a B-29 plane dropped the A-bomb which all but obliterated Hiroshima. At exactly 8:15, as scheduled, 81 percent of the once-thriving city ceased to exist. One bomb, dubbed "Little Boy," exploded with the force of 20,000 tons of TNT. For an instant, temperatures at the epicenter (above ground zero) were millions of degrees. As far as a mile away people suffered burns through their clothing. Factories, hospitals, and homes disappeared from the face of the earth. The few buildings left standing momentarily burst into flame. Damaged buildings far from the site were totally annihilated. First reports indicated 68,000 dead with more injured. That memorable morning, dreadfully burned people moved through the flattened eerily silent city, holding their arms out before them to prevent seared surfaces from touching. In the afternoon, people who seemed at first to have escaped unharmed, died—the first victims of radiation. Hiroshima: *the city which died giving birth to a new era . . .*

Nevertheless, Japan refused to settle for peace.

A solemn-voiced American reporter made the announcement. There followed a questioning silence. What did it all mean— other than that every living thing touched by "Little Boy" was blackened and dead, or waiting to die? Was it possible that the war in the Pacific, a war fought with such barbaric ferocity, was near an end? That the years of horror were on the verge of climax because of yet another more horrible threat: the ultimate weapon? Torn by mixed emotions of hope, fear, weariness, and desperation, people dared not voice what rose within them. Radio stations suggested that people stay tuned for further information as it became available, then switched to popular music of the day.

Never had the Office of Price Administration been so crowded or so hushed. Voices were those reserved for funeral parlors. Even the soft-sweet strains of once-soothing songs became dirges.

"What does it mean?" an ashen-faced Mary Ann whispered as she tiptoed past Marvel's window en route to the boardroom for approval of a tire application. "I don't know what to think or what to do. Nobody prepared us for what would happen in case—"

Marvel shook her head. "I don't know either. Just go ahead, I guess. It's hard preparing for the unpredictable."

Outside, the stately palms reached high for breath, but no breeze came to cool their parching fronds. Had the tides, too, ceased their ebb and flow? Inside the stuffy confines of the handkerchief-size OPA office, even the telephone sat silent. There was only the music which nobody dared tune out lest there be a news bulletin. Marvel's chin trembled with each change of song, for every melody held a special memory or marked a change in her life. But she must not break down—must *not*. A single sign of weakness could peel off the thin veneer of serenity masking the hysteria so near the surface of those around her. The thought kept her going step-by-step.

There was a close call when "Thanks for the Memory" came on the air. Murmuring a hurried excuse, she turned from the window to hide her tears. A pretended look inside the file cabinet moved her from the radio and muffled the sound. Why, oh why did the applicant-in-waiting have to repeat the painful end of the song?

> ...and all the little dreams we dreamed
> That never could come true—
> I th-ank you—so much!

In a single second, memory's magic carpet transported Marvel Harrington across the limits of time and space. She was the little girl with big dreams, winning trophies and not caring, because beyond the window of her small world stretched a wide, green meadow woven of reality, dreams, and fantasy where she could be whoever she chose to be, do whatever she chose to do. The winters of life were not barren periods of brown. They were resting periods which sealed in the sap of spring. And then summer came with its blessed showers to water the thirsting mouth of the earth to produce as it had "in the beginning." Oh, she would help God preserve it...even plan with Him how to cross the great gulf which separated man from his Creator. All this she would do—and more. But she must prepare herself. So on to school...achieving...each step leading up the golden stair...bearing all things...believing all things...

The spelldowns, term papers...onward and upward...for she had a dream that the horrors of the Dust Bowl could not blow away. "Honor thy father and they mother" was a commandment she would obey joyfully. There were moments of sheer fantasy, too—moments in which she was queen of the glass hill none other could climb. And sometimes, alone before her mirror, Marvel would don the white crepe-paper robe with its edging of cotton mink (once worn in a school operetta) and command the sun to stand still. And when Titus came into her life, it did. But the stars danced in the Milky Way. Sometimes they came in daytime, when the two of them sat cross-legged beneath the great oak tree and planned how together they would save the world from doom, putting it back into God's hands where He alone could restore His meadow perfect. Those stars sang then, sweeping closer to earth to light the way for the unicorns....

Mary Ann had no way of knowing what her cousin meant by the very strange words spoken at the close of the tension-gripped day.

"I wish," Marvel said wistfully, "the dreams we dreamed could have been salvaged. I need those dreams to hang my hopes upon."

"You mean like Fanny's clothesline hung the wash? I don't see—"

"Like Fanny's clothesline—exactly! You *do* see. Dreams can be the clotheslines of our very existence, linking our hope with God's promises, aligning our future with the past."

"Maybe I *do* see," Mary Ann said vaguely, "letting us forget this awful present. I used to think of the present—this day, you know—as all we could be sure of. Now I wonder."

Marvel wondered then, too. Maybe it had all been foolish. No, God had told her something. Just what, she couldn't be sure. She only knew that He felt close—*very* close—when, by unspoken agreement, the two of them slipped quietly into the back pew of their dimly lighted church. They knelt in solitude to pray....

That night the family prayed together fervently. Then, without speaking of the earthshaking explosion, they huddled in a circular embrace and wept without shame. Only one person violated the silence—the one to be least expected: B.J. himself. His voice gave its last crack of adolescence when he said, "We have to forgive them—our men who dropped the deadly weapon, and the enemies who gave them no choice!"

"God bless you, my son," Uncle Worth choked, knowing that his child had become a man.

$$* \quad * \quad *$$

August 7 and August 8 soft-shoed past. The three days of waiting as the muted strains of music dominated the radio paralleled the three-day mourning period when the late president had lain in state. Brave they must be, hopeful, in yet another military void.

And then it came: "We interrupt this program for this important announcement!" the announcer said with a lilt in his voice which drew listeners' full attention like a magnet. *"Russia has declared war on Japan!"* The cheer which arose across America all but drowned out the news bulletin's repetition and the reminder to stay tuned for further announcements. The war was over—with one bomb!

The world was totally unprepared for the next announcement. Within hours a second atomic bomb, the "ultimate weapon," exploded in Japan. This time in Nagasaki—with the same devastating results as the one which preceded. Thirty thousand victims lay dead on the streets of another dead city. Nothing remained but the mushroom cloud.

Marvel listened to the reactions of others and shook her head in despair. What was there to be gained by cursing God, holding the Prince of Peace responsible for wars Satan inspired? Or furthering his black kingdom by screaming in the streets, "Strike 'em again—and again—Kill, *kill*, KILL! Make the yellow devils pay!" Didn't they know the wages of sin? For that matter, well-meaning though they were, who would listen to the frenzied cries of overcome preachers standing on the street corners attempting to be heard? "Repent! *Repent!* This is man's final hour! War is not ending, the world is! Alas, Babylon—alas—alas!" None of this was helping.

What *would* help Prayer...serenity...a peace that passed all understanding...and a use of one's talents. A line of the hymn unheard since leaving her childhood home came back, "If ever I need Thee, Lord Jesus, it's now." And the Savior could use *her* and her gift—which was, of course, writing. And writing she must do. Somebody must record history-in-the-making for posterity. Dark days though they were, these too were a part of America's heritage—a vital part, the part mankind *must* commit to memory lest it be repeated. That way alone could good come from suffering.

Marvel Harrington made a wise decision. Her premonition that history would be biased and warped to fit the needs of various writers was correct. Memories can be short, particularly of those with minds closed by prejudice and eyes blinded by ignorance or greed. Lo, there were those among the military, men upon whom Americans had grown up believing they could rely, changing stance even now. The new command-in-chief had blundered, they once said. Japan was on the verge of surrender. Why drop a bomb on a nation beaten to its knees? But now?

First had come Hiroshima. The nation "beaten to its knees" did not sue for peace. Next, Nagasaki. And even on this day of August 9, 1945, a now-sober-of-voice radio announcer said, "We regret to inform you that Swiss news sources relay the message that Japanese leaders have balked at surrender to the Allies. 'The emperor must be spared!' is the hue and cry, based on what they attribute to 'preserving his holiness,' a symbol of their religious convictions."

And ultimately, while the remainder of the world trembled in waiting, it was Emperor Hirohito who overrode his two chief military advisers. The nation "beaten to its knees" must surrender.

* * *

At last, almost four years after it began, the fighting in the Pacific had ended. World War II was over, this was the best-guarded secret of the barbaric war. There were whispers... prayers...rumors...and more prayers. But dare they hope? Nobody knew for sure.

Perhaps the Harringtons prayed hardest of all. They drew closer to one another and closer to their loving Lord, who alone knew what the future held in store. On on two occasions did one of them break the understanding silence, easing the tension with a small serving of humor which heretofore had come as naturally to them as the triumphant crow of a rooster to pierce the darkest hour preceding dawn. From the same kind of hush came Dale Harrington's words: "I declare, if we hug any tighter we'll be tied in a knot." To which B.J. answered, "That's like the tale of *Little Black Sambo* that Mary Ann and Marvel used to read me. Th' tigers kept getting closer and closer until they swallowed each other and turned to tiger butter—unrationed, Uncle Dale!"

There was a blessed release of laughter—laughter which repeated when an echo of Mother's once light touch to life came unexpectedly. "You've all been great—and waiting would have been harder with that. Sure enough, the past weeks have filled up with what Mother used to call 'days for the devil's fiddler'!" When the rest of the family laughed, she laughed with them, only to add: "Now you listen here! When we get the good news, *I'm* bound to be a *she*-devil fiddler. Now stop that laughing. And don't you dare tell that mother of mine when we get home!"

The days dragged on. And then, on August 14, V.J. Day, Americans received the long-awaited news. Radio music changed tempo suddenly, and listeners sensed that something was coming. Silence... a silence broken by a jubilant announcer who blurted out: "JAPAN HAS SURRENDERED—SURRENDERED UNCONDITIONALLY! DID YOU HEAR—UNCONDITIONALLY! IT'S OFFICIAL—AND THE OFFICIAL TIME IS 12:01 BEAT THE JAPS TIME!" There would be no celebrating, President Delano Roosevelt had said. No celebrating? Americans went wild.

Across the country people poured into the streets, church bells rang out, unplanned parades marched wildly, and storms of confetti descended from upstairs office windows. In New York, two million people crowded into Times Square—a great sea of shouting, kissing, horn-blowing celebrants. In San Francisco, sailors on shore leave staged a three-day riot. Streetcars were overturned. Bond booths were ripped down. And every window on lower Market Street was broken. And the Los Angeles area? Carmen Miranda, famous for her writhing dances while balancing a hat which looked more like an overloaded basket of fruit, tied up traffic at the busy intersection of Hollywood and Vine for two hours. Car horns honked a response which screamed of triumph rather than impatience.

The war that roared like a lion had softened the hearts of millions like lambs. The horrifying apocalyptic drama was over. But Americans were drained, weakened, exhausted—and fearful. For over them, in spite of the adrenaline-induced celebrations, hung the catastrophic mushroom cloud of doubt. *The peace treaty was not signed.* And the sense of impending apocalypse of greater measurement yet hung like the other cloud of memory—threatening, but softening hearts more yet.

Nowhere was this more evident than in the Harrington home on Elm Street where the leaves had started trembling again. But the family had each other. "Yet my concern goes beyond these walls. I praise Almighty God that the shooting has stopped. Still, war—like all other tragedies—shakes love loose, makes friends of strangers. Will they continue to care—you know, be nice to each other when life is calm again? We have to keep reaching out—" Dale Harrington said.

"To 'Throw Out the Lifeline' like the old hymn used to say, and I guess still says? Well, there's no time like the present—"

Even as she spoke, Snow Harrington reached down to bring out the violin nobody had noticed propped conveniently near her chair at the dining room table around which they sat. "Open the windows wider!" she commanded. The round, clear notes to follow were produced by slender hands but born of the soul. No, her daughter realized, seeing the tears which glistened in the eyes of her family-audience, such warmth and richness were not those of a she-devil! They whispered of angel song....

August changed to September. There was a remembered tingle of mornings back home, Marvel thought, recalling the brisk air that blushed the cheeks and burnished the soul. Even in California's unchangeable seasons, there hung a feel of expectancy. Strange how one noticed each detail on memorable days. With her, it was concentration on Mother's flower-lined paths which had exploded with color.

On that day, September 2, an allied armada sailed into Tokyo Bay. The tense Japanese representatives, maintaining composure with difficulty, boarded the U.S.S. *Missouri* (the world's largest battleship), and walked the gauntlet of stern-faced Allied officers. MacArthur signed the surrender document ceremoniously. The first two pens he handed to officers who had been rescued from Japanese prison camps just days before (Jonathan Wainwright, who had been forced to surrender Corregidor, and British Lieutenant General Arthur Percival, ill-starred commander of Singapore).

The war of the Pacific, a war fought with barbaric ferocity, had ended officially, but only after years of horror climaxed by use of what Americans called, with painful and often prayerful precision, the "ultimate weapon." And certainly they had paid the ultimate price.

From the *Missouri*, General Douglas MacArthur addressed the American people, underscoring the inescapable moral: "And now a new era has dawned.... Men since the beginning of time have sought peace. Military alliances, balances of power, leagues of nations, all in turn failed, leaving the only path to be by way of the crucible of war. The utter destructiveness of war now blots out this alternative. We have had our last chance. Repeating: If we do not devise some greater system, Armageddon will be at our door!"

7

Aftermath

The shouting was over, but for most people, the war was not. Official records marked the close of World War II as "August 14, 1945, the day hostilities ceased." On what fronts, Marvel pondered, had hostilities ceased? Nowhere was hostility more visible than in signing final terms of Japanese surrender aboard the *Missouri*. Stern-faced victors and frosty-eyed vanquished affixed names to the document in a hush of silence, unbroken by so much as a glance.

For some, the shouting had never begun. Perhaps, those awaiting return of loved ones demurred, then the war will end. Most sober were the wives, parents, sweethearts, relatives, and friends knowing nothing for sure. Were all prisoners released and accounted for? Had MIA's been declared officially dead? Where were the personal effects...proper documents...the remains? Buried in some common grave? Grim though such thoughts were, knowing was better than the uncertainties of waiting. Until then, there could be no healing of hearts—and certainly no celebrating. Celebrating? There would never be wild celebrating for the agonizing number on the home front whose loved ones would never be back. Death's icy touch had left them hurting, angry, and wondering if America remembered the guarded caution in Franklin Delano Roosevelt's voice when he said: "I question that there will be celebration when hard-won victory is ours...rather, a solemn, sacred determination that war must *never* happen again!"

One thing all America shared in common: impatience to return to normal. The aftermath seemed anticlimactic. Warned though they were of long delays, nobody was prepared. Rationing, price control, shortages—none of this was needed. And how could government red tape delay release of service personnel *this* long? Occupational forces? Were such measures really necessary for keeping the peace? Wasn't surrender unconditional? And what's this? Our boys continued to be fired upon by enemies-in-hiding who either had not heard or refused to heed orders to cease fire. Or—perish the thought!—had embittered military leaders of "The Land of the Rising Sun," refusing to see that the sun had set on their "evil empire," given orders that they fight to the finish? It was a time of uncertainty, misgiving, mumbles, grumbles, impatience, and tears. The long road back was slow and tortuous. But it was a time of prayer....

Churches filled up with worshipers. Dr. James Murphy understood. Chaplains' facilities proved inadequate for long lines of service personnel in need of guidance. Synagogues were few. priests were inundated by contrite souls pleading for margins of men-of-the-cloths' time to hear confessions and intercede for forgiveness of sins committed under the stresses of war. Most Protestant churches were locked against "bums" until regular services. But First Baptist retained its open-all-hours schedule.

"Gosh all hemlock! Don't you ever sleep?" young Billy Joe Harrington asked guilelessly.

"Seldom," Pastor Jim answered with equal candor. "The Lord knows I could do with a little help, though."

"'A volunteer for Jesus—a soldier true. Others have enlisted—why not you?' Seems I lucked out, pastor—missed the draft, you know. Not that I'm grievin' a bunch. I've about lost a stomach for *that* kind of combat, but count me in for a TKO with th' devil!"

Marvel waited quietly, wondering just what the minister would assign his recruit. Mary Ann waited, too, her brown eyes meeting Marvel's blue ones once. War had been horrifying, breaking apart her isolation, her self-immersion. "Not that I worry about dying anymore—just Jake's safety, his and all the others out there. But something else, something I learned from you first, then my family, and Kate Lynn's letter—and, well, looking back, from our Uncle Fred. What I worry about is not having finished all I ought," Mary Ann had confessed to Marvel once. She had changed. They all had. The world had. Changes demand risks. Ruts were safer. Pastor Jim knew.

"I'm in a philosophical mood," he said now, glancing at some point beyond the three of them. "Any catastrophe (and what could be a greater one than war?) makes me realize how insignificant our petty differences are. To me, they're reduced to a pile of dust, like this universe can be if that weapon falls into the hands of a madman! Well, never mind me. I've served Jew and Gentile alike and I never felt God frowned on that. My job, as I see it, is to bind up wounds—and we all bleed alike. Agree, you three?"

They agreed and reviewed together the touching incident in which the rabbi, Catholic priest, and Protestant minister had descended to a watery grave with arms about one another, their voices lifted in prayer. The chaplains had refused to abandon the torpedoed ship until all who looked to them for spiritual inspiration were rescued. Before the last lifeboat could reach the trio, the ship had sunk.

B.J.'s eyes sparkled with tears, but his chin jutted out. "So *we* can do that. I can't carry a tune in a sack, but gimme one of those lace dresses and I'll be your choirboy, candlelighter—whatever. Not that I know rabbinic language either. But you know what? I sauntered into a temple and saw an Israeli guy instructing women and kids in th' martial arts. Said they needed to now how to protect themselves, so called it a kind of first-aid course—the means of survival. Oh ho! So I *do* know one word, *hisardut*, meanin' "survival" in Hebrew! Well, we have to help others learn to stand up and fight. Survival, yep!"

"Yep!" Dr. James Murphy said seriously.

Walking home, Mary Ann said quietly, "Well, I guess we've got ourselves a preacher—or a teacher. Unorthodox, grant you, but we help in our own way. I'm learning that. We *have* survived, and we have to keep on surviving—somehow. Better with the martial arts than grabbing our cats and hiding under the bed—"

"Yes," Marvel said softly, then, "there's no hiding place."

"Oh Marvel, we *will* survive—even— Please let me say his name."

"Titus. I'll say it for you." Marvel's gently spoken words surprised them both. "We were a perfect match, a dream come true."

Mary Ann's tone reached the same low pitch. "*Were?* Does that mean hope dies when dreams have to wait? We've all waited. Don't you ever think Titus could have survived—think he might find you? He loved to surprise you. And, oh Marvel, it's later than you think!"

Much later. When had today's yellow twilight been swallowed up by the velvet throat of night? Marvel looked up and thought she had never seen as many stars as hung over them. Just the mention of his name did this? A complete new galaxy opened inside her heart.

"Yes," she said in words too long held captive, now happy to be set free. "I do dream. I guess I always will. Fantasy keeps me going."

"Yep!" Mary Ann in perfect imitation of Pastor Jim's word.

They laughed together...softly...dreamily. The lights of home signaled a welcome. How good that they were no longer blacked out.

Mary Ann's whispers, Marvel supposed, were due to their being so near hearing distance of the family—and a mutual awe of laying out dreams, hopes, and private thoughts. Nothing wrong with fantasies. Everybody had to daydream a bit, her cousin was saying sagely. Take her, for instance. There were moments when she was sure there had been a switch of babies— that Mary Ann Harrington was in truth a somebody else. Mary Ann Riley—that was it. Didn't she look more like Gran'mere than either Aunt Snow or Marvel, Gran'mere's own daughter and granddaughter? And maybe some frivolous mistake was made long before their generation. Maybe a band of Gypsies—*real* Gypsies—had whisked Leah Johanna Mier Riley away or exchanged her, making her just an ordinary babe. Could be...just could be...

Yes, could be! Didn't Gypsies rely on the stars? Stars, of course, even in their kind of society, did not preordain, the Gypsies said. Cornered, they explained their stance away by saying, "Oh, the stars do not preordain the future. They only incline."

"Of course," Marvel whispered back, "*we* are led by one star— the one which pointed to the holy birth."

"Which gave us hope. You say so yourself. And I'm *inclined* to agree," Mary Ann said with the characteristic toss of her black curls that Marvel thought her cousin had put away as dreams dimmed.

They hurried up the steps, stifling giggles like two truant schoolgirls. Oh, it was good to simply let God take care of the future.

In October dark clouds of birds filled the bright blue skies, replacing the blimps of wartime. The Harringtons watched, still fascinated that the migratory creatures winged in instead of out. Downright uncanny, wasn't it? they marveled, how all nature knew when winter was nigh. Back home, of course, the feathered guests would be waiting for signs to change from "time of arrival" to "time of departure." Mary Ann had said at one point that at least neither man nor beast was haunted now by that mocking sign: "Is this trip necessary?" which once greeted all civilian travelers at every terminal. The family nodded, saying that gradually everything pointed to normalcy.

On one particular evening in mid-October, Dale Harrington said, "Ladies, down home the 'frost is on th' pun'kin,' so I've a hankering for pumpkin pie. Guess I'm feeling the call of the wild like those honkers. Hear them? Guess the squirrels are filling their storehouse, and Mother Riley's putting up watermelon rind preserves."

"Feeling nostalgic, eh, Dale?" Uncle Worth grinned. "There's a feel to fall no matter where we are. I feel it. On that pie, we agree. Feels like Ole Man Winter's sealing in all the juices of life, expect those in my taste buds. Remember those persimmons? Man! We ate our share—didn't we just? And persimmon pie—yummy."

Mother and Auntie Rae had sat wordlessly, while B.J. perched like a bird on a limb preparing for takeoff. Now the two women exchanged knowing glances. "We get the message," Auntie Rae said. To which Mother added, "'What'll tom'rar night's suppah be? Two buttah-beans 'n uh blackeyed pea!' capped off by 'punk'in pie!'" Then came their shared laugh that rolled on and on until they virtually ran out of breath in a memory that took them all home. *Home*—and maybe soon...

Marvel's heart winged her back to the persimmon grove momentarily. Oh, those persimmons...so worth waiting for... so inspirational in their patience...recognizing no winter wariness...just patiently awaiting nature's beckon to release the green sap of spring. *Patience*. That word released a memory of sharing the sweet fruit's meaning. First with Titus, and he had understood as he alone understood her every thought, gesture, or glance. And then she had shared with Kate Lynn—Kate Lynn, who asked for a copy of the item Marvel had written for reprint in Baylor's hospital bulletin. Marvel had obliged and promised Kate Lynn a letter—a letter too long postponed, she remembered guiltily. Tomorrow for sure...

But "tomorrow never comes" described the next day perfectly. The schedule was hectic—so hectic Marvel forgot to purchase spice to add to steamed pumpkin from B.J.'s prolific "Halloween vine" until she was well past the corner store. Mr. Simon, a stocky man with thinning hair well compensated for by his flowing goatee, peered at his young customer through thick-lensed glasses. "Ah, my dear Miss Harrington! 'Tis good to see you— yah? I see you pass. 'Tis a lot of hurrying you do—like time. But 'tis good you come, for you should like knowing what the young one does for our people—your brother, yah, my child?"

"Cousin." Marvel smiled appreciatively, paid for her purchase, and hurried away as the fading eyes followed her in regret. 'Twas sad what war had done—sad, robbing the young, sweet, fulfilling joys of holy wedlock, sons as numerous as Abraham's, and blessings of the Almighty. Sad...

Marvel put the pumpkin pie together hastily, the rule being that the first one home took charge. Best use the old standby recipe from their trusted collection. The result was perfect: honey-brown and spicy-breathed. The moment B.J.'s serving came, he grabbed a fork and with his free hand laid a stack of letters beside his plate. "Baylor University—yours, Marvel?" He placed the mysterious letter on top of the stack and, without pausing to swallow, lifted another forkful of pie to his mouth. "Talk about larpin' good—larp, larp—tastes like always—" he gulped. "Out of our mothers' cookbook, huh?"

Marvel tried to conceal a grin. *"Stretching to Survive—"*

Mary Ann made no effort to hide her grin. "You'll have to stretch that breadbasket of yours to survive this meal, I'd say, B.J.!"

There was a round of applause for all ladies... *applause* ... applause.... Mother might have been soloing on her violin— which she would be soon.

"Pastor feels we should go all out for the Thanksgiving service— throw open the doors, have a very special concert, make it into a real symphony of prayer. I want to play for you all—play and pray. But mostly I want to pray to God who helped us win the war!" Mother said.

"That's my girl," Daddy whispered, then hummed, "Seems like old times... seems like old times—" and his smile expressed pleasure.

"And I suppose you, my sweet," Uncle Worth said to Auntie Rae, "will be elbow-deep with pilgrim costumes. Remember, they dressed all in colors like—well, like the persimmon, hickory nut, and oak trees at home after the first frost. Of course, Quakers wore all black and white. But I guess all colors will be there. Pastor Jim likes that."

Suddenly an awareness of Titus crowded in to deafen Marvel's ears to the conversation around her. The oak tree . . . their special oak—was it still there waiting? It had to be—just *had* to. If only it had the patience of the persimmons. Oh Kate Lynn . . . Baylor . . . it all fit together somehow. Her thoughts were jumbled, unclear.

"Are you all right, honey?" Daddy asked gently. "Bad day?"

Marvel shook her head. "Not bad, just busy. Wow! I guess you could call it one of Grandfather's weighty days. Remember how he used to say he might as well be dragging a 12-pound catfish behind him?"

There was laughter. Yes, they remembered. More laughter— the kind that brought tears to their eyes, the kind that expressed joy. Lots yet to be done, and concerns remained. But there was joy. The shared joy set Marvel back on course, reminded her to share Mr. Simon's praise of young B.J. Harrington.

"So," she concluded, "Pastor Jim and B.J. seem to think alike."

The boy was silent, humbled. "I'm glad you told me, Marvel. He said that about *me*—the Jewish man, I mean?"

"Oh yes, and you can feel complimented, honey. Mr. Simon— dear man—is frugal with words. Sort of afraid to reveal the love he feels for the human race, as if he's been hurt by life."

And haven't we all? Marvel thought with gentle understanding. How much have *I* revealed? Would anybody guess that I am so vulnerable? No, outsiders would suppose she was too "sensible" to fall head over heels in love, become so involved that reality and dreams became one? And remained that way? *Yes*, so much to be thankful for!

B.J. was still talking. "—so I know what I want to do now. I mean I *know* now what I want to do later. I'll teach in school and Sunday school And I want to use your history book, Marvel—go back into the past in *everything*. You *will* take a squint at the baseball research and maybe use it? I can tie it in with history, too. It's all important. And then I learned a lot working with all kinds of folks—Mr. Simon, for instance. We have the old Bible in common, and we worship the same God. Yes, I'll go on to school." B.J. turned toward Uncle Worth.

"Whoa! Better slow down, son, before you swallow your tongue—"

Daddy glanced at his watch, seemingly torn between furthering this conversation and getting back to the shift lying ahead. Mother saw, rose, and began to stack the dishes. But over her shoulder, she said, "That's wonderful, and I'm glad the draft is no longer a threat. It isn't, is it? Didn't the draft bill stop with the war?"

In the moment of speculative silence, it seemed easy and natural for Marvel to answer as she did. "Titus will know."

A teacup, one of Snow Harrington's prized collection, clattered to the floor. Her husband rushed to retrieve the broken pieces. "There's some new glue on the market," he said uncertainly.

Mother gave no indication of hearing. "Marvel," she gasped, "you don't mean you still think of this Titus Smith as coming back? He's dead—you told me so yourself. And you suffered in silence."

Marvel felt sick to her stomach. It was the pie. She had eaten too much. "Nobody told me for sure. And yes, I suffered."

"Suffered" didn't cover the grief Marvel Harrington had endured. And there had been none of Daddy's magical glue to piece the broken shards of her heart back in place. But there had been Almighty God to offer her healing. And with healing came hope.

"And nobody told me for sure Titus is alive either." Marvel could have said more, but the room seemed to be tilting sideways. Was Los Angeles experiencing an earthquake, or was the quaking from within herself? Never had she failed to be at the USO...the nursery school...at church...on the job. Was it going to be unavoidable tonight?

The faces of her parents swam before her, their features out of focus. But they were standing, weren't they? They must have collected the remains of the teacup. And Mother was speaking from far away.

"Even if your friend—your childhood sweetheart—did make it from wherever he was, don't you think he'd have been in touch? I—I just can't bear seeing you keep living with a—a *dream*." Mother was wringing her hands, wanting to light-touch the unpleasant talk and not knowing how. "You've grown up, darling, and growing up makes us ch-change. Thank you, Dale—" she gulped, accepted his handkerchief to wipe her distressed eyes.

"And Titus—Titus Smith, wasn't it?—he would be changed, too. You—why, you'd be strangers—"

Strangers. *Perfect strangers*, Titus had called them shortly after the whirlwinds of the dust storm blew them together in high school.

"Changed?" There was a metallic ring in her own voice now. And her head—oh, her head. If only she could rest it on the table. Instead, she swallowed and went on: "We've all changed, and we'll find everything different when we go back home: Grandfather, Grandmother Riley, uncles, aunts—"

"And cousins!" B.J., unaware of the tension, chirped as he picked up the broom and dustpan. "Let's hope so."

"But love doesn't change, Mother," Marvel finished with an effort.

"And that," Auntie Rae said softly, "nobody can deny."

Marvel managed somehow to escape. Already she and Mary Ann were late—very late...at least an hour. She couldn't go. Mary Ann would have to explain. Her legs threatened to buckle.

"I know you need to be alone, Marvel. I—I'm so sorry you had to go through that Spanish Inquisition downstairs. They don't understand, but they ought to. 'Love is blind'? How blind can they be? You're—why, you're cold as a clam. Stay home just this once," Mary Ann pleaded as she trained Marvel up the stairs. "Read your mail and relax, and hold onto that conviction. *Titus will be back!*"

Marvel accepted the letters with an affectionate squeeze of the hand holding them. "You've always said that, and I was afraid to hope," Marvel said thickly. Inhaling deeply, she went on, "Yes—yes to both. I'll stay home because—well, I have to. And yes, I—I'll hold onto the conviction. When two people, so bruised by life, find one another, nothing else matters. Nothing at all."

With a little moan, Marvel fell across the welcome softness of her bed. The pain in her head had lessened, only to be replaced by a white-hot zigzag of pain in her left side. Then it, too, stopped.

Feeling weakened and in need of a drink, she made her way to the bathroom and turned on the tap. One glass...two...dare she drink *three* glasses of water even though she was dying of thirst? Sipping slowly, she drained the glass. And then the room righted itself.

Not that I could have worked, Marvel thought tiredly. Then, with a smile, she whispered: "Where does pain go, Lord, when

You take it away? Into Your fiery furnace with the other trash You remove? Thank You for trashing my sins—my pain. *Thank* You!"

Refreshed, Marvel opened the letter from Baylor University. A check fluttered to the floor. A check for *300 dollars*! A success, she realized for the first time. Her first bona fide check. Focusing on the accompanying letter was a challenge. Might they have her permission to publish "The Patience of the Persimmons" in a newspaper story the university was doing regarding "local authors"? It was their understanding that Miss Harrington was of Pleasant Knoll, graduated from local schools, and formerly associated with Titus Smith in the articles published throughout the state of Texas. They would pay her well, the editors added. She was a gifted author....

The embossed letterhead blurred. Perhaps the letter said more. It didn't matter, for Marvel's heart had soared to unite with Titus in togetherness shared in the articles mentioned by the editors: her "Eyes of East Texas," his "Ears of Austin" which he prepared while attending college in the capital city and working on a part-time job for a family friend, one Senator Cliff Norton. And then they had coauthored the "Heartbeats of America" ongoing series ... one day to become a book ... weaving together the power of fact and the drama of fiction. Oh, it would all come true, they had said then. And it would! Who could separate reality from dreams? It was *truth* that counted. And who could prove truth to the scoffer, the agnostic? They had laughed at Noah's ark, his warning of the flood which would cover the earth eons ago. More recently, they had laughed at the existence of an atom. How could one split the unseen? Marvel sighed as slowly she came back to the here and now. The unseen and unbelieved atom had exploded in due time—exploded and come close to destroying the earth by fire.

And the unbelievers would go on forever denying Almighty God, Marvel thought with her usual compassion. They had not seen Him. Well, neither had she and Titus. But they had touched His face....

"And we will go on writing, my darling, blending our God-given talents: your empirical eye of the journalist, blessed with moral and spiritual vision, with my creative loom of the novelist. All the while drawing from our wellspring of experience, our meteoric shower of star-struck happiness—and our love. This I pledge, Titus."

The letter from Baylor should be framed. Just hours ago she had rocked the family by suddenly turning 180 degrees. For how could they know what she had not known herself? Not completely—until the timely letter completed the 360-degree turn. But for now, just a scribble of her name to the release the editors needed, then on to the remaining mail. No, first she needed the status of the draft bill. Luckily, she found several clippings for the family. And then she summarized them for a column.

On August 12, 1941, the House passed a measure that the press called "the draft extension bill" by a narrow margin— a step future historians may misstate or exaggerate.... In actuality, the Selective Service Act of 1940 provided that drafted men should serve one year and spend ten in the Reserves, subject to recall in the unlikely case of war. In August 1941 the Army persuaded President Roosevelt to support a bill extending draftees' service to 2½ years. "Conventional wisdom" ran rampant. This was an act of renewal. Four years later, just after the death of the president, *Time* magazine referred to the lengthening of draftees' service as "the one-vote margin in the House, when the draft came up for extension just four months before Pearl Harbor." Another recognized reporter wrote an article "The March of Folly," mentioned "renewal of the one-year draft law." Wrong! The Selective Service Act was not a "one-year draft law," therefore needed no renewal. Chances are that readers will be misled into supposing that had the House voted otherwise, the Army would have been virtually disbanded with the Japanese struck in December. Actually, had it been defeated, fewer than 17,000 drafted men would have gone home before the infamous day of December 7. And to those of us who remember, this is understandable. It was a time of disruption and uncertainty. There are those who cry that we were misled by a New Deal president who "sold us short." Wrong again. Details are numerous but, in summary, let us rest assured that if the bill had been defeated, America would have had a larger Army on Pearl Harbor Day—and been better prepared. Its future in this postwar period lies in the hands of the man now serving on the Hill, President Harry S. Truman.

The calendar shifted to November. Fashion-conscious ladies shifted style as well. Something called "the new look" came in: longer hemlines, pencil-slim skirts with modest slits in side seams or back, and parfait colors replacing the drab ones of war. The more daring changed hairstyles radically, shearing their crowning glories of wartime in favor of what busy beauticians labeled the "small head." Happily, they scissored dangerously close to the scalp. All this for the "style setters." The more conservative—the Harrington women among them—altered themselves little. Continuing to add to growing bank accounts (transferred from checking to savings because of rising interest rates), they let down hems until it was obvious that the skimpy hems of the war years made little difference.

"All right," Mother conceded at last, "we'll just have to make a few purchases. And what better timing, what with Thanksgiving near?"

Very near. Rehearsals had been in progress several weeks. Mother and Auntie Rae had more time now. The double shift was over at the defense plant. Not that there was less demand for planes, as the frenzied manufacturing of weapons of war had diminished. Needs now turned to commercial airlines. "People will be flying around like birds," Daddy said. "The prophets of old were right. And the changeover spells need of a new kind of mentality—many leaving, even more coming in."

"And what a change in housing demands!" Uncle Worth added. "Real estate will go sky-high as soon as more building materials are available."

The two men exchanged glances—new shopping centers *everywhere*.

USO centers had closed, as had emergency nurseries. And now the Office of Price Administration was to disperse—a process that consumed all of Marvel and Mary Ann's time, numbing Marvel to her pain and loss of weight.

8

Without Appointment

"Disaster never makes an appointment, does it now?" Grandmother posed the question in one of her frequent letters. The question—more of a statement, really—prefaced a surprising bit of sad family news. Erin and her "bright young husband with a promising future" had taken their battles to the courts...getting a divorce. "And now Dorthea is as hysterical as Eleanore, not that one could wonder at Eleanore's grief—what with her having lost Duke in the war. Still and all, my branches are bent toward the Squire's application of the Scripture: 'As you sow...' But deep down he's terminally ill with sympathy. Keeps shaking his head (yes, still using that miracle color on his hair—has to, he says, now that he's back in banking) and muttering, 'Poor Joseph...poor Emory.' Keeps feeling twinges of guilt, like he was responsible. But I saw: 'Oh, get the world off your back, Alexander Jay Harrington, Esquire! Take a look out yonder at your son, Dale, who had himself sense enough to marry my daughter. And what a *Marvelous* granddaughter *they* produced!' And Worth's just as great...as are his wife and children. He can't wait for you to come home. Alex Jr. never will, but *you* will. Just don't wait too long. Good news comes without appointment, too. I'll try to stop watching the pot so it'll boil!"

Excited talk followed, regrets, a few wisecracks from B.J., and some tentative planning. They would check out the offer on the Elm Street house. No need to get excited, girls. No rush. Yes, of course, everything could wait until after Thanksgiving—*everything.*

91

Marvel heard little other than the hum of their voices. The clippings Grandmother Riley enclosed, undoubtedly to support her opening words since each was annotated with scribbles along the ragged margins, sent Marvel's mind in several directions. Did they remember? Grandmother had asked. Remember? Oh yes...

Near exhaustion, but eager to scotch rumors about his health, FDR rode in an open car through a cold October rain following a 1944 campaign speech in New York. "Defeated?" he quipped with reporters. "Of course not! The American people have better sense than to change horses in the middle of a stream!" But at the very gates of victory, sudden death! On March 1, 1945, Franklin Delano Roosevelt had reported to a joint session of Congress on his trip to Yalta. The audience was shocked. Suddenly, at 63, they realized that the nation's leader looked *old*—and terribly changed. The once-strong man's hands shook as he tried to deliver a prepared speech, usually ad-libbed spontaneously in a jovial voice, now read...his words coming out too thin, hurried, and at points, slurred. And he sat, instead of managing to stand for the first time during his presidency. The man was ill—while valiantly attempting to groom the nation for a post-war world.

The end came on April 12, 1945. When the news struck, millions of Americans, feeling their hearts skip a beat, told one another that the world would never be the same without him. And it never will. For the nation was unprepared for the loss, just as nobody was prepared for Pearl Harbor or for that ultimate bomb. It is up to us to meet the postwar world bravely, *remembering* all these events, resolving in our hearts that they will not be repeated! Herein lies the challenge to all historians.

"And we will try," Marvel vowed, just as she had vowed to protect her parents. Yes, she could find strength to live up to both vows. Sadness and suffering brought out the best of mankind's heart. Like the seasons, the heart's winter signaled approaching cold—until one directed the soul to its Source. Never mind how she felt—forget the aches and pangs. "We can, we *will*, we MUST!"

Conversation stopped. Realizing she had spoken aloud, Marvel said, "You'll want to read this—and there are more. Sweet of Grandmother to send such rich material for my columns— and eventually the book Titus and I planned. More than one, actually—to keep the torch burning in the Statue of Liberty's hand!"

"And use in my classroom. I *am* going to teach. And I'll need books—new ones that tell about the old days and the new ways. You promised to read my baseball stuff and maybe use it, Marvel."

"And I will!" If only things would slow down. Even the dining room was spinning. She reached a hand to grip the table. That helped.

But Mother saw. "You haven't touched your meal, honey." There was puzzled concern in her voice. "It's cat's-eye stew. Remember how you liked it? That was a long time ago—" her voice trailed off.

B.J. was unaware of any tensions, words left unsaid, or skirting of issues. "I guess you put that recipe in the blank pages of your *Stretching* book, huh, Mother? But it came from those Gypsies we met under the bridge when we camped out there. Maybe it'll fit better in your book, Mary Ann. You remember, don't you, huh?"

"Remember?" Mary Ann's eyes had a faraway look. "I remember what happened—and what didn't. I sneaked away and had my palm read."

Auntie Rae gasped. "You didn't! Why, that's superstition— evil. You know what Paul did—denounced it as ignorant. *Denounced* it!"

"Denounce *her* then after we've had dessert. But Mother, you and Mary Ann *do* look a little bit, well, like those pretty Gypsies." B.J. glanced at Rae Harrington as if weighing the idea of saying more, shrugged, and added, "Those people were kind to us— and they didn't know our God who 'dwelleth not in temples made with hands.' But they know now thanks to the Bibles Grandfather wanted passed along. And they didn't hurt you. Come on now, 'fess up, *little* sis. Tell our parents you don't believe in mediums and seances!"

"I 'fess, pest! And yes, I *do* want to use the Gypsy lore—just like Marvel will include them in her Pulitzer prize novel."

There was so much to talk about, the Harringtons agreed, but better postpone it. (Didn't they always because of the pressures of time? Marvel wondered wearily as their voices floated in and faded out.) Yes, it could wait. Deacons' meeting...B.J. had a night game (great lights were on again, huh?), Mother must attend rehearsal, and Auntie Rae would be with her since the backdrop must be hung and curtains adjusted for sound effects. Yes, Thanksgiving...

"Thank goodness, *you* can rest. Can't you finish your tapioca pudding, honey?" Mother coaxed. "I wish you'd see a doctor."

Marvel sighed. They had been over this so many times. There was a shortage on doctors. Older ones had retired. Younger ones remained to check all service personnel before discharge. "I'm just tired, Mother. Please stop worrying. An aspirin would help though—just a slight headache. And yes, I'll drink lots of juice."

"I wish we didn't always have t'be in such a cottonpickin' rush," B.J. complained. "What I know about Gypsies is important—something going on right now. And these famous authors need to check in San Jose before we leave California. It fits in—a mansion that's sure enough haunted and dates back to last century. Man! That place was filled with spirits of the departed—hovered everywhere. Boy, wouldn't Fanny take a shine to that! Don't look at me like that, Mother, please. You know I don't believe that junk, but the poor woman who inherited the house big enough for a shopping center was scared spitless." Giggling, he went on, as a wide-eyed family stared at him: "You see, that medium—a Gypsywoman—lassoed her into believin' there were good ghosts and bad ghosts. People could choose the uppercrust ghosts and let 'em do battle with the evil spirits. We gotta see it. Okay, okay, I see that look. So I'll cut out. But Marvel, what did Baylor University want?"

"That's her business." Uncle Worth's voice carried a warning.

"No, it belongs to all of us. I thought I'd told you," Marvel said vaguely. "My first real sale—a check. We'll have to frame it!" Marvel told about "Patience of the Persimmons" then, about Kate Lynn's part—Kate Lynn, daughter of their beloved Dr. Porter. Yes, he was killed in the war, as was Kate Lynn's husband. Yes, sad, but she was a perfect example of patience...a nurse at Baylor now.

"And that's how Baylor knew about the article."

There was cheering, which did nothing to help Marvel's headache. Surely Grandfather's yell of "Bravo!" punctuated by the rat-a-tat-tat of his cane as it jabbed the floor in wild applause when Grandmother Riley (his "Duchess") walked down the ramp modeling her homemade dress had been no louder. But there were tears in the eyes of those who cheered, just as there had been in Grandfather's so long ago.

Mary Ann must have shared the thought for she said, "Oh, going back to this clipping— You're right, it was worth sending. And Gran'mere sent me some things for my book, even suggested a title. How about *Wisdom of the Ages*? Good, isn't it? You *bet* it's good! Oh, I'm glad she lets me claim kin—be her granddaughter—"

"Me, too—her grand*son*, I mean—but still be a Harrington. So Cousin Erin's getting herself a divorce!"

Somebody was stacking dishes . . . another rinsing in preparation for washing . . . storing food . . . sweeping . . . and still talking.

Too bad about the divorce. How could anything so right go wrong for Joseph and Dorthea? To which B.J. snorted, "What you all mean is *How could anything so wrong go right*?"

"Amen!" Mary Ann whispered to Marvel, then, still whispering, "Gimme those dessert plates before you drop them. You sit down. No, go on upstairs and I'll follow. They're leaving—*go*!"

Once upstairs, Marvel took the aspirin, drank several glasses of water, and sat down to ease the queasiness inside her. Her mind went back to the articles Grandmother had sent. There was more on the late President Roosevelt. These must be saved for reference in preserving history, as the first-read article had suggested. Yes, indeed, this one would lighten the otherwise somewhat grim journey through the lean years of the Great Depression to the awfulness of war—and its shocking aftermath. She read it again and smiled.

All will remember—or should—Franklin Delano's first victory. . . . If not, have an over-the-backyard-fence chat with a Dust Bowl victim. . . . Who knows better than persons who experienced hunger and loss when drought struck without any more warning than the crash on Wall Street which spelled financial disaster? They had a need. He met it. Not without criticism, as history should tell you. Second term, ditto! The third-term issue caused some excitement in 1940, but the fourth-term question aroused little excitement in 1944. By then, millions of Americans could not remember a time when there had been anyone in the White House but Roosevelt. Wendell Wilkie, the utility tycoon, had flunked the test. Who cared that he had flown around the world? (Later there were those who did care—cared a lot.) Wilkie's account of that trip, *One World*, proved to be the most influential book published during the war ... raising more eyebrows than his unsuccessful battle to unseat Roosevelt. *One World* did more than sell two million copies. It helped to create a remarkable shift of opinion away from traditional isolationism.

Up popped the competent but colorless Thomas E. Dewey: young, vigorous, middle-of-the-road. But the GOP nominee made two fatal mistakes. He failed to find a real issue. Then he resorted to faultfinding of a war-weary Franklin Delano Roosevelt. FDR mishandled the Depression ... the war ... foreign affairs. ... *The man was a failure!* Roosevelt chose to ignore the "nipping at the heels" of his opponent. Finally, stirred up, the president, addressing the Teamsters Union, commented in mock indignation: "These Republican leaders have not been content with attacks on me, my wife, or our sons. No, not content with that, they now include my little dog, Fala. Well, of course, *I* don't resent attacks ... but Fala does. You know, Fala is Scotch, and being a Scottie, as soon as he learned that the Republican fiction writers, in Congress and out, had concocted a story that I had left him behind on the Aleutian Islands and had sent a destroyer back to find him at a cost of two, three, eight ... or twenty million dollars, his Scotch soul was furious! Fala has not been the same dog since. I am accustomed to hearing malicious falsehoods about myself, but I think I have a right to resent libelous statements about my dog!"

"Knock, knock!" Mary Ann called without knocking.

"Who's there?" Marvel said the expected words with an effort.

"Cecil. *Open up!*"

"Cecil who?" Marvel said, fumbling with her bedroom doorknob.

"Cecil have music wherever she goes!" Mary Ann sang out. "I have the orange juice—fresh-squeezed. That's what took me so long. Drink up. They're all gone, still fretting over Uncle Joseph's problems, afraid the family's falling apart and all that stuff. I'm still glad your grandmother took me under her wing. But something shook me a little. It was the first time I ever heard Aunt Snow mention—you don't mind if I say it, do you?—you know, her own brothers. I guess I knew they were out there somewhere, but you never talk about that side of you. You're so close-mouthed and I'm such a blabbermouth. Don't answer that! This'll shake you though—what our daddies said. Something like the Harrington brothers were gettin' wider and wider apart, too. Oh Marvel, *we'll* stick together won't we? Us and our families, I mean, well, geographically, in the flesh—physically's the word, I guess—and spiritually? Say *yes!*"

"Yes!" Marvel said once her cousin's marathon of words stopped. Then, gratefully, she took a long, slow swallow of the gold-flavored juice. "I'll miss the oranges, but," she swallowed, "the persimmons—"

"I want to read that persimmon piece and read B.J.'s baseball papers when there's time. And you gotta see what Gran'mere sent me. Some you'll want—all about how the Great Depression and World War II shaped folks. You can bet your bottom dollar on that!" she shrugged. "Always that old saw about the worst of times and the best of times—how we used fortitude and *grit*. Yeah, grit—grits for breakfast like the *Stretching* cookbook says, and grit between our teeth from the dust storms. The best of times? I wonder..."

Marvel finished her orange juice gratefully. "The best in that it brought out the best in us. We trusted God and each other. I'm glad I kept scads of notes and records on it all. How many will believe such a time existed? I'm thinking how people looked at us no differently after we lost everything than when we were *The* Harringtons, 'those banking people.' They kept looking to us for leadership. Never mind what make or model car, or whether we had one—or what kind of shacks we lived in after the old mansion burned. It was what we did, what we said, and what we gave of ourselves—"

"Our hearts," Mary Ann whispered. "I always had Jake. We both had our parents. And, oh Marvel, you and I had each other. Then you taught me how broad love was—you and God—and to simply give *myself*."

The dull ache persisted in Marvel's stomach, but her head felt more clear than it had for weeks. Talk of the writing quickened her pulse, made her fingers tingle to be at the typewriter. She hadn't felt this excited for months. And something told her not to wait, just as Grandmother had urged her Squire's sons not to wait too long to return.

Mary Ann caught the excitement and babbled about rumble seats, shivarees, those "darling bleached-out feedsack dresses," inner tube garters, and cliff-hanging Saturday matinees filled with grand heroes like Tom Mix—and oh, those door prizes. Remember when we Harringtons won 'em all?"

Marvel remembered. Remembered the magic of radio, too ... the medicine shows ... the breathtaking wonder of the circus come to town ... and rationing. While it was too current to be of value now—"Forget it, sweep it under the rug!" people said— rationing was an important part of history, even (Marvel realized suddenly) to returning service personnel. Men and women overseas were elbow-deep in gore, and news was often available, while those in uniform at home were spared the ordeals of shipping with stamps. "Family allotments" meant portions taken from meager checks, matched by the government, and sent home to dependents. Yes, it was good to have all the notes— even those on the days of the big bands: Brown ... Goodman ... James ... Tucker ... Welk ... *Dorsey* (the name brought Titus, never far away, back to stand beside her, his gentle face more real than Mary Ann's). Oh, she would go on and write about all the remembered leaders' "canaries," the name applied to the vocalists of the numerous orchestra leaders. And the songs—oh, the lovely songs! Could she include "I'm Looking Over a Four-Leaf Clover"? Yes—yes, she could, just as she had kept the mysterious dried and preserved clover. One day Titus would explain....

"Sitting here won't do the jobs, but it's good lookin' back on those gentler days of kindness and caring. Dr. Porter made more than house calls, even stayed days and weeks, all the time knowin' we couldn't pay. I could bawl about that. And what few groceries we had to buy, well, we'd say, 'Just put 'er on th' tab, Wilbur!' to Mr. Benson, and 'square with you when th' cotton's baled!' Soooo, why don't I shut up and get crawlin'? Oh, I *do* want to see the president piece Gran'mere sent. Got it handy?" She reached to accept it.

"Oh!" Mary Ann stopped quickly. "This cute part about Fala— Mr. Roosevelt mentioned the Aleutians. Jake's there—he can tell me now. And he'll be back in Ft. Lewis anytime. *No appointment necessary!*"

But Mary Ann's frown spoke of concern.

"That's wonderful," Marvel said softly, thinking how wonderful if—

Mary Ann bit her lip, but nodded. "Oh yes. Only Jake wants to go on home, get on with banking. Not that I object. I don't give a hoot what my man does, just so we can be together. You know that. But I'd planned to stick by Mother, Daddy, and B.J. until we could go as a family. But closing out real estate deals 'ain't what it usta be.' Something else you'll need to use in your book. We didn't used to need a string of Philadelphia lawyers to square a deal—just a handshake."

Marvel smiled. "Don't stop trusting altogether, Mary Ann. Things are just, well, different. Maybe we won't know all the dogs by name when we get back to Pleasant Knoll, either. But we'll learn. Families and friends have kept us in touch."

"And told us the bad news, too—let us see the other side of the coin!" Mary Ann burst out. "I can't let something like what happened to Erin happen between Jake and me. Couples need to be together—"

"We've been through all this," Marvel said wearily. "You're married now, and Uncle Worth and Auntie Rae aren't exactly the 'homeless, rootless, migratory laborers' people used to call us anymore."

"Oh, that sets my blood flowin' the wrong direction! You aren't going to tell about *that*, are you—in your book, I mean?"

"Aren't we off the subject?" *As always*, Marvel thought with the usual amusement at her cousin's detours of the mind. "About Jake: You and he will have to decide. Just remember your vows to him."

"And yours to Titus. That's what you're remembering. Admit it!"

"I admit it."

"'Forsaking all others'—our parents did that. Yes, I'll go. And about Erin, I'm sorry. There's just no right way to do a wrong thing. I'll write him *right now*. You look more chipper—*going, going, GONE!*"

Dear Mary Ann. What would I do without her? Marvel wondered. Always thanking others for what she was—never trusting the precious gifts God had given to her alone, realize what she was giving of herself. What was it Mary Ann had said of my mind once? Oh yes, back in the days of black-and-white movies, Mary

Ann had said, "You see in color, listen that way, write that way—and kinda paint it, you know?"

It was true. And somehow that God-given sense of vision had prompted Marvel Harrington to see a world turned gray with dust in come-alive color—the way it was in the beginning... the way she and Titus would help to restore it. And they would. They *would!*

Smiling, Marvel bent to open the bottom drawer of her desk. She knew exactly where the little item was, the one she had written back in high-school days. It resulted from Mary Ann's comments—and from her deep, once-in-a-lifetime love for Titus. Loving it, he had kept a copy of her "I Saw... I heard... I *Felt* the Sixth Sense of Sadness":

> How sad that mortals are unable to *see* love's color—captives that they are, crouching in their tents of gloom and doom, blinded to light, feet moving in ghostly motion. How sad when they are unable to *hear* love's rustling procession of heartbeats, the rhythm of dream-flutes and dreams-come-true drummed so unexplainably by Unseen Hand... cannot smell love's floral fragrance or the good-earth scent of its restless growing. How sad that mortals must resort to words, the primitive tools clumsily used to express what the heart sees, hears, scents, touches, tastes, and *feels* within the human heart. How sad when mortals cannot care. How can they care, those who have not met God, felt His breath in their dead hearts, and then heard His whisper of love everlasting? The world spins more gently then... in external color. Enlightened, they rejoice and then feel the sixth sense of sadness—because to other mortals love is unknown.

Misty-eyed, Marvel laid the writing of her youth back among her souvenirs. Perhaps it was clumsily written indeed, but she would not change one word. It expressed her feelings then, and it expressed them now. Never mind words. Nothing had changed—not really. Even the yellowing page still smelled of lilacs. Mr. Corey would appreciate knowing that something remained of the box of stationery the newspaper gave her—the only payment for her continuous contributions to its pages. But other rewards meant more than money: appreciation, love, the joy of giving...and togetherness with Titus. There were no tears...just smiles of reassurance. Life had its lighter moments, things would get better. God would see to that. And those who journeyed through those years continued to cling to that conviction. Thank God for that. And now she smiled.

One day passed...two...then three. Marvel managed during those busy pre-Thanksgiving days to write Kate Lynn. She caught herself speaking of Titus in future tense, started to erase the sentence, then changed her mind. Like Mary Ann, Kate Lynn kept insisting that although they were unable to explain the intriguing circumstances, Titus was alive and would be returning. *Oh, please Lord...*

Mary Ann took some more needed time, begging that Marvel add to her list of amusing sightings on churches' outside bulletin boards—some done through poor phrasing, others done "in good faith." But all brought a smile—a touch of humor without making faith a humorous matter. "Like this: 'Trespassers Welcome'?" Marvel asked. "Like that," Mary Ann said. And then they compared lists and penciled out duplicates: "Prayer Conditioned"..."Redemption Center, No Stamps Required"..."How About a Faith Lift?"..."Come On In, We Accept Anybody."

"Hey, get a load of this!" Mary Ann bust out laughing, "'To All Christian Brethren, Merry Christmas—To Our Jewish Brethren, Bright Festival of Lights—To Our Atheist Brethren, Lotsa Luck!'"

"Your *Wisdom of the Ages* book should include that God is the skeleton key that opens all hearts. I never saw that in print."

"It has a *twist*." Mary Ann laughed again. "People seem bent on forgetting simple things like puns, knock-knocks, yo-yos, hula hoops. Oh well, that's the purpose of our books. We learned how to laugh when we had to make do with nothing. And these," she went on with a nod at her list, "can keep folks laughin' and give Satan a jab in the jaw and end *his* laughin'. I'll take over—check with you later. Thanks a bundle—" Mary Ann's hug punctuated the unfinished sentence. Then she was gone with a whirl of her curls.

And Marvel went back to her writing.

"Was America ready for the postwar world?" the reporter had asked in the clipping Grandmother sent—and "Would they remember?"

Believing that her materials covered most of the period between the Great Depression and the close of World War II, Marvel postponed checking details and concentrated on another angle: a General Motors spectacular treatment called "Futurama," which captured worldwide attention at the 1939 World's Fair. Depression-weary America was making a slow return to recovery. Dreams were alive and well. Who needed the nightmare of war in their future?

What did they dream? *Life* magazine expanded upon the General Motors prophecies with unrealistic enthusiasm, uncharacteristic of the publication. How much had come true? Marvel wondered as she excerpted the copy she had held onto, coveting the time to get back to it:

What will America be like a decade from now? Tanned and vigorous people will have learned how to have fun... very fit people who do not care for possessions... are not attached to their homes or hometowns.... Trains, express highways, and planes get them across America in 24 hours.

Americans will take two-month vacations, drive on a two-way skein of four 50-mph lanes on outer edges ... two pairs of 75 mph... and in center, two lanes for 100-mph express traffic. Cars change lanes at specified intervals... signals from control towers which stop and start traffic by radio... out of driver's control... car is safe against accident... raindrop shape ... diesel... air-conditioned... cost $200... highways skirt great cities.

Happy people live in one-factory farm-villages... strip planting... no erosion... federal laws forbid wanton cutting of wooded hillsides... dams prevent floods.

Behind visible America are inventors and engineers—liquid air... a potent, mobile source of power ... atomic energy used cautiously. Power by radio beams... Lanora cell has made all gasoline motors diesels... life is easy... cures for cancer and infantile paralysis have extended man's life span... his wife's skin is perfect at 75... houses light, graceful, easily replaced...

On every front America knows more . . . nearly everyone is a high-school graduate . . . talented get the best
education in the world . . . more people are interested
in life, themselves . . . and making this a better world
. . . politics and emotion still progress slowly. But
these obstructions are treated with dwindling patience. . . .

Marvel's mind spun back as her pen spun forward. Oh, it was
real, that Depression . . . ask the 15 million unemployed, turned
beggars, peddling apples from city street corners to provide
watery cabbage soup for wives and children, praising God for
jobs yielding 200 dollars *a year*. Down South, cotton dropped to
a nickel a pound, then wouldn't sell, period. Floods, droughts,
whirlwinds stole away dreams—but, like pack rats, left something in return: *grit*. The "Dirty Thirties" put America on worn
tires, roaming, pleading, raising Will Work for Food placards in
high hope, only to lower them in despair. Gone all—except for
faith. And faith brought endurance. For who could deny *God's*
prophecies (never mind those of a by-then disillusioned General
Motors Corporation!): "As thy days, so shall thy strength be"?
And they survived!
What had she left out? Very little, except that God blessed
them all with a national sense of humor in oft-unexpected ways—
one via radio magic: family programs for evening listening at the
close of a grueling day . . . soap operas for women who did dread
jobs of ironing, patching, and preparing meager meals. They
could dream—and identify. And dream they did, dreams enlarg-
ing when Franklin Delano Roosevelt took his oath of office to the
tune of "Happy Days Are Here Again!" Dreams darkened when
the president ordered banks closed to halt withdrawal of de-
posits in those panicky days. And then those dreams lightened,
finally to change color completely with the premiere of "The
Wizard of Oz." Linking hands and hearts, all America skipped
with Dorothy, the tin man, the fearful lion, and the brainless
scarecrow, down that yellow brick road of 1939, the year marking
the end of the Great Depression and the biggest World's Fair ever,
"Merry Days at Mad Meadow." Ahead beckoned the emerald city
of prosperity. . . .
The question remained unanswered. "Was America ready for
the postwar world?" But the hour was late. And it was time for

rehearsal. "Lord, give me that promised strength," Marvel whispered, and rose on legs as rubbery as those of the scarecrow.

*　*　*

"It's a Chamber of Commerce day," Daddy said of Thanksgiving eve. Sure enough, it was one of those blue-ribbon days of bronze chrysanthemums and still-clinging golden elm leaves vying for attention. "Work day as usual, but no rehearsal tonight, so I'm feeling thankful already!" They all were and said so in their family prayer.

Marvel looked for changes throughout the day to add to her notes of the present and recorded them as time allowed. There was disillusionment. She read it in the faces of men returning to civilian life after the bitter battles of war. Lines—everywhere there were lines: in grocery stores, at bus stops. Where had all these people come from? They hated lines. Hadn't they had it up to here in the service with "hurrying up to wait" tricks? And where were the jobs they left? Promises to hold their jobs open for them were empty indeed when the offices had closed. And the women who waited—what had changed them so much? Why, they were doing men's work: driving buses, building houses, *heading the families*! That's what! Were men needed at all? Their children no longer recognized them, did not respond to their commands—had become as independent as their mothers. It had felt good to shed uniforms, but moths had had a banquet in their packed-away suits. And what few the insects had not found were outdated. Fitted coats, military presses, and cuffed pants were out—oversize suits, in! Where were all the welcomes they had expected, dreamed of, and prayer for?

In the Bible study and rap session, Marvel determined to continue until the building was ordered vacated. A young man, wearing his suntans stripped of rank and ribbons, said to another: "I don't get it. Barb made such a point of telling me how happy she and the kid were—no problems, none, she claimed— that between you and me, I wondered if she missed me at all! And now," he added bitterly, "who's griping? Oh, that was different, she says—a war on. And everybody envied officers' wives. Me a Second Louie—some rank!"

The other man agreed. Liz wanted him to re-up—keep his rating. He hated it all but, blast it, there *were* rumors of other conflicts. Well, all the more reason to stay out—durn sordid over there.

"Yeah," a third agreed, "still, I miss my buddies. At least we could communicate. We promised to keep in touch. Oh well, a reunion maybe. I gotta bum leg and a bum rap—pension, big joke!"

Totally disillusioned, bitter, and disenchanted, the trio muttered that maybe America hadn't won much after all. Better surrender like the enemies did and expect the conquerors to feed 'em.

* * *

An ashen-faced Marvel strung the words together, racing against time, sorted and labeled data, and wrote a note to Editor Corey. There was no time for addressing an envelope due to an interruption.

"Marvel!" B.J. burst out breathlessly before entering the door, "I saw it take off—the Spruce Goose. I did—*we* did. A girl by the name of Mimi! Hot dogs and cold cats! Mimi got as excited as I did a-about th' Goose—not a bird, not a plane, it's—"

"Superman?" Marvel guessed, glancing at her watch.

"Super-*ship*! A *flying* ship! Big—oh man! A weapon that can win *any* war all by itself. And th' pilot was none other than the wealthy bird who had the Spruce Goose built—owns th' patent and th' corporation. I think his name's Hughes. Funny thing, the name of *Mimi*—"

Oh well, what was another five minutes? Seeing Billy Joe's telltale glance at the floor and heightened color, and recognizing a first love, Marvel handed him a treasure. "Here are your answers."

"Wow! *Whoop-EEE!*" her cousin yelled with such enthusiasm Marvel told Mary Ann a long time afterward that she thought he would have to undergo the National Recovery Act to regulate his heartbeat.

When most of the country hit rock bottom, old-fashioned high society floundered along with it. From the rubble of Newport and Fifth Avenue, however, emerged enough hangers-on to create a glittering, publicity-made, indefatigable set referred to in retrospect as "café society." In reality, the "cafés" were

speakeasies, even though prohibition was repealed in
'33. Phoenix-like, chic restaurants (New York's Stork
Club, El Morocco, "Club 21," and the like) rose from
the ashes with their own breed of firewater. Among
these (dating from 1933–38) were the Grand Duchess
Marie (cousin of Russia's last czar)...Elizabeth Arden
...Lady Astor...Vandervilts...and "Red-Hot Mama"
Sophie Tucker, plus such indiscriminates as a Mrs.
Margaret Emerson-Mckim-Vandervilt-*Baker*-Amory-
Emerson. Then came the ultimate glamour girls, among
them *Mimi Baker* who made her debut in '37. At 15,
Mimi was ravishingly pretty, a precocious spender. So
ostentatious was her debut that even gossip-loving
columnist Elsa Maxwell condemned her as a decadent
aristocrat, while Walter Winchell called her "the *cele-
*butante." Time marched on...Miss Baker became
"Mimi, the Daring" who wowed Wall Street garbed in
floral "Beach Pajamas"—an idea which spread like a
fungus. And somehow, *Mimi began dating the elusive
millionaire, one Howard Hughes.*

"That's it, Marvel, that's it! I saw 'em—th' Spruce Goose—
with *my* Mimi. You'll meet her when we have the big major league
playoff tomorrow. I know, I know, tonight's the program and big
church banquet after it's all over. I'll scram. You'll be along?"

All talk stopped downstairs. The house was silent. Marvel was
alone. *Alone.* "I must go—I *must*," she willed. "They'll worry."

The whole day had been a grotesque dream that didn't happen. Already it was tiptoeing out of her mind, making room for
the roar of her head. The door was only a short distance from her
reeling chair. Surely she could make it, although the nausea was
back, and it seemed so dark. She tried to stand, but a knife-sharp
pain reduced her leg bones to gelatin. Too late, Marvel knew she
had waited too long in making a doctor's appointment. *Dear
God*, she whispered, and pitched forward as the floor rose up to
meet her.

9

The Fledgling

Dale Harrington shifted nervously in the pew of the church. All around him, the congregation was astir with anticipation. From behind the curtain came the soft strains of a violin. Snow! Yes, of course, she would be fine-tuning the instrument, intent on the several solos for tonight's gala Thanksgiving celebration, unaware that their daughter was late. Marvel—their Marvel who had never been late in her life. Some father he was. Hadn't he been poor at all else? A has-been baseball player who never made it to first base...a disappointment to his father. The Harringtons were *alway* bankers until Dale the maverick came along. And then, worst of all, he'd failed his family—made them into near-paupers rather than admit he was a loser at farming while shifty-eyed bankers took all. A good father would be out there looking, and he—why, he was afraid to look up again even now, because Marvel might be missing.

Once more. No sign of her. This time his brother followed his gaze. "She's late. Should we go?" Worth whispered.

No, it was too late.

Dr. James Murphy was reading the welcome address Marvel Harrington would have delivered without notes. Did he imagine that their pastor's voice was choked by emotion? No, Snow had noticed, too, as evidenced by her unscheduled playing of a soft, sweet, melodic accompaniment to Marvel's words:

Autumn is the loving arm of God placed around the
shoulder of the world....August stopped sulking at

107

the first September rain. A sort of gentleness sets in as summer yields to fall—which, God willing, all mankind feels toward one another. A mysterious haze changes the perspective of the landscape. Hills are more distant, more aloof—appearing easier to scale. Trees huddle closer together as if in united prayer. The atmosphere is spiced with quince... farmers fill silos with fat pumpkins and peanut-hay, remembering to leave the gleanings for animal friends over whom God gave dominion. Bright-eyed field mice search the stubble for overlooked grain. Ducks muffle their hymns on the pond. An indefinable sense of satisfaction mellows the world with a shawl of loveliness. A crisp north wind lifts the luminous haze, reveals the fire that the aspen and pen oak have kindled on the hillsides to mingle the wood smoke with maple syrup, ribbon cane, or molasses, depending on what section of God's magnificent earth one occupies.

The Harrington men looked over their shoulders. Maybe Marvel was detained—had taken a back pew. She wasn't there. She was not coming, their eyes signaled. They should go, but was the timing wrong? Snow Harrington's strained gaze said she knew, and yet, the show must go on! And what's this? Pastor Jim was *what*? Already Dale Harrington had missed something, but he managed a nod of encouragement to his wife. Soon she must solo... such a lonely word.

...and the sunshine has more substance as if it were melted down like our human hearts. October's bright, blue weather seems but a fleeting interlude—a warning that we must love, cherish, and remember, when stronger, sharper winds have stripped the trees of color and the birds have flown away. The foot of anticipation steps toward Thanksgiving! The theme of autumn is harvest... God's harvest—a time of storing and praising the almighty hand that feeds our hearts, our minds, our bodies, and our souls!

Snow Harrington's music became more triumphant in "Praise God from Whom All Blessings Flow." Applause followed. And as it faded, Pastor Jim said quietly, "And now, repeating what I managed to say before, let us make this Thanksgiving the most joyous ever, for it is a time of storing memories of friends in my own bleeding heart—as *I will be leaving my God-given friends!*"

His voice broke, and Snow Harrington's solo began....

But Dale and Worth Harrington had slipped from the church. Word traveled from eye to eye. The Harringtons needed no words in time of family crises. No need of a clock, either. Time had no meaning. Togetherness told it all—the kind of togetherness which took them to Elm Street...home...and the crumpled form of their beloved Marvel. There was need of a doctor, then the Great Physician on high.

"Operator? This is an emergency—my daughter—a matter of life and death! Elm Street Ten. No, we *haven't* moved her. Covered with a blanket? Of course. Stop *talking*, you idiots, and get rollin'!"

Numbed by shock, the family joined hands as they dropped to their knees and raised their voices in fervent prayer. One minute...two...or were the clocks and watches ticktocking hours away, praying with them for the welcome wail of a siren? And then the ambulance came.

Only once did Marvel stir slightly with a moan too small for others to hear. She longed to reassure them, tell them she was all right. *Trust—they must trust God.* The pain was gone. She felt nothing, just a strange lack of emotion, an inability to move her lips. Had she ever known such complete numbness, such detachment, as if she were suspended above the scene, a spectator looking down? She was seeing the bereaved, and yes, watching herself through closed lids as they all pressed closer to assist white-coated men lifting her weightless body. Yes, she had experienced this when Titus was reported missing...again, when he was presumed dead...and yes, when Philip's plane exploded. *Dead*, both men were dead. So this was what it was like to die, without a chance to say, "Farewell, God is waiting."

There was a blinding red light. Then the darkness closed in again.

* * *

For five days Marvel lay in a coma. Even then, she drifted in and out of consciousness. People hovered over her—of that she was certain. There were voices, but the words were jumbled ...faces she could near-recognize, only to have them blur and then fade completely. She must *try* to hear the starched words of nurses, grim warnings from one of the several doctors, consoling phrases of another.

Through the surrounding mists of semiconsciousness, she was totally aware of only two things: Either her body was bloated beyond recognition or a heavy weight lay across her middle, and she was dying of thirst. "Wa-ter," she tried to whisper, but the word stuck in the parchment-papered throat. Again... try again...

Someone must have heard. From faraway a voice said, "No... can't risk... ether makes one sick... stitches tear. *No!*"

That someone laid ice to her lips, then floated away.

The wave of nausea passed and Marvel opened her eyes, wishing she could shade them against the light. The hand stroking her hair stopped. "Oh darling, don't try to talk. We've been so anxious—"

Mother. "Then it's not all over?" Marvel wanted to ask. But she felt too empty to speak. It made no difference... no difference at all. Mother always cried when she was happy, laughed when she was sad....

Once in the dark of night, Titus came. There were no words, no need for them, just the gentle understanding in his eyes. He held her hand and smiled crookedly. Of course. Hadn't he suffered because of her own pain? But why the uniform? Somewhere buried deep in her subconscious, Marvel envisioned the lean physique clothed in slacks, football garb, or *shining raiment....*

Was he leaving? She must plead. "Titus...?" she whispered faintly.

He nodded. "Yes—I know." More voices, then quietness up and down the medicated halls of the sleeping hospital.

* * *

Bit by painful bit the story came together—enough for a brief synopsis, at least. Someday, perhaps, Marvel Harrington would appreciate details of the event which was to change her entire life. But for now, even the briefest outline was a struggle—the segueing of faces, voices, and meanings in a strange, new world.

Or was it her old world seen from a new light?

The family cared deeply. They were so open with words of love, yet restrained, as if something lay between them unsaid.

Daddy told her all about the Thanksgiving program and the events which brought her to this place, but stopped short of saying what happened here.

"When you're stronger, baby, we'll talk then. But for now, you need rest. So 'Hush, li'l baby, don' say uh word, Daddy's gonna buy yah uh mockin'bird....'"

Mother's tightly laced fingers were her segno to Daddy's words. Repeat: *Rest, get well, rest...*

Marvel felt confused, helpless, pressured. All she wanted was their honesty. What has happened to this body of mine—this temple of the Lord? What are the damages, the costs of maintenance and repair? And then she would feel guilty, and a fresh wash of weak tears would trickle down her face. In wordless prayer, she found solace, but His answer seemed somewhat the same: "Come unto me, all ye that labour and are heavy laden, and I will give you rest."

The lethargy lingered. Thoughts jumbled together, sometimes bright, clear, and transparent—sometimes clouded and unreal. Pastor Jim came to say good-bye. Marvel would never know, he said, what an inspiration she had been—including the Thanksgiving writing. Marvel knew, didn't she, that Mary Ann had forwarded it on to Baylor, along with the other seasonal portions to accompany it? No, Marvel did not know. But now she remembered having labeled it for mailing.

"Oh—oh, we'll miss you," she said brokenly. "Must you go?"

He nodded gravely. "It's wise to change when my finger won't plug the hole in the dike anymore, make way for younger blood. I feel I've fulfilled God's purpose under circumstances that led me to meet needs in a way some call unorthodox, unseemly, and against tradition. But, like my blessed deacons Dale and Worth, I just plain hunger for home, where everybody turns out for church and prayer meeting, not waiting around for times to get tough before calling on the Lord. 'Bible-belt folks' they call us—praise th' Lord!"

Marvel smiled wanly. Yes she knew—she knew.

Dr. James Murphy was embracing her tearfully when a stranger soundlessly walked in. Obviously Jewish, the man was elderly, his eyes compassionate, his body stooped by the years. He stooped even more when he bowed politely, a gesture which revealed the white crocheted kippa covering the balding head. Rising, he peered uncertainly through thick-lensed eyeglasses, first at Pastor Jim and then at Marvel. He *was* here, wasn't he—not simply a part of the recurring unreality in which she longed to feel a part, but dared not? Feeling would bring only the dreaded pain. Her world was safer.

"May I enter, my child? Ah, you sir, the preee-cher, yah? 'Tis many blessings you have brought my people, and I shall see you no more. Both be leaving, yah? I bring God's blessings."

"And in His name I thank you, my brother," Pastor Jim replied, his voice trembling with emotion.

In Marvel's turbulent world, it was inevitable that a third guest should float in on the wings of a floor-touching cassock. "I have lighted many a candle for you, my sister," the priest said. "We share so much, remember so much together. And you have made my people your people, as well you should. For do we not recall reports of Catholics and Protestants, Social Democrats and Jews, those thousands whose lives ended in deadly cremation—only to be reported as dying of *natural causes* in that purgatorial darkness where only the hand of God could touch their souls: *Nazi Germany!*"

The blinding white hospital cell became a church, a synagogue, a cathedral . . . the brotherhood of man under the Fatherhood of God. For then, as it had been when the ship sank during the height of the war, the three men of God embraced. . . .

The healing process came soon afterward. Marvel had witnessed a miracle—a miracle reserved for her Creator's use *in His time*. Heretofore, images, their features blurred, had been an unfolding saga in black-and-white celluloid. Now, while she still viewed the world through a shifting of transparencies, they took on color, their depth increasing with each breath. She inhaled deeply as nurses had instructed. So what if it hurt? There was born inside her now the overwhelming desire to feel, to learn, to know. Oh, she was still a fledgling—depending on others for food and water. But now she wanted to fly from the nest. Once upon a time, she had known the feel of wings—independence. What kept her from trusting her wings now? Fear? Lack of trust? Fly she would, the fledgling in her resolved—else she would forget the skill, become helpless, forever dependent. . . .

"Hi, Marvel!" B.J.'s voice interrupted her reverie.

"Hi yourself, cousin! How's our Harrington heir?"

Billy Joe made no effort to hide his excitement and happiness. Oh, how great she looked . . . everything was bound to be okay now—*everything*! And oh Marvel, how scared he was! But now she could listen to what the guys told her. They had won without him!

"Oh honey—you didn't! You missed your game—because of *me*?"

It didn't matter—it didn't, he insisted repeatedly. And the team did more than that. Prayed—they actually *prayed* like they'd seen Uncle Dale do when he was manager. "And me, I taught 'em words don't matter, just so they talk to God like He was there—because He *is*!" B.J. paused only long enough for Marvel's nod of approval and then added humbly, "I guess I've influenced them—like you and Mary Ann shaped *me*. And just one thing more—th' guys took me serious-like about visiting th' sick, came here to peek in at you, even with that 'No Visitors Allowed' sign on your door."

"I'm proud of you—so proud! We all influence one another—it takes us all. So go ahead, be a teacher—you're one now."

"Yeah, I guess I am. Holy smoke! And I didn't even know I was a writer either until your check came. Know what I did then?" His voice dropped to a conspiratory whisper. "I took the bull by the horns and put some ideas your daddy gave me together for a sports magazine our school library had in the morgue—and I hit a homer. Paid me *ten bucks*. You will read my whole book?"

"Every word," she promised softly, knowing now that the feathery feel of her wings was real, that she could soar on the wings of an eagle—without a safety net. God would bear her up, sustain her.

When Mary Ann made the daily visit (more than one, her cousin was to reveal later), she gasped, "Marvel! You recognized me. Don't deny it. Oh, I'm so happy I could cry!"

And she did.

Marvel reached out a comforting hand. "Don't cry, Mary Ann—please don't. We have everything to live for. I should feel tired, but I don't." It was true. With each visit, she grew stronger and more convinced that she could trust her wings—not panic and drop at Satan's beck and call. Not that she would take soaring for granted. Oh no—it was a matter of knowing now that life held no pain too great to bear. God's love was stronger than earth's gravity. He would hold her aloft. "Tell me about Jake— everything about you and your husband!"

A strange look crossed Mary Ann's face, a look which changed to understanding in a way that tattled rehearsal. Mary Ann *had* told her, but she had known even then that Marvel did not comprehend.

"I—we—" she hesitated, dabbed at her tear-dampened eyes, and went on, "Jake was here, you know. He's family, too, and only family and ministers could visit. He was in such a rush to get home, he still had his uniform on—" Mary Ann stopped, a look of horror on her face. "Oh, shut my mouth!" she all but screamed.

Jake was here. Jake was going home. And Mary Ann had stayed. This time it was Marvel who wept. Never had she loved her family more. Never had she felt so humble. But words could never express it.

"You've all been so wonderful," she gulped. "I—I feel like Pollyanna. Oh, not the all-giving part—more the all-broken part, when everybody came to say how perfect she was. And she knew better."

Low-pitched voices just outside the door said others were coming. Mary Ann looked relieved to be spared an attempted answer. But there were questions Marvel needed to ask—answers she *must* have.

"Wait—it's Mother and Daddy. They'll tell me about—well, the medical details. But only you can tell me this. *Titus*—he was here, wasn't he? I mean, he was with me all the time. I felt that. But was he here in person? The truth, Mary Ann—did I just dream Titus, too?"

"Not here exactly, but proof—the next-best thing," Mary Ann whispered hurriedly. "Jake *did* see him. He knew Titus, remember? Knew your picture, too. Yes, Titus showed Jake that Kodak shot I took on the road—the one of you shading your eyes—"

And the one the young soldier tried to tell me about, Marvel thought with sad regret. Oh, why hadn't she listened to the words of the boy at the USO? Instead, she had jumped to conclusions—wrong ones. He was lonely, in need of company, seeing the girl he left in another, as she had seen Titus in Philip. Or maybe he was making advances, testing the waters with the old line, "Haven't I seen you somewhere before?" But he *had* mentioned a photo—

"—and he *was* in uniform—"

"Titus?"

The old Mary Ann was back. With a toss of black curls, she laughed outright. "Of course, Titus! Isn't that this most wonderful man in the world's name? Pushing me for answers, then paying not a penny's worth of attention—you and that brother of mine! His head's in the clouds over this Mimi-girl. You'll have to put Titus through this deprogramming when we all get home. Ooops, somebody's coming. Hi!"

The parley had ended outside the door. But Marvel's parents did not come in as she had expected. Instead, it was one of the several doctors—the most gentle, as she recalled. A Dr. Finstead?

"Hello, doctor—Finstead, isn't it?"

The doctor nodded, and even while going through the professional routine of studying the chart at the foot of her bed, feeling her pulse, and cuffing her arm for a blood-pressure count, Marvel was aware of the scrutiny of his eyes. "Much pain—tenderness?" his hands were pressing the swath of bandages carefully.

Marvel tried not to wince, biting her lip to hold back a moan.

"It's a long incision of necessity, but the three of us agreed on what had to be done. Fever's gone—all vital signs normal. It will take some time, but we need to talk," he said seriously.

"Yes," she murmured, aware that the words would spell change.

Dr. Finstead drew a chair alongside her bed and took her hand.

He tried to be kind, and she tried to be brave. Both were surprisingly successful. How much did Marvel remember? Very little—just blurred images, snatches of conversations, and sounds. Warning signs? Well, fatigue, nausea now and then—and yes, some dizziness when the pain came. And it did come more and more often—so often that she named it her Great Pain "when it outgrew me and I felt I sat in the lap of it," she admitted. Rest? There was no time. The night she collapsed? "I did?" she asked dully.

The doctor inhaled deeply. "There were signs then, warnings. There usually are, but—" he let his breath out slowly, "nothing would have prevented this, my dear. I'll be blunt. That's best for us both in the long run. I'll need to ask you two related questions.

She waited.

"We doctors respect our patients' privacy, but we do need to know all circumstances. Are you by any chance married?"

Surprised, Marvel answered the question with another. "Why—what ever gave you such an idea? Married—did someone—?"

Dr. Finstead shook his head, then combed his crew cut needlessly with uncertain fingers. "Nobody suggested anything, but you did talk a lot about someone by the name of Titus. Of course, you were delirious because of the fever." The man appeared to be relieved. How strange—until his next words came. "I needed to be sure. You see, I asked permission of your parents, and had there been a spouse, he should have been consulted in such delicate matters."

The remainder of the explanation came out in a jumble. Her appendix had ruptured . . . peritonitis had resulted . . . sulfa drug failed for her . . . penicillin (still risky because of possible severe reaction, but wasn't it a miracle that the first shipments were returning home from the war?) proved effective and surgery could be performed. . . .

"I see," she said slowly, not seeing at all, "but I would like to know what the diagnosis was—all of it."

"Of course—and the prognosis as well."

Without hesitation, the doctor told her then. It was necessary to remove most of her reproductive organs. There was no alternative for she had had a "close call." It was regrettable.

"Regrettable? What you're saying is that I will be unable to bear children, isn't it? But you did the best you could, and for that I thank you. But what was your other question?"

The doctor was near retirement, and his eyes spoke of admiration and respect. Most women would have wept, asked all kinds of questions as to whether they could hope for a fulfilling relationship in marriage. There was something special about this young lady—special and rare. That was it. She held some pearls of wisdom. Unemotionally, Marvel Harrington had posed a question. He must respond.

"You have enough ahead of you just recuperating, and you must be very careful, take it easy. And if you will promise that, then I can promise full recovery. Yes," he nodded, "the prognosis is good! And here I am, your doctor, needing to assign you yet another task. You see, your parents are laboring with guilt. I had to have parental consent before removing the diseased organs. Can you help them?"

Could Marvel help? Hadn't that been the story of her life? But there was not a hint of former feelings of having too much responsibility. Something strange and beautiful had bloomed insider her. And she knew then what God's purpose was in her life. The call was loud and clear. Help others? Of course, she could—and would.

"That's the best way I know of healing—helping others!" Marvel all but sang out. "I will let Mother and Daddy know everything is fine." And as for Titus—it would make no difference... none at all.

"Out of weakness I am made strong—Paul speaking. And well, it's not the road I take, but how I take it—*Marvel* speaking."

"I would expect something like that from you, and yet, I marvel at your courage. I prayed along with your family, you know."

"And *I* would expect something like that from *you*," Marvel said softly. The smile she gave the doctor was tremulously radiant.

* * *

The road back was fraught with difficulty. Most patients would have turned back, given up, or lain helpless when they stumbled and fell. But Marvel Harrington had a nobler cause now, a surety of destination—a surety which, surprisingly, Mary Ann shared.

"I know—I sure enough know," Mary Ann said, her head bobbing up and down in confirmation. "I was there with you, you know—or *did* you know? That specialist called in from San Francisco kept saying we could talk you through—that you heard. And Somebody else heard, too, and answered our marathon of prayer. Anyhow, God told *me* what to do, too. I have changed my mind—my plans—"

"Not about Jake!"

Oh no, not *Jake*—nothing could change her love for Jake. She had to stay with Marvel—Jake knew that, just as *she* knew Jake needed to go on to school (scholarship waiting under G.I. Bill. No time to "fiddle around."). She would work when they all got back. Business administration Jake was taking, and some course called "Great Religions of the World." So Mr. and Mrs. Jake Brotherton would take their rightful place in Titus County, East Texas, U.S.A.—bring it all together "like a bevy of quail." Wasn't that the way life should be?

"Yes," Marvel, accustomed to her cousin's circles of thought, answered. "And we know that all things work together for good to them that love God—"

"—to them who are called according to *His* purpose," Mary Ann interrupted. A look of pleasure crossed her face. "Oh, I love that chapter in Romans. It says it all. Hear this! I've memorized it—*me* the scatterbrain . . . all about our being God's heirs . . . our Christian hope through Jesus . . . His elect, the conquerors! Oh, I saw *you* conquer. And, to think, I now understand," her voice slowed, "what you meant a-about—Frederick Salsburg's last hours being beautiful. You said he changed and he—okay, our Uncle Fred—made us *his* heirs. It's not the money. How much do we need? It's that he *did* learn love."

Marvel's throat tightened as she nodded. No, not the money. For her, the symbolic legacy meant even more—the pearls, the beautiful pearls she would wear for Titus. *Yes!* She, too, loved the eighth chapter of Romans: "Nor height, nor depth, nor any other creature, shall be able to separate us from the love of God. . . ." Neither could those forces separate her from the love of Titus Smith. God would not allow it!

"The way we were is, to a melancholy degree," she said more to herself than to Mary Ann, "the way we still are."

Mary Ann was laughing and crying. "Beautiful," she murmured in something akin to reverence. "You understand me—you and God. We'll make that trip home together, see the changes, then see more at home. Things'll be different, but the same." Her tears were gone—laughter had conquered. "Jake'll become a regular squire. Won't Grandfather be proud? Remember how he used to say, 'Now, boys, in my time the customer was God! Why, we'd no more take advantage of him than we'd rise and fly. We felt if we did the right thing, profits would take care of themselves. Never had to rob 'n steal 'em blind. Why, illegal acts would've soiled the Harrington family name!'"

Marvel remembered. Later, she promised herself, she would allow memory to go back for more. But for now, "And your plans? You said they had changed, I believe?"

"Oh yes, like I told you, going through all this (seeing how life can go wrong) why, Marvel, everything can look so bright one minute and return to dust the very next. Left me feeling all quivery. This book of mine has to count, have something lasting—history that honors God. I feel changed, along with you. Soooo, I've done a lot of Bible reading, made notes—and guess what! People go around usin' expressions they don't know came right from the Bible—people who never darkened the church door. Downright morose, ignorant."

"So you plan on including them in your book? Great!"

Mary Ann's excitement mounted. In a voice which rose with each word, she began recalling examples: "apple of His eye... knock and it shall be opened... out of the mouths of babes... bridle your tongue... weigh the balances... blind leading the blind... bone of my bones... render unto Caesar... And I have all the references for the sayings. So many like 'cup runneth over,' 'drop in the bucket'—on and on. B.J.'s putting them in alphabetical order. You'd be surprised—"

No, not surprised, Marvel thought as she tried shifting to a more comfortable position. B.J. was bright, just enjoyed cat-and-mouse games—"hiding his light under a bushel." Probably he would work the idea of team prayer into his baseball writings. Baseball... Daddy...

Later Mother plumped Marvel's pillows and checked the water pitcher, hovering like the self-sacrificing mother bird who needs to wean her fledgling from predigested morsels (in need of weaning herself from ill-placed guilt). Marvel thanked her gently, then reassured her that she would be walking soon—trying her wings, so to speak.

Snow Harrington's face was pale, drawn, and filled with restraint. "Oh, that's wonderful!" she exclaimed. "But—" her lovely hands moved as if to applaud only to stop in midair uncertainty, "are you—?"

"Strong enough? I *will* be. I have the doctor's word on it. He and I had a long talk, and everything's going to be fine."

Dale Harrington covered the distance between himself and his daughter's bedside in one stride. "You—you don't blame us, baby?"

"Oh Daddy—*blame* you! I detest that word, especially for my parents. I never blamed you for anything in my life—which you saved, by the way. You did what Titus or I would have done."

Mother fumbled for a handkerchief, her relief pathetically obvious. And Daddy did little better at disguising his emotions. His words were disjointed, contradictory, and more adolescent than B.J.'s had been two years ago. Her parents wanted to escape but remained, needing reassurance that they had done the right thing for her.

What safer ground than normal behavior, everyday conversation?

"I hope you're baking fruitcakes, Mother. I'll be bringing my appetite home with me. I've missed your cooking—and our talks. That reminds me, Daddy. Thank you for the help you gave B.J.'s baseball project. Later I'll look over all his work. A check—imagine!"

Suddenly the three of them were talking at once, planning the future, reviewing the past—too rapidly at first, and then in a normal flow of words. Grandmother? Oh, she called every day—*every* day. "Oodles of news" she said. But in general, things were looking up, except for her and the Squire! They were looking *down*—down the road, that is, watching for their two younger sons to come home.

"Your grandfather keeps his hands on the purse strings," Daddy chuckled, "but Emory and Joseph are back in their cages."

"Oh Dale, you make it sound like cells!" Mother laughed.

"And to me it would be. 'Oh, Give Me Land, Lotsa Land....' Well, we'll get it, huh, Marvel? Grass is mighty green back there now. We'll go when my girls are ready—but to the farm, not the bank!"

Mother nodded an implied "anytime, anywhere."

Marvel remembering her desire to delve into the Harrington background again, posed a question which put her father on familiar territory and restored his sense of security completely. "Of *course*, we want to build back. That's home! But I do want to hear more about Grandfather, Daddy. Banking's a part of my heritage, too. Wasn't the first bank founded in 1910 by his father, or was there one before?"

Long before, she learned, as Daddy talked animatedly. But 1910 was correct for the immediate family history. Sons Alex Jr. and Emory joined the firm in the twenties—eventually, so did Dale. And Marvel knew the story from there. They did workups. Started out as "runners," shuttling documents, then were promoted to the "cages": handling loans, mortgages, doling out cash (until the crash on Wall Street). But now they were more like salesmen, visiting a handful of big-business banks—bidding, one might say, for customers...trading, stocks, bonds....

"Alex lives on Easy Street up there in Oregon. Talk about diversifying! Your Uncle Emory and Uncle Joseph could have struck it rich, but you know the *why* of their choices. Father got himself downright disillusioned, lost all the old punch there for a while. But like others of Wall Street's old guard, he's bounced back. 'Feelin' his oats,' Mother Riley says (he paused to wink at his wife, and they shared a laugh like old times). Even adorned the walls of Harrington banks, Inc., with grainy photos of men in black suits and bowler hats his Duchess says looks like undertakers, old citations—and family group pictures—"

Mother's hands met in applause this time. "And why not? Tell your daughter the whole story, Dale—that you're on the board of trustees!

Marvel breathed a silent prayer of thanksgiving. She could soar now—as could they! Their plumage was altered, and they were no longer earthbound. God would continue to nourish them in His formation.

10

Emergency Measures

The war's ending created major problems for the chief executive of the United States in both international and domestic spheres. Harry S. Truman was destined to serve as vice president only 83 days. Then, at the time when the nation needed him most, President Franklin Delano Roosevelt died without time or strength enough to groom his successor for the presidency. In a heartbeat of time, the quiet-spoken "Farmer Truman" became the hard-boiled leader dubbed "Give 'em hell, Harry." Educated by the school of hard knocks, he proclaimed himself "a plain old-fashioned Democrat" . . . like it or lump it. There was a job to do, and he'd do it! "Stubborn as a Missouri mule" in self-selected simile, Truman was decisive, outspoken and without fear or favor in his dealings at home and abroad. He was honest, but inflexible—a combination which enhanced his reputation as a leader to some, while inevitably made him powerful enemies in other camps. So what? "If you can't stand the heat, get out of the kitchen!" he barked.

At first the Harringtons paid little attention to the controversial discussions of Mr. Roosevelt's successor. He was no FDR, but who was? The man was an omnivorous reader, said to have read every book in the local Missouri library in his teens. So one could guess he would see that monies went into the education coffers. Alexander Jay Harrington, Esquire, proclaimed Truman a "self-made man, not afraid of dirtying his hands." And that, he said, "I could take a shine to!"

Worth Harrington laughed. "*Shine*—the kind on a silver dollar! Harry Truman began at the bottom and pulled himself up by the bootstraps in banking, you know. Father *would* like that."

"True—yep, *true* of *Truman*," Dale agreed. Marvel, still hospitalized, only half-listened, more interested in noting that her father had taken to teasing again. She saw then that the light had come back into his eyes . . . that they were startlingly blue again. And the color seemed to deepen as he talked animatedly about the president's grasp on agricultural matters. Grew up on a 600-acre family farm, Daddy said . . . said they were the happiest years of his life. Biggest mistake was in leaving, but World War I took him away from his wife, Bess, and their one little girl. Oh, church-goers they were, too! But there was a minor depression in '21—oh, nothing like Wall Street, but enough to clean Truman out in a business venture he made.

"Yes, I remember now. He refused to file for bankruptcy, didn't he? Said no man of integrity would do that. So he's a man of honor."

The conversation had dwindled then, but they were to remember it later—remember and wonder if their assessment had been correct.

The family was much more concerned with matters at home. Recovery from the war was sure not breaking any speed laws, was it? More men were applying for unemployment insurance than expected. Rent was out of control since ceilings were lifted. And where were all those building materials supposed to be so readily available once the war was over? Oregon was filling up with lumber mills, according to Alex Jr. Everybody who owned so much as a handsaw was scalping the hills. Disgraceful, wasn't it—if one could put much stock in rumors—that so few could buy boards here? Yet ship it out, some said, to *Japan*? But real estate was booming. Was *everybody* in California coming to the Northwest?

Patience was the watchword. Automobile factories were making noises in Detroit. New models would be out soon—most without all the chrome and other extras which added nothing except to the cost. "A return to simplicity," they said, "and best get orders in *now*. Waiting lists are long."

Longer than employment lines? Harrington men questioned. Longer than lines of traffic leading *out* of California? For yes, there was a mass migration now, since defense plants were closing down in most instances, maintaining skeleton crews in others. Too bad about that "Spruce Goose" deal. If it had worked, production might have perked up. Not that it mattered to them personally since they were going home, but the whole of the national economy was important. Good sign, though, all those male faces back on campus thanks to the G.I. bill.

Most important factor of all was right in their immediate family. So much depended on Marvel's recovery—*everything*. Until she was strong and well again, all else was on hold. Not that she doubted—not anymore—even though Snow Harrington had paled at the scars on the otherwise perfect young figure. "Think of them as life-saving scars," the doctor had said. Marvel had watched her mother look up at him trustingly, heard her say, "And you are God's medical missionary. She'll heal, just as she has healed us. We've changed during all this."

Change? Yes, they had changed. It was God who changed them. But now He used them to help Him change others. So many miracles had taken place. Look how He had gathered a city in need to assemble under one roof. A short time ago, had someone revealed a Jewish faith, most worshipers at First Baptist Church would have raised eyebrows—possibly in scorn, or more likely to say, "What does that mean exactly? A Christ-killer?" To be answered sadly, "No—no, the Romans were that. It means that we celebrate Hanukkah, the Festival of Lights." Catholics would have said, "The miracle of immaculate conception, begotten of God to the Virgin Mary—blessed art thou among women. It means we celebrate with confession, High Mass, and lighted candles." And Protestants would have said simply, "A day set aside for remembering the birth of Jesus Christ, our risen Lord and Savior. We celebrate with loving praise in music, song, and feasting—inviting all who will to join us. Come!"

And this was the miracle—that they *had* come! Even now, Mother was rehearsing for a cantata, planned for Christmas Eve. Marvel would be discharged by then. She *must* because—well, just *because*.

"Because why?" Marvel asked of Mary Ann when she brought the little radio to the hospital room, saying that there was some interesting news going on. And did Marvel know President Truman was to speak? Most knew what he'd accomplished—or hadn't, but this was special.

"You must come because," Mary Ann answered between plugging the radio into the outlet and shoving bouquets aside so Marvel could reach the dial, "Aunt Snow wrote it. It's her symphony—a cantata instead of a Christmas sermon. Pastor Jim's gone, you know."

Mother wrote it... a dream come true! And now her cousin was telling her more—that Mother's refrains would be somewhat like subjects Jake was studying. "Christmas Around the World," she'd call it, and wasn't he taking that "Great Religions Around the World," course? There would be the lighting of a menorah, candles, and strands of lights everywhere... Mother soloing in "Ave Maria"... and some peculiar sounding music from something called the *Judenplatze* (odd Jewish name, having to do with ancient history). B.J. knew more about it than she did, Mary Ann said with no small degree of pride. "I guess Auntie Snow wants this to be a memorable Christmas, her way of saying good-bye—telling everybody that for this one night we can praise God, the Father of us all," Mary Ann tried to explain. And Marvel understood.

* * *

Resting after her around-the-halls exercise, Marvel switched the radio on. The voice of a news reporter sounded subdued, apprehensive. The president would be addressing the nation soon, and perhaps the listening audience would appreciate a quick review—taking note of events leading up to this day, he said hurriedly.

Yes, literally. Marvel fumbled clumsily for her pen and pad.

The man knows how to take command, organize, relegate duties... doesn't hesitate to do so. Events have been fast-moving—too fast? History will tell. ...This president halted further lend-lease operation... realized Europe's bankruptcy and, contrary to his personal record, advised Congress to sign a bill lending 3.75 billion dollars to Great Britain. Lots of money but famine conditions demanded it! Allies owed the United States 42 billion dollars and over a quarter of which the Soviet Union owed. Still, a monetary exchange was preferable to pressing for early repayment. Next, the big question: Wouldn't it be wise to share the secret of the atom bomb with the United

Nations "when enforceable safeguards could be devised?" Doggedly, Mr. Truman pushed on, born leader that he is: self-government for Puerto Rico and the Virgin Islands...statehood for Hawaii and Alaska... independence of the Philippines republic...faster, faster...

Real problems reared their ugly heads. He was accused of a "get tough" policy toward the USSR... "headed toward the same old isolationism of prewar America." Isolationism? Generalissimo Chiang Kaishek had struggled for years to unite China when Japan attacked in '37. "If China ventures to fight the Japanese," Chiang prophesied, "the Communists will attack from the rear and chaos will swallow our country." China did fight, and, after the Japanese surrender in World War II, Chinese Reds did attack from the rear...and communism seized power in China.

There was embarrassment on the part of Truman, so he switched tactics quickly to another front. Better study Germany's food and collateral...send relief for liberated countries "before other powers take over."

Hearing was difficult, strain as she would. Nurses padded in and out on this pretext or that, and patients, often accompanied by their visitors, came from adjoining rooms and stayed. Talking among themselves, each had a pearl to cast before deaf swine: "Truman, that—well, now I know why his parents never could agree on what the *S* stood for in that middle initial. *Shippe* for his pappy's pappy or *Solomon* for his mammy's pappy. Hah! Shudda been *Shylock*. Solomon's a tightfisted Jew name, hmmmm? *S* is for *shyster*!" (Marvel longed to order him from the room, but another uninvited guest had challenged him, and she did want to hear the broadcast.) "Share the atom bomb secret! Is the man crazy!" *"Herbert Hoover*—Yes, Truman's nutty as a fruitcake! Herbert Hoover advocated the 'trickle-down economy,' and where'd that put us? Smack in the middle of the Wall Street crash—that's where! But what can you expect from a black Republican?...Hey! It's more like what you can hope for with a nigger-lovin' *white* president—war, that's what. And mark my words, we'll be back in one!"

Talk stopped then, Heated words dwindled to a whisper. For words which rocked the walls of the hospital room shouted a message.

> We interrupt this program of news analyses to bring you this bulletin! *Two Puerto Rican nationalists have made an attempt to assassinate Harry S. Truman!* Stay tuned....One moment please—this note just handed me states: *One would-be assassin killed.* What's this? *His accomplice wounded by the president's guards.* News of the president as soon as it is available, but suspects are apprehended!

Moments later in the tomb-like silence, there came the news the world waited for: "It is our pleasure to announce to you, ladies and gentlemen, that Mr. Truman escaped unscathed! Repeating: President Harry S. Truman is unharmed. We now return to the regular program."

There was a reshuffling of feet as everybody talked at once. Marvel felt herself exhale. then, murmuring a soft prayer of thanksgiving, she strained to hear what might come next. To her immense relief, the former reporter was back at the mike.

> Sobered as we are by the frightening news, we must all be surprised to learn that, although delayed naturally, the president has announced that he will not be intimidated by—and I quote—*two-bit jackals.* If he got all shook up over threats on his life, he'd be barricaded in like Adolph Hitler! This is America, land of the brave! Getting rid of such trash would be like trying to drain the ocean with a dime-store sieve! So, who can help but admire a leader who bounces back with this announcement that he *will* speak—just as soon as he washes the smell of those two from his hands....Meantime, a guess at what Mr. Truman's message may center around surely some kind of emergency measures.

The reporter guessed right. Summarizing almost breathlessly, he made mention of Truman's policies, his disregard of prophets and poll takers, and his amusement at public name-calling: "Dixie-crat," "Missouri Waltzer," and the "Great Loser."

128

"One day they'll eat crow!" he said. And the good sports among them had done just that! But on the grave side, the president had outlined a program aimed at preventing further spread of communism in Europe and Asia. Congress listened to his joint-session address and provided for unification of the armed forces "and whatever else may become necessary in the event of further invasion by Communist neighbors."

The president's radio broadcast to the American people was brief, perhaps due to the recent attack on his life. Or, more likely, based on his philosophy that "less is more" when slapping a still shell-shocked nation with the likelihood of another attack from communism, the faceless "Judas."

Ladies and gentlemen, American intelligence has warned free countries of the world over the years of the enemy of democracy. And now the threat is very real. An attack on the Republic of Korea by North Korean Communists is inevitable. This, according to foreign policy, demands instant support of the victim should this occur. In such event, I, your president, would be compelled to proclaim the existence of a national emergency. For, even *now*, our homes, our nation, all things we believe in are in great danger!

A shaken president left the podium, and a member of his Cabinet completed reading the speech originally to have been delivered by Harry S. Truman. It would probably be necessary, the man at the mike said, to create an Office of Defense and urge continuance of American foreign policy along the lines of the past years. He ended with a quote: "Because it is morally right and because it is the best insurance against world enslavement by Community power!" *Emergency measures*, he said...

* * *

Christmas Eve brought lamentations by the Harrington family. White-faced, they gathered around Marvel where they talked with one another and with God. Only He would know the answers.

Mother's face was tear-stained. There was something so girlishly appealing about her, so delicate, frail, and blonde, Marvel thought with a warm rush of compassion. No wonder Daddy loved her so much. And love her he did, just as he loved her replica, their daughter. "The product of our love," Daddy had said with chest-swelling pride—a fulfillment their child could never know, their eyes said sadly. No amount of reassurance could convince them now. It would take time. *And now, tonight of all times, I had to strike one blow more. I can't go....*

"Mother, Daddy—all of you—I have a very special present I want—"

"Anything!" they chorused before hearing more.

"You're to go on with 'Christmas Around the World.' If ever we needed that, it's now. No, no backing down. You promised my anything, and I believed you. Christmas is a time of *believing!*"

Outside the hospital window, the sky was darkening. Soon night would be coming down. The sprawling city was agleam with prewar strands of colored lights. There was the jangle of Salvation Army collection bells, punctuated by a coin-drop note. Families were beginning to assemble for feasting and festivity, while memories and miracles mingled. *Home*, each heart was saying in its own language. Marvel looked at the faces around her and saw remembrance—and regrets. She, too, remembered. Was it only yesterday—or was it a million year ago—that the entire Harrington family clustered around the hearth and sang together their very favorite Christmas carol: "O Little Town of Bethlehem"?

"Mother," Marvel said suddenly (scarcely aware that they were caucusing, pondering just how to handle the doctor's refusal to discharge her until tomorrow), "you must include the line we loved. You remember, all of you, how we sang it together: 'The hopes and fears of all the years are met in thee tonight.' That Phillips Brooks carol rings as true now as ever—the hopes and fears. Hope has to fill our hearts. Play it for *me*, Mother. Play it! And I'll hear. I'll do even more: I'll write something special to the music I hear. And oh, Mary Ann, you mailed my winter contribution to Kate Lynn for the Baylor bulletin. So improvise—you can read this between scenes the rest of you will be reenacting. A copy's right there in the nightstand drawer."

"Traitor!" Mary Ann hissed, but her lovely dark eyes were ringed by unshed tears. "Well, you know what?" she whispered, her face hidden behind the curtain of black curls as she rifled through the drawer, "I agree about the hopes and fears: hope of life, fear of death. They've filled our lives since the Creation, I guess. And I'm here to tell you in no uncertain terms I'm downright happy that Jake had gumption enough to get out while the gittin' was good. Who gives a hoot about keeping some silly rating? When World War II ended, we thought it was the war to end all wars. And now, take a gander at what's brewin' over yonder."

"Come on, can it! Want us to be late? I'm Joseph, you know, Marvel—sportin' a beard, no less. And you'll never guess who'll be Mary in the nativity scene. Don't even try. I didn't think she would—"

Self-consciously, B.J. stopped. His boyish face stained with crimson blush, then drained of all color. The young man was in love!

"Mimi? Oh B.J., that's a wonderful Christmas gift!" Marvel whispered. She saw his look of pleasure. And then her own heart filled up with love and longing. Was this the first time she wondered, that—incredible as it seemed—the realization came? Why, B.J. was as old as she had been when Titus came into her life! Their private miracle had been so simple—just the joy of being together. And as love grew, their miracle enlarged to become a miracle performed by God Himself. *Hope*...yes, there was hope along with fear. And hope was the stronger. They *would* be together. There *would* be "peace on earth"—within the human heart.

Marvel urged the family on to the church. This would be their last Christmas in California, she promised with a conviction she did not feel. Memories of warm, safe holidays felt so near she could reenter the scenes before the president spoke. And now they were remote and unreal to a mind caught up in the vortex of a whirlwind of emotions. Another war... Wasn't war the only thing she had ever known? Compassion and concern had driven her to listen to the first rumblings of the Spanish Revolution, which surely must have taken Titus on his secret mission of reporting for the Associated Press. And long before, as America grappled with the Great Depression, there had been rumors— muted whispers that a world was afraid to listen to and be warned by: the massacres, the persecutions at the hands of frenzied Nazis. Jews? None in these parts. Oh, except those in some of the business districts, speaking their strange language, always slapping signs on store windows reading: Forced Sale ... Great Sacrifice ... Liquidation! Oh, not that they wanted them killed—just out of sight, out of mind....

But Marvel Harrington had cared—cared with a passion. They were God's people. God loved them, as He loved all other peoples of the world into whom He had breathed the breath of life. And eventually the entire world cared, caught up in a blood-bath that required far greater sacrifice than the Yiddish signs foretold. And now? *Oh dear God*, her heart cried out, *not again. Not again!*

"They've gone. You convinced them. But for the life of me I don't see *how*," Mary Ann whispered brokenly. "Yes—yes, I'll read what you wrote, if I don't start bawlin'. Oh Marvel, something's wrong. You—you look like you witnessed the Holocaust ... the end of the world!"

"And I have," Marvel heard herself say from a distance, "unless we give the world hope again. Read what I wrote—read it loud and clear. It's the beginning of the relay we talked about—a torch—"

"A torch!" Mary Ann repeated—and caught it. Minutes later, she read:

> Winter is sitting down with loved ones, families, and seasoned friends, talking and remembering. Fat bears have gone to sleep. Wasps have abandoned their gray-sponge nests and given up their sting. Night becomes a quiet thing. The glow of the moon deepens ... and flirtatious stars wink from God's firmament, lighting the way to eternity. A first snowflake ... a shimmer of silver on the pond ... the cry of a lost goose in need of love's company ... a beaver reaching for one last twig ... and nature beds down for the long, white sleep. A death of sorts? Not really ... for, beneath the ice of winter, the pulse has not been lost. Nature awaits the green call of instinct, while those of us who know Christ await the golden blast of the trumpet, as the heart unites with God. "Fear not ... tidings of great joy ... peace ... good-will!"
>
> The Creator of the earth and its peoples has arranged the seasons and set them in motion. And now December's world adds another backlog and reaches out to embrace

family, friends, and neighbors and insulate against the cold. For now there is time for togetherness as nature takes a glad day of rest, the Sabbath of the seasons...a time for mankind to tramp the forests in search of holiday greens ...a time to envision angels smiling in the snow...a time of baking for sharing...a time of rehearsal...for Christmas is nigh. And now—*What is Christmas? What MUST it be?*

"O Little Town of Bethlehem" captured the anxiety and yearning of the human heart that first Christmas—one that remains as timely today: "The hopes and fears of all the years are met in thee tonight." The sweet story of old began some 2000 years ago in a little Middle Eastern village. "Just an ordinary night," most people of Bethlehem would have shrugged, as they went about in their business-as-usual manner. Ordinary? Not to Joseph and Mary—alone... away from home...sheltered by a stable. They prepared to give birth to a child by a miracle neither of them understood.

The miracle was God's. In the midst of the hopes and fears of ordinary people, He did the extraordinary. "For God so loved the world, that he gave his only begotten Son, that whosoever believeth in him should not perish, but have everlasting life." Was there mention of code, creed, or color? No—Jesus came to all...and so it is that we have "Christmas Around the World!"

There wasn't a dry eye in the house, Mary Ann was to explain in a glowing report the next day. Fact was anybody caught dry-eyed would have been lynched or hanged right there. Why, the sexton himself would have said, "Here's th' rope!"

But for now, alone in the hospital room, Marvel kept her promise. To the soft-sweet strains of Mother's music, she added to the Christmas message—hearing with her heart the voice of the violin blended with the Voice from on high:

The little town of Bethlehem is only six miles from Jerusalem. But it represents a long, hard journey for so many people to undertake...the journey to understanding who Jesus is and His purpose. For in Bethlehem we see the manger, the stable in which the Christ Child was born. But in Jerusalem, we see the shadow of the cross falling over that holy birth...and then the empty tomb. The manger shows us the humility of Christ. The cross shows us the power of the risen Christ—and His power over death! Only Christ can make a difference in our world. And if ever there was a need to increase our prayers and our proclamation of the gospel, it is now! Christ our Savior, the Prince of Peace, is the hope for each of us, whoever we are, wherever we are—our individual hope...and our hope international! Truly, there must be a "Christmas Around the World! in the heart of every Christian. Pray together tonight, tomorrow, and forevermore. Together we can light a world of darkness.... Let the doubters and scoffers know that our loving Lord is more than a myth or a fantasy. This Christmas can make a difference in this world and the world beyond. Unite in love, and keep the candle of love aflame in hope and peace!

* * *

Christmas Day was truly one of celebration. Marvel was released from the hospital after a month's confinement within the white-walled prison. Color had never looked more beautiful. She touched every item of furniture, feeling the cool loveliness of it. And surely the drapes had deepened in shade. Roses from the garden tickled her nostrils, mingling with the spice of evergreens. Could there be a battle between good and evil? But there was—there *was*—outside the protective shelters of American homes. In Korea (maybe all over the world if the red flag of communism continued to raise over peoples unable to resist invasion), the grinning skulls of Satan's army would mock the free world.

But this day, Marvel determined, was designed for peace. The late-rising sun strung pink banners across the eastern sky. And in the elms where a few golden leaves still clustered, bird twitter spoke of spring.

The family's excited talk drove all concerns still farther back into the recesses of her mind. Last night's triumph was still fresh in their memories. Each must be heard. Just how, Marvel thought with fond amusement, presented a problem, with all talking at once in much the same manner of the birds outside the window. "Oh, they *loved* my music—my first but not my last cantata...."

"Sure thing, only Aunt Snow should have called it 'Dynamics of Diversity.' You should've seen the different people I beat outta the bushes when the guys and me—*I* went lookin' for ever-greens—"..."My son's right. If there's one thing we had in common, it was our differences—"..."*Our* son. And just look at the greenery they found and told about—" "Well, I'm your daughter! Don't I get a say? Or do I just disappear like a runaway balloon? Marvel made the program. Oh Marvel, that beautiful piece of writing!" They all agreed on that point and on a good many others as they talked throughout the memorable day. Up to and including B.J.'s comment that there were some Japanese men in the congregation—which showed that maybe there were some good guys among 'em, after all, "*Loyal* is a better word, I would say," Marvel interjected softly at that point. To which her cousin nodded and proceeded to tell about the "loyal" (not "royal") Japanese-American squadron which contributed so much during the war...had to fight behind the lines for their own protection, but moved on to the front and earned all kinds of medals.

"Sort of like me," Dale Harrington grinned. "The behind-the-lines business—pushing and shoving platforms for these stars. Only when do *I* get a medal—huh, Snow, my pet?"

"If you mean that stomach is growling like your voice, my husband, you'll get your rewards! I'm trying to remember why I married you."

"Because I said the minute I saw you, 'There's the fair maiden I'm going to marry.' You were starry-eyed, sweet 16, and *claimed* you could cook! Now, now—no throwing pillows. This is a time of peace!"

A time of peace. Marvel had never felt more peaceful. She was home—home with the family she loved more dearly than life. What richer gift than knowing that they returned that love? And now they had stopped hovering. They were happy—radiantly so. Even teasing again!

"Smell my frankincense and myrrh?" B.J. asked Marvel.

It was Daddy who replied, "Ummmm—Marvel would rather smell food."

"You mean her father would!" Mother laughed. "I give up. I'll get the feast going. Mother sent gifts even though I asked her not to. Oh, just small things, she said—didn't want us carryin' big stuff on the way back. You know, there were some funny things in her letter—"

Mary Ann winked at Marvel. "Funny, *ha-ha* or funny, *strange*?"

"Don't correct your elders, Miss—uh, *Mrs.* Priss!" B.J. muttered. His words made little difference. Mother hadn't heard. So, undaunted, she went on talking about Grandmother Riley.

"She quoted—who was it, Marvel? 'Home is the place from which when a man has departed, he is a wanderer until he returns.' Who?"

"Sir William Blackstone," Marvel supplied. "Tell us more."

"Like I said, Mother gave funny little hints. She loves beatin' around the bush, creating mysteries—said we could figure it all out. She and Father Harrington have something too big to carry—"

"A cow?" Mary Ann giggled. "That *would* be hard to *tote*!"

"Why, Mary Ann!" Auntie Rae said in astonishment. "You're rude."

"—sent this," Mother went on, "sayin' we could guess what our homecoming present would be. She and the Squire had one and it was just about as showy and big as that console radio, but not as big as the piano."

Marvel expected to see the figurine Grandfather said he wouldn't take a "pretty" for—the hand-painted replica of the Duchess of Devonshire sculpture wearing the plumed Gainsborough hat. It was his gift, his expression of love to his Duchess. The little collector's item, though plainly stamped "Made in Japan" in prewar days, became Grandmother Riley's treasure. Later their granddaughter was to wonder what could have made her think they would part with it. What they did part with was something of intrinsic value to Marvel—as they'd known it would be. She had shared the secret sealed inside this crystal ball.

Instinctively, Marvel lifted it from the tissue-lined box. Underneath lay a hastily scrawled note: "Found this at an auction. Hadn't seen one for years. Doubt if owners knew its value, its power."

While the others concentrated on the "big secret," (Could television sets be available?) she tipped the water-filled ball and waited in anticipation. And sure enough, the pink-and-white swirl of minute snowflakes dropped to leave the inside tree trunk bare. Fascinated, she moved the ball to an upright position. Immediately the snow became petals, and then blossoms clustered to the parent trunk. *Cherry* blossoms. She squeezed her eyelids shut. Even then she saw clover on the ground below...

and Titus, standing arm extended, offering the only clover with four leaves.

> I know a place where the sun is like gold,
>   And the cherry blossoms burst out with snow,
> And down underneath is the loveliest nook
>   Where the four-leaf clovers grow....

When she felt a tear slipping from between her closed lids, Marvel walked weakly into the kitchen. She was pouring herself a glass of water when Mother rushed in to scold her gently. "We were to wait on you, hand and foot, darling, and your job is to get well!"

"I'm all right, Mother," Marvel said, gulping the water.

Her mother looked uncertain, and then told her that dinner would be a surprise, "but I'll share it with you. Your grandmother sent a huge home-smoked ham—not one of these deli things with paint-on smoke flavor. This," she confided while checking her *Stretching to Survive* cookbook, "is the old-fashioned, sugar-cured, hickory-smoked kind. *Shhh!*"

"No need to shush me," Auntie Rae said softly. "I'm in on this, you know. Here, I found the method we used for baking. Ummm, our men will go wild. We'll fix the sweet potatoes the old way, too. You know, bake 'em in their skins, let the caramel sugar drip from the fork-prick testing. I'll do that. Now, where are the cakes Marvel asked for? Marvel, you go rest, sweetie. Keep the others out for us."

Her assignment was easy. The "others" were occupied.

"—so I was right glad I'd kept this piece so I could share, showing we do have common history. Mother wants some of the vegetation for that *Stretching* history. You'll get to share some if you behave yourself, big-little sis. Goes along with your history. No, too lofty. Belongs more to Marvel—or *me!*" He waved the clipping daringly near Mary Ann's nose. "Listen to this!"

"We *did* listen!" Mary Ann said tartly. "Heard all about *trees*—"

"But he was right," Uncle Worth said quietly. "The fall of man is associated with trees: the tree of knowledge which led to disobedience back in the Garden of Eden."

Daddy nodded. "And the wood of the cross, which some call 'the tree,' led to redemption. I guess early Christians used evergreens."

Oh, they did, they did, Billy Joe insisted, and began a long question-and-answer game. Mistletoe? Well, a parasite but clung to the soul of the oak during its "winter death." Fir? Not really Christian, was it? But Queen Victoria decorated the trees with lights ("And that," B.J. said triumphantly, "went along with the Jewish Festival of Lights'!"). Holly? Yeah, hard to believe, but a lot of Christians held tight to old beliefs and symbolisms. "Holly" meant "holy," white flowers, Christ's purity . . . red berries, drops of His blood . . . thorny leaves the crown of thorns. Yule log? Oh, forget it. . . .

It was B.J. who stopped the game. "I should've been a wise man instead of Joseph. Weren't *they* smart? And they were as different as that mixed audience we had. Agree on that?"

"Agreed, so hang that on our tree," Mary Ann smiled.

Marvel followed Mary Ann's dark eyes in their travel to the corner. There stood the smallest, most straggly branched tree she had yet to see. But it looked like Christmas, decked as it was with ropes of red and green ribbon, a strand of colored lights awaiting a touch of the switch, and one tinsel star on the topmost branch. Soon glowing bulbs would illuminate the room. The the little winged angels, set here and there, would appear to take flight, singing as they hovered above the holy family carvings, awaiting their miracle in the scattered hay below. Marvel's heart filled up with love—the kind that added a sacred holiness to her own family who had done this for her.

"I hope," B.J. hesitated now, seeming less certain of himself, "I was right. I mean, reading what I did about the wise men. It *seemed* right. But you know what? I got to thinking what Pastor Jim used to quote so much—the proverb about every way of a man being right in his own eyes. But it *did* feel right what with all that come-one-come-all audience. Anyway, I said it was an ancient tradition—the names Melchior, Caspar, and Balthazar— kings of Persia, India, and Arabia. It's not gospel truth, is it?"

His father smiled and went to straighten one of the angels. "Don't need another fallen angel, now, do we? And listen, son, I wouldn't worry about the identification of those men. We'll read Matthew's account if those cooks of ours ever get the fatted calf ready for Marvel's homecoming. My, my!" Uncle Worth grinned. "Good help's hard to come by. Oh, I see you're still stewin', B.J. I guess I need help, Dale."

"With the angel or the wise men?" Daddy teased before turning soberly to his nephew. "Matthew tells us all we really need to know about those mysterious Oriental travelers. They journeyed by faith to Bethlehem to worship Jesus, brought Him precious gifts in tribute to His sovereignty over earth, heaven—and death. God's Christmas gift—"

"To all," B.J. nodded. "Not to just one person or one country, but one *world*. I do like that part about '*they* fell down and worshiped him.' That means *everybody*. Yeah, I'm glad I read it. You know, I got to thinkin': I betcha some kids picture Jesus with yellow skin and black skin. His story belongs to 'em all—every human being."

It was a dream Christmas...perfect...so peaceful...so— well, *perfect*. Marvel felt all tensions and concerns melt down like the candles on the Advent wreath—a first for the Harrington family, especially for her.

The house filled up with laughter and savory scents. Wasn't it wonderful having all the larders full, being able to reach in and pull out needed items? No wartime rations. They had everything anybody would need in case of unexpected emergencies. (After all, who knew what emergency measures life could demand? But *they* were prepared.) And no more of the Great Depression hunger. Auntie Rae stopped to bite her lip, the dish of pickled kraut in her small hand forgotten. Something was wrong.

"No hunger?" she asked softly. "Something's crawling around 'way back in my head. It just keeps gnawin' around like a Christmas mouse."

Uncle Worth took the relish. "Merry Christmas, my pet! You've been working too hard—giving too much of yourself. That's what."

"Not enough. Christmas *is* a time of giving. All right, I've reached a decision, and all of you are involved. Th' meal's ready, but *I'm* not—not until we have an old-fashioned Christmas like back home. Why—why" Auntie Rae's fragile little being was trembling in excitement as she jerked off her apron and flung it on the nearest dining room chair. "Why, shame on us. Jesus would be sad at finding no room in the inn of the Harrington hearts. We've got to feed the hungry. Marvel, you rest." And Auntie Rae began dragging baskets from cupboards and filling them with fruit and baked goods.

For a stunned moment, the family looked mystified. Then memories of holidays past set them in motion slicing ham, wrapping cookies, and stuffing corners with jams and relishes. In no time at all, both cars were packed with gifts, gift givers, and suggestions as to which needs should be met first. Marvel stay behind? Forget it.

A homeless man trying to sell buttons clipped from discarded clothing found in trash barrels had captured B.J.'s attention. One skinny arm reached out to show his wares. The other wound around a dirty bedroll—his "home." "Poor guy—poor, *poor* guy!" B.J. muttered. "Didn't I tell you right? Don't, *doesn't* he look right smart like a rag doll that leaked out all its sawdust? Huh?" His voice broke.

Before anyone could answer, the gaunt old man dropped his only earthly possessions to accept the food offered him. "God bless ye!" he cried. There were tears in the eyes of the givers as they nosed to the shack to which Auntie Rae pointed next. The wispy woman tenant favored them with a toothless grin. "I knowed you'd come, beautiful lady. I jest *knowed*. God sent yah!" Rae Harrington smiled and handed a basket to the shriveled piece of humanity. The response was a smile of contentment. And then she floated away toward her humble abode like a dried-up elm leaf which had clung to the parent trunk long after its sustenance was depleted by dormancy.

Miracle after miracle followed, showing the truth of the biblical declaration of "more blessed to give than receive." There was an ancient man in threadbare clothing ambling through one of the back streets, his birdlike claws clutching scraps of paper he distributed in what appeared to be a nightly circuit. A few fell on the rocky soil of indifference and became wads of crumpled paper to be giggled about or shrugged off. Others fell on the fertile soil of acceptance Filled with equal effervescence of the season, believers rewarded the beggar with a coin which clanked loudly in the proffered tin cup. *Pick it up or risk being haunted forever by this memory*, Marvel willed herself. With an effort, she leaned forward to retrieve one of the soiled notes. "Merry Christmas!" was scrawled inside. Touched, she fumbled in her purse, found a five-dollar bill, and dropped it soundless into the cup. The stranger squinted, unable to believe his eyes. "God bless you real good!" he choked, dabbing at his watery eyes with a tattered sleeve.

"Oh, Marvel—Marvel," Mary Ann whispered. "That gave me goose bumps. Let's find a place for you to wash up. No need though," she said in resignation. "I heard Daddy and Uncle Dale say we— Oh Marvel, we're going down to the ghetto where the winos are. We can be—"

"Killed? Where's your sense of adventure?" B.J. demanded as they began climbing back into the cars. "You wouldn't miss it for the world. You're not foolin' us for a minute. You've seen this stuff before. You'll be in the big middle of it before we get to eat!"

His predictions proved to be right—right for himself!

But first they would venture into the poorly lighted alleys and, ignoring the warning by a lone policeman, shake the drunken from near stupors and feed them the first food they'd had for months. In the beginning the half-clothed men—their prematurely aged faces blurred by accumulated pain and want—were startled, afraid. Then, seeing the food, they grabbed like starving animals. "Oh, those eyes—I'll remember them forever," Mother whispered desperately to Marvel. "You shouldn't be here, Marvel."

Marvel moved closer to her mother, embraced her, and said gently, "This is *exactly* where I should be, Mother. Otherwise we'd be Scrooges."

Snow Harrington straightened. One could feel the renewed ripple of strength in her. Self forgotten now, within her heart she was playing her violin. . . .

"Leave my garbage be, you tramp. Get out or I'll kill you!" The insulting threat boomed from the proprietor of a restaurant where leftovers should have been plentiful—food, but not for the hungry.

"You—you dog in the manger!" B.J. boomed loudly—too loudly, for a crowd was clustering. His father tried in vain to reach him.

The man rushed toward B.J. as if to do him harm. "Why, you green upstart! Don't know much about good-for-nothing filth like these losers, do you? Better get streetwise if you hope to survive in these parts. The place is crawling with greasers, gooks, wops, niggers. Ain't safe for a greenhorn like you. So no more loitering. Your kind's not needed here. My advice to you is—"

"Mister, my advice to *you* is to leave my son alone—" Uncle Worth began.

"Yeah—you do that, mister!" One of the men on the street yelled. A chorus of threats from men swinging clubs followed. The owner of the restaurant made a dash for his back door. And the Harringtons backed from the alley. "'Charity never faileth,' stranger!" one of the street people called out to the surprise of all. "Merry Christmas!"

"Well, B.J.'s right. Christmas *is* for us all—up to snuff or not, as Mother would say. The Spirit's alive and well," Mother observed softly, a tear glistening on her Dresden-china cheek. Daddy kissed the tear away and stroked her face with loving fingers.

"Christmas is the exception which breaks all rules!" he announced, as if the idea were new to him. "You're right, all of you. This will be our best Christmas ever—in California, that is. It's like we were back in the heartland. And praise the Lord, we will be next year. And now," he laughed, "about the traditional feast—"

Before he could complete the light thought, the figure of a fragile woman loomed suddenly from the darkness to stand directly in the path of the car in the lead: Daddy's! With a screech of brakes, he managed to stop. Uncle Worth came close to rear-ending his brother's car. The girl was frantic. What tragedy could have befallen her to so blanch the face of one so young that she appeared to wear a mask of death? There was suffering in her eyes, hysteria in the wave of the arms. "Help, *help!*" came the scream like a siren in the night. What followed was a montage of confusion, for the girl was on the verge of giving birth and her husband was not to be found. "Probably at one of the bars," she sobbed. "He ain't been right since he got home from the war. Oh, help me!"

Bruce (and she described him) was a good man—he really was. The couple was just down on their luck . . . not able to afford this baby or a doctor. And she was so ugly, she sobbed, so unappealin' to uh man—all bloated like this (more tears followed by a scream of pain as she crumpled to the floor of the dirty apartment called home).

The Harringtons went into action. Snow and Rae knew the routine, having taken first aid. Their daughters had learned so much from the home economics teachers—Marvel, especially, having worked so closely with Kate Lynn and her father, Dr. Porter. The men? They'd find that young whippersnapper. And they did—just in time to hear the lusty yell of rage from his firstborn. It was that sound more than the coffee, they all agreed later, that sobered Bruce. He—why, he was a father! He knelt beside the bed, kissed his wife while weeping openly, and held the now-sleeping son in his arms, whispering, "I never knowed it could feel like this. I jest never knowed. Now I got me somethin' to live for!"

It was then that Daddy reached into his pocket and drew out a small New Testament. Why postpone reading the Christmas story? Dreams came alive in the poverty-stricken quarters as the young family heard of the other Babe's source of strength and healing. And love curled around Marvel's heart as soft as smoke. God always kept emergency supplies....

The night's encounters created a sort of holiness to the Harringtons' evening. Heaven came down to shower them with stars—fusing past, future, and present together in blinding radiance. Never had food been so delicious, Mother's playing so inspired, their carols so triumphant—*never*!

11

A Day of Reckoning

January and February filled up with impatience. Impatience! Pink, red, and white, the irregularly spurred *impatiens* refused to wait for summer, choosing to break out in glory to rival gold-throated daffodils. The four elm trees towering along the fence line strung their branches with spring green without having slept at all. Ever-blooming roses still bobbed on the backyard trellis. And now the yellow climbers opened tightfisted buds to rival the crimson braggarts. Looking down on the spectacular display of nature, Marvel felt the same triumphant stirring within herself. "Home—home by Easter!" the Harringtons had decided. And she would make it. In fact, the Lord was as good as telling her so, she thought, as closing her eyes she inhaled deeply. Oh, the aroma!

The rest had been good for her. And so many things had happened—all of them wonderful! For instance, there was the mail. Remembering, she smiled.

"What's so funny?" Mary Ann demanded, coming in all fresh and smelling of violet cologne, her dark curls still damp from their morning shower. "Lucky you—getting to stay home like this and loll around while the rest of us slave away! What's this? Letters to answer?" She hurried over to give Marvel a hug. "Not until you read this fat letter from Kate Lynn. You, she, Uncle Sam, *somebody* owes me something! Boy! The news in this envelope better be good. I had to pay extra postage before that grumpy mailman would let me have it. But wait!"

Mary Ann's hand was a restraining order.

"I gotta go, so I want to tell you that Jake's writing me every single day. *Hurry*, he says. And he wants me to come on to school and be with him, so you'll get your wish. I'm going to *Bible* school!"

But before Marvel could comment, her cousin was rushing on. Oh, just thinking of her husband made Mary Ann's heart go bumty-bump. And she'd never get over it—*never*! Not even trying, Mary Ann said. Oh Marvel, love was for all ages. Look at her: in love with Jake before she was born. And the four of them *would* have the double ceremony and live happily ever after like their parents—and (she whispered) like I do believe Grandfather and his Duchess will! *Titus will be there!*

Marvel's heart gave a forceful thump, just hearing his name. Oh, she understood all right. She smiled again, moved to such depths she could not trust her voice. Yes, Titus would find her. When Mary Ann was gone, she opened Kate Lynn's letter quickly and found her fingers trembling. Somehow she knew it would hold something special.

She was not disappointed.

Kate Lynn was finding solace in her work, had learned to be content. She had suffered losses in World War II—known sorrow with all of its tears. And now, oh surely, a third war wasn't in the making, but:

> You know, the people of our generation are the makers, not the readers, of history. Looking back at your columns (and they're featured along with other "News and Views" now—more on that later), I see you've made a kind of political timeline: Franklin Roosevelt '32–'44, the Great Depression . . . then *boom*! World War II. Maybe the country blamed the man, but "blame" got him reelected not once, but twice! And think what we will about Harry Truman, Mr. Roosevelt's death put him in the Oval Office. What a period of uncertainty for all of us. There's talk of this Korean conflict . . . scares me silly. . . . What is this "Cold War" talk? But he's proving himself, facing down Stalin. And we used to think of Russia as our ally.
>
> I get so confused . . . and nothing in comparison to what you must feel what with all this talk about enemy countries holding our men prisoners, refusing to answer our questions. You can bank on this: Bill *did* make contact with

Titus. Don't know what happened or why. It goes on like the "Ma Perkins" soap opera. But this I can tell you (and this column—just who does it sound like? Appeared right alongside yours, and bears me out!) Titus *will* show up. So knit yourself a dream and purl it with fact—that's your style!

Now read the clipping and (I'm quoting *you*. Me? I can't write worth a hoot—except patients' charts): "To paraphrase Lord Alfred Tennyson, 'We see things as they are and ask why. Better we should see things as they could and should be and ask *why not*! And Marvel, please—*please*, honey—have faith, like you taught me to. The *Baylor Bulletin* published everything Mary Ann sent of yours back when you were so sick. You're *famous*. They're sending you a big check. This went to Associated Press and showed up—you guessed it—right beside you-know-who's piece. No byline on his, of course, but his quote is *exactly* like yours. It's a signal of some kind: "My day begins when the sun chins itself in the eastern horizon and ends when it tucks its chin beneath the covers of lace-bound cloud banks in the west. The shadows lengthen and disappear—and my calendar day has ended. I can never repeat it, but I can remember ... another day doing what I hope the Lord intended, but without a certain someone so necessary to perfect the day. But I shall remember its beauty, knowing that nature teaches and the Bible instructs that everything has a beginning and an ending. And so I press it between the pages of my calendar heart as I would press a four-leaf clover. One clover leaf is for hope—hope for tomorrow!"

The words blurred and then faded. No amount of squinting could bring them back into focus. For Marvel Harrington was weeping brokenly—and the shower of her hot tears had washed Kate Lynn's pen strokes into rivulets of blue ink. Titus had to have said that!

Had there been a shred of doubt remaining in her mind, Kate Lynn's letter would have removed it. Why then must there be tears? Because they had been dammed up so long that an emotional overflow was essential to total healing. When at last the flood subsided, Marvel checked the calendar. Easter came in early April! Small wonder Mother's violin responded so joyfully

to "Easter Parade" and "Alleluia! Christ Arose!" There was triumph in the hands that touched it.

Without further readings of the printed material, Marvel
responded to the burst of joy within her. And quickly she typed:

> *Welcome, Spring!* Who can resist your wonder?
> Fuzzy leaves unfurl as nature's newborn frisk in exu-
> berance of post-winter warmth. Days lengthen and
> brighten, melting away ice on the ponds and worries
> locked inside our human hearts. Oh, youth and vigor
> of you, Spring! You make the bewhiskered dance and
> bid us all to come back to the old tire swing beneath
> the oak. There we soar—and our hearts soar even
> higher. The world is resurrected. And we love as we
> have never loved before!

Was it afternoon already? It must be, for B.J. was hammering at
the door. "Marvel—mailman! Lucky you. Here's another check
from Baylor, I betcha! Want me to open it? Oh, can I come in?"

"You're already in," Marvel laughed. "Yes, you *may* come in."

"And *may* I open the check?"

Why remind her cousin that he meant *finish* the opening? He
had the envelope partially slit. The size of the check did not
determine the value. Its worth was determined by what message
of hope and good cheer her writing may have given to students of
Baylor University or patients at the institution's hospital. But B.J.
was too young to understand that. Actually, there was doubt in
the eyes of many adults when she tried to explain. Right now her
own eyes were beginning to ache. She slipped into the bathroom
and splashed cold water on her swollen face. Even above the
faucet's force came B.J.'s whistle.

"Wow-eee! If I had this much money, I'd pop the question to
Mary-Mimi—I sure enough would!"

"*Mary*—Mimi?" Marvel called, toweling her face.

"Uh-huh—what I call her since the Christmas play. And she
calls me her Billy Joseph. She knows I'm goin' to school—wants
me to make something of myself. She'll 'keep,' she says—" B.J.'s
face flamed with embarrassment when Marvel reentered, and he
turned to safer subjects.

Speaking of money, did Marvel know Dizzy Dean had what was
called the "million-dollar arm"—and Grandfather said he had a

mouth to match? Yes, just between him and Marvel, B.J. had a "sneakin' notion" that Grandfather felt so bad about keeping Uncle Dale out of baseball that he'd been sending tidbits like this one about the Diz....

Yes, Marvel remembered. She should. Hadn't she and Titus talked about Dizzy Dean back during high-school days beneath their oak-tree heaven? The 1930s? Could it possibly have been that long? The baseball player butchered the king's English, and Titus had laughed in his memorable way. But Dizzy Dean did furnish some comic relief, an escape.

"I guess," Marvel found herself saying slowly now, "he did have a good right arm—the so-called 'Okie Kid.' But maybe he contributed more to some people—helped them keep a sense of humor. Baseball was so important then—back during the Depression. It was a rough time."

Billy Joe's answer came as a surprise. "I know. I understood better than the rest of you thought," he said seriously. "That's why I kinda slanted my big paper toward the past. I-I feel like a dog, nagging like I do, but if you'd just scan my paper. It *is* important. We're going home after this year, you know—Easter, if we can."

"And we can, B.J. I'm sorry about the paper. I'm the one who procrastinated. Of course I'll read it. The mail can wait."

His face lighted as if she had touched an electrical switch. "Oh, my *marvelous* cousin—oh, la, la!" he sang out, "Marvel, Mary Ann, and Mary-Mimi—mmmm, good!" Looking a little guilty, he took the paper from behind him then in a way that made her smile. He knew she was an easy mark. The whole family was toward B.J.—and each other!

Thrusting the manila envelope into her lap, B.J. turned to hurry out before she could change her mind. Then just as quickly, he turned back. "Oh, forgot to tell you. There are some pretty good offers on this house. But nobody'll decide, you know, until we *all* have a say."

Marvel nodded. They were close and that was wonderful. But she remembered, too, that "Marvel, you decide" would always prevail with her parents. It was so much a part of them that they probably no longer were aware. It made no difference. She would honor them forever. Marvel realized then that she, like her parents, had forgotten the exact beginning of her lifelong commitment. But Titus had understood, for he had made a similar vow in regard to his older sister.

The door closed behind B.J., only to reopen. "Hey, did you feel a shake—a kind of tremble?" he asked anxiously.

"I'm not sure," Marvel said truthfully. But now she *was* sure. There was a gentle sway, and then it was gone. "Nothing to worry about."

"For me it is. I remember when our shore got a bombing. Oh, I know the War Department shushed it, said it never happened. Mustn't tell people the truth—we'd lose our cool, and all that junk. Whadda they take us for anyhow—a bunch of idiots? I know when I've been shot at and, yeah, it scared my pants off." B.J. paused and then went on, "I never did tell anybody, not even my family. But you read the piece on the paper. Somehow they got in here—hit the California coast like up in Oregon. No wonder Aunt Eleanore got all shook! Not that it'd take a lot to make her teeth rattle. Door's rattlin' now!"

"Billy Joe!" Mary Ann said sharply from behind him. "Didn't think I heard, did you? That wasn't nice. And *we're* going back, too. Call us sneaky, too?"

Her brother drew weapons from his arsenal of words. "Ha! So *I'm* the eavesdropper, am I? Good example of Gran'mere's 'kettle callin' the pot black' or 'castin' stones from glass houses.' Come to think of it, who casts the first stone according to Jesus? Chew on that!"

Mary Ann winced. This called for a detour. "Oh, that reminds me. I received a wheelbarrow load of magazines—tear sheets, yes, some for all of us—and a letter a mile long from our sweet Gran'mere. I'll have to sort through it all on the way back like you did coming, Marvel. Real estate's boomin', you know, and I think our daddies have something brewing when the time's right, due to the boom—"

"Me and Marvel—Marvel and I *heard* the boom!"

Either his sister failed to hear or chose to ignore the remark. Remembering the geometric corollary, she plunged from one point to another in a straight line. B.J.'s face registered relief, his eyes signaling Marvel that the "shelling incident" was their secret.

Grandmother, it seemed, had "bushels of news," but this Mary Ann must share or she would burst. B.J. winked at Marvel. One of the family's shared jokes started with Mary Ann having used the expression years ago. "Don't do that!" Uncle Worth had said. "We'd have to stitch you up with black thread—plum out of white." And Billy Joe's serious observation had set them rocking with laughter: "Oh, big sister, you'd be a black-eyed pea!" But let sleeping dogs lie. It simply wasn't wise to interrupt again.

"Miracles happen. We all know that, so it needs no proving—but this? Now, who would have believed it? I'm puzzled—not doubtful, but puzzled about that silly hair-growin' quackery. Remember how our grandfather kept using the junk on his head on the sly, but his Duchess leaked the secret. Well, it's workin'—or *something* is. He found a whisker where the full moon used to show. Got so excited he plain forgot Gran'mere 'didn't know' and had her look! It sure enough was a hair. Just one, mind you. But now he has her look every single day with a magnifying glass. She claims her eyes are failing, but even she can see fuzz all over. Says she feels to be sure—" Mary Ann said.

"She *feels* our grandfather's head?" B.J. gasped. "Next thing you know, they'll be gettin' hitched!"

"Of course, they will, silly. Love's never too old—"

"Or too young," B.J. said smugly. "I believe her—and *you*."

"Well, that's a switch," Mary Ann grinned. "You're smarter than most brothers, and not a 'pest' anymore. But before you go getting a swelled head, let me finish my story. They know Grandfather will never grow a bush like those banking ancestor pictures on the Harrington Bank walls, but what the heck! If it makes him feel better— Oh, here's a poem Gran'mere sent to drive her point home. You'll remember, both of you. We got an ice-cream soda at Strong's Drugstore for memorizing this in Sunday school. But who wrote it? And her copy says *tree*. I think we used to say *pine*. I'll start—you'll remember then."

If you can't be a tree on the top of the hill
Be a shrub in the valley, but be
The best little shrub on the side of the rill,
Be a bush if you can't be a tree.

When Mary Ann paused, Marvel said, "Yes, we learned it as a pine. As to the author, it seems to me that Mrs. Key mystified us all with the word *Anonymous*. We thought that was the writer's surname. It applies to our Christian calling. We're not all given the same gifts, but we can use what we have for God's call, as well as in all else. I was about to go ahead, but I see you're waiting, B.J. Go ahead."

He did, prefacing his quote by saying it was right for baseball:

> We can't all be captains—there's got to be a crew.
> There's something for all of us here.
> There are big things to do, and there's lesser to do
> And the task you must do is the near.

The three joined together then as they said the final lines with conviction born of experience. Children of the Dust Bowl, forced into premature adulthood during a war that was ended but remained unsettled:

> If you can't be a highway, then just be a trail,
> If you can't be the sun, be a star.
> It's not in the job that you win or you fail—
> Be the best of whatever you are.

There was silence. Then B.J. signed. "They looked down their noses at us when we did manual labor, but we *worked* for every stinking cent on the road. Nobody picked grapes better than us Harringtons!"

Mary Ann flinched. "Ugh—don't mention those vineyards. I still get hoppin' mad. But we made it, and I do believe did some good—"

"We did indeed," Marvel reassured her. "Our parents, teachers, ministers—and, yes, our neighbors and friends—taught us well. That early training sticks. We learned not to judge, but to measure. And we try hard to measure people by their character—not by their jobs, but by how well they do them. And certainly not by their money!"

Stirrings downstairs said their parents were home. Shortly afterward, Marvel scanned Billy Joe's paper, "Take Me Out to the Ball Game!" He had covered all bases, she realized with increasing amazement, as her eyes skimmed the lengthy contents. Most theorized that the cradle of the game was in New York, originating possibly with an Abner Doubleday... a loosely regulated game called "town ball" back in 1839 or so... finally came to be called "baseball." Why? Due to diamond-shaped dirt field, each point a base. As to baseball greats, there were many. "The Babe" needed no last name, but for history buffs, it was *Ruth* (yes, just like the gone-to-war candy bar)! Babe Ruth had to be the all-time great, having hit his sixtieth homer on September 30, 1927—the "big crash" that rivaled Wall Street's! Then there were other long-gone favorites—favorite parks, in addition to New York's: Ebbets Field, Forbes Field, Shibe Park. And now the game was finding a field in Japan—a game unheard of in that faraway land. Why did baseball become as American as apple pie? The game provided well-earned Saturday afternoon recreation for people of all ages in the 1900–1930 period. Then came the Great Depression. America needed *escape*, its sense of humor, and a clinging to something of the past. Nobody asked "Yogi *who*?" They knew. And how did the greats come to be great? By giving to the world the best that they had...being the best of whatever position they played...being the best of whatever they were.

With tears in her eyes, Marvel penciled an A+ on B.J.'s title sheet. Oh, there would be teasing, she knew. After all, it was she who said an A was tops, so there could be no superlative. But she was so proud of her cousin, her father—all the family, in fact.

And now—*oh, please God, be with me as I do this!*—Marvel must look at the clippings Kate Lynn had sent, attributing them to Titus.

* * *

It all began for this writer on a "lend-lease" basis ...lent by an unnamed news international on a short-term basis. All things must have a beginning and in like manner, all must have an end. The world was created by the hand of the Almighty. Ultimately, it will be destroyed. And for a time it appeared that mankind would be the hand that reined down the fire of destruction. New traditions were born out of the chaos to follow. Are "loans" ever returned as God commands, pressed down and running over? Not in war, for ultimately all wars become an Armageddon of sorts, a battle between good and evil. And in the heat of all this, it becomes impossible to sort the enemy from the ally. Mankind is jumpy, cautious, fearful, and suspicious....Wrong prisoners are taken...wrong vessels sunk...wrong planes shot down, often under "friendly fire." War becomes more than a word—it becomes an emotion. Officers become enlisted men, ministers man guns singing, "Praise the Lord and Pass the Ammunition." All reporters, the wounded, the Red Cross ships merge with the vessels of war. Flags mean nothing, and reporters, crawling on their bellies, lose all track of time and distance—intent only in getting the story to press and finding a source who hopefully can be trusted...a someone to tell our loved ones we are alive but trapped. We did what we could, helped as we could, working alongside apple-green soldiers packing rifles from World War I, until we, too, were discovered....

Marvel's heart beat against her rib cage unmercifully. But the article was either an excerpt or a reprint. War became an emotion with her, too, roiling inside, begging for more. There could be no doubt that this was Titus' style. So what had happened? The words surely could lead to only one conclusion. Titus, her Titus, was taken prisoner. That explained the MIA—but the "declared dead"? Hurry, *hurry*, HURRY! her thudding heart cried. She must read other items.

August 7, 1942—eight months to the day after Pearl Harbor. The first wave landed on Guadalcanal's Red Beach. Six months of history would be written in blood there on that 90-mile-long jungle island... desperate men fighting desperate battles in that disease-infested, sodden jungle, without rations or sleep, nights broken by screaming of bombs and screams of dying men. But God was with us. Guadalcanal was the turning point—the stepping-stone to invasions of Tarawa, Saipan, Pelelu, Iwo Jima, Okinawa...closer to Tokyo. We stuck to our posts, performed every duty—driven by the primitive urge for survival. We lost good men, and a few of us tried to pray for our enemies, only to end up crying out of the depths of agony: "Oh God, how did it all happen?"

Squeezing back tears, Marvel read other excerpts. What did it feel like to die of hunger? one of them questioned. First, one dreamed of wild mustard...something he'd never sampled. He smelled apples—apples on those stinking, cold dirt floors where one tried to ignore the stench of rotting flesh and human waste. And then one retched at the sight of molded rice shoved through prison bars between beatings. Freedom would come. . . . He'd be reunited with that person left waiting. God *did* answer prayer. And he would say her name over and over, keeping her memory alive, making himself bearable to himself . . . for one knew when his body was dirty, his clothing ragged, and his teeth loosening. In moments of panic, one listened to imagined sounds of the underground radio sometimes smuggled in out there in the war zones. And at last it no longer mattered. One's mind wandered and, as the sky lowered with approaching unconsciousness, the prisoners of war wondered vaguely where lost members of the body were buried and if markers stood above the graves. A cross? No—one had need of the cross here . . . not to bear, but to lean on. . . .

Marvel gave way to the tears then, weeping as she had never wept before. "Oh, my darling, my darling. It *is* you, isn't it? What have they done to you—*what?*" And for the first time in her life, Marvel Harrington knew what it was like to know hatred, to taste the searing liquid fire and feel it turn solid—a weight too great to live with. The world turned to mist before her eyes. Light-headed, she gripped the corner of her desk for support. If Titus had died, now she was dying with him. More—she must read more. Fighting off the grip of lethargy, she grabbed at fragments, wondering in what chronology they had appeared. One spoke of atrocities inflicted on those "like this writer who is a conscientious objector based on moral and religious principles" because "we are scorned as if we were lepers—*cowards*, they call us, *spies*." Another made mention of the writer being in uniform (reporters in uniform?). "At first, we were supposedly quislings. We would collaborate—anything to save our own necks. Americans were stupid, afraid to die."

The item was ripped badly, but Marvel was able to gather from the lines that, after papers were processed "showing us to be officers," the inhumane treatment turned to cunning. Our minds did not match those of the superior Japanese empire peoples, although rank spoke of a sharper mentality. But we would break under more gentle persuasion—unless we were *spies*. If so, the choice was clear: "Serve as a double agent or be riddled by bullets of a thousands guns."

And then—wonder of wonders! A short clipping fluttered from the stack. And it had to be the most recent. Oh, it *had* to be!

> But strength returns. Teeth tighten. And apples are as crisp and crunchy as remembered when one can bite into them again. But the wild mustard I can do without. There remains work to do. The world is not yet free. But keep that torch of freedom flaming to light our way home, remembering ever that hearts, too, can be healed.

Joy blazed through Marvel's being. Weightless, she felt herself cradled against the man she would marry, his tears mingling with her own as his lips brushed her cheek in a first gentle kiss. "Marvel—my Marvelous, my Marvelous," Titus chanted, as if her name were a prayer—the prayer he had prayed throughout their ten-year gulf of separation. Every sacrifice they had made was worth this moment.

"Forgive me, Lord, for ever doubting," Marvel whispered as she doubled up in prayer. "Forgive my unworthy thoughts. I can and I *will* forgive those who spitefully used us—hating only their sinful ways. This I can do through Your love. All things are possible now!"

"Oh Titus, I will make it all up to you, for you will be back. The war is over—and you are free!"

"Marvel?" Mother called softly from the foot of the stairs.

"Coming, Mother!" Marvel sang out. "I'm starving. Be forewarned that I'll wolf down my supper. Are there any apples in the house?"

* * *

Dinner was festive as Marvel had known it would be. She had felt joy floating up the stairs at mention of her returning appetite. It was true. She had not felt this ravenously hungry for years. Titus was right. Hearts could be healed—bodies likewise. Hurriedly, she splashed cool water on her face, fluffed her hair, and—with a longing sidelong glance at the lengthy article titled "Can Courts March God From Our Classrooms?"—quickstepped down the stairs. Giddy with happiness, she yearned to share Kate Lynn's letter, but decided against it. Titus was, as always (unless

Marvel was pressed), her secret. The decision was of no consequence. The air was charged with excitement—the kind that rarefies and makes spiritual.

"Oh, here's my hungry daughter now!" Daddy announced unnecessarily. "Sit down, sweetheart," he urged, pulling out a chair for her at the table. "Here's my Goldilocks one!"

"My, my!" Mary Ann laughed. "Don't *we* look like the cat that swallowed the canary! B.J.'s gone for your apples—says he can't trust *me*. I just might be the wicked witch after Snow White's daughter!"

"Oh, praise the Lord for—for all of you," Marvel managed.

As if on cue, they all sang out: "Praise God from whom all blessings flow. Praise Him, all creatures here below...."

And they found much to praise Him for.

B.J. brought the apples and news. Polishing an apple on his sleeve, he munched as he reported: "Man stopped me outside, sayin' he wondered if we'd sell the back lot (get this!) for a baseball field. I didn't know him, but he knew *us*—mostly because we know the game."

Daddy and Uncle Worth questioned one another with their eyes. "Good news, I reckon," Uncle Worth grinned. "Still, we're not sure."

"Several inquiries," Daddy said mysteriously. "We'll see."

There was general talk then, centering around the planned trip home. Grandmother had her heart set on Easter. Great! Easter it would be. Mother clapped her hands with delight and began talking dreamily.

"Mother has planted hollyhocks along the fencerow of the old hotel she runs. Remember how she always said she wasn't planting just seeds but more like a legacy? She used to do that even when we rambled around in covered-wagon days. Deep down, I think my mother needed roots. We'd ramble on then, so she never got to see the hollyhocks bloom or make the pretty colored petals into fairy wings for my dolls like I tried to do for our Marvel. Remember, honey?"

"I remember, Mother. Mary Ann and I played 'house' and decorated make-believe walls with bouquets like you arranged for church."

Mary Ann's black curls bounced up and down. "They came up volunteer—year after year, until the drought. I guess there has to be a day of reckoning. Seeds quit multiplying. People stopped sharing."

"But their legacy lives on," Auntie Rae smiled. "We can plant new seeds now, watch them mature, then see their resurrection come spring."

"Spell that with a capital—Resurrection! It'll be *Easter!*" B.J. trumpeted. "Don't I get a reward for my news—an oatmeal cookie?"

"Count us in!" Daddy interrupted his private talk with his brother to say. "Let's take a plate of goodies and coffee to the living room. I'd like to hear the evening news."

Minutes later, they heard:

Primary elections are in progress. Postwar America is mired in an economic and political quandary, insidious and complex. Historical reference? There is none. Problems were easier to identify in past administration: Civil War (Lincoln), World War I (Wilson), a disastrous depression and onset of World War II (Roosevelt), then postwar recovery (Harry S. Truman). Ah, but the man was to inherit more—much more. American values are at stake. The very foundation of democracy and freedom for all nations are seriously threatened. We stand at counterpoint, caught between hatred of war and our commitment to other civilizations. How quickly the world can change. The Cold War is no longer a secret. It is an open threat. How foolish we were—how faulty our thinking. The Soviet Union, always a questionable ally, now looms as a full-fledged potential enemy. Oh, to read the tea leaves...

Events moved with cyclonic speed for the farm boy from Missouri when Mr. Roosevelt died. Following a secret meeting with Churchill and Stalin, the demand for unconditional surrender was repeated for a last time by the Big Three. Lest we forget, a lone bomber flew over Hiroshima days later. Sunny skies smiled down upon a shrugging city... until fire rained from the cloudless sky. Warlords dropped to their knees. But what mind could grasp that new source of power, or read the intentions of Russian leaders' minds? An uneasy peace followed. We *wanted* to believe, but could we? And can we even now? Uneasiness has dimmed exultation. War had become so terrible that the United Nations formed a charter. War must not happen again. We must work together as one world. One world? With Germany split in half and rumors of war on other fronts running rampant, while America still searches the rubble for its dead or missing? After affixing his signature to the document, President Truman told the American people: "What a great, great day this can be in history!" *Can* be? It *must* be, listeners said.

Wars, always ending raggedly, confronted the nation with readjustments of peace: war contracts canceled... workers no longer receiving overtime pay...strikes... demands for ending wartime restrictions...unemployment...disillusionment...broken dreams.

And now, pledged to support the United Nations, America is caught between idealism and isolationism by its promise to "unite efforts for collective defense for the preservation of peace and security." An adage of our grandparents comes to mind: "jumping from the frying pan into the fire." Are we to jump from the hot war into the cold one—meaning, in simple language, to free nations of the world facing the aggressions of communism? As Berlin is divided, so is Korea. Allied powers agreed long ago that the thirty-eighth parallel would divide Soviet-dominated North Korea from the Republic of South Korea. Reliable sources now hint that the agreement is being violated. Our reserves will be recalled....

The Harringtons stared at one another in white-faced horror. Surely the affable, smiling "man from Independence" would be relieved to bow out of politics.

"Americans get the government they deserve!" quips Truman. We can hope and pray that voters make right decisions in the upcoming elections. *We are facing a day of reckoning!*

12

Earthquake!

Oscar Bancroft was not a man to inspire confidence. He was muscular and fit in appearance (due, he said, to lifelong following of Bernnarr Macfadden's *Muscular Fitness* advice). But his steely eyes studied the two Harrington men in appraisal. That he was up to something was evidenced by his approach to the matter at hand. This family was easy prey, probably in need of cash—putty in his hands.

"We'll be in another war, probably less than a week from now," Bancroft said in the voice of a patient whose doctor has said has a rare and incurable disease. "A third world war could alter our civilization forever. But of course you know that. You do listen to the news?" The man's voice said chances of their understanding were unlikely. "Controls will tighten and—mind if I smoke?"

Reaching into his pocket, he withdrew a cigar. "Join me?"

"Neither of us smokes, thank you," Dale Harrington said tersely. "And Mr. Bancroft, this business won't take long. May I ask that you postpone smoking? Now sir, exactly how much are you prepared to offer? My brother and I understand that you want only the back lot."

"And for a baseball diamond. Wasn't that what you said to my son, B.J.?" Marvel overheard Uncle Worth interject.

The man hemmed and hawed, obviously surprised at their directness. "Well yes—temporarily. What I mean is that there's to be nothing written down, no such contract. Who knows what war would do to our economy? This prosperity won't go on forever. Best sell now while prices are up. In fact, I think you'd do well to sell it all."

"We plan to—and we have other offers," Daddy assured him.

The visiting man gasped, then quickly faked a cough to cover his surprise. "I see. I, uh, see. In which case, I'm prepared to make you a better offer and—" he paused as if to cinch the agreement, "Oscar Bancroft offers cash on the barrelhead."

Marvel laid her writing aside and inhaled deeply as she glanced skyward. Directly overhead, the blue was blinding. But on the horizon white clouds piled up—some silver-lined, but others turning dark as if portending a storm. Below, the oranges bloomed on and the annuals were budding. She inhaled again, letting the fragrance fill her lungs, while memories of Grandmother's hollyhocks came trooping back. With all her heart she longed to go home. But principle counted with the Harringtons. *Don't deal with this man*, her heart willed.

She should have known they wouldn't. But it was a relief to hear their voices break the heavy silence below, hear their blunt refusal.

"Let's have it!" Daddy said abruptly. "Bring your terms out in the open. My family isn't accustomed to beating around the bush."

Again the man's voice betrayed him. These people were less enthusiastic than he had expected. Better change tactics. Marvel listened in disgust as this con artist/Prince Charming emerged.

"It's easy to see that you gentlemen are well versed in business matters," he said smoothly. "Tell you what. I'll *double* other offers. That's twice what it's worth, but I know folks like you'll snap it up, so I've brought along a pen for signatures."

"Hold your horses!" Uncle Worth said in an angry voice. "Pretty sure of yourself, aren't you? Just what do you mean by *folks like us*?"

"Don't bother answering, Mr. Bancroft. The answer is *no*. Folks don't need a ream of paper like that sheaf—notaries, lawyers, and the like. Where we come from, a handshake is a gentleman's agreement. *Folks like us*, anyway. I think you'd better go now before I say something I'll regret."

"Regret—*regret!*" the man sputtered. "You'll regret this all your lives. I'll see to that personally. I know your kind."

"You should! You've been following us around!" Daddy said heatedly. "And I wouldn't be making threats, for that's what your words amount to! You see, we've investigated your kind, too, and the law is on our side. You never planned for a single minute to have a ballpark. You planned the space for parking. At least you could have been truthful. You applied for a liquor license. That we know."

"A bar! A bar in this quiet neighborhood—on the sly!" Uncle Worth all but yelled. "Get out before I throw you out. *Go!*"

The man went.

* * *

Mary Ann trotted out a 1930 edition of Macfadden's *Physical Culture* after Oscar Bancroft's visit. "How dumb! Where's his barrel chest and skintight trunks? That crook had better practice what he preaches, huh, Marvel? Claiming to be such a specimen of good health, and all the time suckin' on those foul cigars. Guess he just wanted to throw up a smoke screen—one our daddies didn't fall for. They've got another deal going. But look at this magazine, will you? I guess muscle's muscle and fat's fat— and never the twain shall meet!"

Marvel had been busy opening mail of her own. But now she turned partial attention to her cousin. After all, checks came almost daily now from limitless sources. All received prompt attention, however, for always she hoped for fragments concerning Titus. And often they came. Maybe today would offer more. If so, she wanted to read the messages in privacy. And what was it Mary Ann had said about "another deal"? Something to do with sale of the property? There was no time to ask, for Mary Ann was pointing to pictures and very aptly comparing the articles to physical fitness programs suggested in current publications and to the calisthenics touted by the armed forces. The programs were, Marvel realized suddenly, so very similar to home demonstration, home economics, and domestic science courses. The difference, it seemed, between the then and now was people's reasons, feelings. Then, homemakers were health-conscious. Now (the Hollywood influence?), men and women seemed consumed by a certain body-consciousness. Sort of sad.

"I can't believe this!" Mary Ann exclaimed. "It's like I'm Rip Van Winkle waking up after that 20-year sleep: eyelids at half-mast, looking for changes—and not seeing any! Take a squint at these titles: 'How to Avoid Heart Disease' . . . 'How I Keep My Beauty'

... 'The Fat That Kills!' Sound familiar? It ought to. It's in our mothers' *Stretching to Survive* recipe book! It's all coming to me now—how all our writing fits together: exercise in baseball, nutrition, history of all this and how it works in hard times, war times, *all* times. And who, I ask you, doesn't want to be fit—and beautiful?"

Nobody, that's who, the two agreed, as they delved deeper into the dog-eared magazine: academics, health tips, stretches and exercises, beauty tips, recipes, healthful eating. Familiar, but—

"I see what you mean," Marvel said. She did and she didn't. For when, moments later, Mary Ann's sparkling brown eyes met Marvel's thoughtful blue ones, the brown ones looked uncertain. "I have an idea. I'm not even sure how to share it. It's not new—not old either."

"Now there's a riddle," Marvel laughed, trying to hide concern.

Mary Ann did not return the laugh. She seemed to have floated into a world of her own making, seeing a future that stretched ahead mysteriously, one she was not ready to share. And with it came an unrelated question. The look had gone as quickly as it appeared.

"Look at these recipes—just look: succotash and yummy sautéed sardines on toast, lots of fresh fish and poultry, raw fruits. Salt, lard, and too much sugar are no-no's. Can you beat it?"

"History really does repeat itself—for better or for worse," Marvel nodded, looking at the *Physical Cure-all* columns of testimonials from "previously bloated" individuals who found physical salvation in Battle Creek Health Foods and Pettijohn's Bran Cereal. Oh, the rewards of roughage, the advocates claimed, with fringe benefits of soothed nerves, stimulation of the adrenal glands. Not to mention what proper diets did for the skin and hair. "I remember Grandmother telling us all this, and I see it repeated in *The Baylor Bulletin*, as well as on the back of some of the clippings Kate Lynn sends me. Remember how we girls were to use pure castile soap and rainwater for our shampooing, followed by a lemon rinse—"

"Only we couldn't afford lemons," Mary Ann said with a sad smile. "Well, we have 'em now. And we can buy them by the dozen at home. But we *did* have vinegar. Our mothers made it—"

she broke off then and burst into laughter. "Oh my! Some of the thoughtless things I used to say to Billy Joe back in his baby days. When he cried, I'd say, 'What's th' matter, crybaby? Cryin' because the vinegar's mother is dead? But people now wouldn't even know what I meant by 'vinegar's mother.'"

"Well, *we* know. That's what counts—shared memories. Homemade vinegar did have a mother—a slimy membrane that came from yeast. We had to add that or it would have turned to wine—"

Mary Ann's shoulders shook with laughter. "And *we* would have been turned out of the church!" Then, sobering, she said, "Good for a family to have private jokes. Oh, it'll be good to be home! Not that we'll show up wearing false eyelashes and peeling to make ourselves tanned. We'll be just like Mrs. Sutheral and Miss Ingersoll taught us: *ourselves*, but luckiest ladies alive to have found the two dream men—without those sickening ripples of muscles and Atlas poses! Wow, let's stick with the ice-water rub and witch-hazel splash to close our pores, and do like the teachers said: 'Let the natural beauty shine'!"

There was a lull in the conversation, but it hung unfinished. Marvel's mind skimmed the words quickly for clues, as one does when considering purchase of a new book. In like manner, she closed it.

"What's troubling you, Mary Ann? The deal on our property?"

Mary Ann denied having more knowledge. They would know more after tonight. It would be out in the open, a matter of family domain.

"Then what? Everything's *cousin*-domain with us, so tell me."

There was a slight hesitation before Mary Ann burst out: "I'm going on to Bible school like I told you, and Jake and I'll be together."

"You told me and I'm happy for you. So now, that new-old idea?"

"I still don't know how to put it but, Marvel, I want to be an instructor in, of all things, home economics—like I told you, putting all my experience, research, even my *feelings* into it. And I'll tie God's teaching in, too—about duties to mates, the sanctity of marriage, and more! Do you realize how much advice on nutrition the Bible offers? I can do it—I *can*!" Mary Ann's eyes were dancing.

Her enthusiasm was contagious. Marvel felt excitement well up inside herself. "Now, that wasn't so hard to say, was it? And I'll answer your question before you ask. You're a natural!"

Their joyful embrace ended the matter, or so Marvel supposed until she felt an unnatural stiffening in Mary Ann's body.

"Forgive me, Marvel—oh, I'm sorry. I shouldn't have mentioned all this junk—all about perfect bodies. Don't look at me, just listen."

"To what? Your sobs? Why on earth *shouldn't* we talk about all that? I enjoyed every minute, and we had some good laughs!" Marvel found herself smiling—as usual, comforting the offender. Only what was the big transgression? "So what did you do or say?"

"Oh, I—I could cut my tongue out. It's my worst enemy! I for—for—forgot *your* body being so carved up, so scarred. Oh Marvel, will it make a difference between you and Titus?"

The question caught Marvel by total surprise. A difference? What difference did *scars* make? They showed healing.

"Would it make a difference to you if Jake had scars? You know it wouldn't! And Titus? I know how I feel about *him*. I want him to feel whole—but only for himself, not for *me*. All I care about is finding him alive. If God will just send him back—"

"Oh, He will—He will! You *know* God will!" Mary Ann cried out passionately. She drew back then, blew her nose, wiped her eyes, and whispered, "Oh, thank you for letting me forgive myself! I've wanted to talk about this for so long. I'm glad we had this talk!"

Marvel was glad, too. And appreciation would deepen, as time would tell. Tonight their world and lives would change in a totally unexpected manner! But for now, they parted with another hug.

Alone, she could open her mail! Looking at herself in the mirror, Marvel saw that her Harrington-blue eyes were bright with secret. There could be no doubt that there would be word from Titus. And she must read fast. Twilight shadows were gathering. Could dinner be far behind? Again she smiled, remembering sharing with Titus about Mother's heavenly blue morning glories...Morning Glory Chapel, named for her vines which entwined the little church...and Titus' reaction. "*Harrington*-blue? Let your family call those eyes by whatever name. I like heavenly blue better, 'my beautiful lady in blue.'"

Editor Corey's letter brought the usual check, together with a note saying that Associated Press would be in touch with her. Checks would come directly from them now. Mr. Corey hoped Marvel had found time to read the "mystery columns," and had a hunch that AP would be asking for the whereabouts of their columnist, Titus Smith. Asking *her*? How ironic, Marvel thought fleetingly, when she had posed the same question to the syndicated source so many times, only to receive what amounted to a rebuff. As to her own columns, the editor wrote, they improved with each writing. Just when could he expect the first installment of the book-length story she planned to write? It would bring her a fortune now. Meanwhile, she would please note the recent review given on her more current columns. It was short:

> Writers, like actors, generally hold mirrors in front of themselves. Those protective mirrors cover their own emotions, as professionals are trained to do. But those following the work of Marvel Harrington will note a change in style. The promising writer has changed along with this changing world. This child of the Great Depression was compelled to grow up before her time by circumstances over which she had no control: the awfulness of World War II. Its private hurts, its hopelessness led the stoutest souls to quiver, the most faithful of hearts to ponder: "Did I deserve this?" Not so with this natural-born writer, and not so with her highly respected colleague. The two of them teamed together have matured. And now the windows are open in their maturity, to let readers see inside. Nothing is held back. They let you see their tears and yet retain the essence of their own personal dignity.

Together. What a beautiful word! It was one Marvel refused to question at the moment. She must scan the column Kate Lynn sent and of which Mr. Corey unknowingly had sent a duplicate. Quickly, the blue eyes danced over the column, her heart dancing with each word:

> Yes, the Supreme Court can order God from our classrooms. It *did*! Instead of being neutral, the U.S. government has turned hostile toward all religions …all because of the obscure figure of speech "separation of church and state" used by Thomas Jefferson in a letter in 1803. John Jay, our first chief justice, said: "Providence gave us choice. It is the duty of a Christian nation to choose Christian rulers." John Quincy

Adams, sixth president, said: "The highest glory of the American Revolution was that it connected government with the principles of Christianity." And now the foundations of our Christian heritage are threatened. Will there come a day when prayers in public schools are forbidden... when God's blessings can no longer be a part of our children's and grandchildren's opening exercises... and prayer will be forbidden in graduation ceremonies? God forbid! Only a national spiritual awakening can regain our posture. And so we wait to see what President Harry S. Truman—noted for standing above the grind of political machinery... decisive, and as honest as his devout Baptist parents—chooses as priority. He knows we stand on the brink of another war. He knows Christians could become the endangered species where worship is prohibited—another Nazi Germany... just as our forefathers knew. I wish to God that we were of "like mind" today....

A tinkle of the small crystal bell Daddy gave Mother as an anniversary gift interrupted Marvel's reading. *He knows about Truman—Titus knows!* her heart sang over and over as she answered the crystal-bell summons where B.J. was holding court.

"Ho, hum—another so-called fire drill today. Remember Jimmy Trout, Uncle Dale—the outfielder who *looked* like a fish? Still does—ogling at Mi-uh, a girl I know. He fell for this drill hook, line, and sinker—that red hair standing up in spikes. It looks like it was whacked off by some barber school dropout, anyway. When that alarm sounded, he up and yelled, 'Fire!' Shucks! There wasn't a fire—not with the teacher's command to *drop.* You all know what that means—"

Mother all but dropped the baked beans and Auntie Rae's face whitened even though she went on slicing the Boston brown bread that her busy hands found time to make fresh. Uncle Worth was the one who spoke.

"Yes, we know. We should, as often as we practiced. Drop, curl up, roll yourself beneath heavy furniture or something else for cover. Sit down, son. Want this good food to go up in *smells*?"

The family sat down. Daddy asked the blessing, and the two men began to dish up the beans and pass the generous slices of bread.

Mother passed home-pickled peppers and pear honey, but needed reminding that butter came first. "Not butter—margarine. Better for you, and less expensive," she murmured, her mind obviously elsewhere. "Not that we have to pinch pennies, and our emergency shelves are well-stocked. Butter—uh, margarine, Marvel? No?"

"Marvel can't reach it," Mary Ann laughed.

Auntie Rae quickly took the dish from the slender hand that held it. "Here, B.J., you send it on. I guess we're all wondering about that drill you mentioned. We practiced all that in Red Cross, first aid, then at college. 'Be Prepared!' was the watchword. But now that the war's over—well, what reason except fire?"

"Where's this family been? We're almost in a third one!" Billy Joe sputtered. "Ummm—bread's good with butter 'n jam!"

He swallowed with an effort, the butter dish still held high. Shared laughter relieved the tension. "Let's not borrow trouble, particularly not tonight," Daddy said, his blue eyes suddenly brightening in eagerness to please. "Worth, you tell the good news!"

Uncle Worth looked a little sheepish. "I—I can't take credit—"

Neither of the two men took "credit." With a rush of words, they gave a quick account of their latest offer for the property on Elm Street. Could the family believe that the heretofore quiet residential area was now zoned for business? There would no longer be a Los Angeles proper—if, indeed, there ever had been such. The city had always been afflicted with "urban sprawl," which Daddy laughingly compared to a woman's—uh, *some* women's "middle-age spread." Yes, Uncle Worth winked at him to add that it was nothing like, say, San Francisco's "corseted city center."

The two of them turned businesslike in a twinkling. "The point is," Worth Harrington said quietly, "we have a bona fide offer to sell to a large grocery chain, a part of this neighborhood shopping center. Dale and I've checked it all out. It's all in good faith: no fraud, deceit, or under-the-table deals. And the price, wow!"

His brother leaned forward and the amount he mentioned as offered by the developing company caused his son to whistle. "I'm ready to vote!"

"The neighbors?" Snow Harrington wondered. "Do they know?"

"They know, darling," her husband said reassuringly. "They've *all* decided the issue. The Harringtons are the only holdouts. I know how you hate moving, Snow White. You and Rae have been bricks—all of you have. And it will mean another upset—"

"Not this time!" Marvel was surprised to hear her mother say. "We're going home."

It was hard to hold back tears when Daddy leaned his head very close to Mother's and, unaware that his daughter was watching, eased his arm about her waist. Mother's cheeks flushed, but she looked calm and shiningly beautiful. Daddy looked as if the storm he had dreaded passed over, dropping only enough rain to dampen the garden below. And now the sunshine in his eyes lifted the blossoms as if they offered praise for the shower. It was a beautiful thought—one which was to shatter, like all else around them, after one more comment.

"Oh, one more thing. Rae, you've always loved the trees, and somehow I think you'll be pleased to know this will be called 'The Elm Street Shopping Center.' Kind of nice?"

It all began with the trees—at least, for Marvel. Automatically, she glanced at their tops when Uncle Worth mentioned the elms. And it was as if a wild wind had swept their heights, causing the leafed-out branches to claw at the sky, then sway in dark dance against the windowpanes. Was that "rumble-*boom*!" thunder? The earth shuddered, and leaves rained against the roof with the force of machine-gun fire. Triggered by the jolting force, alarm signals split the air. And, simultaneously, sirens wailed and dogs howled in pain and warning. Some evil force might well have taken hold of the globe in a mad attempt to remold its skin, only to have it crumble, distort, and fracture beyond human repair. A curfew bell tolled.

"Drop!"

The word must have been chorused by the entire family. Providence, it seemed, brought them together beneath the dining table. Above them, the vibrations continued ... swinging, swaying ... the shock first shattering glass ... the second booming as if a steamroller had passed over the house on Elm Street Ten. And then the shaking stopped.

Earthquake!

Did someone say it, or did they simply know? One thing was certain: The hysterical screams in the unnatural silence following the quake spelled disaster. Men, women, and children had violated all rules of safety and gone out-of-doors. Fearing they would be buried alive beneath the tumbling structures of their homes, they had rushed into far greater danger—from falling objects and electrical wires, in particular.

"They'll be electrocuted," Daddy said in a voice kept carefully level. "And they'll clog the streets—leave no room for emergency vehicles." Even while speaking, he backed from beneath the table.

Uncle Worth reminded him of another danger. "Or they can fall into crevices, fill up hospitals—"

B.J. bounded for the door. "I'll go warn 'em!"

"*You* will stay right here with your mother and sister!" Uncle Worth said sternly. "No back talk—not one word, you hear?"

Mother rushed forward. "You men don't mean you're going out there, too. Oh Dale, I won't let you! I'll help you!"

"The best help you can give is prayer, Snow. I'll take no unnecessary risks. I love you too much. I *have* to go. Marvel, you'll—?"

Calm Mother. Marvel nodded. And the slam of the front door said they were gone. She took a deep breath, then reached to touch the knotted hands.

"We've been through emergencies before, Mother. We all know what to do. Daddy's right. Let's pray that the water mains and fire-fighting equipment aren't rendered useless. From what I've read, I believe it was a small quake. But we'll have to wait for reports from the local seismograph. The danger is fire."

"That's right!" Mary Ann agreed hurriedly. "Now . . . that prayer. Make it short and powerful. Then let's get to this mess."

Without further words, they joined hands. Gripping as if doubting all laws of gravity, they lifted their hearts in silent prayer. *"Amen!"* B.J., the self-appointed man of the house, said loudly. Then, grabbing the broom, he set to work, while barking orders in a way that made the rest of them smile. The atmosphere changed to one of preparation.

Mother would get out all her first-aid material, she said. Good! Auntie Rae said, and hurried to sort unbroken containers of food from the mass of splintered glass. Mary Ann, bringing a mop, said she'd prefer having the fire department hose the tile floor.

The cleanup job was done in short order, even though they stopped periodically to give one another supporting hugs. Even Billy Joe, being "in charge of operations" now, took part in the family embraces. It was he who said practically, "People'll need more than bandages, you know. They'll come in here like a pack of hungry wolves. We can stretch yesterday's stew—make a mountain of sandwiches. And I picked a small ton of everbearin' strawberries. Nothin' left to do but work!"

"Does this Minnie Pearl know how to cook?" Mary Ann giggled.

"Mary-Mimi!" her brother said indignantly.

"Aha!" Mary Ann teased as she hurriedly measured coffee. "So that's her name! 'How old is she, Billy boy, Billy boy? How old is she, charmin' Billy'?" she sang a snatch of Grandmother's old song above the splash of water as Marvel filled the kettle for tea.

Mother and Auntie Rae, engrossed in meeting anticipated needs, did not look up. But Marvel's setting the kettle to boil captured Mary Ann's attention. "Did you learn to like that stuff— hot, I mean—from Philip? It's too late to think of iced tea, so I wonder—"

Feeling color stain her cheeks, Marvel answered honestly. "It *is* late to steep tea, and I guess it would take more ice cubes than we have. But somebody *could* prefer it. It's soothing. Only that wasn't really your question, was it? You're wondering about my feelings for Philip, and I wish I could make you understand. Philip's gone, Mary Ann," she said gently, "but everyone who crosses our lives leaves a part of himself. Yes, including Philip. Only it wasn't the same was with Titus. Nobody could replace those feelings—*ever!*"

Tears filled the other girl's eyes. "Like Jake, I know—"

Meaningless babble of people too frightened to utter meaningful words drowned out further discussion. Where had they all come from? Marvel wondered as the multitude pushed in. Another emergency, indeed. And the Harringtons met it as they had met those preceding.

"I'll take the baby, ma'am," Marvel said to a weeping woman who was holding the infant so tightly the tiny legs were purple.

The woman surrendered the baby mindlessly when Mother rushed forward to say, "The baby's in good hands. Let me bandage your arm."

Mary Ann had scooped up two whimpering toddlers. "Sh-h-h, we'll find Mommy and Daddy. Let's have cookies and milk while you tell me their names. Ummm, I make the best raisin cookies in the world—"

B.J. darted ahead to set out the heaping platter of cookies he had arranged. "Mommies and daddies like cookies, too. They'll be here faster'n you can tell me where you live. You'll see—"

"Nah-uh!" the larger of the two denied stoutly. He pointed a small finger to the house next door and grabbed a fistful of cookies.

With a satisfied look, B.J. whispered to Mary Ann, "And yes, Mary-Mimi *can* cook!"

The bandaging, feeding, and soothing went on and on in seemingly endless bedlam. A relative calm came at last among the women and children. But the men continued to talk excitedly as they drank coffee, forgetting moderation. Emergency shelves were emptying as home-prepared meals gave out and, in desperation, Mother and Auntie Rae opened canned salmon and replaced sliced bread with crackers.

"We're to the point of picking up crumbs of the loaves and the fishes," a tired Auntie Rae confided. "They're bottomless pits."

It was all to change—a far greater problem to replace it. But for now, the men—obviously in need of releasing tensions and concerns—talked on. "You can tell how close these quakes are by the *earthquake sounds*! This was a biggie—had to be as it sounded like sharp snaps, the kind that brings down mountains and tear away boulders!" one man declared. Discussion of sound followed. Sounded like heavy equipment passing over bridges, bulldozing houses.... More like dragging furniture over all the floors ... thunder ... explosions ... distant cannons ... steam boilers exploding ... an armada of planes.... One thing was certain, if a body ever witnessed an earthquake, he'd know when one came.... Nobody would confuse it with distant gunfire....

In the midst of the heated discussions, nobody noted the higher-decibel scream of sirens on emergency vehicles until the room filled up with smoke! And then there was the tumult of screams: *"Fire!"*

A stampede followed. Nerves, already taut, snapped. And, like cattle, the flare of a match would have set them running out of control. There was no reasoning with the mob—not with the crimson tongues of flame licking ever higher, while black smoke roiled with satanic fury, obscuring all vision. "Our *houses*! We *have* to get there—all we own's tied up!" some screamed. Others were more concerned with personal safety. "These buildings will *all* go. *Run for it*—run for safety!"

The real danger lay in panic. Marvel remembered warning that even a small earthquake could become a major catastrophe by starting a few fires. And then people virtually committed suicide by rushing into the very mouth of disaster. It had happened in San Francisco....

Something clicked in her mind then. "Mother!" Marvel cried out, her voice echoing loudly in the rapidly emptying house, "Your violin! Play something—anything, just hurry! Stand by the window and *play!*"

Snow Harrington, who had been wringing her hands helplessly, did not hesitate. This she could do. And she did. Softly, sweetly, and poignantly, the strains floated to the milling crowd. Mother's eyes were closed to the horror below. Neither did she see nor would she ever know how many cinder-blackened faces looked at the upstairs windows in awe and turned back to safety. But not all—*oh, dear God, not enough!* Bodies, their remains wrapped like mummies, lay in rows along the sidewalk until loaded ambulances could take them to the morgue. Marvel choked back tears. Mary Ann retched. And Auntie Rae's eyes searched the crowd for her son.

"Oh look!" she called over her shoulder. "The deacons have come. They're all together—the deacons. Worth—Dale—oh, there he is! There's Billy Joe out there with the police, safe and sound!"

Mary Ann ran to the window. "And—and directing traffic!" she choked through a torrent of tears. "He's a good kid. *Oh, thank God!*"

Auntie Rae's face softened. "Then why do you tease him, honey?"

"Just so I can console him, hug him, tell him he's no pest!"

The nightmare ended as nightmares do. At least there was a semblance of order. But for some it would never end—not for those whose loved ones were lost. As the Harringtons were to learn later, the casualties were greater by far than first thought: loss of life was higher...more were injured...and the unexpected dragon of despair, the inability to cope—the wounds which could not be bandaged.

But tonight was sufficient unto itself. So thinking, Marvel rushed onto the porch to see how she could help from a safe distance. The others followed, with Mother continuing to play soul-touching music as if her inspired fingers had forgotten how to stop.

A crowd assembled around them and cameras clicked. Marvel pointed out remembered faces to Mary Ann, and they drew the owners into conversation. How could they help? Mary Ann asked, and listened to answers Marvel failed to hear. Another familiar face loomed from the sea of others: none other than Oscar Bancroft! The shifty-eyed man attempted a quick getaway when he saw her recognition. He would have slithered away had he not been surrounded by three Harrington men, flanked by an unlikely mixture of police and deacons!

"Mr. Bancroft, I believe you're trespassing," a man in uniform said matter-of-factly. "This has happened before. Do you wish to go peacefully, or would you prefer joining me in a ride to head-quarters?"

A second policeman addressed Daddy. "I doubt that you or your neighbors will be troubled further," he said reassuringly. "But should he surface again, we need to know. He's barely within the law."

"Thank you, Mr. Harrington," one of the spectators said. "It seems a shame—a downright shame—that we have to be strangers until disaster strikes. A shame, too, that we'll not get to know you better—"

"Harrington, did he say? I need some information. I'm from the *Los Angeles Times* and I need some quotes. Your daughter," the reporter said as he scribbled notes, "was a writer, I under-stand—"

"Leave my daughter out of this!" Daddy said shortly. "And I am not qualified to assess the damages. End of quote!"

Daddy hurried to her then. "Don't answer anything, honey—promise? I'll explain it all later. We have to be cautious."

"That will be easy, knowing you as I do," Deacon Gregory smiled. "Strange thing, Dale. These quakes are tricky. We didn't feel so much as a tremor at the church. We heard the news on the radio."

Then it was a small quake, after all, Marvel thought with a sigh of relief. Oh, if only those people had not ventured out. Aloud she said, "Would you and the others like coffee, Mr. Gregory? Do go inside anytime. I need to check on families of those who lost their homes and loved ones. I feel so inadequate. Still, we can pray—"

But to her surprise, no buildings had burned and to her relief, remains of the dead were gone. "What happened? I mean, how did this all start? Broken power lines—but no buildings?"

The fireman to whom she spoke was accustomed to disjointed questions and able to explain quickly. No broken lines, just a short resulting in a blown-out transformer. Trees caught fire. There would have been no problem had occupants remained inside. And, as for loss of life, it was too bad when people behave so irresponsibly.

Sadness filled her heart. She felt oddly guilty. Surely there was something she could have done—*something*! Well, there was something she could do now. Cupping her hands to her mouth, she heard herself shout, "Come inside *everybody*! Come in for coffee and prayer. It's not the end. It's a time of prayer and a celebration of life!"

The response was overwhelming. Drop biscuits would take only minutes....

13

Aftershocks

When the first clear light of morning seeped across the sky, the blue dome looked freshly scrubbed and clear of smoke as if a storm had passed. Which it had, a disheveled but oddly contented Marvel decided. Contented? Yes—not with the horror of it all, but with a fulfillment that comes from meeting needs as they arise.

Nobody had slept. There was neither time nor desire. And now there was more—big things and little ones. Much to talk about—when the time was right. "The phone's out," Uncle Worth announced. "No big deal, except I'm wondering if Father'll hear about this."

"Probably," Daddy said. "The media covers the sensational. Good that the power's on. No time to read the papers, but the radio'll cover it all. We'll see which fault was responsible."

He didn't, however. Neighbors were wandering around aimlessly. "I'll have to check on them first. Then there are matters for us to talk about. Rumors are rampant. It's like the fires back home—remember the wild tale?"

"All too well," Mary Ann said with a shudder. "I smell violets in the garden—a little bunch would help us feel back to normal."

Agreed, they said, and repeated the word when B.J. announced that he had ever intention of going on to school. Time here was short, the A-double-plus paper was due, and he needed to confer with teachers, tell them he planned to leave before the term ended.

Dazed, the Harringtons moved about setting the place in order, scarcely making mention of the bizarre realities of life on Elm Street. Instead, they commented on the unseasonable warmth, how sticky they felt—blaming temperature for their drained feelings. The neighbor across the street was enormously pregnant, and would they still be around to help her at delivery time? Best not restock too heavily, so much packing to do, the woman said vaguely. The house no longer seemed friendly. ... Maybe they shouldn't have made the purchase. A good investment, she and her husband had said at the time—yes, affordable and out in the suburbs... *but now*?

Marvel felt their uneasiness but made no comment. She was engrossed in human interest stories for Associated Press, another angle for Kate Lynn, still another for Editor Corey. Then she must record all these happenings for that someday book. The time was near.

The epicenter, according to radio reports, was over 100 miles away, and even there the earthquake was relatively mild. Not that facts could counteract the wild claims of neighbors who made no effort to readjust. The ground had yawned open, they said with certainty, swallowing hundreds of helpless people, some houses, and, undoubtedly, some entire villages in this crazy state. Who could believe reporters? Liars—all of them. The quake was awesome, and next time this whole street would drop into a bottomless pit, not leaving a trace! Roads, *everything* ... and the rocks and mountains would fall on them. No escaping them— *none*!

"There isn't a single piece of evidence of such a happening," Marvel heard her father try to reason. "Use your heads."

Daddy's reasoning did no good. They'd better clear out, another group was saying foolishly, before the meteor swarms came—and then the thunderstorms and tides preordained to wash this whole state out to sea. Oh, it would happen. It *would*! And they didn't plan to be here.

She knew then that the neighbors would be leaving because of the unsubstantiated accounts. Sighing, she returned to her research:

Fire is the gravest danger when an earthquake strikes. What happened here is mild compared to damages experienced April 18, 1906, in San Francisco, for instance. Building codes were less stringent then, and the quake caused property loss of some 20 million dollars, whereas fire which followed caused an estimated 400 million dollars damage. Imagine 520 blocks—25,000 buildings—going up in smoke. The Great Panic, many reporters called the disaster—referring to panic on the art of the city's dwellers themselves! An interesting sidelight was the survival of St. Mary's Cathedral, said to have been filled with early-morning worshipers that fateful day. A reporter of the time wrote a firsthand account:

> Dawn broke over San Francisco on what promised to be another peaceful, warm spring day. The huge clock at the Ferry Building at the foot of Market Street ticked to 5:13 and stopped. One quake, followed by an aftershock one minute later, tore the heart of the bay city asunder. The worst quake in American history accounted for 500 dead, 1500 injured, and 250,000 left homeless. Fire raged until sunrise three days later. Streetcar tracks bent and twisted like ladies' hairpins. Hysteria reigned to increase the casualties. The militia came, followed by the National Guard, all assisting local authorities. "The city filled up with dope addicts ...looters...thugs," one of the commanders said. "We did what we could, but they became raving, screaming animals."

But *hope*—there is *always* hope! Hope wears many faces. On those, the darkest days in San Francisco history, it was a *jewel*. As the city lay in ruins, a certain brightness came with the arrival of a lovely young actress named Izetta Jewel. She opened as leading lady in "Salome" at the Colonial Theatre on Market Street. The building, under construction when disaster struck, escaped total destruction by its manager quickly dousing falling sparks with buckets of water. And so it was that, in that partially constructed and partially destroyed theater, the brave young actress sang her little heart out before a packed house... boosting morale and sparking the 15-year comeback of a city that refused to die. "I had to come," she said simply. "Music soothes the soul." And today, for those with imagination, the sounds of waters along the bay mingle with echoes of Izetta Jewel's golden voice. And for the few survivors who may have been in that audience, a remembered line may return—and hopefully live forever: "No star is ever lost we once have seen. We always may be what we might have been."

Marvel's fingers, as inspired at the typewriter as her mother's were with the violin, strummed along the keys. She prepared various versions for the planned sources and made notes for herself. Now, she smiled, Mother would understand how her daughter came to think of the soothing effects her own rhapsodies would bring on Elm Street.

And then came a sudden aftershock. The slight tremor lasted only a split second. But for the people who themselves had become the "raving, screaming animals," it was of far greater magnitude.

"We're leaving—we're leaving *now!*" they chorused.

Marvel rushed downstairs, heard a few harsh words, and turned away sickened. They turned deaf ears to the reasoning around them.

"I hoped you wouldn't see, Marvel," Mary Ann said. "You're doing something to help others, and there was nothing you could do to help out there. It's never let up—see? They're all packed. They're crazy, I tell you—crazy! They'd *kill* anybody who tried to stop 'em!"

"But their furniture? It makes no sense. Just hours ago they risked their lives to save it. And now *this*?"

They were gone. Every house except for Elm Street Ten stared vacantly as if in accusation of these departed inhabitants.

Defeated and weary, Daddy and Uncle Worth stood conferring with the deacons and several strangers in business suits. The Harrington men had turned toward their own house when a second group of men cruised to a stop and the inhabitants called them aside. All voices were low-pitched. Only gestures up and down the street and occasional nods and shakes of heads indicated that a conversation was in progress.

What happened was incomprehensible at first and remained unbelievable even after Marvel understood. The families, none of them natives to the state, made ready to escape immediately following the earthquake. And instead of calming down, they became more frenzied. Smiles vanished. All hope and brightness faded. Carried away on a wave of hot anger mixed with despair, they lashed out at the world.

"You should understand!" the men taunted the Harringtons. Understand? Yes, Daddy and Uncle Worth said, they understood hopelessness all too well. "Then you know what the Good Book says...." And by various quotes taken out of context from the Bible, the neighbors made their stance clear. Like magicians pulling rabbits from hats, they conjectured: "We're commanded to take nothing with us.... We're not to look back.... And we're to take no heed of what we're to eat or wear!"

One man, a little more controlled than the others, said that the property was worth nothing—nothing at all—since this catastrophe. Nobody of sound mind would build here now. Daddy suggested that they had no way of knowing, that they must wait and see. But wait they would not. Never mind the property, the furniture, *anything*. Safety of their families was paramount—particularly "with the missus here ready to deliver. You men know what the Bible says about a woman in travail!" Their investments were worth nothing now—no way could they recover their money. And loans? Let the sharks take over....

"And that's exactly what such men as Oscar Bancroft would have done," Daddy said tiredly. "Worth and I just couldn't let that happen."

B.J.'s face lighted up with a triumphant grin. "And no Harrington worth his salt would have let them leave empty-handed! Why, the salt would have lost its savor. Grandfather would die of shame—"

"So what did you do?" Mother asked anxiously, her voice hoarse and tight. "You didn't—?" Snow Harrington's hands knotted in fear.

"I did—or, rather, *we* did, if I'm understanding your concerns. And I'm sure I am, darling. Yes, the men you saw—the first ones—were insurance adjusters and the second were—uh, representatives of the loan companies. Help me explain this, Worth. I'm having trouble."

Uncle Worth did his best. Both groups would be in touch—as would men appointed to purchase the property for the shopping center. Meantime, the Harringtons had purchased the property— well, "sort of."

"*Sort of?*" Auntie Rae whispered. "What does that mean?"

"That the final decision rests with the family," her husband said.

That startled her. "Then we won't be going home?" Auntie Rae did not look directly at Uncle Worth when she asked. "That's it?"

"Nothing's decided. Everything's up in the air. We need your help. It's been a hard year—a hard *ten* for us all."

He hadn't answered her question. There was an unnatural silence, a strange, secret discord. All the safe security of family togetherness seemed to be slipping away. Something called constraint hung over them like a pillar of smoke. "Oh, how did we get into all this?" Marvel longed to cry out, her throat swelling.

Half-truths and indecisions would solve nothing. Somebody must make a move. In a voice she hoped sounded cheerful, Marvel addressed them all. "Of *course*, we'll be going home. Now, let's all relax and be happy again. The Happy Harringtons!" She turned to her father then. His drawn face showed fatigue and fear of mismanagement. "Exactly what are we talking about, Daddy? *Money?* State your cause, sir!"

The gentle command, spoken so lightly, hit its target. His blue eyes were round with awe, but the contour of his face softened in relief. "Money, yes. We may have made a terrible mistake—"

Mother came through then. "You haven't made a mistake, no matter what you did. *Tell* him, Marvel. Make him believe *you!*"

"You heard the lady," Marvel smiled, reaching out to squeeze his hand. "Why are we borrowing trouble? We've no idea how much this will take. Maybe," she managed to laugh, "we'll be borrowing *money* instead. *I* just may have a surprise!" Even as she spoke, a plan was formulating in her mind—one she would share with her father, her eyes promised. They had a small fortune, and she could add to the coffer by submitting the first installment of the novel promised to Mr. Corey—the fact-fiction accumulated over this trying decade.

The tears welled up in Mary Ann's great, dark eyes would wait no longer. They overflowed in a happy sort of way. "Now," she sobbed, "we know what to pray about!"

Time passed quickly—so quickly that Marvel felt as if they were sleepwalking. But it didn't matter, for the Harringtons were a close-knit family again. These were no ordinary days. But had anything in their lives been ordinary? "It's one judgment day after another," Mary Ann said, as people trooped in and out of the house in a never-ending line. "But I'm not afraid now—even of the Big One. We'll be okay. We're prepared!"

"The Big One?" B.J. asked on the fly, as it was his job to let the plumbers, the electricians, insurance adjusters, and assorted others in. "Earthquake? Nobody knows when those'll come!"

"No, silly! I mean *the* Judgment Day. We'll be prepared, I tell you. We know the verdict. Christ found us 'not guilty'!"

"Amen!" Uncle Worth said from behind her. *"Dale!* They're here!"

"They" were the planning committee members for the proposed Elm Street Shopping Center. The three men conferred briefly with the Harrington brothers. No damage to speak of... not that it would have mattered. All buildings ("Yes, sorry, gentlemen—including your place of residence") to be razed... replaced by quake-safe structures. Entire area rezoned for business. The only problem might lie in the immediacy of fulfilling the agreement. In short, "Sign and vacate!"

"Just like that?" Daddy's voice held a certain wariness. "But the loans—what about the loans? My brother and I—my daughter—"

"Yes, Mr. Harrington, it's part of our business to investigate such matters. All arrangements are made." The man who seemed to be the spokesman for the trio looked thoughtful while Daddy and Uncle Worth looked anxious and touchingly protective. "The developers are in your debt, gentlemen. Legal problems would have stopped the operation had you not assumed the responsibility and procured their signatures before they left so unexpectedly—leaving no addresses."

Was she hearing right? The men were telling Daddy and Uncle Worth to name their price? Marvel's heart beat far too loudly for her to hear the words. But moments later, her father had bounded up the stairs to whisper excitedly: "Oh, Marvel—my Marvelous! We did it! We pulled it off, you and I. Nobody else knew—not even your mother. And now I can repay you—and more!"

"Oh Daddy!" she whispered back. "It wouldn't have mattered. What matters is your happiness, and that we can go home!"

He hugged her tight. "Praise the Lord for you! Could He possibly be as pleased with you as I am? Yes—yes, of course He is! You see, we did more for *Him* than we did for our neighbors."

The two conspirators hurried downstairs. Nobody had missed them, for everyone was talking at once. "I spilled the beans!" B.J. said in greeting. "It's all done. Debts'll be paid—everything's settled—well, except for my fee for services rendered. Good news, huh?"

Mother rushed forward to embrace them but stopped with arms extended. "Oh—oh, I just thought— What about all that furniture?"

"Give it to the poor—the unfortunates we cared for on Christmas," Auntie Rae said happily. And Mother's arms completed their circle.

"Maybe," Mary Ann said later, "not everybody needs to comfort other people in order to feel comforted. I don't know. But we Harringtons do because—because, well, that's just the way we are."

"Thank you for saying that," Marvel said humbly. "I always felt that I was *different*—afraid to be myself. But it's all right to be different, isn't it? It's the way God wants us to be. And Titus always understood. Oh," she said dreamily, "we could be ourselves."

"And you will again, Marvel! You *will* if you'll get off your duff and get on the stick. Shooo! Get upstairs and get us out of here. Finish that writing project I know you're workin' on. I'll take over down here. Oh look! You're not needed—sorry! Here come those sweet ladies from the church. There are nice folks everywhere."

Marvel, feeling that she could embrace the whole world, rushed back to her typewriter to reread what she had written. "We are finished!" she had begun, quoting outgoing President Herbert Hoover's words of surrender at the beginning of the Great Depression. Drawing from her exhaustive research and documented proof, she had allowed the creative loom of God-given creativity to mold characters . . . fabricating here . . . fictionalizing details there. Taking up where she had left off, Marvel Harrington's fingers rippled across the typewriter keys, addressing timeless themes while traversing beyond personal experience. Readers would see the vital importance of merging fact with fiction—see and appreciate! Never once did she doubt that the two could coexist, or that a publisher would see its value as a novel.

Only once did she pause to listen to the news. The warnings remained.

So we can assume that what gave NATO teeth was American possession of the atom bomb. Have we forgotten so soon why we built the nuclear weapon? Fear of Adolph Hitler! But the bomb fell on Japan, sparing untold thousands of lives both there and here. But other potential enemies emerge. Let the atomic bomb be our warning. NATO tells the Soviet Union that U.S. troops will be stationed in Europe. Surely Stalin will take the warning to heart, preferring to return to friendship as opposed to allowing the "Cold War" to become another 'hot" one. But our armed forces are preparing. Never mind propaganda and 1939 isolationism! Only moments ago, President Harry S. Truman's pledge was "to support free peoples who are resisting attempted subjugation by armed minorities by outside pressures." He meant no more, no less. America will keep this pledge . . . use troops as we used bombs to bring freedom both at home and abroad. . . .

There would be war. Of that Marvel was as certain as publication of her book. Time would prove her right. But for now, two jolting events lay ahead for which she was totally unprepared. Both proved to be "aftershocks," and both were mysteries. One led to renewed hope. The other, unlike the convictions regarding the inevitability of war and the ultimate success of her completed book, she knew nothing about. The aftershock proved greater than the warning "quake."

In her rush to post the finished installment, Marvel all but collided with a mail carrier on the sidewalk. "Sorry, Miss," the uniformed postman murmured in embarrassment. "I was craning to see a number on this house—*any* house. There seem to be none. The fire, quake, something took 'em out. Not that it matters. Can't read numbers *or* names on this backup of mail—looks like it went through a flood. Can you help? So many changes—" he went on while withdrawing remains of an envelope. "Know anybody by the name of Marvel something—or something Marvel? I have dozens of empty ones, but—"

Whatever else the man said went unheard. Marvel had grabbed at the piece of mail, managed to identify herself and thank him. The empty envelopes were of no consequence, she agreed hurriedly. And no, she could not make out addresses either. But this one held a message—only a fragment, but a message all the same. Only a miracle could have held it in the shattered, misshapen envelope. That miracle was glue. Somehow the scrap had attached itself to the flap in sealing.

Even before reading the blurred words of the single paragraph, Marvel knew the source—not the where or the when of its mailing, just the *who*. And that was all-sufficient. God would take care of the rest. There was no signature, except that of love in her heart.

> "Hope deferred maketh the heart sick; but when the desire cometh, it is a tree of life" (Proverbs 13:12). How timeless—even when so long deferred. But is this Scripture not a similitude to *our* tree, the old oak awaiting our return? (The crumpled paper was blotched, the words unreadable, until the beautiful finale.) "One leaf is for hope'...for hope never dies. Pushing up the very lid of its casket of despair, Hope springs to life, restored, refreshed, more lovely... eternal for those who love. *Wait for me....*

The barely discernible words dissolved completely in the wash of Marvel's tears. "Titus," she whispered, "Oh, my darling!"

The handwriting had told her what lack of a postmark had not. When she jerked the fragment from the envelope's remains, Marvel expected—well, what *had* she expected? Certainly not to be transported back to sit with Titus beneath their private tree. Or had she ever left? All barriers of time were erased in that flight. All the beauty and love of life existing between Marvel Harrington and Titus Smith remained. They dreamed in that world. They *ruled* it....

In that frame of mind, the hawker of newspapers failed to penetrate her ears. "EX-TRA! EX-TRA! *Read all about it.* More victims than expected in deadly quake—some leaving no next of kin! EX-TRA! EX-TRA! City's only edition listing *names of the missing!*"

Neither did other members of the family hear, engaged as they were in shipping furniture of their own, delivering to the needy the possessions left behind by fleeing neighbors, and loading their separate automobiles. In a final gesture, Dale and Worth Harrington closed all accounts with the local bank and signed forms for having funds transferred to Harrington & Sons, Incorporated, Titus County, Texas. First, of course, they had the California bank deduct a tenth, as usual, for First Baptist Church. Yes, their tithing money—but this time there was to be an additional offering, and would the bank please hold said offering until Easter? "Some Easter egg!" a surprised young executive exclaimed with an unaccustomed whistle. "More like a *nest* egg!" Regaining his composure, he expressed appreciation for their patronage, saying it was a "pleasure indeed" to have been trusted with such a substantial account. "And why not?" Daddy repeated, having asked of the "privileged young man," "Hasn't the Lord entrusted us with far more?" To which Uncle Worth had added, "We were the earthly custodians only. Now, it becomes our real estate in heaven." And Billy Joe, not to be outdone, said, "As they say back home, it's gone home to roost!"

And so it was that the Harringtons had no inkling that their own names appeared on the list of victims of the "great earthquake" which didn't happen—or of how far-reaching were the emotional aftershocks.

* * *

The time had come. "Thanks to nature, spring mornings return the early dawns winter stole behind our back. Ready, everybody?" Daddy called out.

"More than ready," Mother said, her lovely face blooming like flowers so soon to be bulldozed to a premature grave. "We're going home!"

Home! Marvel's heart, once seemingly immune to joy, leaped up to join the few stars which had forgotten to dim their lights. Yesterday's miracle letter had heightened her awareness of feelings for Titus. Even *love* seemed inadequate to express it. Titus was—well, Titus was so much of herself that God might have taken him from one of *her* ribs—taken flesh, nerve, and sinew to shape him. They were *one....*

"Come on, dreamy-eyes, let's go see our men!" Mary Ann whispered, seeing right through her. "I'm riding with you. We'll talk and plan. B.J.'s riding with Mother and Daddy—*sans Mimi!*"

"I heard that!" B.J. said, giving his sister a playful shove and hurrying to join his parents before she could retaliate. "The guys on th' team agreed. And no, we didn't *vote* on it! But Mimi's as fickle as Erin and Cindy—wantin' me to hatch up another Spruce Goose, all for the love of money. Bleaches her hair, hates cats, claims it takes no brains to teach. Get th' history books ready, girls—'n fit *her* in!"

"*Some* first loves don't last," Mary Ann sighed, climbing into the car beside Marvel. "We're different. Ours did!"

Mother overheard. "Mine, too! Oh, what a courtship we had!"

"Amen!" Daddy said, then pointed to the face of Oscar Bancroft, who was trying to dodge headlights. "Oh ho! Th' buzzard's too late." And then Daddy quoted his banker-grandfather's motto:

"When a man with experience meets a man with money, the man with experience ends up with the money; and the man with the money ends up with the experience."

14

Along the Way

The Harringtons pulled away from the Elm Street curb, Daddy's car leading the caravan of two. Occupants of neither vehicle looked back. Good-bye, ocean. Good-bye, palms. Good-bye all pages of a now-closing book. Good-bye carries a ring of finality. But the story had not ended, Marvel knew. The setting for the final chapter would be back in the heartland . . . back to their heritage . . . back to their roots of joy, with installments unfolding along the way—more than they knew.

Mother reached for a box, pulled out Daddy's socks, and began mating them, cuff to toe. That she took pleasure in small domestic services for the man of her life showed in the smile playing at the corners of her mouth. "Finished!" she said, rolling the last pair into a neat ball. *Finished:* the socks—and life in California.

"Leave plenty of room for my Achilles heel?" Daddy teased. Then he turned serious. "Why on earth must you do that *now*?"

"Because it's still too dark to mend!" she quipped lightly.

"We're not poor any longer, Snow. I can support us, so why waste your precious talents like that? Where's your violin?"

"On the pillow behind the girls. Where else? All the changes since we came will form another symphony. Then there's your poetry, honey," she called over her shoulder to Marvel. "You *do* keep writing it?"

"She does, yes," Mary Ann answered for her. "Quote that 'return' one. Didn't know I saw it, did you? Don't answer. Just say it."

Marvel obliged with a lump in her throat. She'd written the lines for Titus and held onto them, too heartbroken to complete the poem. Then came the long, dark years of waiting and waiting... the trying to go on even after hope had died in her heart. Finally—like a dream, fleeting and fast-fading—he had come. Not Titus—Philip, so like him. Could she give voice to the lines? Couldn't she pretend she had forgotten? They would know better than that.

Expectant eyes turned her direction. "Please to begin," she smiled.

> There's sweetness in the word "return"...
>> Today I long to go
>> To an old familiar place
>> My childhood used to know.
> The landscape seems more lovely there
>> In sweet-remembered charms
>> And I feel the hills reach out
>> With smiles and loving arms
> To bring me back across long miles
>> And equidistant years
>> To daisy-dotted meadows
>> That never heard of tears.

When she stopped, there was applause. *Bless them, Lord*, her heart said softly through threatening tears. Though she loved them with an undying passion, there remained a part inside her she could never bring herself to share with them. Locked away was the verse written when Philip entered her life so briefly. He was gone. But the poem, like his brief-passing memory, remained. With all her heart, Marvel hoped that he had found God before the horror of war snuffed out the young officer's life. And an inner voice whispered he had. But the closing verse of "Return" she would never reveal to others:

> Of course, it's home I speak of;
>> And for those I lost I yearn....
> And though I'll not be going back,
>> I'll let my heart return.

"Well, it's home we're heading for," Daddy said happily. "Back to neighborhoods where everybody knows everybody else—

simpler times filled with summer evenings in the porch swing lickin' away at a double-dip ice-cream cone from Strong's Drugstore. Yep! *Returning* like our talented daughter said. Set that poem to music."

The sidelong glance Mother gave Marvel showed a strange hint of concern. "The poem *is* lovely—musical, too. But, like Mother used to say, 'The past is a nice place to visit but not to live in.' She meant memories, of course. Everything's different now—all of it."

Marvel understood then. *Titus,* her mother meant. But the comment required no response. And Daddy had covered without knowing.

"But before you work on another composition, practice up on this! 'Take me out to the ball game; Take me out with the crowd—Buy me some peanuts and crack-er jack, I don't care if I nev-er get back. Let me root (*Come on, ladies join in!*)...'"

By the time the sun was fully awake, occupants of the lead car were laughing and linking their voices with him: "Let me root, root, root for the home team, if they don't win it's a shame—For it's one, two, three and you're out—at the old...ball...game!"

The subject turned to agriculture, beginning with—according to Marvel's quick notes: "Agriculture, history of:

The long arm of the American economy always encircled the "Land of Plenty's" history. The land's agricultural wealth kept its machinery humming. Before the Wall Street crash, which led into the Great Depression and for some hard-hit states, a simultaneous drought, the outlook was bright. There would be a bumper crop, those in the know predicted. Nobody challenged. Americans were too eager to believe. Those little leaks of problems on the Big Board? Pshaw! Rumors, sheer rumors. Look at the land under cultivation. Look at the yield. How much last year? Some 2.5 billion bushels of corn and 825 million bushels of what, wasn't it? Oh, that was in '29? Well, the outlook was even better now.

Brokers on Wall Street cared little about farmers. Their concerns loomed larger: investments in food processing, packaging, and distribution. And agriculture had come of age with the infusion of mechanical tractors and other equipment. The dirt farmers? Pity the poor devils, but what did they know about national economy? So Wall Streeters thought—if they thought at all. Farmers weren't consumers, unless (they joked feebly) one could call eating what they produced *consuming*! Banks were another matter . . . could be counted on since they were as ruthless and self-serving as Wall Street investors. How true! Fishy-eyed, flint-hearted bankers of the thirties moved in to foreclose on the "little man" after the market debacle. Oh, the ends justified the means, they rationalized. Sophisticated Wall Street investors adjusted their diamond stickpins and took a "broad look at national economy—not the individuals." And one by one, then by the thousands, "little farms" faded into the past.

Herbert Hoover, whose administration had crashed along with the stock market, tried to restore a calm he did not feel. "The trickle-down plan *will* work. Words are of no importance. *It is action that counts!*" Those words appeared in bold print. People read no farther and, preferring not to *think*, they cheered! All brains suffered withdrawal, an indulgence denied small investors, like farmers, who lost their all. Dictator Joseph Stalin rubbed his palms together with satisfaction and chortled. "So goes capitalism . . . the New Communist Russia has no need of it!" He was compelled to shift that stance, of course, during World War II!

There was much more to write—so much. And write it she would, Marvel promised herself, turning her eyes to see the ever-shifting (and totally unrecognizable) scenery beyond the windows of the car.

"None of it's the same—absolutely *none*. We wouldn't fit in, would we?" Daddy asked of his riders.

"We never did!" Mother said hastily. "Look at how the signs have changed."

They looked. Sure enough, instead of "Help Needed" or "Help Not Needed," signs now read: "Apply with Union" or "Union Controlled."

"So the labor unions have taken the reins on farms, too," Daddy said slowly. "Organized labor has done a lot for wages, hours, working conditions. John L. Lewis was a self-made man, truly—self-educated anyway. Never got beyond seventh grade, but more than his eyebrows were awesome! Did you know he read the entire Bible, the *Odyssey* the *Iliad*, and Shakespeare's works? Pretty good for a coal miner—"

"That doesn't make him holy!" Mother said with feeling. "I saw some things take place in the defense plants I'd rather forget."

Marvel's parents went on with their labor discussion, but Mary Ann turned to whisper with a shudder, "And *we* saw worse right out in these orchards, groves, and—oh Marvel, those *vineyards!*"

"I know. You're remembering the owners themselves. The very men we thought we could trust tried to take advantage of our innocence. Well, we learned. And anyway, it's all behind us."

"Not quite!" Mary Ann said fiercely. "I still get mad every time I think about it—good and mad! I know it's a sin, but—"

Let her talk. It would be good. But her cousin stopped and looked, asking questions with her eyes. *Is it all right to be angry?*

For a fleeting second, Marvel Harrington wished that people would ask fewer questions. She was no expert. How had she managed to give that false impression? And then she, too, felt angry—angry at herself. If she could help, it was God's will that she should try.

"A lot of people quote part of Ephesians 4:26, I think it is. Anyway," Marvel said slowly, feeling her way along as she spoke, "the one that says 'be angry,' and they stop there. But there's more to it. The whole Scripture is 'Be ye angry, and sin not; let not the sun go down upon your wrath.'" She intended to go on, but Mary Ann stopped her.

"My stars!" she gasped. "Did the sun go down that night?"

Marvel laughed. "Silly! The sun goes down every night. But, the sun had set before we attended that so-called *vendage*. We'd put in a hard day's labor in the vineyards before we went. 'Mademoiselle, will you do me the honor of being my private guest?'" she mimicked. "As if we had any choice! So—well, you can see, the memory raises my dander, too. But I can put it in proper perspective now—even (laugh this one off, if you dare) use it for the glory of God!"

"Well, for *heaven's* sake!" Mary Ann exploded. Then, as usually, she repented. "No pun intended. Oh, bridle my tongue, remove my hasty heart. But I still don't see how being hoppin' mad can work for God."

"We *all* feel. That's what life is: *feelings*—not good, not bad, just a part of life. Dear Mrs. Key, our Sunday school teacher, was such a love. But she taught us it was a sin to be angry. And I know now that I didn't conquer feeling angry. What I did was hide it, push it underground. So the dragon I conquered was of my making, without learning to handle it at all. Actually, I did that with all my emotions, I guess. It was okay to be angry, but I sinned—"

"By hiding it," her cousin finished. "I see. But I *don't* see how we could have used it at that hateful *vendage* thing."

"Maybe we *did* use it." The words were as new to Marvel as to Mary Ann, and their taste was as sweet as the last of the harvested grapes. "We were scared that night—and on some of the other nights—at the injustice we saw in the fields: the tongue-lashings, the long hours, the mistreatments, taunts, and insults. We were good and mad about it all, but we made a difference—all of us. We shared, comforted, tried to cheer the homeless wanderers. Our parents handed out Bibles, Mother played her violin, Auntie Rae shared her recipes. In one way or another, we told the story of Jesus. I never realized it until now."

Two fat tears rolled down Mary Ann's cheeks. "I'm not mad anymore."

Marvel squeezed her cousin's hands, having little doubt in her own mind now that undoubtedly there would be more opportunities ahead for the family to make use of the definition. "For ye have the poor with you always."

Mother and Daddy were still discussing agriculture, making excited plans as to how they would restore the vast Harrington lands. "Oh," Daddy said suddenly, "hear ye, hear ye! I want you all to learn something. We were all in such a mad dash we never got around to sharing letters and all that. But one came from Father that'll interest you. Can you hear back there?"

"Listenin' with both ears," Mary Ann giggled. "Just don't ask me to share what my *husband* wrote! Tell us about Grandfather, sure!"

Grandfather, otherwise known as Alexander Jay Harrington, Esquire, of Harrington Banks, Incorporated, Daddy told them (trying to keep his face straight with the pretentious title) had taken a downright healthy interest in the old home place. He, of all people!

Marvel had a healthy interest, too. And what her father went on to say caught his niece's interest as well . . . history.

"It seems that our nation's first president very well could have had another 'first' to his credit. Any of you know that the father of our country was the father of agriculture so to speak—agriculture as a kind of science, that is? Yep, George Washington raised wheat, corn, and tobacco on his 8000-acres Virginia plantation."

"The Indians raised 'Cain' long before that," Mary Ann giggled.

Even Mother joined in on the teasing. "No cotton? Stop, you're breaking my heart. Sorry, darling, I'm joshing. I love hearing you talk!"

"Then don't interrupt again—yah hear, my pet?" Daddy commanded, his tone stern but his eyes twinkling. "Just don't think our generation was the only one to plow through droughts. Washington learned how to rotate crops and preserve the land—even to breed better mules."

"Interesting, Daddy," Marvel said with true appreciation. "So George Washington was a struggling farmer like us. Save Grandfather's letter. I'm trying to preserve history like it is. Otherwise, it's lost and it takes years—if ever—to show historical people as human beings with so many similar feelings. All those tribulations began so very long ago, didn't they? I'm thinking of the *Old Testament*—the lean years and the fat. And Daddy, I'm remembering something about the labor leader you mentioned. It was John L. Lewis who said, 'Labor, like Israel, has many sorrows. Its women keep their fallen and they lament for the future of the children of the race.'"

"All that shows the face of the world better than paying homage to big bands and such actors and actresses as Norma Talmadge, Gloria Swanson, Harold Lloyd—dot, dot, dot," Mary Ann said thoughtfully.

Mother was quick to protest. "Oh, I don't know. They're a part of our past. And I have some material my own mother sent about—well, I'll let you read it all. Right now, why do we have to be so serious? Let's have fun! Me? I have a special request. Oh Dale, I want to see the nurseries so much—all those fields where the seed companies raise their flowers. I used to order so much. Could we?"

"Of course *we could*!" he laughed. "Any other requests?"

Well, the highways had changed. But if possible, why not stop by that oasis, the date shop called "Valerie Jean's"? Then there was the Salton Sea. After that, "The shortest distance between two points..."

The little date shop wasn't little anymore. Neither did it stand alone in the desert heat. Fruit stands, each offering produce it claimed was less expensive and of higher quality than that of competing neighbors, lined the new stretch of highway. Where once only a few palms had hovered, now there were countless gardens of them, each tree hanging heavy with fruit. "Valerie Jean's" had changed ownership. There was such a person? one of the several clerks asked. Just a name as far as he knew. But previous owners had "struck it rich" during the war. No sugar, you know, and what with all the convoys passing through—well, why not "make a killing"? Those guys in uniform were hot and thirsty, so they gulped down date milkshakes by the barrel— never you mind about the price. Wanted to send stuff home, too, so locals "contributed to the war effort" by working 24-hour shifts to stuff dates, make date candies and zillions of other goodies... packed, wrapped, mailed... with a charge for each service, naturally.

Naturally? There was nothing natural about it—just plain greed. But yes, the Harrington family would appreciate the recipe book. No olives, preserves, dried beef, or souvenirs, thank you.

They were readying for a hasty departure when the exciting action took place—one which turned their disappointment to delight. Two neatly groomed Chinese men stopped to ask for a road map.

"No road maps without a purchase," a busy young clerk snapped.

The men did not understand. "We do not wish land—just land map," one said, bowing politely from the waist.

Either the clerk failed to hear or chose to ignore the words. Daddy and Uncle Worth stepped forward, purchased dates at an inflated price, and handed the map to the Asian guests. Pathetically pleased, the men bowed humbly. The Harrington men bowed in return.

In whispered tones, the men told an incredible story—one which would linger with B.J. forever. For they had played an invaluable role in the life of his much-revered Col. Jimmy Doolittle who staged the then-daring attack on Tokyo. The desperate raid on Japan had come on April 18, 1942, just four months after the Japanese attack on Pearl Harbor. It was a daring strike the B-25's made—"foolhardy," newspaper reporters said later, since it inflicted no mentionable damage. But nobody could deny that the timing was right. And who could have imagined the vastness of the fringe benefits? American morale needed the boost. The Doolittle raid boosted sales at theater box offices as well, since "Thirty Seconds Over Tokyo" depicted its history.

And now this!

"Did you not know," one of the Chinese men asked in broken English, "that honorable men must land? Scared we were—just Chinese peasants in rice fields. And scared we are now—"

The second man bowed again and continued his companion's account of the raid. "American men scared, also—lives trusted in these hands. Big American men in little Chinese workers' hands—but we help. And we thank you. Sometime maybe we go back, but not now, no safe. Go back, get broken wings—for people we owe. Church help us escape—no can tell all. But you so kind. You help Chinese get map. No read Santa Rosa—navi-gator live Santa Rosa. Smuggle us there, yes?"

Daddy spoke slowly and clearly, pointing out and marking the route for the two frightened men. Uncle Worth assured them that they had no cause for fear, that they were safe, as were their "secrets" shared with this family. The American navigator the Chinese befriended would be kind.

"Get me a picture—oh, *please* do, Marvel!" B.J. begged.

It would mean the world to him, but would the refugees be frightened by the thought? And was it thought proper for a woman to ask permission in their culture? On sudden impulse, she suggested that it was a "man's job."

Bowing as the Chinese rescuers had bowed, B.J. addressed the men in a manner that brought a look of pride to his father's eyes.

"Gentlemen, you are the *real* heroes. You helped America win the war! Would you do me the honor of letting me take your picture?"

The two men appeared miraculously relaxed. Their faces crinkled with a broad smile. "Thank you!" they said at the snap of the camera. And with many a "God bless you!" the strange reunion ended.

* * *

Highways were smooth and well-marked for the remainder of the trip. Motels, advertised well in advance by colorful bill-boards, bade the tourists welcome miles ahead of their location. The scenery was disappointing in general. But there were exceptions. And each stop brought unexpected highlights, each a part of the passing scene in history. But, in resignation, the Harringtons accepted that, in another form, history would repeat itself—until the Final Battle.

The Salton Sea, normally some 280 feet below sea level, had dropped over the years, leaving a salt-crusted shoreline which smelled of dead fish. No boats dotted the murky marsh. The only sign of life was a cluster of rusting vehicles topped by worn canvas. Probably abandoned, Daddy observed, for surely no man would bring a family here for an outing—most certainly not to live. Nothing lived in such an environment. But, behind them, Uncle Worth had turned toward the desolate remains. There was no choice but to join him.

"Why?" The one-word question was all Daddy could manage in the violent burst of desert heat.

"Because I thought you'd missed the sign," Uncle Worth answered, "and I remembered Mary Ann wanted to see the place."

"Well, I've forgotten why," his daughter answered for herself. "Check the map and let's get out of this witch's oven!"

As the men looked for a shortcut, B.J. called, "Keep the air conditioner going in those cars, please. My feet are fried!"

Unexpectedly, a gaunt figure emerged cautiously from what had appeared to be an abandoned hammock swung beneath a sheet of ragged canvas.

"Need help getting out of this hole?" he asked curiously. "I tried for years. But what with both my wife and car ailing, I had to give it up as a lost cause. Still, I *do* know the route."

Marvel caught enough of the conversation that followed to warrant braving the heat to hear more. Mary Ann scrambled out with her. Any subject holding B.J.'s attention under that merciless sun must carry a powerful punch! Their hunches were right.

"So, you see, the Japs *did* strike the West Coast. I was a lot younger then, and too many people said I imagined the whole thing. If my imagination were *that* good, I'd be writing books so as a one-armed man I could afford medical aid for my wife. What they were really calling me was a *liar*! I'm used to name-calling aimed at me—being a 4-F'er, *draft dodger*, lazy cripple lapping up cream. Well, let's face it, I *am* a failure. But a *liar* I'm not! Being from the Bible Belt section, I'm a dyed-in-the-wool convert to Christianity. Oh, would you like a copy of the report that appeared in print? Somehow, I want to convince you—"

The man calling himself Leon Gill rushed inside his sad abode. Daddy and Uncle Worth exchanged a few quick words and nods, both reaching for their billfolds. Their offspring noted the move, but spoke of the validity Mr. Gill's clipping would give to accounts of the war.

"'Specially for me—as you know, Marvel," B.J. said proudly.

There was no time to say more. Leon Gill was back. B.J. accepted the newspaper account and hurried to the car for the dates. "A sick woman over there needs 'em worse than we do," Marvel heard him explain to Auntie Rae. How thoughtful! She would add a Bible.

Mr. Gill accepted the bills (one hundred dollars the men told them later), and turned away to hide his tears. "Please accept this gift for Mrs. Gill—together with our prayers," Daddy said quietly. "You see, we, too, are Christians. And all we do is for the Lord."

"Thank Him for me," the man tried to smile. "Tell Him I'm too broken up inside right now to talk, but I'll find my tongue tonight. Oh, my goodness sake! What's this, *dates*? My wife's crazy about them—and a new Bible? Oh, what a sight! I've found my voice. Let's pray!"

"Maybe we should have offered more," Daddy said uncertainly when they shopped for the evening. "Or should it have been less?"

Uncle Worth looked thoughtful. "We're expected to be good stewards, be cheerful givers. But we have to be *wise* ones, think before we invest Someone else's money. Tithes are God's—but gifts?"

Mary Ann squirmed. "We have to figure just who the *poor* are. We'd be crazy not to. Remember Tansy and her wild tales—how she came from that mythical 'lost colony'? We bought her story and paid for it! Living in a boxcar, my foot! She picked your pockets!"

The family shared a laugh. The scheming little tramp had taught them the valuable lesson of wariness. That was a part of stewardship.

"You're no Scrooge, my darling," Mother said reassuringly. "The beautiful part is that you gave at all. I'm proud of you!"

"None of our men are misers," Auntie Rae said in her usual sweet way. "You tithe, pay taxes, take care of us, and still give. And Worth, you taught our son to share. *You* wanted those dates, B.J.—"

"Yes, Mother," B.J. admitted stoutly. "But I wanted to give them to that poor one-armed man more. We Harrington *men* aren't selfish!"

"I'll give you a nightmare for that!" Mary Ann threatened. "I'll set off a bomb in the desert of your mind. Remember the sand dunes—how you got lost and big sister came looking for you? Well, I'll get retribution. You hit a sore spot, you know, bragging about the Harrington *men*. Who feeds you, looks out for you—all that stuff? Selfish? Hah! We pay through the nose for you—on the installment plan."

After more laughter, the family reached an agreement: Everything they owned, they owned by the grace of God. That included *love*. That closed the conversation, except for a whisper which only Marvel heard. "We Harrington women *are* selfish about one thing: our men! We absolutely refuse to share *them*!" Mary Ann's dark eyes found agreement in Marvel's blue ones. *Marvelous-blue*, Titus called them, she remembered dreamily, wondering just how many miles remained.

* * *

B.J. was to share Mr. Gill's newspaper article with everyone within hearing distance in the immediate and distant future. And, since, he, too, had witnessed the small but significant incident, he would decide it deserved a reading audience. Meantime, the family could share, he said reluctantly. Marvel first—because she believed him!

Shelling of the Pacific shores was one of America's best-guarded secrets. The nation was reeling from the attack on Pearl Harbor. Censoring news not yet ordered by President Franklin Delano Roosevelt allowed for the lone leaked report, never echoed again. "We interrupt this program to bring you this radio bulletin. A Japanese-manned, armed submarine has struck at the shores of California. The 1-17 attack represents the first enemy strike on our mainland since the War of 1812!" Not a major incident in itself, shattering more nerves than property, the strike confirmed public fears. The enemy was capable of bringing the war to America's doorstep. The hushed-up attack hastened the roundup of 120,000 West Coast Japanese-

Americans. And the report was put under wraps, as were other incidents to follow, in order to avoid panic. And now only firsthand reports fill in the blanks. "How could it have remained secret?" one woman is quoted as asking. "Why, all sirens went off according to plan. There was total darkness, broken only by searchlights crisscrossing the skies." Countless witnesses gave various descriptions: "like a distant cannon ...whistling noises spaced between thumps...bright flashes as if an oil field had been struck...an eerie caterwauling...a sickening sensation like a quake." These descriptions came from those who peered from behind darkened windows to view the dusk-shrouded Pacific shore. The incident was covered up—as it is today by the beginnings of what is to become a golf course, we hear. Let us hope there will be a marker to commemorate the attack and serve as a grim warning to future generations that *it can happen here*!

There were other reports, the articles went on to mention, all minor—except that they occurred on the mainland!

"My sakes!" Mary Ann gasped before surrendering the newspaper account to her brother who was *the* star witness. "Listen to this: 'Japanese sub fires at Oregon coast. Jap pilot bombs Oregon forest. Japanese balloon bombs explode in Northwest' all 'without effect' they claim. Who're they kidding? No wonder Aunt Eleanore panicked—demanded to be taken away. And Aunt Dorthea along with her!"

"Those two would go bananas at seeing a mouse!" B.J. declared.

* * *

Marvel focused her eyes on the orange groves, seeing first how the trees lined up diagonally and then vertically, depending on one's vantage point. Try as she would, she could not single out one tree individually. They were marching armies—no, families, united in purpose. And then all illusions faded. The car's speed picked up and the groves were but a blur. The trees, like history, would fold into the past. Already the scene had changed. The landscape—once flat—was more rolling. And the highway came alive suddenly with *people*.

Daddy who had busied himself with the map during the rare silence, had noticed, too, as evidenced by his remark. "Well, I'll be! I guess the postwar problems are bigger than we knew. Look at that one!"

A middle-aged man, wearing an ill-fitting army flight jacket and unmated shoes (neither of which fit), swung like a gong in a bell between two crutches. A sign across his chest said "Vet Needs Help."

"Ugh! I can almost smell him," Mary Ann gasped. "Dirty's no name for it. And look alongside him—a guy too lazy to stand up, lying there smokin' like a stove, and still holding out a cup. Let him have a dime and he'd blow it on booze. Soooo, why am I feelin' guilty, huh?"

"Because you care," Marvel said softly. "I feel guilty, too."

"Try not to, girls. We want to be Good Samaritans, remembering the battered traveler on the Jericho Road. But we have to be cautious Samaritans, I guess. Some of them are frauds, but there *are* the needy."

Mother looked up at him with respect. "Father Harrington would buy that, darling. Remember how he kept saying charity begins at home? Hadn't we better wait, contribute to our church and, well, sort of check on the others? I don't want to be selfish, but we were dirt poor and we never begged. We *worked*. But now I wonder if I can enjoy the flowers!"

"You'd better, my love!" Daddy said with a playful pinch of his wife's arm. "I'm driving pretty far out of our way to see the display. It must be something—even marked on the map. You'll love it."

They smiled at one another affectionately, trying to pretend they did not see the lines of probably panhandlers—professional bums, beggars, derelicts, winos, and people who simply found work distasteful. Marvel and Mary Ann talked in low-pitched voices in the backseat of the car while Mother tried to talk cheerfully of flowers.

"Gran'mere used to say that giving beggars money just encourages them to be lazy, but I—well, Marvel, I sometimes cough up a dime in those tin cups. I guess tin's back from the war?"

Marvel laughed. "I'll check that out. And meantime I guess you can afford *ten* cents if they can afford a *tin* cup. We've worked so hard, tried to save every cent, and succeeded by the grace of God—"

"And hard work! My stars! There's been no time to count savings. What're we worth? I mean in cash money? I know our worth as God's children. Oh, there I go again switchin' sides. But-but that man, the one with a face that shakes like pudding every time he waves that newspaper. Isn't he one of God's children, too? And that newspaper's the only roof he owns—and us rich!"

"Hardly that," Marvel murmured. But she felt confused and strangely accountable to the needy, too—if needy they were. The reasonings of her upbringing suddenly felt outdated. They didn't work in the world of today. Then she, like her cousin, felt trapped in a quagmire of contradiction: wanting to ignore the misery, make herself believe that a shave and a little ambition would solve their problems. And more for herself than for Mary Ann, Marvel found herself dragging out the parable of Lazarus and the rich man.

Mary Ann groaned. "Oh, why did you have to do *that*? If you wanted to make me feel worse, you did it up in ribbons. I'd drag out some of my heavy artillery arguments and shoot down every word. Only I can't, and you know it! I started all this, and hate myself for it. I had to up and mention those losers as being God's children, and that's givin' me gooseflesh. *I'm* the one who'll end up with the nightmares I threatened to give my brother. If those creatures belong to God's family like we do, I—I've got this nightmarish notion He'd be totin'—*carrying*—pictures around in His heavenly wallet like our daddies do."

The idea was ridiculous, so why couldn't she laugh? Because it made sense in a senseless kind of way. Somebody had to love those lepers. The world was changing, yes, but love endured. The matter would take prayer and more prayer. Taunts and over generalizations hurt. How well Marvel Harrington remembered. But she had love—always love.

Dale Harrington had turned onto a side road. The flower gardens were in sight. Marvel saw a breathtaking wash of color spreading before them. Admittedly, she felt relieved. One needed to see God's glory, lean on it, learn from it. Monumental answers then bloomed....

What appeared to be thousands of acres painted the earth, some in untamed wildness as if tossed carelessly by Mother Nature. Others stretched in never-ending lines as straight as arrows. Most spectacular, if one could compare, perhaps were the gigantic designs... the nation (each state in a different color)... a likeness of the American flag, the stars and stripes rippling with each breeze... and the pristine purity of a white cross so large it spanned one entire hillock.

The family stood speechless in admiration. Daddy and Uncle Worth removed their hats in respect and B.J., whose head was bare, placed a hand to his heart. But not Mother. Never, ever had Marvel seen her so excited, so happy. She ran from row to clump, pausing at intervals, and eventually disappeared over a little rise without so much as a backward glance. Moments later, looking was not enough.

15

Shortest Distance Between Heart and Heritage

Where had they been, this vast audience congregating around as Snow Harrington drew the bow across the strings of her violin in a long sustained note? Swaying gently with the spring breeze, she appeared to be a part of the floral landscape, the main attraction. As the single note ended, the very blossoms seems to pick up the echo and hold it in their petals. The wonder filling her daughter's heart reflected in the eyes of those around her.

Closing her eyes, Mother gave herself completely to the majesty of the wondrous beauty of her surroundings in an inexplicable way. In the world of music, she was secure, happy, at home. The wild, sweet music she played that day came from a repertory of her heart. Another of her symphonies? Marvel was uncertain, since none of it sounded familiar. But the sad-sweet strains communicated to the multitudes closing around the performer. For the melodies awoke in each listener the subtle, unseen pull of a homeland—a link with the past which, like the tide, ebbs and flows at the bid of the moon to join the land to the ocean. Like the tides, they left, they returned—but always they were inescapably linked with the past, the lure of home.

The whispers of those around the Harringtons said as much, and the tears in their eyes told the same story. One man gave way to sobs. "I want to go home," he said brokenly. "Not just a house. My *home*—where people know my name. Time and distance have diluted maybe, but they can never destroy—not my memories of home."

Marvel could understand. They all could. For Mother's music stretched a verdant carpet of farmland before them, then decorated it with cattle grazing peacefully. The tempo changed and the scene shifted to budding orchards... freshly turned earth ... sweet clover... with the sound of church bells declaring it was the Sabbath, a day of rest.

"I could use a good cry myself," Mary Ann whispered.

Marvel squeezed her cousin's hand, not trusting her voice. She, too, wanted to weep, and for the life of her could not have said why. Anything seemed possible in this atmosphere—*anything*. It could be raining, and yet she could be standing in a pool of sunshine—she and Titus, alone, seeing their shadows and laughing and believing it. Startled, she stiffened. That was dangerous thinking. *Oh no!* her heart cried out. *Please, Lord, don't allow it all to have been a dream of my own making—one I created and let myself believe!*

Thankfully, the tempo changed. The notes were more lively, more recognizable. Bach, wasn't it? Each bar was busy with sound: big-city traffic... taxi horns... Baltimore, Boise, Dallas ... Anywhere, U.S.A. Tears changed to smiles, and the audience bobbed and swung to and fro. They were a part of the act now. Before the musician was a Pied Piper—no, more of a *sand*piper, tolling them from her nest. But now she sent them home.

When at length the strange performance ended, there was wild applause. Then, in appreciation, listeners showered Snow Harrington with coins. Her eyes were open now. She was back on earth, giving the impromptu audience a graceful bow followed by a shake of her head at their offering. More applause, and then a shower of bills fell at her feet like confetti.

"No, no! You misunderstand!" she cried. "I was not invited— or paid. I can accept nothing. I—I may have been out of place—"

"No, my dear lady, you were *not* out of place!" a man (later to identify himself as manager of the vast acreage) said loudly enough for all to hear. "I should like to take you and your family on a tour of the grounds." Then to the audience, he said: "Please respect the lady's wishes. Her invaluable services were a gift."

Mother smiled sweetly. "Thank you, sir. And to you out there, a very special thank-you. My family is among you. I am in need of nothing. But—but it would please me if you would take the donations and share them with the needy. You'll find them lining the highways."

Behind her, Marvel heard her father cough. "I've never been so proud of your mother," he whispered huskily, and hurried forward to tell her so himself. Marvel felt her own heart swell with pride in them both.

Uncle Worth, flanked by Auntie Rae and B.J., signaled Mary Ann to join in the tour. But neither she nor Marvel moved, caught up as they were in conversation between two returning servicemen.

"Bad as I want to get home, that concert was worth the delay," the younger man said. "Yes, get home, marry my childhood sweetheart, and have ten kids. I'll raise 'em right, teach 'em to hate war and love God. But I can't let my girl see me all wasted away like this. I weighed in at 175 and weighed out of that Jap prison at 102. Oh, I'll eat my weight in beefsteak, vanilla ice cream, and Ma's biscuits. I'll never take anything for granted again—whether it's a sunrise, my morning coffee, a blanket, Ma's wild blackberry jam, or a page in the Bible."

"Yeah," the man beside him said reluctantly. "Maybe I felt like that once, back when I believed it was for a good cause. Well, they won't trap me into another fracas. I'll hide out, lie, cheat—anything it takes—just like that lying military did to us! Ha! Forty percent of us POWs died in Jap prisons? Good publicity—just enough to make people back home mad. Seventy-five percent's more like it. Bein' in the Navy, the enemy put me out to sea in Jap hell ships where they starved us, beat us, and let us rot in rags and loincloths. Then, of all the gall, they killed one man right before our eyes and ripped off his uniform. And one by one, they'd line us up and take pictures of us, taking turns wearing that one U.S. uniform—all for identification, they claimed. And, by God, American officers did it, too. Want a Bible? Not me! I'm not even going home where I'll be exposed to religion again. They betrayed me—every one of 'em! I went in there a stupid believer, but my eyes are open now. Religion, family—my gut's full!"

"I'm sorry, and all I can offer is my hope that you'll feel better one day. Hope was all that kept me alive. I saw so many die, but I kept hoping as a means of survival. Then I felt something inside me change. I began to *believe*, buddy. It can work both ways, you know. You see, I was agnostic when I was drafted, and I came out with a shouting kind of religion—not the summertime kind, but that for a lifetime. People I hitched a ride with wanted to see the flowers, so it brought us together. I'm glad—for who knows? Take that 'Amazing Grace' hymn—"

"That's a *hymn*? Save it for the black-faced minstrels. I've heard it eleventy-seven times from those clowns."

Stunned, Marvel and Mary Ann looked at each other. The stinging words may have stunned the younger speaker, too. But he, like themselves, must have sensed the need to let both matters drop. The two servicemen went to other topics. When had they known the long war was over? When the Japanese colonel offered the commander of the American prisoners his sword! Well, really, when troops painted POW on the barrack roofs and Allies parachuted enormous drums of rations, even candy and cigarettes . . . like dreams come true. The man who served in the Navy was flown to a hospital ship in Tokyo where (for public relations, he said bitterly) the red carpet was rolled out. The young infantryman was flown to an American base in the Philippines. Neither could be released until their bodies healed. But their minds never would. There were handshakes, backslaps, and then, surprisingly, a parting from the Navy man.

"Well, buddy, we survived—so I guess we never gave up!"

"Oh Marvel, did he mean—could he mean he'll *think*?"

"We can hope. That's what the one who found God said brought him through: *hope*. I've survived on it. Our family always hopes."

"I know, I know," Mary Ann choked. "But sometimes I wonder— 'specially after hearing guys like that talk. Just what's happened inside the men we love. Deep down, you know?"

There was no time to answer, and Marvel was relieved. For she wondered about more—much more. The dragons of doubt, ever-present beneath the thin veneer of faith, were attempting to claw through at Satan's beck and call. *What is Titus like inside?* they jeered. *Inside when there's no reason to hope the outside man is alive?* Surely Portia Francisco's sudden appearance, her tiny self shorter than the bowers of flowers, was a divine intervention.

"Mrs. Francisco here wanted to meet you, Marvel. She loved Aunt Snow's music and has read your newspapers columns. Well, let her tell you. Her story's more exciting than ours!"

B.J.! A million questions came to mind, but the where, why, and when of this meeting were of no consequence. It was the *who*. And Mary Ann's brother was handling that by making introductions and doing a commendable job. The wee lady's body, Marvel saw (without appearing to look down), rested on a wheeled platform concealed by a ruffled skirt.

"Your writing has helped me live with this freak body," Portia said sweetly. "All my life I have prayed for a normal body—and I had the faith, I guess to believe that I might grow legs. But never, ever did I dare hope to meet *you*. Oh, the luck of the Irish!" she twinkled.

Marvel smiled in admiration. "Greetings, Cousin Portia! We, too, came from the Emerald Isle—at least, some of my ancestors. If my work has helped, then I have fulfilled God's purpose. But I tend to question that luck has much to do with your acceptance of what you call a 'freak body.' I'm more inclined to remember the words of Jesus: 'Daughter, thy faith hath made thee whole.' Lovely, isn't it?"

"Well, one thing's for sure!" B.J. piped out, "You're no leprechaun. They're grumpy fairies, and you're not Grumpy—he was a dwarf!" Realizing what he had said, B.J. blushed. "Oh—oh, Mrs. Francisco, I didn't mean that the way it sounded."

"I'd hope not," Mary Ann said quickly. "I apologize for my brother."

Portia laughed again and waved away all explanations. "I've been called worse. And Master Harrington, those mythical leprechauns were demoted gods whose status dwindled after Christianity enlightened the island. I guess I'd be grumpy, too!" Her laughter rang out like the tinkle of silver spoons. "You want I should tell my story?"

They wanted.

And the story Portia Francisco told was suitable for all their use. It was rich in history. It awakened a new compassion for the truly handicapped who refused to lay down the Christian armor. It was filled with courage. And to add color, the gracious lady (and the amazing husband who was to join them moments later), then offered all the pictures Master Harrington wished to take— a never-before, she said.

Gabriel Francisco loomed like a giant, casting a shadow of his 8′–6″ height over the young Harrington audience. His talon-like hands carried a placard reading: "The World's Only Half Living Woman and Her Giant Outer-Space Husband!"

Both Franciscos laughed. "What those people who exploited us meant was the world's only living half-woman—meaning size, I guess. But we let it pass. After all, it could have an uglier meaning. Follow my meaning?" Gabriel paused to ask.

"Hermaphrodite? Homo—"

This time B.J.'s sister clamped her hand over his mouth. But it was no use. He talked between her fingers, "G-go on—with sto-ry!"

They all laughed then, comfortably, beautifully. And the story continued, folding in as if it were a part of the floral scenery.

Portia O'Malley was born without legs—or money. Money was a necessary evil, so face it! Why not capitalize on her "freakiness"? And God had been good to her. He had provided her with the world's greatest man (and laughingly, no, she did not refer to his outer-space height. After all, he could carry her and did!). What's more, God saw to it that both of them were very successful—had been the biggest sideshow attraction from 1936. The circus? Yes, until the great fire that swept it from existence. Then they had played the carnivals, fairs—anything that welcomed "unusual people and animals." But now the circus was coming back. Where? Why, Texas of all places.

Billy Joe whooped. "See? What did I tell you—great news, huh?"

"Perfect," Mary Ann breathed, to which Marvel said, "Amen."

"Well, in the beginning, the Creator gave Adam and Eve dominion over the animals," Gabriel said in pride. "And we're going back for the end—the end of the way for us, anyway. As freak performers, that is. But we'll have dominion over freak animals like five-legged cows, dwarf horses that forgot how to grow, blind tigers, and lions without teeth."

"No cat with nine tails?" B.J. teased.

Gabriel's tone matched B.J.'s. "No, just cats with nine *lives*."

"You two will undertake the task all alone?" Marvel asked them.

Oh no, they told her. Other aging and tired circus and carnival performers and workmen would work with them. The performers had always operated as a family. Everybody worked. They pooled their resources, counted out pennies, ate from a common pot. After all, they had to look out for themselves. They were good for nothing but a laugh wherever business led them. There would be an interesting assortment of honking-nosed clowns, fire swallowers, strippers, fat ladies, acrobats, trapeze artists, roustabouts, and "freaks."

"I'll serve as a kind of ringmaster in the sky, what with my advantage of height. Outsiders scorn us, so we take care of our own needs. We're the doctors, teachers, preachers—and when it comes to cooking everybody's got a finger in the pot."

"Gabe here takes charge of the outside, being the ringmaster," Portia dimpled. "The patriarch. Fine! But I'm the matriarch of the kitchen, the low-down cook. I can out-scoot anybody—"

"And can she cook!" her husband extolled. "Talk about creative cooks! My wife's more than a sideshow feature. We made do with what we have, feast or fast.Our favorite dish is stew, the strangest of all concoctions. I remember," Gabriel gazed off into horizons only he could see, "one special time after the Greatest Show on Earth was gone, we had no meat—not much of anything really but vegetables. Portia improvised. 'The show must go on,' you know. And guess what she did."

"Made cat's-eye stew?" B.J. guessed.

"The only eyes we had were in the potatoes," Gabriel said soberly. "But our queen of the kitchen up and added peanut butter. We had a barrel of that. Good? It was delish! Our all-time favorite."

"Or course—" Marvel said haltingly. "Yes, it would be. Filled with protein—no fat needed. And it would thicken. Auntie Rae will want to try that, Mary Ann."

But Mary Ann had gone. Moments later she was back, carrying with her a copy of the diminishing supply of recipe books.

"*Stretching to Survive*— Oh, lovely!" Portia clapped dimpled hands in glee. "Recipes—just the kind we need. One for absolutely everything. And all on a shoestring budget. Just one thing missing: a recipe on how to grow legs. But who knows but what stretching will do it!"

There was laughter—the kind that circus people know, with tears in the eyes of the clown. Time was getting away. That they all knew reflected in the more hurried talk and actions. It was B.J. who thought of the Bible (a gesture which brought coveted praise from his sister). Marvel asked if the wonderful couple would like copies of her poems, and what about "The Patience of the Persimmons"?

Portia was weeping now. And touchingly, Gabriel—looking like an average-sized man on stilts—awkwardly reached down to dry her tears.

"Just look at what you've done for us. And we've done nothing at all for you," Portia said humbly, still mopping at her tears.

"You've filled our hearts with gifts," Marvel said.

This time it was Mary Ann who said "Amen!"

No gifts? The young Harringtons were silent as they returned to cars where their parents, laden with every conceivable type of seed, bulb, and tuber (each marked GOVERNMENT INSPECTED), prepared for departure. Marvel and Mary Ann knew—and B.J. was learning—that there were reasons why God peopled the earth. Reasons, too, why instinctively they felt the need to go back—go back to their home, wherever home might be, and go back to their "kind" . . . back to their beginnings . . . on earth as it is in heaven. And from a historical point of view, Marvel realized that the Franciscos had represented the passing of an era. Their acts and services, once valuable, would reach the same grave-yard as vaudeville, sideshows, minstrel shows, and (sadly) summertime revivals. Good in their time, people might say, if they noticed at all—unless they were captured by a pen such as hers. *Thank You, dear God, for my gift*, she whispered.

* * *

Dinner was a gala affair. Mother was ecstatic about the flowers, about her music, about life. If the world had problems, Snow Harrington had forgotten. So low tides had pulled them out to unfamiliar seas? High tides would bring them back. Or they would battle their way upstream of some river tributary, like salmon heading home, against all odds, "bearing all things, enduring all things." But for now, she was resting in the eddy of quiet waters in total peace.

"I'm too excited to eat—let alone *cook*," she said dreamily, even though the family had insisted that they seek a motel with a kitchen instead of looking for a restaurant. Discussion began with the youngest Harrington.

"And we, my dear," Daddy joked, "wouldn't put our lives in jeopardy by sampling your wares. Not in this faraway mood!"

"No problem. I had a special reason for wanting a kitchen. *I'm* gonna cook!" B.J. announced. "And you'll have cat-'s-eye stew!"

Uncle Worth seemed genuinely amused. "*You?* You, cook? You mean to say that would be safer? Let's see, cat's-eye stew dates back to the encounter with the Gypsies we met on the way to California."

"Sweet of you, Billy Joe, real sweet," Auntie Rae said, unconsciously using her bedtime-story voice, "but stew would take too long."

"Not the kind I make," he said with a wink at Marvel and Mary Ann.

His mother looked uncertain. "Frozen vegetables help, but chicken takes hours, honey. I know you've had kitchen experience, but—"

"I said *no problem*. You're all on kitchen patrol. So set the table! Mary Ann, Marvel, and me—*I*—will shop. It's our secret!"

B.J. marched out in renewed independence. His appointed helpers followed, both of them restraining smiles while, paradoxically, bonded in secrecy and something deeper: another tradition added to a common past....

The stew was no "reasonable facsimile" of goodness. It was the real thing, exceeding all the promised perfection—good to the last sop!

After a dessert of sliced honeydew sprinkled with ginger, Mother reached for her violin again. "A feast like this calls for a celebration."

It took so little to set the Harrington kin singing. Togetherness was a piece of home all its own, an airbrushed haven that Currier and Ives could not imitate. It was colored by love set to music.

They sang in wild abandon, forgetting their surroundings, following Snow Harrington's lead: the old hymns...the soft, sweet echoes of home...and the rollicking rhythms that made the tickle box turn over.

The sudden knock on the door went unnoticed, as did the second. On the third try, a threatening voice accompanied the pounding.

"Open up! Open up this minute!" the motel manager's voice commanded angrily. Daddy and Uncle Worth rushed to obey.

Then shortly, they returned. "I'm sorry," Daddy whispered, "real sorry. It's the first time I've ever been threatened because of my wife's beautiful melodies. We're about to be arrested for disturbing the peace!" He looked ready to laugh.

Suddenly it was funny—very, very funny. So funny that they all burst out in peals of laughter. B.J. said he wished he'd gone to the door. "I'd have said that I'd poke him in the nose except that it's 'Be Kind to Dumb Animals' week. And he's a jack—uh, a mustang!"

Auntie Rae's mouth opened as if to reprimand her son, then closed. She appeared almost relieved when Mother spoke. "I didn't know this week was special for animals, B.J.," she said innocently. "Maybe it's the humane society after me for *cruelty*—saying my playing hurt their ears. Well, I'll not bother anybody or anything, will I, when we get home? I can play to the flowers I'll grow—acres and acres—"

"You bet you can, my pet!" Daddy said excitedly. "So which route do we take getting out of here?"

"A straight line is the shortest distance between two points, according to the geometry theorem you drilled into me, Marvel. Ugh! Memory of that thing still gets me. Remembering that stupid stuff made me gag on your stew, big-tiny brother!"

This time Rae Harrington did speak. "Mary Ann!" she said gently, "Now, I know you're teasin', but you know very well that stew was out of this world. That goes in my recipe book for sure."

"He knows I was teasing, Mother. Didn't I help brew the concoction? B.J. brought some interesting people into our lives."

There followed an exchange of the day's experiences, with everybody talking at once of counting blessings brought their way and the blessings which hopefully they had been in the lives of the givers: the music, the recipes, and the Bibles.

"Oh, that reminds me, Mother!" Mary Ann interjected. "I want you to see the research I've done. The history of biblical foods is amazing."

"And I have a very special poem for you," Marvel said. "Then Mother, you'll create a symphony, won't you—combining taste buds with the buds of spring? Say, that's a pretty title: 'The Buds of Spring.'"

"I'm tasting it," Mother smiled. "Heavenly—like angel food cake."

"Great, Snow White!" Daddy said. "Well spoken, for the air is lighter up there. Absolutely *no* devil's food. His chair's vacant!"

Briefly, the talk turned sober. There *would* be some empty chairs back home. They must expect changes. After all, their journey had been more than the poetic "over the river and through the woods." True, they'd ridden the rapids, managed to stay afloat in the impossible whitecaps of alarm clocks, schedules, and demands. But time had not stood still for those left behind. Mention of the vacant chair served to remind them that there had been deaths, Erin's divorce, casualties of war...

"Don't spoil a beautiful day," Mother whispered. "I should call—"

"Let's surprise them. We'll soon be home," Uncle Worth suggested.

"Let's!" Mary Ann sang out. "Okay—shortest distance between heart and heritage!"

16

To Gain a New Perspective

At times, the car poked like a balky child. At others, it hummed along, hungrily gobbling up the miles. Marvel knew the illusions depended on her mood. Did other family members share the same unspoken uncertainties? *Home . . .* they were going *home.* The place which had felt so close during the long years of planning now sounded strange and faraway. *Oh Titus, be there for me,* her heart begged. *Be as you were—inside!*

Even as she and Mary Ann sifted through the assortment of notes and clippings, her mind ran carefree to the meadows of the past. It must have been the ragged sigh that alerted Mary Ann.

"Sort of doin' battle with the past, wondering if people and things will be changed? *I* am. I feel all churned up inside, doing combat with memories. We—oh Marvel, we'll be changed, too. Will Jake understand?"

"Of course," Marvel reassured her. "I guess we're afraid to hope. Another disappointment would simply be too painful—"

"Stop sayin' that this minute! You're just getting cold feet like any other bride-to-be—prenuptial jitters! We formed some strong bonds."

"Yes," Marvel said, wadding discarded items into tight balls, "and, in a sense, established some new traditions—all good in themselves. But they haven't mellowed with age, become the real thing. I *need* the past."

A sudden blast of the horn stopped the conversation. Dale Harrington's voice was excited. "Look! A car with a Texas license plate—heading the wrong direction. I could tell those refugees a thing or two. Oh, there's another one behind us!"

As the car in the rear window drew alongside them, the driver signaled Daddy to roll down his window. "Hi, y'all!" he yelled across his lady companion's head. "Hi, yourself. Your mouth's open!" Daddy called, knowing that any Texan would appreciate the old greeting. Occupants in both vehicles laughed and waved as the other car moved past.

It was only a simple gesture, but somehow it brought home closer. And suddenly Marvel could picture it all again. Home ... there was no place like it. She would slay the dragon named cowardice. Now! Do away with all those taunting ghosts—for that's what they were, those fears. Ghosts! They were nonexistent—just Satan's sly proxies from past hurts programmed to scream "Boo!" in her weaker moments. They were his way of blocking her view of problems of today—not problems really, more the gaining of a new perspective. Those "ghosts" could live in the past from now on. Wasn't that where they belonged?

"Let's sing!" Mother called over her shoulder. "Beautiful, beautiful Texas—land where the bluebonnets grow! We're proud of our forefathers—land of the Alamo!..."

On and on they sang, changing songs, changing lanes. But Marvel's mind remained on the bluebonnets, the low-growing annual lupine of Texas with its silky foliage and dainty blue blossoms—their state flower, wrapped so tenderly away with her other memories of home. "Bluebonnet blue," Titus had said of her eyes before he came up with the name of "Marvelous, *my* Marvelous-blue!" It was Titus who told her of the blossom's history. Bluebonnets, sometimes called cornflowers, originated in Scotland. No, not the flowers—a wide, flat, round cap of blue wool or—and he'd laughed—one who wears one. "And you, my darling, wear them in those *Marvelous* eyes!" Remembering, she sang louder.

The singing ended where it began. "Encore!" Mother commanded, and they sang "Beautiful, beautiful Texas" again.

"We'll sing 'The Eyes of Texas Are Upon You' tomorrow," Mother said breathlessly. "But right now," and she dug in her handbag to find a lengthy magazine article, "I want you girls to look at this. Mother sent it. Interesting—and such a precious name! 'Bluebonnet Theatre'—right in Culverville. Listen, 'Silents Make a Silent Comeback in Matinee Idyll Style.' I'll toss it back."

214

"You caught the bouquet!" Mary Ann laughed with her trade-mark toss of curls. "That means—"

"I know what it means!" Marvel said a little more curtly than she had intended. "Let's read about the silents," she said more softly.

Mary Ann looked at her warily before saying, "I love the name, too. And you know what? Bluebonnets will be in full bloom at this time of year. So much rain'll bring them popping up to see what all the rumble's about. Funny, how those seed lie there dormant for years then, like the old movies, wake up double-quick, huh?"

"You're right. Nothing in nature is lost. Mother will want to make one more stop. And I guess we wouldn't want to miss the sight."

They took turns reading—sometimes skimming, sometimes reading excerpts. Reopening the movie houses, often restored to their former grandeur, seemed to be a new frenzy in the enter-tainment world—a need to return to the former glory, real or imagined...a form of escape. It all went back to the Roaring Twenties, the heyday of Harold Lloyd, Mary Pickford, and Doug-las Fairbanks in those heady days before the great crash... when things were "normal." But the news now was the rapid-fire spread of "recapturing what was lost"...and spreading like Ber-muda grass! First hitting the big times with their wonders: California, naturally...Philadelphia...Chicago...and now, sur-prisingly, revisiting the hard-hit cities of the Dust Belt. "After all, was the 'Bible Belt' a synonym of the 'Chastity Belt'?"

"Wow!" Mary Ann gasped. "That was a tacky thing to say. Let me read that thing. I—I guess I'm surprised Aunt Snow'd let us see it. Well, we're on a third-generation street now, so what cities did this piece refer to as hard-hit?"

Taking the pages from Marvel, she read aloud: "Oh, he—she—the writer mentions Kansas City, Oklahoma City, Austin, Dallas, San Antonio, and then covers a flock of them with 'and smaller towns scattered throughout the states.' Nobody thought they would survive, he says? Nobody thought any of us would either—except us. We weren't doomed. We fought our way back from scratch! Tickles me now, some of the things they said about us. Said we were too dumb to know better! Well, praise the Lord, for dumbness. We kept our noses clean!"

There was much more. "I'm getting hoarse," Marvel said. "It will be nice when we get some kind of cooling system in cars so we can hear ourselves talk. Sometimes," she laughed, "I'd like to hear what I have to say. But maybe it would be like the car radio. Not once have we used it. It's like we were avoiding the news."

"I *know* I have. I just wanted to think *good* things."

Marvel had caught sight of something more she wanted to read. But the conversation between her parents caused both her and Mary Ann to listen while they let their voices rest. Mother was wondering how the passengers in other cars knew they hailed from the great state of Texas. Didn't the license plate say California? Yes, but for sentimental reasons Daddy had kept the Texas flag sticker on the back bumper. Would Texas require a driver's license? Daddy didn't know. There was so much they would have to find out.

Turning attention back to the article, Marvel read aloud:

> Sometimes the past seems so near, the present so distant. One can measure history by its dreams. But dreams can tumble into nightmares. And the greatest of these came with the great crash. Those were the days when Rudy Vallee crooned... a privileged few owned radio sets... women voted for the first time ... "modern" women bobbed their hair... and anyone with gumption borrowed on life insurance and bought common stock low, for they were sure it would go up. Or so it seemed. A decade later the president was telling them not to fear fear. A million people were seeing the U.S.A. by boxcar, and the safest buy down on Wall Street were apples peddled by hungry street vendors! At that corner of the universe, day turned to night and dawn would be long in coming. Rarely has a dream of so many collapsed so abruptly into such despair... or buttoned down world finance so permanently... redirected the course of history... or left a memory so stinging. But we were blind, sandwiched between two world wars... and blindly we dreamed.

"Stop! I can't stand anymore," Mary Ann said. "We know all this—how prices had gone up like women's hemlines and come down even faster. Don't get me wrong. I'm glad we're preservin' history. It serves as a guide to the future. But *God* doesn't live in the past. He's right here—and He wants us to be happy!"

"Oh Mary Ann, thanks for reminding me. What would I do without you?"

"Don't try," Mary Ann said airily. "I agree with one thing that rambling article said: that we could measure the feelings of the generations by its movies. Ours today sure enough play second fiddle to those romantic movies they used to make. There's too much bombing, violence, hanky-panky. They used to be lessons in love-proving that sad can be beautiful, too. I have another piece on that. Here it is! I'll name some films. See if you know the years."

Mother and Daddy overheard and took part in the game with them. *Casablanca*? 1942...*The Philadelphia Story*? 1940...*Wuthering Heights*? 1939...*Camille*?...1936...*Gone with the Wind*? ...1939...*A Farewell to Arms*? 1932. They all graduated with honors.

How ironic that the Harringtons should hear a similar recap on the radio broadcast that very evening in their motel. Similar—but more frightening! For it carried a grim warning none wanted to hear.

The world changed suddenly, silently with the great crash. No more rules...a violent game of manipulation ...looking for and finding suckers to dump. The last of the big spenders sat their days out in darkened theater-like settings, watching the new prices on ticker tape flashed on the big board, flowing past like a river of fortune. Women, new to this man's world, watched the readings change on a translux machine as they snuggled in plush chairs in stock rooms of hotels. Slowly, but surely, as the great bubble of unrealistic dreams enlarged in preparation for bursting, there were other excesses. Manners and morals of the Roaring Twenties were over. It would end, they said, and it did! Came the Depression. It too, would end—and it did—in *war*. But wounds leave scars.

Memories come back, sometimes in song. America was singing "Don't Fence Me In" when the attack on Pearl Harbor came as suddenly, as silently as the great crash. All America stopped singing then just as the nation stopped singing "How Ya Gonna Keep 'Em Down on the Farm After They've Seen Paree?" in World War I. Many galloped out "where the West commences," and maybe they knocked down the fences in their escape. Certainly, the Japanese bombing changed the complexion of the United States forever—the work, the play, the private lives of every citizen. The war dragged on from 1941 to 1945.

Then the mushroom cloud over Nagasaki loomed, dissipated . . . and RKO Radio Pictures was hard at work again. *The Best Years of Our Lives* was their first release. The film attracted America because of its timeliness. Veterans were coming home, and not always finding home as wonderful as they had dreamed it. Statistics bear this out. A year before war commenced, America's divorce rate was 2 per 1000 population. By 1945 it was 3.5. And it continues to mount, with predictions that the rate will reach 4.7. The world had turned over during the absence of the servicemen. Fighting for survival, they knew little of women's streaming into the workplace and had never met "Rosie, the Riveter," knew little about women's shift from the home to labor or professions, and even less concerning the rising divorce rate. Blissfully unaware, they marched home—only to come face to face with the staggering news.

"Well, for cryin' out loud! How depressing. We've read all this!" Mary Ann had darted cross the room in seven-league steps to the radio.

"But we haven't heard the news for a while," Uncle Worth reminded her. "They'll get to it. And in the meantime, honey, it's good for us to remember the Depression, the war, and count our blessings. Unemployment of the Depression's over, and shortages of the war—"

"Still a shortage on good wives," Daddy said, reaching affectionately to take Mother's hand. "Yes, I'm right glad God thought of mates—and families. Guess we'll keep 'em around if they'll scramble to the kitchen. Say, there's an idea! Scrambled eggs and cinnamon toast!"

Mary Ann had sat back down with an exaggerated sigh. Marvel, torn between lending a hand in the kitchenette and remaining for possible news, decided on the news. Neither of them could have known that the words to follow would come as a shock—one which would shake them all with greater intensity than California's minor earthquake followed by the inevitable aftershock, to send Marvel's heart soaring with new hope. No, *more*—a kind of *knowing* certainty that hope brought. If only—

This reporter, along with several other undercover reporters who worked tirelessly gathering classified information for our wartime president, generally under assumed names, now know the new concept of the monstrous A-bomb. But then we knew only what we saw, thanked the Lord that we had escaped its hellish fire, and made every effort to smuggle the "harnessed power of the sun" information to the White House through the wire service. Any security I may have felt melted down in the devastation left in its wake. But now, after these years of hope, my knees tremble with foreboding. It's no longer a secret, Intelligence Forces have alerted us. "Expect to hear," they say, "at any given moment that dread message: 'We interrupt this program to bring you the following special report ... the Soviets just exploded an atomic bomb!'" We should have known the impracticality of the hope that our country could maintain a monopoly. "Alas, Babylon!" We should have known not to link arms with communism. We should have read the prophecies!

"End of Hoover's New Era—end of Roosevelt's New Deal—beginning of new threat!" Daddy groaned. "But," and he brightened, "beginning of the new perspective. Let's head home!"

"Bark is willing!" B.J. near-shrieked. "I guess grandfather was right. He's a right smart smarter than we thought."

The two men agreed, laughed, and said he should be. After all, Alexander Jay Harrington, Esquire, dealt in *securities*. What was greater security than *home*? Good title for a bank: "Home Security"!

"The only security I want is my husband!" Mary Ann whispered fiercely. "I'm going to Jake the minute I get home. Nobody can stop me!"

"Nobody will try. We're all shaken by the news. Only it's not news, I guess," Marvel said disjointedly. Titus had told her. Yes, *Titus*! She knew now that many of the news releases she had saved were his writing. Every clue was there. Detail could come later. For now, the overall picture was enough. Titus Smith—by whatever name—had been, among other things, an eyewitness. All foolish fears, misgivings, doubts, and dragons of flagging faith underwent a filtering system. She felt purified, humbled, and so joy-filled that the glow must show. How could I have expected myself to know? she wondered now. Or put such demands on myself? Only God knows all. A Christian mind is a trusting mind—a dedicated and growing mind! And now the mind of Marvel Harrington was a stable mind, for its anchor was in the mind of God. And there she would be stayed on Him. When tomorrow's news broke, it would not shatter her peace.

"Come unscramble those eggs and dunk toast in coffee! Come on—scramble, hear?" Mother called gaily. And Auntie Rae giggled in the background.

They scrambled.

Daddy asked the blessing. They talked in general terms about concerns of the news, agreed that it was important to keep informed, but realized that even the commentators saw "through a glass, darkly." Auntie Rae passed extra napkins and said how nice to have paper good back. Then they talked of feeling an urge to get home where there would be a smidgen of peace, no radio for a spell, not even a newspaper—just *talking* all day and all night through!

But there was an undercurrent of anxiety. Evil things *do* happen to good people. They trusted the Lord's wisdom—not to be confused with man's tendency toward a blind faith that was self-serving. Life was short. It should be spent in loving togetherness....

Marvel listened as the talk flowed past. Inside was an urgency unshared, a need to read one item in particular. Yes, Titus would have been that eyewitness. She hoped and, yes, she would pray that he was not still on watch. One war was enough.

Managing to smuggle the item into the bathroom, Marvel scanned it hurriedly. It was hard to see by the dim light, and the words flashed off and on like traffic signals with the throbbing of her heart. Even so, the words sang across the columns: *Titus, Titus!* It was his work. Nobody could imitate his style:

Nobody who cares can deny the cruelty of World War II, especially someone who *saw*. And yes, I covered it all, beginning with the atrocities in Spain. The impact on all Americans was as powerful as the death-blow which ended the war. We changed...the entire world changed...but America most of all. We are no longer an isolationist country. We are a superpower—

a role we share, perhaps temporarily, with a hostile and uneasy Soviet Russia. Sobering...particularly for those with deep religious convictions...for we cannot condone killing! But we are charter members of the nuclear age, and we must learn to live with it as we learned to live with the Great Depression...or see our nation and its people blown to smithereens. The responsibility rests upon our shoulders uninvited ...but face it we must! All is not dark...God is not dead. So look at the impact of the war: Can you accept that perhaps dropping the A-bomb was the most humane thing to do? Its use saved the Japanese from extinction...and love the enemy we must. Victory saved us from a barbaric world dominated by Nazi Germany and militarist Japan. Let us never forget that our hard-fought victory brought an end to the Nazi slaughter of Jews in Europe...too late, God forgive us, to save the lives of almost ten million of them...but sparing countless additional millions.

"Occupied?" B.J. called with a knock that said "Time's up!"

"Coming," Marvel said, torn between amusement and irritation.

The new perspective, Daddy had said. And Titus gave it definition. A new triumph—for truly the end of World War II gave birth to the United Nations...inspired hope that it would endure where the League of Nations of World War I had failed. "United we stand," Titus went on, "for in God we trust! The sum of the two addends equals discouragement to Russians who might push farther into a divided Germany or draw us into an ugly localized war in Korea...a promise of more blessed years of peace in this postwar world—so starved for love. I have fought the good fight. Now my heart turns home...."

17

Dare We Believe?

There may have been more to see, who knew? Who cared? The Harringtons were too caught up in exhilaration to take note. Each tried to camouflage the yearnings in idle conversation. But it was no use. Each time, the talk harked back to memories of the past. "I guess we never left home—not really," Daddy said at last.

"Strange, isn't it?" Mother answered. "Close as you and I were to each other, and close as we all were to each other, I felt a kind a sadness—guilt maybe—about the part we'd left back home. It was like, well, the way I felt about Eleanore's threatening to leave Emory. How could she divorce the past? And me all the time thinking the same about home—how people can be side by side and be so far apart. Or be miles apart, separated by miles—but together."

Snow Harrington had rambled, but they all understood. Talk stopped then. Marvel and Mary Ann lost interest in sorting their collected materials, neither able to concentrate. The clutter became too much. Oh, they would go back to it: go back to the concerns of others...get caught up again in the work of the kingdom...back to school...back to "normal." But now just getting back home was enough. Their minds could hold only small things.

"We'll count signposts or power poles," Mary Ann said mindlessly. They tried, but the markers seemed to dissolve. And there was silence.

Looking back, the trip seemed short. There was no problem at the Arizona border. Actually, inspectors cared little what tourists took out. They were concerned only with what came in by way of plant life. Mother's lovely eyes enlarged when the inspector demanded curtly that all such items be declared. Oh, the seed, bulbs, and tubers! But she had forgotten that they were stamped GOVERNMENT INSPECTED. Mother cried quietly, a joyful sort of crying, as jealously she hugged her treasures to her heart once they were hers again. These represented life—the new life which sprang from the death of departure.

Then suddenly they were in Texas.

A chorus of joy filled the Dale Harrington car. "Something exploded inside me!" Daddy said excitedly, and his hands trembled on the steering wheel. "I can just hear B.J. yelping 'Hot diggity, we made it!'" Mary Ann laughed. "Me—I feel light as fluff, like my insides were nothing but cotton-candy stuffing!" Mother mimed the playing of her violin as she, Mary Ann, and Marvel turned to make two-fingered V's of their fingers to Uncle Worth's family and see the victory sign returned. Home...they were going home.

"This sky—has it always been so big, so blue?" Marvel murmured. Inside, she felt the fade out, fade in of scenes—past and present. Hollywood seemed far away, shallow, tinsely. The past felt closer. All the self-expectations and how to fulfill them came back, as did Titus—and their tree. "The tree of life," he'd called it because the tree represented so much—its protective branches shielding the two of them against the evils of the world. There they plumbed the depths of their hearts together, developed in one another a certain grit, stubborn determination, and unshakable faith which gave them the courage to journey away, knowing they would journey back. Couldn't they take life in stride now, endure, knowing love conquered all?

Marvel's heart was lighter than air, and surely each slight bend in the highway brought more brightness. Daddy saw it, too.

"Father says there's been excessive rain. Obvious, isn't it? Everything's so lush and green. Everything's good—even the weather!"

It was true. This was dry country. The rains seemed timed just right for their homecoming, Marvel reflected with a smile. Downpours had stopped now, coming only in moderation, and (seemingly) only at night. Each leaf and blade of grass glistened, and shallow water stood between endless rows of planted crops.

Suddenly the car nosed up a slight knoll, and there they were! A million bluebonnets rippling as if set to music, a "Rhapsody in Blue."

Breathtaking as the wash of color was, the Harringtons did not linger. Marvel made notes. Mary Ann and B.J. took pictures. And the men discussed crops, banks, and the proper order of pulling off their surprisingly early homecoming. The older folks might not recognize the children, who were children no more, so wouldn't it be smarter if Daddy and Uncle Worth just up and knocked? "That'll knock their socks off!" Daddy predicted, his sparkling-blue eyes made more so against the blue of the flowers behind him, purpled in anticipation.

Mary Ann winked at Marvel. "Won't know *us*? Ha! Just an excuse to be first," she said knowingly. "Fine. It's '*Hi*' 'n '*Bye*' for me!"

"Let's go—anytime you're ready," Mother said breathlessly.

Daddy laughed. "What! No symphony? No violin? No *seed*?"

"No nothing!" Mother said. "Oh what a surprise we'll be!"

Surprise? What a pebble-word—one which would set ripples reaching farther and farther in a spine-tingling kind of way.

* * *

Leah Johanna Mier Riley answered the door in her stocking feet.

"I'm coming!" she said, swinging the heavy door open wide to accommodate the group. "My word, I thought a flock of peckerwoods attacked!"

Well spoken for in the end—preplanning forgotten—the entire family had knocked. But something strange was happening. Did nobody else note the blank look on Grandmother's face, as if she failed to recognize her own? Marvel wondered. Mother didn't notice.

"Peckerwood! We haven't heard that word since we left home. It's woodpecker, Mother." Snow Harrington laughed merrily.

Perhaps it was the laugh that did it. Instead of opening her arms as one would have expected, Grandmother's face lost all its color and she dropped backward. Grandfather reached her just in the nick of time. Without looking up, he laid her motionless body on the nearest couch and began speaking in low, soothing tones.

"You'll be all right, my dear one—just lie still. I'm here. You'll be all right." And to the surprise of the prodigals at the door, Alexander Jay Harrington, Esquire, began massaging the stockinged toes one by one with practiced hands. It was too much when those hands moved to the ankles of the patient and then upward.

"Say, can't we come inside?" Daddy demanded. "We're home!"

"And hey! What's this? What's going on here?" Uncle Worth asked suspiciously. "I wasn't born yesterday, Father—"

"*Father?*" Grandfather said dull-wittedly. "What—who—?"

Then he, too, looked in need of first aid. Frightened now, the family pushed in. Mother leaned down to check on Grandmother. Daddy and Uncle Worth bent awkwardly over their father. Marvel and Mary Ann rushed to the kitchen and returned with two glasses of water, cold compresses, and a bottle of smelling salts. There was bedlam, in general. And why of all the times would the youngest Harrington choose to take a picture of such a scene?

The smelling salts worked. At least they brought the owners of the rambling old hotel from the semiconscious state. But the shock remained. Both faces looked blank—blank and frightened!

"It can't be—it's not possible!" Grandmother gasped. "Dare we believe?"

"An apparition!" Grandfather, still holding Grandmother's foot, said harshly. "Only I don't believe in such. And I don't believe *this!*"

It was not the homecoming they had expected. And now the returning families were as puzzled as those who had waited for them so long. Admittedly, there had been no advance notice. But since when had the Harringtons stood on formality? The welcome latch was always out, a candle of welcome burning in eternal flame.

"What's the big problem, Father? I thought you understood—" Daddy began, then stopped just short of embracing Grandfather.

"You're dead, that's what! *Dead.* We've grieved and now out of nowhere come strangers claiming to be my sons!" Grandfather sounded angry now. "I think I understand. You're after their inheritance!"

"*Our* inheritance!" Daddy was angry now himself. "That's unworthy of you, Father. When did Worth's family or mine ask anything of you?"

Mother still hovered over Grandmother. "*You* know better, Mother. I know it's a shock, but it ought to be a happy one."

"Snow White?" Grandmother said, raising on one elbow."Oh, my precious. It *is* you. I prayed, I cried—and then the furniture came—"

"And the money," Grandfather muttered."We read about it—"

Marvel was beginning to understand. They *read*. That could mean only one thing: the earthquake! Of course—the hurried departure...shipping the furniture...transferring the bank accounts...

She was ready to attempt an explanation when her father spoke for himself. "Let's skip the details and put our time to better use, like praising the Lord that newspapers can be wrong!" Quickly summing up the circumstances, he concluded: "So, you see, we didn't spend our portion of goods in riotous living in our journey. Actually, I believe the story goes that people rejoice and kill the fatted calf in such instances, anyway, Mother Riley," he grinned.

"Mother *Harrington*!" Grandmother announced proudly and, suddenly healed, sprang to her feet. "We planned an Easter wedding—"

"Easy, Mother," Snow Harrington cautioned, motioning to Auntie Rae to join her in supporting Grandmother. "You want to be in fine shape for the wedding. *Wedding*—did you say wedding?" she gasped.

"Oh, you'll be in great shape by then," Auntie Rae said softly. "Easter's close. Let's see, isn't this Good Friday?"

"*Good* Friday indeed!" Grandfather near-shouted. He picked up his forgotten cane, rapped on the floor, and became the patriarch. "Meet my bride, the Duchess Leah Johanna Harrington. We needed one another when—when the news came. Oh, there's a wealth of things to tell you. But like you said, son, it's time to rejoice! I believe the father took compassion on the prodigal, and fell on his neck and kissed him instead of falling on his own face like I came near doing. My sons were dead and they live again. They were lost and now are found. Let us eat and be merry—dance and make music!"

And "fall on one another's neck" they did—the whole lot of the clan knotted together tightly, weeping, laughing, praying. The music would come later with Grandmother Harrington at the piano and her daughter by her side playing the music of the spheres. And while the voices raised in praise might prove no match for the heavenly choir, it was an earthly facsimile. Nobody would sleep—or want to.

But for now, it was Billy Joe who brought them back to earth. "Take a look—see? I'm all grown up—a real he-man—a Harrington with ambition to match! But we Harringtons need food. Don't I smell scalloped potatoes, Gran'mere? Now you *know* I'm alive! The dead don't eat potatoes!"

* * *

A flurry of activity followed the strange homecoming. Grandfather pointedly ignored his returning sons' suggestion that a reunion could wait, and waved away all notions that they could be tired or have other matters needing attention.

"Tired—at your age?" he said in rebuttal. He was fit as a fiddle—only used the walking stick when the callus on his right heel started acting up. As if to prove it, he hurried to the new corner grocery and came back with two loaded shopping bags. Daddy and Uncle Worth were yessing their father as always. In no time at all, they were suited in their Sunday best and heading for Harrington & Sons, Inc. What could be more important than family—and investments?

Grandmother's cheeks rivaled the scarlet climbers entwining the freshly painted pillars of the large multi-gabled building. Both had weathered many a storm and endured with a flair. "I'm fine—just fine. Oh, the Squire takes good care of me—meets my every need. *Here, get these aprons on and let's get going, girls!* Back to that husband of mine . . . well now, he knows every trick in the book about a woman's needs—like massaging my Achilles' heel where it tends to shorten when I'm exhausted. And," she paused to grin wickedly, "he knows I—well, respond. I'm here to tell you, it's more sensuous than emptying bedpans."

"*Mother!*"

Grandmother chuckled. "All right, *be* stuffy! Your daughters understand. You get on with your sweet potato peeling. *They know!*"

Yes, they knew. Mary Ann needed to call Jake, reassure him that she was *alive* (not that he didn't know, for she had written daily). But, well (giggle, giggle) her voice would be "more sensuous." if the family insisted she stay for that silly reunion, Mary

Ann would have a grand mal, she fumed. Marvel smiled absently, her mind busy with organizing the search for Titus. Of course, there was a need to call Editor Corey and update her writing assignment. Then—

Neither she nor Mary Ann could gain access to the telephone, however. Grandmother, having put Mother and Auntie Rae in charge of the kitchen, made a series of calls. Neighbors, friends, the church—all must know of the miracle. Then there were Dorthea, Eleanore, and the remnants of their families, she said vaguely . . . and others. . . .

In the end, members of the Harrington clan gathered, made a painful effort to establish a warmth they'd never felt in reality (without finding a calm in the confusion because of moanings and groanings—which turned to accusations), but carried on because of the senior Harringtons. And, admittedly, the Easter service was rooted in glory.

Meantime, Mary Ann reached Jake, made plans for joining him Monday. And now—in broad daylight—puffy-white dream-clouds floated in a full-moon sky. Mary Ann waltzed to the dulcet tones of the Ink Spots wafting from the radio: ". . . the day we tore the goalposts down . . . we'll have these moments to re-member. . . ." All the world was beautiful.

Marvel could only sigh. Goalposts meant football. Football meant Titus, their dreams, their "moments to remember." Dreams, yes—dreams and stolen moments. But life had denied them the sweet joys of youth. A deep sadness for what might have been welled up inside Marvel Harrington for herself, for Titus, their generation, and the world. How ironic that Titus Smith, the only man she would ever love, would be captain of the football team, and she had never seen him play—didn't even know the rules of the game. Well, take heed, sad heart. Who cared about such a trivial matter now? They would wipe away all tears forever and live out an end, if not a beginning. Look at her grandparents!

Heart pounding at the thought, she placed the call to Mr. Corey.

Never had Mr. Corey sounded so excited, so happy. "Oh wow!" he exclaimed in that ghost-of-Virginia-to-Texas drawl. "I'm right glad bein' in touch. There was that quake, conflictin' reports— then silence. Sure had us worried. You'll need to get in touch—"

His voice trailed off as if he were in search of something. "I *am* in touch, Mr. Corey. Didn't my columns reach you, the book?"

"Yes, yes—was tryin' to find the address. Well, a couple—but to know you're alive and kickin's something! Mankind, I guess—and he, they, all 'em'll be just as glad. Life's been dark as a tropical jungle, but you've turned on the light! First we'll talk book."

"First and last, I'm afraid—at least, for this time," Marvel said gently. "You see, I'm on borrowed time with this phone."

"Apologies, sweet Marvel," he said quickly. "But you stay in touch, hear? And don't hang up. Your address'll be on what I need *pronto!*" Mr. Corey was feverish with excitement as he tried to explain.

Two publishing houses were vying for rights to a book by Marvel Harrington, whose writing they had admired over the years. One (he chuckled) was the higher of the two bidders, and offered an advance royalty, *"ad vomit!"* (another chuckle), but published in mass paperback. Didn't hold a candle to the other. *The White Flags of Triumph* would appear in hardcover...far more reliable...hold greater promise. "And hear this! Their prestige's lip-smackin'. Not that we care about the spotlight, but we *do* care about this here: Editors all but guarantee it's on th' way toward the coveted award of you-know-what! A real feather in your bonnet, darlin'. Now, all they need's th' end!"

Marvel was silent.

"Say *yes!* Hurry up—I can't wait," he almost shrieked. "Fix it!"

"I can't, Mr. Corey. You see, I—I don't *know* how it ends. It's in the Lord's hands."

"Then hurry Him up a little! Oh, strike that. But you made a believer outta me. Nothing's impossible with Him—or *you*, honey."

"It's impossible for me to know the future, Mr. Corey."

"But Marvel, honey, listen: I've seen a heap more of life than you. I know talent when I see it. I saw it in you years ago. You're in charge of this book. Now, lift it up—let it soar after all this poor girl's been through. Newspapers are one thing. Fiction's another. It's not like the facts of life. You can shift it like sand."

"It's no fiction, sir—I mean, not exactly."

"I *know* what it is, and so do the dozens of agents tryin' to get their meat hooks on you. Ignore 'em—you're gonna put me up yonder seein' as how I discovered you. Already they're comparin' you to Hemingway, Steinbeck, and Tillie Olsen, callin' you a

literary journalist—givin' readers the ole one-two of fact with all
the romance of fiction. Don't hang up on me. It'll come to a happy
ending, I promise!"

He *promised*? How could he or anyone else promise that?

In a quickly stolen moment, Marvel looked t her memoirs, her
scissored excerpts, and—for the first time since they arrived
home—at the treasured souvenirs. She'd been far too shaken to
rejoin the family after talking with the editor, and had taken that
way of regaining composure. Had she promised A. Thomas Corey
a happy ending? That was what he asked for—and promised.
How strange. And in an equally strange way, the man was right,
although in a totally different manner than she would have dared
dream.

* * *

The increased noise level said the other two Harrington sons
and their offspring had arrived. Marvel hesitated before going in,
conflicting emotions battling inside her. It would be nice seeing
them all again, but why was she trembling? They were family. The
terror had something to do with the uncles, aunts, and cousins.
True. But something else had churned this highly emotional
state, this breathlessness. Oh, of course: the book sale. Wasn't
that a proper ending in itself, what she'd always wanted? *Success?* Her writing and, of course, helping her parents reestablish
their dreams? Daddy would have his land now and Mother would
have her house. They would be among people who cared. *Home.*

"No!" Had she said the word aloud? Marvel wondered in
confusion. If so, nobody heard above their own voices. Relieved,
she pursued her thinking. The book meant nothing—nothing at
all without Titus. There could be no pretended "happily ever
after" without him. Yes, or course, she had colored scenes,
fabricated names, and fictionalized some details for the editor.
He had told her to for the ongoing series which unfolded in the
daily newspaper. But the news coverage furnished had been
black-and-white facts, just as Titus was the essential component. Titus was real. No, she could not—*would* not—change the
hero of her book, the love of her heart....

Some of the acquaintances made during the long absence had
blossomed into friendships, Marvel thought fleetingly as her

eyes panned the room. "I've found closer kin and more comfort in meetin' all you girls here in the OPA office," Marie had said. The spirited redhead's "Johnny" had "come marching home," bringing his young wife joy and his captain's friend, Marvel Harrington, heartbreaking news of Captain Prinz's demise. Yes, she could understand how those bonds could tighten. But they were not family. And never did one feel the magnetic power of family more powerfully than on holidays. Tomorrow was Easter—*together.*

The house smelled of baking ham, candying potatoes, Easter lilies—and the heavy perfume that was the trademark of Uncle Emory's women ("harem," Grandfather had sniffed). "Now Squire," Grandmother Riley Harrington had scolded gently, with a twinkle in her Gypsy-dark eyes. "The stuff's potent—*strong*—but 'twould be, you know, coming from Strong's Drugs and Sundries!" Memories, ties—small but as potent as that odor. Remembering, it was easy for Marvel to smile as she rushed in to embrace each member in turn. Sights, sounds, and scents blended in a blur of her overworked senses in a kind of impressionistic art.

Recall came when Mary Ann presented a review in realism. "Uncle Joseph and Uncle Emory look the same, except for the pouches in th' middle. And they'd better start on that Creole Colorback stuff Grandfather uses on gray at the temples. My sakes, Marvel, I wouldn't have recognized Aunt Dorthea—stuffier than ever, both ways! That dress was tighter than skin. Well, like mother, like daughters—"

Mary Ann rambled on. Erin "drove her geese to bad water," but had found another man already. And Cindy—*Lucinda!*—had fallen in love with a chiropractor—a *married* chiropractor ("Put that in your pipe and smoke it! Grandfather's livid about the fornicatin' around!"). Poor Aunt Eleanore wasn't with it...far gone as Fat Elmer used to be. Well, Aunt Dorthea had done one good deed and tried to get her grieving sister-in-law into her bridge club—an embarrassment when she kept insisting she'd read all the cards, yesterday's mail.... Ironic, wasn't it?

"And sad," Marvel said softly, as the blank face of Duke's mother came floating back. "Aunt Eleanore's haunted by his memory. Ironic, yes, that she'll be institutionalized where Elmer was—"

"Oh, she'd be better off, I—I guess. The only holdup is that uncle of ours. Wouldn't that grab you? Not because he's any disciple of 'in sickness and in health'—nothin' so noble. It would be as disgraceful as declarin' bankruptcy or gettin' divorced, having her committed!"

Put her away, shut Aunt Eleanore from his life—as she had shut herself away from the world. As if his wife, mother of his two sons, had never existed. Did a man have that right?

"Sometimes," Marvel said slowly, "I wish I'd accepted Dr. Porter's offer of a medical scholarship and gone into nursing like Kate Lynn. Doctors in the service dealt with shell shock and battle fatigue, and there just has to be treatment for people like our aunt. Being disturbed and depressed is a lot different from being insane or deranged."

"Like the Thistle? Oh, Elmer's gone, and it's not right speaking ill of the dead, but rememberin' him still gives me nightmares."

Marvel had nodded. Better to daydream and think ahead to the rest of her life with Jake. Yes, oh yes, Mary Ann agreed, going on to add that her plans included going on to school—*Bible* school—and working on her book of familiar sayings originating in the Bible (for inclusion in her book, plus working for hire). And then (breathlessly) there would be a family, of course.

"Being in love the way we are— Well, we're like my parents and yours: *in love and bound to stay that way.* We want to procreate, make another *us.* Oh Marvel, we can have such beautiful children—like B.J. Remember how sweet he was, how his hair curled around his earlobes? I love it, but I loved everything about that little pest!"

Did her cousin see her wince? Of course. When did Mary Ann ever miss a trick? She was apologetic immediately. "Oh, I forgot. You *wanted* me to and I did—forget about the surgery, I mean. No children—ever—"

Yes, she had put the surgery from her mind and her heart, told herself it wouldn't matter to Titus—been affable, placid, self-assured. *Then.* But now a demon of doubt probed her self-conscious. A baby . . . a baby for herself and Titus . . . theirs. It had mattered when Titus thought *he* would be unable to father a child. So why wouldn't it matter that *she* was flawed? Titus' long-held doubt about himself had kept them apart. Suddenly came the ugly suspicion that he may have wanted children himself.

The illusion, startling and frightening, became a living thing. The child she would never have . . . dimpled, fat-cheeked . . . smelling of lilac talcum.

"Oh Marvel, I *have* hurt you. I have a gift for that! I'm Icarian, forever soarin' too high for safety without using my noodle. Sometime my wings'll melt like that mythical Greek god all because of my sinful tongue. Oh honey, you look like you've seen a ghost—"

Marvel laughed, feeling the blood rush back to its normal flow. Thank God, the silly illusion had dissolved. "We talked such trivia before—remember? Ghosts live in the past, if ghosts *live* at all. But a ghost of the future? No way. Those so-called *ghosts* are just an excuse to keep us from facing present problems." Feeling strong now—strong and free—she plunged to complete the thought lightly: "Our present problem, as I see it, Mary Ann, is deciding what to wear to the early service. We may have to adjust some hemlines for the 'new look'—slit a seam for the slashed sides. No time to shop."

* * *

Triumphantly, the eastern sky blushed pink with promise. Distant chimes rang silver "Alleluias" to Easter's glory. Songbirds joined in sleepy-time chorus. The Harrington household scrambled with organized confusion. Coffee perked while hot cross buns added warmth to the kitchen. Easter lilies nodded in a first breeze. And Mother joined Grandmother at the piano, making ready to accompany her with the violin in an impromptu special for Culverville Baptist Church's sunrise service.

Yes, Grandmother explained quickly, Pleasant Knoll would be joining the larger church for its special dedication. "You see," she explained over her shoulder as she searched a hymnal, "it's been refurbished—something to behold. There'll be crowds at all three services, so shake a leg, grab a snack and we'll have pecan waffles and honey after church. Snow White, I can't find that dratted sheet music. We'll play by heart. Then let's be bold! You play that symphony you're working on and I'll follow—"

The Squire laughed merrily. "She always gets herself in a dither when she's happy, that Duchess of mine. But I'll jolly her out of it. We do that for each other. It's our bonus from a lifetime of preparing. It pays off, like I tell investors. Your grandmother, Marvel, is a brave one—never gets scared except when she *sees* fear. So don't get all lathered up when they play. Those two'll be church-stoppers. Well, time's a-wastin'. Don't know why I'm using it up like a sentimental silly. It's just that that lady saved my life—made me stop wanting to just up and vanish, get rid of *me* so I wouldn't be in the way—"

B.J. giggled. "Vanish—like blow away? We'd have found you, Grandfather. Couldn't do without a stubborn boss. Hey, let's not bother with the *vanished*—just the *famished*. Let's grab that food while it's friendly!" Laughter rose to mingle with music as they munched.

"Ready, everybody?" Grandmother, looking from Fifth Avenue in the white suit with primrose hat and gloves, called out. "We have to be early. Oh, my! I forgot to say we're all to sing with the choir!"

"*Ready?* Nobody's ready for *that!*" Mary Ann exploded.

Of course, they were, Alexander Jay Harrington said with authority... wonderful example of what family was all about. And being a model family took no rehearsing—just wise investment! Ready? Oh sure, according to the youngest Harrington to carry on the family name. After all, he was used to wearing those "dresses," and his hair went along with such garb better than his cousin Thomas' crew cut. Mother wore an old but becoming apple-green dress (Auntie Rae having lowered the hem last night), and her heavy hair hung loose and spun-straw golden. "Smashing!" Daddy whispered as he straightened the back seam of her new nylons. Uncle Worth gunned the motor of the waiting car... and they were late!

When the telephone rang, Marvel hurried to take the call. Uncle Emory was detained unavoidable. Oh, not for long (*of course not, he was a banker!*), but Aunt Eleanore had trouble dressing. Would the family go on? He would join them at the church. Yes, Marvel said, *she'd* wait.

"Go on, all of you—*shoo!*" she was ordering the family moments later. "Uncle Emory's coming by, and we'll bring the lilies. *Go!*"

There was no time for debate. Grandfather gave her an appreciative hug. "God bless you, Marvelous Harrington. You've made this the most wonderful Easter of my life—brought us a miracle, all of you, rising up from the grave the way you did! Then—then," he choked in uncharacteristic emotion, "it's our last Easter together, what's left after our losses. Next—Eleanore, Cindy, maybe *all* of you—"

"Not *all*," Marvel promised, snuggling against his broad shoulder.

Were those tears in those Harrington-blue eyes? Grandfather would never stand for such weakness. Didn't proof lie in that dignified exit, the long black-wool stride marching as if his cane were tapping off the marble-floor distance between him and a prospective customer seeking an income-property first mortgage?

Outside the world was alive, breathing like a creature—a world singing of renewal. The oaks had cracked their heart-shaped buds and given birth to tiny flittering shadows of lime-green leaves. The air was thick with the raw odor of apple orchards in full blossom and beds of brilliant blossoms in Easter-egg colors encircled the white purity of Grandmother's well-timed lilies. They had bloomed out in glory on exactly the right day. But of course, Marvel realized. Easter was to have been Grandmother's wedding day. She breathed deeply, feeling that she was inhaling the world, as she and Titus had breathed it into themselves. The two of them belonged to the world and it belonged to them...in the Beginning...before the *fall*. "I've never gone beyond it, and I never will," Marvel Harrington whispered, not sure if she addressed the words to Titus or to God— or to both of them. Heaven and earth would become one someday. Dare she believe it would be today?

18

Seamlessly Wedded to Actuality

Always-a-deacon Emory Harrington dutifully placed the Easter lilies at the altar and made a side exit to rejoin his wife. Marvel sat with her until he returned. Then, relinquishing the space to him, she backed to an unobtrusive pew at the rear of the church. It was too late to join the choir. The first number was in progress, so she opened the church bulletin. It was difficult to make out the words—even the text—in the dim light. Some chaplain would be in charge of the dedication to follow the program. But why strain her eyes? The victorious singing had swollen in praise, then softened to a prayerful stop. It was doubtful if Grandmother could see the back pew. But just in case, there must be no doubt or fear reflected in the eyes of the audience, Grandfather said.

Mother stood, closing her fingers about the neck of the violin, then closing her eyes as well. Her gifted hands touched bow to string and the beautifully restored Baptist church changed instantly to a great cathedral—seen first by the violinist, then by the whole congregation. Music of worship . . . music of praise . . . a tongue universal speaking to all races, codes, creeds—in need of no interpretation. Oh, surely Aunt Eleanore would understand. God would speak to her.

Now the piano joined in softly. Christ no longer hung dying on the cross. He was a risen Lord . . . *here* . . . walking with them. And Mother was playing for Him. The music was different now, softer, sweeter, more intricate, yet without hidden meaning in the melody. Marvel was overcome with emotion. Mother's symphony—

and Grandmother was following as she had promised. Marvel wanted to weep but dared not. Harringtons held promises sacred. But her vision blurred, and she could never remember at what point the music ended and the Easter message began.

It was all so dearly familiar: the church, the message, the text, even the voice. Hurled back through time and space, Marvel was clutching a copy of the program she, as usherette at Titus' graduation from Culverville High, had handed guests. Speaker of the evening: The Honorable O. Marcus Bradford, retired chaplain in the United States Navy. "I wish," said the speaker, "that together with your diploma, we of another generation could place in your hands a safe and secure world...." Commander Bradford had read the story of the Creation and laid the destiny of the heartland in their young hands—to recreate, he said, "into the land of perfect environment, the Garden."

Marvel, a "captain's" (captain of the football team) "beautiful lady in blue" in her borrowed dress and single strand of pearls, now sat in the same church... heard the same message as if past and present were joined together in "the coat without seam" witnessed by those who knelt at the cross. "But we are not to lie at the foot of our crosses, do nothing for this world...."

Too caught up to glance upward, she could only listen:

So how did we lose it, that blessed garden of perfect environment where the deer and the buffalo roamed freely, nibbling of calamus and saffron, frankincense and myrrh? Can we hope to cross the great gulf separating us from home?

In the beginning, it was good—and God smiled. His smile created a rainbow circling about His throne, a promise before its time.... The lion and the lamb lay down together beneath the tree of life whose eternal bloom perfumed the splendor of the flowers with cinnamon—and God smiled again... as the heavenly odors reached for the four corners of the heavens where wheeled countless galaxies of stars His holy hands had flung to separate darkness from light. Then male and female created He them... bone of one bone, flesh of one flesh—breath of one God....

The rainbow curled around Marvel's shoulders, so naturally, so right, for heaven had come down... and the unicorns were back. "They were naked and not ashamed," the speaker would be saying. There was no cause for shame in a world of perfection. What God had brought together, let no man put asunder by shame. God had smiled on them. They were good, never having tasted sin.

The speaker's voice sounded far away, penetrating her inner ear, but Marvel's heart was far away. Beneath the mighty oak which shielded the two of them from the wickedness of the world, she and Titus had glimpsed that glory in their unflawed innocence, if only "through a glass darkly." But when the risen Christ came back to claim His own, that which was imperfect would be cast aside. No longer would there be evil, the cause for present shame. Surely God must no longer be smiling, when nakedness was no longer without sin . . . indeed, sold for the love of money. And when money shines, morality fades. And darkness is upon the face of the earth. . . .

> We face a choice this Easter morn, for we have that priceless flaming sword of free will. Yes, there is the dark side, the threat of nuclear war . . . annihilation of mankind. But the Creator whose fingers created all things beautiful gave us the Prince of Peace. Would the One who allowed Himself to be crucified—and yes, forgave His crucifiers—push that nuclear button? Remember that the grave was not His goal. No grave could hold His Spirit. He rose that we may live. "Follow me!" the risen Lord commanded . . . and haltingly, inconsistently, we stumble to obey. He forgives, and by the grace of Almighty God we stumble on . . . and will until the glory of His being fills the earth as the waters fill the sea.

It was. It had to be Chaplain Marcus Bradford. The voice, the words, the emotions the man lent to his message could belong to none other. Marvel's head jerked upward and instant confirmation came. Older, of course—older but still arrow-straight and in his gold-braided uniform. Joy flooded her body. The years between melted away, and within her a voice longed to call: "Yes, we can go home!"

In a need to see a familiar face, to share the recognition, she glanced at those seated nearby. It was futile, of course. The years *had* passed. And then, caught by the loveliness of sun streaming through the cranberry-colored section of a stained-glass window, she saw the words which erased all joy from her heart. Smith...In Loving Memory and she could read no further. Escape, she *must* escape—*now*! Stifling a groan, she edged silently toward the back exit.

What caused her to look back? That, Marvel Harrington would never know. She knew only that all reason had drained from her being. For there, in the front row, sat—oh no, it couldn't be—it could *not* be Titus. Why, then, did the expressive gray eyes lock with her blue ones and gradually, ever so gradually, turn from gray to black? Titus...Titus, *here*—and in the same type uniform as that worn by the speaker? Her overworked mind was playing tricks in déjà vu.

Grandfather was right. Only it was not the aunt who would be committed. It was his granddaughter. Outside, Marvel ran breathlessly, not stopping until she reached the safety of Grandfather's inherited ancient limousine.

* * *

The day went quickly in a pilgrimage of the past blended with plans for the future. Grandfather polished family traditions until their shine rivaled that of his treasured gold watch. Never mind the prickly pain of the years. Search out the sweet berries of togetherness. Carry on in true Harrington heritage. "And that's an order!" he said, holding the family Bible in one hand and his reminding cane in the other.

"Did anyone get home with a program?" Marvel asked repeatedly. Nobody did. And nobody showed interest. The men engaged in talk of political debates, banking business, and the upsweep in world economy—dodging all talk of war. Aunt Eleanore napped, and other lady members of the first and second generations mingled their loves of music, recipes, families, and the church. Yet in all the confusion, a calm reigned in the kitchen. Tables bloomed with traditional foods, armloads of lilies, baskets of brilliantly painted eggs, and waxed flickering of candles on polished silver.

The telephone rang repeatedly, mostly for Mary Ann. Bright-eyed and glowing, she had tried to say something to Marvel as the two of them spread the handed-down (but still snowy) hemstitched tablecloths and brought out the holiday china. "Oh, I *told* you it would happen . . . I knew. How did you feel? Could you *believe* . . . ?" and such broken phrases were all she could manage. Then it was Jake calling again.

Outside, birds continued the symphony Mother had begun at the worship in song, not seeming to mind the competitive *dribble-bounce* of the third-generation Harrington men's basketball. "It's no challenge reaching that hoop now," Thomas complained."They've lowered it—maybe for Monica, s'pose?" "Nope!" B.J. said, "*We've* lowered it—grownup, you know. As for Monica, she might break a fingernail." B.J. told his cousin about baseball then . . . Uncle Dale's game. Yep, been around since the 1800's . . . an American heritage . . . belonged to the people, this family *especially* . . . a part of a book they were writing. "We're *legend*!"

Through the maze of her own thinking, Marvel noted with satisfaction that the two boys were forming a bond. Thomas would need the security of family love and loyalty, having lost the older brother, his idol, and now perhaps losing his mother as well. "Oh super! we'll be in the same grade. And I want to try out for your team, Billy Joe!" "*My* team—yeah, I reckon so. And how about tomorrow for school and organizin' the team? You help me get squared away." "And I can be on the team, sure enough, Billy Joe?" "If you'll call me B.J.!"

Marvel smiled. Wouldn't Cindy and Monica be pleased? All other efforts to draw the cousins into the conversation had failed.But no, they were busy, they said. Both had plans of their own as soon as this "tiresome" dinner was finished. When could they use the phone?

"Right now!" Mary Ann answered for herself. "Oh Marvel, you'll help me, won't you? Jakes's found a place—got me enrolled for tomorrow. I'll be in touch, and you tell me *everything*. Oh, how proud you must be of him—sooooo handsome and so, so, so *so-so*— Oh, help me—have to be on that train *tonight*!"

Nothing she said made sense. But nothing was making sense to Marvel. Except that Mary Ann must leave sooner than planned —or did that make sense either? And what was her cousin trying to tell her—the coded message about *him*? Him *who*? *Titus?* The very thought set her pulse pounding, and then there was no pulse at all. Titus lived in memory only . . . *in memory* and in déjà vu on stained glass.

It did not occur to Marvel Harrington, torn apart as she was emotionally at that time, that Mary Ann was unaware of her quick exit from the church. And they could not share a common memory in the remainder of the Easter miracle.

* * *

Mr. Corey himself answered Marvel's early Monday-morning call.

"Ah, Marvel!" he said with a lilt in his voice. "So you have the ending for that book. Good girl."

"No—no, sir, I don't. Nothing comes out right."

It came as no surprise that the editor would be disappointed. And disappointed he was. The telephone lines echoed with his sigh.

She owed him an explanation. But how could she explain this wavering uncertainty inside her? There could be no happy ending—no ending at all until the writer knew. Perhaps the book should be scrapped?

"Nonsense," he scoffed. "Anyone as young, as gifted, as inspiring as you can't find life this complicated—this uncooperative. What's troubling the guy?"

"Who?"

"You know who—your hero, the man you built your life around."

"My life?" Marvel gasped, suddenly afraid of being found out. "You mean my book? That part's—uh, fiction. I mean, it's a novel—"

A. Thomas Corey mumbled something Marvel was unable to hear. It sounded suspiciously like "Who're ya tryin' t'fool?" But aloud, he sounded encouraged and excited. "No problem then. Novels can be changed in a twinklin'—like lives. Our job's to blue-pencil the downbeat, edit the mistakes. There's been enough sadness. Give 'em what they'll go for—true or not true. Give 'em happy. It'll work out. I can edit, but I can't write your life story—I mean, your character's. And besides," (he was mumbling again) "my lips are sealed—but *match* it."

"But—but it wouldn't be true. Oh, what do you mean, *match*?"

"For goodness sake, honey. I thought the blame thing was a novel!"

Marvel hung up in confusion, unable to distinguish between

fact and fiction anymore. She would search for an answer, she promised—meaning it literally. Her search would start this day.

And start it did—with some startling results.

* * *

Dale Harrington had waited long enough. "Three days here, and the old home place waiting for us. Ready, honey?" he asked Marvel. Ready? No—not really. But Mother was waiting, as was Grandfather. And what's this? Grandmother, too? But guests were due at the hotel . . . a matter the hosts waved away airily. Uncle Worth and Auntie Rae would handle it all—sort of prepare them for taking over. Taking over? It was all happening so fast. Not for the senior Harringtons, it seemed. They had had years to think this whole thing through. Son Worth was a natural with all his banking experience. Of course, he would be spending time at Harrington & Sons, but as (*ahem!*) an executive. And that wife of his was right handy, having mastered the art of keeping a proper house and cooking for the multitudes at the orphanage. Always frugal, that one . . . had to be—scrubbing floors, washing windows, pruning roses—and she could learn about hollyhocks. And certainly she knew nourishing foods!

The rolling green countryside stretched before them briefly —too briefly. Marvel needed to see something familiar, a solid anchor. The entire scene might well have been one of the wartime structures hit with the force of an iron ball swung from a wrecking machine, demolishing old and overworked places and replacing them with the new. Was life to be like this for her, only in reverse? A destruction of all the beautiful yesterdays and ushering in of an unfamiliar present, untempered by time? The land seemed to be watching her (accusing, welcoming, or simply awaiting her reaction?). Grandmother! *Grandmother* (still talking about plans for Uncle Worth's family and ignoring her daughter's) was watching—not the land. Marvel swallowed hard and tried to smile.

Moments later they were home—or where home used to be. The persimmons were gone, as were the giant oaks that bordered the bottomlands, standing guard like bearded prophets. No houses anywhere.

"Coming home's always a jolt, isn't it just?" Leah Harrington asked nobody in general. "The Squire and I now, we're different.

We've been here through thick and thin, watched it all happen gradual-like. It's hard telling it all on paper—like describing an old Western movie. Who could make listeners hear the gunfire?"

"It's beautiful—so beautiful!" Mother was clapping her hands in glee. "Our own house—a real home soon. Oh, dreams *do* come true!"

"Yes, my pet, of course they do," Grandmother answered, but Marvel sensed that the words were addressed to her. "Dreams come true when we let them—maybe even help 'em a smitch. Not saying we ought to let go of the past—just hold onto it like pictures in the family album, you know? There's got to be changes, but my, my! Sometimes the most shriveled-prune babies plump into real beauties."

Later, Marvel promised herself, she would dissect the words, examine them one by one. Surely, there was a way to bring together joyful yesterdays and joyful todays. Like love, they must not be put asunder. But now was no time for thinking. There was too much background noise: laughter, voices, and the rattle of papers. For Grandfather had with him the ancient blueprint of the original Harrington home!

Now Daddy was as excited as Mother. "Oh, what a treasure, Father!"

"Ummmm," Alexander Jay Harrington said, without attempting to hide displeasure. "Lots you didn't know about. Well, shall we say *buried* treasure? I never took a shine to my son's being a farmer, you know, but I hung onto the map. Lots of space, choice of sites." His cane swept over the carpeted green vast acreage of natural pastureland.

"Fanny—the Bumsteads—Morning Glory Chapel?" Marvel began.

Gone, all gone, he explained. Fanny's family felt the pull of home, too—"'way down South in Dixie." "Cap" Bumstead, like all other neighbors, sold out to oil companies. The Harringtons were different: "an island of green surrounded by a sea of oil." So be it. They had better sense—and anybody with the sense God promised a goose could figure out a map of Eden. Why, every animal would need grassland for grazing. But drilling for oil? To bring in money, the root of all evil?

"Well said, Father. But money's right handy," Daddy chuckled. "I think it's when we make money an idol that God has to become an iconoclast. As to site, let's use the original. It'll be the same but different—I mean a restoration of the state I hardly remember."

"Oh, but *I* remember! You can depend on me. I'll be underfoot."

Daddy winked at Marvel, his face shining. There was so much to be done, but he would love every minute. Wasn't this their dream? Something stirred within her then—neither the old joy nor the recent pain. Just a kind of peace at knowing her dreams would be fulfilled—in part. She had honored her father and mother. And now they were like happy children "knee-deep in daisies and head-over-heels in love." Ready to start a new life.

Right now Grandfather was pacing off dimensions of the great house-to-be, taking yard-long steps—without aid of his cane! Daddy was penciling the map with figures. Mother and Grandmother followed close behind talking flowers. "Gardenias and poinsettias grow like stinging nettles in California. But oh, Mother, they can't hold a light to our white violets, black-eyed Susans—and just wait until you see all the bulbs and seed I brought back. No need ordering from those catalogs. Ummm... those purple carpets of bluebonnets."

On and on they talked. Hollyhocks, there must be hollyhocks—and a wide lawn. Digging out Bermuda grass was like shaking somebody loose from his hair, but they'd do it. They'd cheat a little, Grandmother conspired. She'd plant flats of annuals, transplant after the house went up...a "cheater's garden." Who cared? They'd be together.

Grandfather stopped suddenly. "Marvel," he called over his shoulder, "you asked about the little church. All the chapels were our missionary projects—remember? Not many members stayed put—sold out, you know." (He stopped to mop his brow with an initialed handkerchief.) "But the few congregations united with Pleasant Knoll First Baptist. Say now, wasn't that Culverville church something to behold? No wonder the donor came back for the dedication—same party who had the old Smith Hotel refurbished. Have you seen the place yet? It's ancient—been there a coon's age."

Marvel stopped walking, stopped breathing. Coon's age? She was the coon's predator...a coon hound, seeking out a trail... sniffing, baying...then frozen immobile...unable to move, to think. *The donor?*

"Who?" she managed through stiff lips. But Grandfather didn't hear.

"Never dreamed Frederick Salsburg had such assets in property and money—or could be so benevolent."

"Uncle Fred—what did he have to do with—with—*what?*" This time Marvel's voice was louder, although her words made little sense.

Grandfather's mind had gone back to the Harrington acres. "Smart of you, son, holding out for the land. If you're still bent on cattle, we may want to accept an offer from the Armstrong brothers. Want to swap a gigantic herd of registered whitefaces for a loan. They're setting up a big business, so if you would be interested—?"

Yes, Daddy would. Wouldn't Marvel? His blue eyes were wide and luminous with excitement. Yes—yes, of course, his daughter agreed, meaning it. But all the while her heart was praying, *Please—please let my grandfather get back to me.* With head throbbing, she tried in vain to divert the conversation. But Mother and Grandmother's voices were buzzing in her ears. They must get to the nursery, check out availability of the native sweet gum trees—big ones so they'd color up this very fall. Couldn't "cheat" on trees. And later an orchard. Tomorrow—there just wouldn't be time left in this day, they said regretfully.

No time. She must find a way to interrupt—just *must.*

Grandfather may have noted her silence. His eyes worked like newly sharpened pencils. "Sorry, sweetheart," he said. "We men got caught up in arithmetic. It can wait. I've got the original bank notes, loan agreements, and such in my folder back at the hotel. Always keep extra copies. So we'll talk at home, Dale. Let's see, you asked about Frederick. Let's think—" And he was doing mental arithmetic again. "Holy cats! What *didn't* he own? Seems he's served in the First World War with this—uh man, army buddy, some relative of one of the Smiths. Of course, there are so many Smiths—it's a common name. This one wasn't related to the others—fact is, the name wasn't the same."

Winded, Alexander Harrington paused to mop his brow again. "Ah yes, it comes back," he said, taking coveted time to fold and crease the handkerchief before replacing it. "T. Lee—odd name."

Confusion replaced the sense of peace. Wasn't the name vaguely familiar?

Auntie Rae had sliced apples and popcorn, waiting. Everything looked peaceful and happy—except her eyes. There was anxiety in the glances at Marvel, as if a message of desperate urgency waited. But who could deliver words unrelated to Harrington holdings "out yonder" or "hereabouts"? Beautiful day ... marvelous day ... dogwood in bloom on the farm ... and guests taken care of at the hotel. "Everything went fine—the bank treated me royally, Father. Want to see Dale, too," Uncle Worth hurried to say. "No problems with fixing meals or settling guests. This woman of mine put me working, even peelin' more spuds than a tub would hold. Something *scalloped* with ham! You'll get a sample if B.J. and Thomas left any. But, oh, that phone!"

"It rings constantly," Grandmother laughed. "Get used to that. And it'll get worse, with all of you home. Wait'll news spreads you're safe. I'm spreading the news that you survived, after all. The church will put you—all of us—right to work. Then that friend of Jake's wants to see you, Marvel. You'll just have to see how nice that new garage is. He's single and sure to be singlin' *you* out. But he's got some competition, I'm guessing—another interested party."

Auntie Rae waited for her mother-in-law to finish. She must never "butt in." "Marvel," she said softly then, "you're to call the number there on the hall table. It's important. He *must* have your answer."

Mr. Corey, of course. Well, she couldn't give him his answer. The book could not end until everything was wedded seamlessly—actuality and dreams....

19

Captured in Infinity

Windows were open wide to let the before-dawn breeze come in. The forsythia graced walls of the shadowy hotel with gold, like a sunrise before its time. If Marvel had hoped for privacy, she was doomed for disappointment. The family and guests were assembled at one long table in what, hopefully, would be a one-call breakfast.

Soft prayers ... sharp shrills of the telephone ... muffled conversations ... and then, one by one, diners drifted away. The two guests remained—nobody Marvel knew or cared to. One was fat, had no neck visible above his tight collar, and a regulation Marine haircut. His dark suit was new enough to make him squirm. The other was a pale blonde with an equally pale face, probably a 4-F during the war. But his suit was black like his partner's. She failed to catch their names.

"Good luck, their showing up," Grandfather announced. "Would you believe these fellows are contractors—sort of architects, in fact?"

No, she wouldn't. The two looked more like morticians. But Grandfather was a good judge or character. Let him take them along in search of materials while Mother and Grandmother searched the nursery. She, too, wanted to go into the county seat—but alone. Her search was private.

B.J. left early, wishing to get in some baseball practice before school commenced. But shouldn't Marvel be with the family as they made choices? No, Grandmother said on her behalf. Marvel needed time for writing and (significantly) returning phone calls. Marvel nodded, planning on neither. Her only call would be concerning the bus schedule.

Moments after their departure, she hurried past the flower garden, so filled with daisies, petunias, marigolds, and snapdragons it was almost comical. And there were more to come. Every square inch would fill up with new life. Renewal . . . survival . . . faith in tomorrow.

Marvel's tomorrows were filled with Titus. Everything was a part of him—so much a part that she'd taken to wearing blue almost exclusively. "My beautiful lady in blue" Titus had called her, saying she made him ten feet tall when she turned those *Marvel*ous-blue eyes on him. Today's dress was old, but the blue was unfaded, as she hoped her eyes would be. For they must recapture the past—and they would. They had held onto one another throughout the years—held tightly, as if they were afraid. Yet somehow they lost one another—temporarily. But— and her excitement mounted, as the bus swept along the paved distance—they would find each other. Perhaps this very day, she dreamed on.

Culverville, like Pleasant Knoll, was vaguely familiar—but changed like the pictures in Grandmother's album. The cemetery she had originally planned to check was there. But the Veterans' Memorial Cemetery was new. It bloomed with American flags and white poppies. The bandstand remained as a reminder of the free concerts beneath the stars. And, as promised, there where the silent movies used to beckon they beckoned again in hearttugging nostalgia. With its renewed grandeur, the new theater was truly a palace. "An acre of seats in a garden of dreams," Grandmother had called it. Marvel felt numbed, asleep, unseeing.

But she was wide awake when the bus pulled up to the curb in front of the high school—or where the school once stood. A new one was in the making. And their tree—oh, their tree of life was gone!

Tears blinded her—tears she blinked back. As her vision cleared, she saw that, although the giant oak had succumbed to the weight of its years or fallen prey to the teeth of a saw, the enormous log body remained. Sadly, she sat down on the cherished trunk, letting her fingers slide over the textured bark, remembering how she and Titus had measured the seasons of their love by its rough surface—nourishing the leafy green of spring, whispering soft warnings when others intruded. Then, in autumn, it burned in a burnished gold. The great trunk, lying like a stricken giant, stretched motionless—awaiting death. And then came the startling realization that, shattered as the old oak's base might be, a miracle was unfolding. It was not dead. It was still breathing. I had to be, for the trunk continued to nourish the many unremoved branches that reached out hopefully with leaves still crisp and green. And there on the prostrate tree, Marvel felt a lifting of the spirit, a brightening of the already-bright day. She seemed to sit in a charmed circle of certainty where nothing unpleasant could happen. Even in this world of hazards, God protected His children with legions of angels.

Marvel closed her eyes and lifted her heard heavenward, letting fingers of the warm sun stroke her face. Behind her closed eyelids, Marvel saw a shadow pass fleetingly, like a windblown leaf freed from the parent trunk—visible then gone. Startled, she blinked, then lifted a hand to shield her eyes against the blinding surroundings.

"Don't move—you're the picture, my talisman!"

The deep voice, so soft, so gentle—just as she'd remembered.

"Titus!"

"Marvel—my *Marvelous*!"

Who spoke first? Neither of them would remember—ever. They were together. He loved her...she loved him. The air sparkled with the undiluted intensity of pure joy. They had been on a long, lonely journey. But the tortuous odyssey was over. They were home. *This was no dream.*

"Titus?" A question, half fear, half wonder.

"Yes, my darling—your Titus."

She had forgotten how gentle that beloved voice could be. Its gentleness loosed something sharp in her chest. She had forgotten, too, over these long years that it hurts to love. Love, so beautiful, so perfect—like her cherished pearls—could bring the release of tears.

Titus eased his remembered height onto the trunk of their oak then, carefully, as if she were made of spun glass, he helped her shift positions so that they sat on the grass, leaning against the log. The bark was rough—a matter he took care of by folding his light sweater to cushion her back.

When he placed a protective arm about her shoulders, Marvel felt shielded from the world. They were alone again on their glass hill. Why then was she crying? "Oh Titus—Titus, all those years—wasted."

"They weren't wasted, my darling. They served a purpose."

His arm tightened, and tenderly he drew her head against the warmth of his wide shoulders. There she nestled against his chest like a child. The tears kept falling. She wept for the years of waiting, the uncertainties which still lingered but no longer mattered, and for the misunderstandings—irretrievably lost. Could she ever make amends? And then she cried for the joy of reunion.

"Oh Titus—I—I wanted to be beautiful," she sobbed.

Titus' laughter was low, intimate. "You *are* beautiful," he murmured huskily. "More beautiful than ever. I've never seen you cry, Miss Marvel Harrington. It's all right to cry." And there were tears in his voice as he blotted her cheeks with a handkerchief.

When she began to tremble, Titus pressed his cheek against her gold hair where, he used to say, sunbeams like to hide. He murmured words of consolation, words she would never remember—except that they took the edge off her pain. Then, tilting her chin, he brushed his lips against her wet eyelids, her damp forehead, her tear-smeared cheeks, her hair again.

Marvel, curled up like a kitten against his chest, never knew at what point she was all cried out, or when they began saying a million "I love you's" to each other.

"Oh Titus—Titus. God forgive me, I was afraid it was all over—" she said, her voice still trembling.

"Over?" he said, and his laughter was a whoop of joy. "No, my precious. It's not over. Like the old song says, 'It's only just begun'!"

Marvel sighed deeply, contentedly. She dared not trust her voice. And there was no need for talk—not now. Everything had been said—everything that mattered. A sacred silence fell between them.

The two of them talked then—talked for what must have been two hours. And the bloom of youth was back. There was so much to say, so many questions to ask—probing deeply into the past. But not now. It could wait. And so they spoke of trivial matters of their shared past: old times, old friends, the things they had enjoyed together—and those which they had missed. Both spoke with candor. They had always been able to talk without hesitation, and the same feeling remained. There were no with-drawals, no denials, and if there were bombshells to drop, they could wait.

"You've lost that down-home accent," he teased. "But *you* haven't changed. But then I never expected you to go Holly-wood."

"Never. And the accent will come back—like the past. It's there."

"Just stay the way you are—the way we were, the way we will be forever. We've a big assignment to do, you know, Marvel *Smith!*"

"Oh Titus, how can I talk when you say such things?"

"*Don't* talk. Just turn those big Marvelous-blues up here to me—yes, just the way they were in that snapshot—that look of expectancy. Oh, now how can *I* talk?"

Silence again. Then it was broken by Titus. "Just tell me one thing—why you left the dedication ceremony. I couldn't follow. You know why. But my heart followed. It was meaningless with-out you, *us.*"

His groan made her heart ache even more. "But the window," she whispered, wishing they could have postponed the ques-tions.

Absently, he was stroking her hair again. "I don't understand," he began in a faraway voice. For the first time Marvel realized how tired he sounded. "Keep your head there, darling—stay close," he said anxiously when she would have lifted her eyes to study the lines of fatigue she knew would be there. "I can't risk losing you again—nothing on this green earth can keep us apart, short of God's will. *Nothing!*" he repeated, this time fiercely. "No matter what happens, I'll love you always—remember that." His cheek pressed harder against her head as if to hold her captive. "Ummm, still feels like polished oak."

Marvel was unable to think of her hair—just about his words. *No matter what happens.* What could possibly happen now?

A little frightened, she snuggled closer. "The window?"

Titus reached for her hand with his free one and gently began to stroke each finger as if counting off the years of separation. "Oh," he said at last, "the memorial to my family. You saw 'Smith' and *ran!* I understand. For my family, yes. My mother who died when I was born, the father I never had a chance to know, my sister who sacrificed her life for my upbringing. You knew Lucille was dead, too—that I'm the last of the clan?"

Yes, she knew—or suspected. Her letters had come back marked "Not At This Address." There had been no opportunity to check, but—

"We'll visit the cemeteries," she said softly, brushing away the niggling dragons of doubt that threatened this otherwise flawless reunion. "This moment belongs to us—these *hours*, I mean," she went on. "It's a time for the living—not for the dead."

It hadn't come out right, and Marvel regretted the words. Somehow the conversation went back to the dead in spite of resolutions they had made. Marvel remembered Frederick Salsburg's friendship with Lucille's husband? Yes, Titus had mentioned that, as had her grandfather she recalled now but made no comment. It was because of her step-uncle, Titus told her then, that his sister all but lost the Smith farm—not that it was of any value, until the oil boom. And then? Marvel questioned. Unbelievable, Titus said—another miracle.

"The same man gave the land back, forgave the mortgage—all because of *you*! He never told us about the will. Then you—"

"Me? I don't understand."

"Neither did I until I heard the story of the deathbed scene, your being there when your uncle—step-uncle—passed on. Your grandmother told me. I guess you told Frederick Salsburg about *us*—"

Marvel shifted her position, shook her head slightly as if to to clear the memory—or wipe it out. "That was a long time ago, but yes, I remember confiding in him. But you mentioned my grandmother. How—?"

"How did I know the wonderful lady? Oh, we've been in touch for, I guess I've forgotten how long—even grieved together when we both thought we'd lost you. Oh Marvel, there's so much to talk about. It's all been so long in happening and yet so slow. I—I feel as if I'd been underwater long enough to drown and I'm just coming up for air."

She understood. Being with Titus had restored the vital juices of life, love, and purpose within her own veins. She was vibrant, renewed—in love with the same man, *completely* in love, consumed, possessed. Love, like tears, had been too long withheld. Yes, she understood Titus' reaction to their meeting now after all these years. Two people in love, knowing each thought, each gesture—total commitment to *total strangers*. For the years *had* happened. Something in his tone of voice had frightened her—leading Marvel to sense uncertainty.

Should she be cautious? Life could fall into a new perspective. Suddenly their world spun off-center. Where was the boldness Marvel Harrington had planned? The surety that nothing could change?

"Maybe—maybe we should give ourselves time," she murmured, "instead of trying to swallow everything in one big gulp."

It sounded so logical, safe, sound—to her ears if not her heart. It was in need of punctuation, of course. And so she tried to pull her hand from his, but he held on. In fact, his grip tightened.

"Give me the other one," Titus said softly. Marvel obeyed. He squeezed it hard, then touched the ring finger reverently. "Here I want to put our symbol of love—my mother's wedding ring. A pearl. I wanted to tell you, but hoped you'd be wearing your pearls somehow."

"Oh Titus," she breathed, all misgivings washed away suddenly. "I would have, only I didn't know. Not for sure. I kept praying—"

"Just as I did—yes, praying and calling the hotel, without leaving my name. Why? Silly of me, sentimental. But you know I love to surprise you!"

Titus was back, no longer a stranger. Life was out in the open again. Marvel snuggled closer. "No more words. We've a lifetime to talk."

Silence closed in, broken only when his arms closed around her shoulders as his hands clasped prayerfully beside his half-hidden countenance. Sighing deeply, he released her with deliberate effort. Silence again, only now it was changed, charged. She had seen his life story etched in new lines on the dearly remembered face, the desperate dedication touched by loss—triumph mingled with failure. Her lips parted in question, which he silenced gently with a touch of his forefinger to her lips. Their eyes locked, and the expression there was astounding, revealing. Once gray shading to black with feeling, they were now leaping with fire. Hazel, Marvel thought dazedly, hazel-*tiger*. "'Tigers'—wasn't that the name of your team?" she whispered from beneath the slight pressure of his finger. Titus confirmed the question, promised thickly they'd see a practice game soon, then lowered her head to his shoulder. The game no longer mattered since she had identified the expression in his eyes. It was, she remembered happily, the look of victory after his football team had won.

The slant of the sun shifted downward, and Marvel's stomach gave a warning growl. How could she feel embarrassed when

Titus was apologizing profusely, berating himself for neglect? Saying he could have, *should* have taken her to the Smith Hotel. He wanted her to see it...all refurbished. Naturally, he was staying there while in town for the dedication—and to find her.

Naturally—yes, it *would* be natural to stay at the hotel. But "while in town"? Did he mean temporarily? Titus gave her no opportunity to ask. "I have a decent car now," he was laughing, "one that doesn't backfire—one that has better manners and can't honk us apart. It's at the hotel. I walked—part of my required daily dozen. We can see the sights together going back for the car. I'll take you home later."

"No," Marvel protested quickly. "I have my bus ticket to Pleasant Knoll."

"Oh darling, we don't have to pinch pennies," he laughed.

"I do, though. Pinch pennies, I mean. Not that I mind *giving*. In a way, I guess, I've given my life away to my family, the church, the needy—and most of all to God. I don't mean to sound pious."

"I know. I know because we're alike. We belong together."

"Oh Titus, there's plenty of me saved for *you*—my heart!"

"I know," he said again. "You must feel all used up, and wonder if you gave too much of yourself to life. And now you want to wake up again, let that person inside you escape and live. We will!"

Marvel's heart took up its song again. Titus understood because he was speaking about himself, his feelings. Then he said *we*. Of course, it was *we*. They were engaged and, thank God, *together*—ready to restore, to rebuild, to fulfill their dreams.

"'We can. We *will*. We MUST'" she sang out.

Her mood was contagious. "Amen! 'We have nothing to fear but fear!'" Titus answered their mutually loved late president's quote with another, as he helped her to her feet. They stood facing each other, hands entwined. He leaned toward her slightly. She waited breathlessly.

And then their privacy was invaded by a curious mockingbird perching on the new-growth leaves. The feathered intruder was so much a part of the scene, the two stood mesmerized, feeling that the winged creature belonged within their Eden. The bird twittered as if tuning his vocal instrument, the way Mother prepared for a violin solo. Two notes...three...eight...and then no longer afraid or self-conscious, the mockingbird burst into a full-throated tribute to a magnificent sunset in the bluebonnet state.

She must hurry to catch the last bus, but not before making arrangements to meet Titus again tomorrow. Come for her? No, later—when the time was right. Just now he was her secret—*please*. Titus did not push her. "But I'm old-fashioned," he whispered at the bus stop, "so I'll want to ask for your hand—never mind your maturity. Then you *will* wear the ring," he urged, "after I speak to your father?"

"With pride!" she smiled tremulously as the door swing open.

Then, blowing a little fingertip kiss, she boarded the bus with a pounding heart. When the bus rounded the corner, Marvel glanced back. Titus stood where she had left him. Hands cupped to his mouth, he had taken up the mockingbird's song. Even from a distance, she read his lips: "Oh, the beautiful lady in blue."

In her state of euphoria, it did not occur to Marvel Harrington to question the why of Titus Smith's wearing a full-dress uniform at the dedication, or any of the other whys of their yesterdays . . . his secrets or her own. For she had revealed nothing. The two of them had talked about everything—and nothing at all. So ended a perfect day.

* * *

Excitement had reached a feverish pitch in the household when Marvel returned—a sort of hysterical zest. The family, carried away with successes of the day, drew her into the in-progress conversation as if she had been along. Oh, the flowers. Oh, the trees. Oh, the everything: seed, fertilizer . . . herd of cattle . . . grain and hay . . . fencing! But most of all, the enthusiastic planning for the replica of the rambling mansion! Wasn't it wonderful, Marvel?

Yes, it *was* wonderful. Never mind the long, hard labor of building, the maintenance and repair afterward: leaking gutters, roofs needing replacing. For now, life for them was a garden, as it was with her. A *talking* garden proclaiming: "We went, we saw, we conquered." Or: "We're surviving, we're thriving, 'We're drinking from a fountain that never shall run dry—for we are dwelling in Beulah Land!'"

"Oh Daddy!" Marvel, caught up in their exuberance now, exclaimed. "I've thought of the most wonderful name for the new house."

"*Our* new house, sweetheart," Daddy whispered softly from where he stood looking at tentative sketches the new residents of the hotel had drawn. "Certainly, you'll be paying—*have* paid." Then, lifting a new book on agriculture, he pounded on the dining room table for attention. "If I'd had a cowbell, I'd have rung it. Marvel has something to say! Every new house deserves a name, agreed?

"Beulah Land might be nice for our *Paradise regained*—"

Beautiful, beautiful, they said in one voice, then went on with their planning. They would close out the deal on the cattle tomorrow morning, unless Marvel wished to look over the herd? They would take a final look at the Harrington homestead in the afternoon, before actual building commenced. Unless Marvel wanted to put her stamp of approval on it all? But the new men were doing an excellent job. And Marvel supposed they were. Impressions were fragile creatures, colored by moods. "Judge not, that you be not judged," Jesus had cautioned. But last night there had been a mote in her eye, and she was easily contaminated by fear—fear that she would not find Titus. The two young men were imposters, losers who lived in some slum, supporting themselves and the mangy hound (who was chained to the caterpillar-tented chinaberry tree) by robbing the blind—including her seeing-eye grandfather.

Today the beam was plucked from her eye, and the world and all that was in it were beautiful, reborn. The Bible made it abundantly clear for the seeing (and Marvel could *see* now!) that there is no fear in love. And she had found love—her love, *Titus*! Even the young men at the table looked cleaner, more intelligent. Already, as the others cleared the table, Samuel Cox and Herman were paying three-months' rent in advance, not with counterfeit bills but a check on Harrington & Sons, Inc.

Forgive me, Lord, her heart whispered, as she rose to help Auntie Rae shuck the first-of-season Golden Bantum sweet corn. Mother and Grandmother hurried in to join them, both still talking flowers and native-to-the land sweet gum trees (listed in catalogs as "Liquid Amber" because of their polished variables in yellow-orange and scarlet tones in autumn). Only one regret tugged at Marvel's senses: a secret desire to share the biblical origin of the home's name. Isaiah, the prophet:

> Thou shalt no more be termed Forsaken; neither
> shall thy land any more be termed Desolate...and
> thy land [shall be] Beulah; for the Lord delighteth in

thee, and they land shall be married. For as a young man marrieth a virgin . . . so shall thy God rejoice over thee.

"Beulah" translated to "marriage"—marriage to Titus . . . marriage to the land . . . their pledge . . . their promise . . . a part of their vows.

B.J. burst in, his face red from running, hated black curls plastered to the round forehead. "Just in time—in time for reservations! Both for those roastin' ears. Save me a peck of butter—and ought I don a face mask for this? I—we—Thomas and the other guys want some land out yonder, like for baseball, Uncle Dale—because you're elected unanimously as manager. Oh, and some room here, too—in back of the hotel. *Please*, Grandfather, we want Harrington & Sons bank to be our sponsor—and the Baptist church to be our spiritual sponsor!"

Alexander Jay Harrington's chest expanded in girth. "And just who'll be the *spanker*?" he asked matter-of-factly. And his blue, blue eyes locked in obvious pride with those of his two sons.

Their dreams were coming true. All were back to the heartland.

Auntie Rae interrupted Marvel's thoughts to whisper: "You took care of the phone calls, honey? I don't want to meddle—but you did?"

"You never meddle," Marvel assured Mary Ann's mother. "And yes, I responded," she added vaguely.

Auntie Rae looked as if she wanted to say more, but she was not one to press. And Marvel did not want to be be pressed. As soon as the evening's meal ended, she planned to disappear. Nobody would miss her.

Mr. Corey was waiting for her to return his call. Surely by now Marvel Harrington would have the ending for the book. Yes, waiting.

But although she paused at the telephone, Marvel Harrington did not call. Something held her back.

That night she stretched luxuriously, had a long talk with God, then, exhausted, prepared for a night of wonderful dreams. Sleep overtook her immediately. And the dreams were beautiful—at first. The rolling grasslands reached into foreverness, freshened by last night's rain. Skies flamed red-orange with sunrise . . . opening white-petaled lashes of snoozing daisies, alerting a

million honeybees to gossip and sample the hidden sweetness
... lowing cattle, unbothered by hammer and saw of building,
nibbled contentedly. Soon Titus would join her, see the beauty of
the Harrington dream-come-true.

Titus came. Above the drone of the bees and rustlings of sky-
brushing trees, she heard the purring of the new car. All chrome
and glass, it glinted with sunlight as Marvel's heart went out to
meet it. Then the dream turned ugly, frightening. Magnified by
the sun's glow, the oval headlights elongated like those of a
heavily lidded animal—a man-eating tiger, those amber eyes
fixed on her: its prey. Raising its forepaws, the beast prepared to
spring. And she could not move.

Marvel awoke with a scream. Her body and bedding were
sweat-soaked, and she was exhausted. She staggered to the
bathroom and, in the half-light of early day, stepped into the
shower. Turning her face to the nozzle, she welcomed the pain of
its full force. What horror water failed to wash away, the brutal
toweling would blot out. Already her mind was clearing, but not
glowing like the angry pink of her skin.

Only a dream, others would tell her undoubtedly, in need of no
interpretation. Perhaps. At that moment, however, the dream
was significant—a warning. Today she and Titus must dig into
their past....

They didn't, of course. Early though she was, Titus was waiting for her at their fallen tree. Both of them ran, hands outstretched in greeting, laughing in the sheer joy of being together.

"Have you had breakfast, darling?" Titus questioned eagerly.

"Well, no," Marvel admitted breathlessly. "There wasn't time—"

Wonderful, Titus said, and then went on to sketch out their
day. Breakfast at the Smith Hotel. Oh, she must see the old
place—theirs! Then they would stroll leisurely up and down the
old streets, note the changes, particularly at the church. So
many memories stored there.

"Our past," he said gently. "And then our future."

"Yes," she murmured, the dream having faded into the shining
vision of unexplored horizons. Tonight she would call Editor
Corey.

The hotel was as she remembered: old and new, so that the
rambling building looked unchanged. Rocking chairs remained
on the honeysuckle-shielded porch, vines' heady sweetness
mingling with fresh coffee. Titus seated her at the farthest table

from the door in a shadowy corner. "I'm glad you wore blue again—our color, our 'something blue'." And the way he said it was like a vow. "Someday I want to go back to the beginning of our *once-upon-a-time*, but not now—except that I wonder if that holds a special meaning to you, too?"

His eyes probed hers, as if expecting a certain answer. Just what—if anything—she was not sure. "Everything we did had special meaning, Titus," she whispered truthfully, then blushed as he squeezed her hand.

Their meal over, Titus and Marvel, with hands joined, strolled the streets, pointing here and there, remembering together—two truant children, guilty and deliriously happy, borrowed from tomorrow's world.

"Beautiful, isn't it?" Titus said as they paused at the church entrance. "I marched down that aisle alone once, then said good-bye on these steps. Never again—no matter what happens. Promise?"

"I promise. I promised a long time ago. Nothing's going to happen."

Titus stumbled but righted himself immediately. "Sorry. Guess I'm in too big a rush to show you something." And with that he pulled her toward the back of the enlarged building. "Look!"

"Oh!" she gasped at sight of the flower-surrounded fountain. "Oh, I just never dreamed—how beautiful, and so large! My, my!"

He gripped her hand harder and harder as excitement grew with the explanation. Large, yes—and with a purpose. The fountain should be in front, passersby would say. But no, the pool below represented far more purpose than "show." A baptistry, he told her with a joyous laugh—the very water of life! Oh, wasn't it, well, *heavenly*?

Marvel nodded, too overcome to speak.

Titus led her closer to it. "Stand real still," he told her then, "and look with me." They stopped and Marvel followed his glance.

He was staring below the sparkling fountain, his eyes peering at the gently rippling pool at the base. And there n the silver surface the morning sun floated, as if captured in the depth. Time stood still.

"Oh Titus," she whispered, enraptured. "It's like God's promise, His whisper of eternity. It's like *we* are caught in that reflection—captured by His love, our love for each other and—and—"

"I know, I know, darling—and our love for others, our service." Almost unconsciously Titus had drawn closer to encircle her waist. "Hold onto the reflection with both hands—with your heart. It's like, well, a holy particle of His infinite space—belonging to *us*."

* * *

At the close of that perfect day with Titus, Marvel placed the call to the editor. The story had been graphic, starkly bleak, she said unnecessarily. For history was not always beautiful. But the fiction? Yes, she could take control of the ending. *Maybe*, she faltered uncertainly.

"You *know* you can—you—*they're* together," he said knowingly. "No more waiting, except on the part of the publisher. Give 'em hope. *Now!*"

"One can't hurry life. We're captured in infinity...."

20

Now,
Once Upon a Time

Titus called early the next morning. Grandmother Harrington summoned Marvel to the telephone, detaining her only long enough to suggest that it was high time the rest of the family met Titus Smith in the flesh. After all, he was to be one of them soon, she said adroitly. "Make it Sunday. We're having the gospel bird then!"

"Chicken," Marvel laughed, pushing past her grandmother.

"Watch it! Is that a proper greeting for a man who loves you?"

His optimism was contagious, electrifying. "Oh Titus—"

"Good idea your grandmother has. Some lady. I'm half in love with her—no need being jealous. Just shows how much I'll love you in our golden years, understand? Yes, I accept the invitation!"

Titus talked rapidly, and all the while Marvel's heart drummed as if to drown out his words. She was not to be concerned, for the two of them would talk before he asked for her hand in marriage. Fine, she tried to tell him. They had three days. No time at all, Titus responded, for he had an "appointment with destiny"— *their* destiny which would be spelled out after his trip. Trip, Titus? A hurried one . . . he would get the paperwork going, some wheels turning somewhere—ram it down somebody's throat if he had to in his eagerness to get back to her.

"My strength's back, mind clear, just in a fever to see my Marvel. I love you. Oh remember, darling 'I love you for a million different reasons—but most of all I love you 'cause you're you!'" He sang in memorized song.

"Yes, I remember. *Ditto*. Oh Titus, I love you. *Hurry* home!"

He must go now—simply must. She would receive a package Titus had mailed last night—yes, today, by Greyhound—something they had discussed.

Frustration and tenderness washed over her when the phone was silent. Two people in love waiting all these years, only to have their relationship grow silent like the telephone. Promises, promises—and now Titus was going away again, disappearing as he had done before? Something inside her shriveled. Her only emotion was anger—anger akin to hate. "We'll never be together!" she sobbed, pounding the hall table.

Having lost sight of all save the three marathon days ahead, Marvel called Editor Corey. It was no use. The ending was wrong, she said.

"You're out of your mind!" A. Thomas Corey shouted. "I had such high hopes for you, for us all—such confidence. Why, you—you're the *giver* of hope! I let it rub off on me, mailed the book on to the publisher as a surprise! He swallowed it without chewin', and now you pull this. Okay, give that blasted book a new title: *The White Flag of Surrender* and trash the thing!"

And with that, he hung up in a rage.

The man's words stung like a venomous viper. But in all due fairness, she had them coming. The Lord Himself would be frowning on the wavering uncertainty, this satanic doubt that His committed servant had allowed to enter her heart. "Forgive me, Father," she whispered, "for these childish games I've been playing with Titus, my family, the world—and (brokenly) most of all, *You*. Strengthen me. Remove fear from love."

Colors of springtime came back. The house, the world were no longer gray.

The family was jubilant when Marvel said she would be free to join them on the next trip to Beulah Land. Daddy folded her in a bear hug, face lighting with pleasure. "Today—we're going *today*. All of us!" Mother clapped, said something about a new strain of roses, and Grandfather, first wondering aloud if the bank could spare him (then mumbling a "*maybe so* with Worth there"), said he would join them. "We'll all go 'if the creek don't rise'!" Grandmother winked at Marvel. "We'll go if we have to *swim*, Squire. Take a gander at the fried chicken and deviled eggs our Rae's prepared!"

* * *

It was remarkable what the crew of men had accomplished. Grounds were broken, raked smooth, immaculate. One section blazed with roses, marigolds, and phlox... another with half-grown leafy sweet gums, still green with approaching summer but promising their autumn fire... and the mansion-like house Marvel faintly remembered was underway: stakes driven, corners squared, each room designated by heavy twine. And there, unbelievably, lay a high pile of lumber, crisscrossed to dry.

Alexander Harrington noted the puzzled look on his granddaughter's face. "The shortages? Well, it pays knowin' the right people. And wait'll you see those cows—stately, fit for us Harringtons." His sharp blue eyes studied her features then, as if she were applying for a loan. "Say, aren't you looking a pinch peaked? Small wonder—still, better have the Grand Duchess brew you a tonic, put some flesh on that frame. If those cows' bones made such a showin', no deal. Just joshing, my sweet."

"Well, I'd hope so. Mind your manners, Squire!" Grandmother ordered, then grinned as her husband quelled and hiked away in mock fear. "He's right, Marvel hon. You're lookin' bruised. Those beautiful blue eyes are not filled up with gaiety. Something wrong between you and Titus?"

It was easy talking to Grandmother. And suddenly, childishly, her story poured out. As always, Grandmother understood. "You've been apart a long time, and anybody readin' those columns you and your young man write would know how much the both of you've suffered, get a whiff of what you've been through. Yet love conquers all. But wait a minute—is it *you* who's holdin' back? Have you told him about your surgery?"

The surgery! The operation which had robbed her of the ability to conceive. It was the first time recently Marvel had thought of it consciously. Now the ghost of memory rose from its grave hauntingly, the reality she had supposed put to rest. She had painted it out. Why then did tears gather in her throat at the thought? *Oh Titus, we have to talk....*

Auntie Rae, pink-cheeked and a smudge of flour on her nose, met them at the door excitedly. "Guzzle your fill of lemonade in a hurry. "There's scads of mail, letters, and a package for you, Marvel! Calls—here, check the menu, Mother Riley, uh, Harrington. There's Irish stew and fresh peach cobbler." She leaned over to pick up the mail, and Marvel caught the familiar scent of Mary Ann's lilac shampoo. If only she could see her cousin, talk things out. Then, blessedly, she saw an envelope addressed to her in Mary Ann's round, childish handwriting.

She would open it first, then Kate Lynn's (so *she* knew Marvel was home?). The package from Titus she would open last—her bonus, her *big* bonus, for it was heavier than Marvel had expected. Curiously, she shook it gently, a child again at Christmas, guessing what was within...anticipating.

> Oh Marvel (Mary Ann said in part), I feel downright mushy—being back with Jake again....It's the thrill of being buckled to love and loving it...the old, the new, our plans all rolled into one. So new, so astonishing ...like sunrise and sunset together...a first firefly, first ice-cream cone, a first puppy, first football game ...so *connected*...eternal freshness. And school? You had to push me like a wheelbarrow, but it's *me* pushing me now. No, it's God, not pushing but leading...leading both Jake and me. Thank you for just everything, honey. And oh, Jake saw Ttius here. You ask him, he'll remember. By now you're together. *Hold tight!*

With scarcely a pause, Marvel ripped Kate Lynn's larger envelope open, scanned the contents, then went back to crucial sentences. *Slow down, Marvel*, she laughed at herself. For she had let two sizable checks slip to the floor without noticing. Who...what? She must reread.

> Mary Ann sent your address—oh, welcome home! I'm bursting at the seams with news...but first about the checks. Remember the items you sent after the persimmons piece? Here are checks. They want permission for reprints. You are *famous*...and your publisher for the book has been in touch. You're sure to be nominated for the Pulitzer for "fiction." Only those of us close to you know it's more than that—all that primary research—for we were there with you and Titus. It's *true*. Truth *is* stranger than fiction. So John (more about him later) says you'll probably be nominated for preservation of American values—real history—and we're losing so many of those values,

the kind we thought were here to stay. Were we dumb, blind? I don't believe that. We were innocent, gentle, and caring. And some of us still care, thank God! But sometimes I feel *old*—or *did*. Then here came John! He's a doctor, I'm *his* nurse—both ways! I got that youth back, what we all lost growing up like we did. And I've lost so much, so many: my parents, my husband... Oh, my heart still aches with losses. Nobody can replace them, or *help*. But God showed me how to go on another way, brought me John. Ours was a cautious kind of love. I couldn't *believe*, couldn't trust myself. Then I got thinking of *you*, how you forced me to pass that stupid geometry. You were so patient, but taught me to trust myself. I felt so guilty when I was drawn to my doctor, like I was unfaithful to Bill's memory. But God took me by those starched shoulders, gave me a good shaking, and let me know it was all right to love again. And oh, honey, love *can* be beautiful the second time around.

Happy for her friend, appreciative of the checks (Oh, Titus would be proud of her!), Marvel let her eyes sweep the crowd of words remaining. Later she would read all more carefully, after opening the package from Titus. *Titus*... What had Kate Lynn said? It took courage to return to the letter, both because the package beckoned and because of the fear of something half-remembered but vital. There was no choice. With practiced discipline, she picked up the tossed-aside letter.

I am so thankful that Bill and Titus did find each other before the war took my darling from us both. Give him time. He'll tell you.... And remember the patience of the persimmons as he wipes away the long years. He needs to talk... good therapy, but it can't be rushed. John knew Titus, you know—served with him. They experienced those exploding bombs with courage... put other men's bodies and souls together so bravely. But after it was all over, wow! bombs commenced to explode inside *them*. It takes a lot of mental push-ups, but Jesus sticks close by their sides—and ours. They *want* to live, love, and be loved, and are shoulder-deep in religion. And they have *us*. John says I'm just what the doctor ordered (the Great Physician and Dr. John Neal!). And your highly-decorated Titus couldn't have a greater wife. You have everything to offer in his chosen profession. We're so proud of you both. I wish Daddy could know. He always knew you'd do something great, and now the two of you will be even greater—*together*....

I do want your Aunt Eleanore to find help, too. It's waiting for her—unless she just gives up hope, has no will to live. We see so much—*I* see so much of life's other side. It would be easy to let today's world take us hostage—brainwash us into thinking our parents were wrong. Some fiend must have done that with our boys overseas. Oh, the sad sight of these pitiful orphans of war, fathered by American soldiers. Well, they didn't have people around like John and Titus to tease them back to sanity. Have to laugh at John's telling what he told the guys when they were all disoriented and mesmerized with seducers (or *were* the seducers, the "one-nighters"): "Get with it, men! Some of you're so preoccupied if I told you to 'keep your pants on,' you'd look to see if you're half-naked!" *Have* to laugh to keep from crying... all these babies and no arms to hold them. Wish I could bunch them all up and take them home with me. And now another war in the making ... our men leaving again ... this insane arms race ... a button to push...,

Marvel read and reread Kate Lynn's letter, a war raging within herself. It was both heartbreaking and heartwarming, both clear and cloudy—a gray haze lined with silver. Two convictions, however, emerged from the confusion. Her love for Titus Smith had grown over the years, and she would meet that unidentified "chosen profession" unflinchingly on any terms. And yes, together they would make God's ways theirs. God needed people who remained stubbornly true to His cause.

The magical contents of the mysterious package held Marvel spellbound, as they were supposed to do. In delicate balance between thoughts and emotions, she lifted the six-book collection of imaginatively colored glossy hardback books from the box. A "starter set," an enclosed printed note explained. A *Now, Once Upon a Time* set by T. Lee (pseudonym for the most literary of literary journalists...locally known contributor... widely acclaimed...so factual, yet keeping a part of himself locked away...a beautifully absurd rhyme-and-reason sense of humor which surfaces in what the author proclaims to be a "logically insane world of the absurd" for children). Local folks could take pride in the writer's achievements, and the world could be thankful that war did not claim the dedicated man's life as reported. He lived to open the eyes of even the most squirmy child...making creator, Creator, and Creation one....

Salsburg, oil, books. Grandfather had mentioned them all, and now they all connected. "Something we've talked about," Titus had said. Locally known failed to describe it. Cushioned as she was against the shock of seeing the author's name in print, why did she sob at the dedication—sob so hard Grandmother's call to dinner fell on deaf ears?

> To laugh often and much: to win the respect of intelligent people and the affection of children; to appreciate beauty, to find the best in others, to leave the world a bit better whether by a healthy child, a garden patch, or a redeemed social condition; to know because you have lived.
> This is to succeed.
>
> —Ralph Waldo Emerson
>
> Dedicated to Marvel, the God-given candle of hope, whose love light burned more brightly in my darkest hour!
>
> —Titus Lee Smith

It must have been by the blessed ministry of angels that Marvel managed to get through the meal. Though her eyes might be red from weeping, the rest of her must be glowing. For inside her a candle was lighted.

Mr. Corey called just as Marvel finished her peach cobbler. He was eager to make a reconciliation. Yes, yes—she *could* finish the book.

"But give me a little time, Mr. Corey. After all (and it was easy to laugh), we aren't recording observations of last year's wheat crop—"

The editor laughed with her before saying, "Right, we're not dealin' with post-abstracts. And you're not a dispassionate observer. This book will shove you head and shoulders above the titans of fiction. For you're in it—you and—oh, why dance around the candle? You and Titus!"

"Yes," she breathed into the phone held by her shaking hands. "I mean we're both in it. But this has to have a perfect ending; *you* said that. I'm no painter or composer whose work improves. This is my best!"

Still glowing, Marvel rejoined her family—only to be summoned to the telephone again by Billy Joe. He heard her whisper, "Titus," then had the grace to leave them alone. After all, the family should know.

"Everything's perfect, my darling!" Titus said excitedly, "I'm coming home—home to our *Now, Once Upon a Time.*"

21

Come Then,
Let Us
Go Forward—

Awake well before the alarm rang, Marvel dressed quickly, the Saturday-morning world feeling as light as an iridescent bubble in which she floated. The white slacks and tuck-in blouse ... blue platform sandals ... matching blue scarf knotted at her throat ... worn with a smile on her lips which wouldn't rub off. Then she rushed downstairs.

Early as she was, Titus was waiting. The faint dawn light reflected on the hood of his plum-and-beige two-toned car. Unconscious of motion, Marvel was suddenly caught in his embrace without the overture of holding hands. Reluctantly, she felt him push her away. Thankfully, not far—just far enough to smile gently down into her face.

"Just a routine eye exam," he whispered huskily. "Yes, they are. They are as lovely as I remembered. Is that love in those blue irises?"

Marvel felt color rise to set her face blazing. Then Titus was settling her close beside him in the cushiony privacy of the car. It seemed natural that they should whisper, laugh, and make light jokes as Titus drove with one arm about her shoulders. Natural, too, that he should take her to the Smith Hotel. Mary Ann was right ... a first taste, yet familiar. He leaned down before opening the door to kiss the tip of her nose. "Welcome home, my darling— our back table, of course?"

Tomato juice had never tasted so tangy, bacon so crisp, scrambled eggs so fluffy, biscuits so light, coffee so bracing— never. The grinning cook, peering periodically from the wide

268

kitchen, may have wondered how they knew, what with gripping hands across the table between bites. Breakfast finished, the two laced fingers and went to visit the cemetery where Lucille was laid to rest. His sister's dreams, too, had come true.

Again, by unspoken agreement, they drove straight to the remains of their tree. There, in the unpeopled silence, it was inevitable that Titus should draw Marvel into the warm circle of his arms and brush her closed eyelids with small kisses—right and natural that it was she who reached arms up to draw his head closer until their lips met in a first gentle kiss. Feeling the throb of his heart, Marvel sensed the torrent raging beneath the gentle pressure of that kiss.

It was she who drew away at last, knowing that they must talk. "I wish—oh Titus, I wish our *Once Upon a Time* could go on forever," she said shakily. "I loved your books. . . . I love you. . . . I love life."

Titus traced her cheekbones gently with his fingers. "I know—" he whispered raggedly, "but I wish we could skip the talk, just be married."

Married. Like breakfast, never had a word tasted so good.

But suddenly it happened, just as Kate Lynn had said it would. Titus was sketching the years of their separation—haltingly, at first, and then in an underlying tide of words beneath the calm surface. It was all there, of course, spelled out in his columns, his letters, his calls—all repeated in her daily writing . . . *waiting* . . . listening . . . *waiting* some more, praying . . . and in the pages of her book-to-come. The nightmare through which they both walked began, of course, with Titus' "brief assignment" in Spain. *And from there, Titus, can you tell me now?* Most of it he could reveal, although portions were still classified "for my own safety— and yours." Chapter by chapter, he would tell her details. Didn't they have a lifetime for that? For now, just the peaks and (with a groan) some of the valleys.

Marvel would remember the monstrous tyranny of Nazi domination and persecution, although only a whisper reached America's ears. Yes, Marvel remembered. Peace-loving, God-fearing Titus County, East Texas, hadn't dared face the truth— "put any stock in such tomfoolery"—in the grips of the Great Depression and the drought. Nevertheless, calamity struck. Great Britain, struggling to cling to democracy, felt the grind of pitiless oppressors' boots first. Belgium fell . . . and one by one the United Kingdom was no longer united. Mussolini ordered Italy to war. France surrendered... and evil threatened the world. There was mass confusion—and yes, Titus was there, first to cover the news, always trying to reach Marvel, let her know that although Associated Press sent him, the government *ordered* him to remain, gathering classified information for the Intelligence Office. Secret, all secret. *But there were no letters, Titus. No anything—just silence.* He had written, but censors ...lack of trust...turncoats...spies...

"But my article of faith was that you'd *know*—deep in your heart, *know*—I was alive to keep my promise. Pearl Harbor and Europe became one—a theater of puppets staggering through a hellish nightmare of blood, toil, tears, and sweat...everybody forgetting lines."

Trembling, Marvel noted the beads of perspiration on his high, intelligent forehead. "I know, I know," she murmured repeatedly. And the words were true. His smuggled-out columns had told her.

In no particular order, Titus told of meeting up with Bill Johnson, his cocaptain on the Culverville Tiger team, who would tell Kate Lynn...same with Duke...and then the clover brought by a forgotten comrade—showing his only picture of her, hoping the G.I.'s mind would make a copy.

"I know, darling. But the MIA report—and then—oh Titus—"

It was his turn to whisper, "I know." Then gripping her hands, as if to hang onto sanity, Titus fell silent—with so much left to be said.

"A part of me died when that 'must be presumed dead' report went out. You'd hear. I just prayed you wouldn't believe it. And then, *oh, dear God!* It was for real. Accused of spying, I was made a prisoner of war—treated with respect at first, in case I knew more. Oh, it wasn't a cozy POW camp with movies all night, but what happened later is too horrible to remember—beaten, battered, broken—"

"Don't say anymore, darling. It doesn't matter," Marvel insisted.

For the moment, it didn't. Until memory of the uniform—

Fortunately, that is where Titus' story resumed. Allied planes buzzed the enemy camp, sweeping low—too low. Shot down— all of them. But somehow Titus had managed an escape...was picked up by a Red Cross ship. Aboard that ship—yes, even with its flag plainly visible—it was fired upon, sunk. With him was the only other survivor, a young doctor named John, morally opposed to war like himself. But there were other needs to fulfill—physical and spiritual. Could they reconcile, mediate, be of service? Aboard an Allied sub which risked the lives of non-English-speaking men to pack them in like sardines, Titus and John Neal (*shades of Kate Lynn!*) promised God that if they survived they would devote the rest of their lives serving *all* peoples!

"I didn't know exactly how, but God led me," Titus groaned. "On that ship of mercy were the twisted bodies and souls of men who'd survived and wished they hadn't—screaming, begging for lethal injections, praying, or cursing God. Only one medical aide—and a chaplain whose faith and order we never knew. It didn't matter—"

There was so much Marvel wanted to tell him. About Kate Lynn. About Pastor Jim. About herself and how she had come to accept the religious preferences as Dr. James Murphy had taught her. She opened her mouth and then closed it. For tears were streaming down Titus' beloved face to mingle with her own. They embraced and clung, in new tenderness and understanding. Fact and fiction were *truth*!

"Now, about me, darling," Marvel began at last.

But Titus gathered her closer and said, "I know all I need to know. Unless," he smiled that seldom-smile, his gray eyes turning dark, "you want to reassure me that we're going to be married. I love the words."

"Oh Titus, you know we'll be married, that I love you, but—"

"But nothing!" he said, kissing her again and again. "I know—"

But you don't know about Philip. Overwhelmed by the depths of their all-consuming love, Marvel decided that segment could wait. Someday she would tell him, for husbands had a right to know everything.

She asked him instead if he had ever seen her—not *her*, not Marvel Harrington who was soon to become Mrs. Smith, just likenesses, well, in the faces of others. Only a million times, he said—around every foreign corner, on the faces of the deep, everywhere he looked.

Titus was so certain, so sure that all was well, wasn't he? Usually he was a wonderful listener. Not so today. *His* was the untold story.

Inhaling deeply, Titus said slowly, "That was unfair—my pressing you for another promise, when I haven't told you the part that matters. Oh, I pray as I've prayed so many times the most important burden of guilt I carry will make no difference— the profession I *have* to follow, while knowing that I can't do it alone. I need you—"

Before she could answer, his flow of words continued. "You liked my books, you said. That's when I changed my identity, took up a pen name. Meeting the chaplain on that ship changed my life. I knew then—"

While John worked with the medic, Titus made the rounds with the chaplain, saw him minister, felt the sense of God's presence. It was he who witnessed a man reborn—Titus Smith reborn in spirit and in identity... T. Lee, a chaplain, with a cross swinging from a chain about his neck. He saw the workings of God's grace, each patient providing new insight, new challenge. And it all happened as columnist-turned-chaplain crawled about on his hands and knees. Yes, really!

The image was comical. Perhaps because Marvel's heart could absorb no more, she asked, "Crawled—you were that seasick?"

"Seasick, heartsick, frightened—but determined to see behind every set of eyeballs of those suffering, so I could see life and death as they saw it. Crazy I guess, but that's what some thought of Thoreau's claim that crawling around in the meadow let us see life from a new perspective. Like four-legged animals—or babies in this strange world. And," Titus said brokenly, "it made praying with them easier, down on my knees in prayer. They knew I cared—*really* cared. Can you understand?"

"That you want to be a chaplain?"

"I *am* a chaplain."

In a little impulsive gesture, all innocence and careful, Marvel touched his face as she had dared venture in high-school days. "But the preparation—schooling, ordination? I *don't* understand. I think as always that you are dedicated. We have no choice, we never did—"

"You mean," he gasped almost inaudibly, "You will? *Oh Marvel*—"

Titus stopped breathing as he waited, looking down at her uncertainly. Marvel saw a thinner, older version of her high-school sweetheart. That was superficial; inside he remained unchanged. Tears gathered in her throat, forcing little sobs as she tried to whisper: "Oh Titus—I *will*, whatever it is you're asking, I will, just never leave me—"

She was in his arms then, and the years stretched between them melted away. *"She will! SHE WILL!"* Titus shouted to the world around them. Then tenderly to her as his hand touched her hair, stroked her brows, traced the planes of her cheeks: "How could I have forgotten how *Marvel*ous you are, how precious? Oh, thank God the other guy didn't get you—you're mine!" And in a way making reality sweeter than dreams, Chaplain Titus Smith's lips closed possessively over those of the woman who would follow him to the ends of the earth.

In the blur of words that made no sense, yet all the sense in the world, Titus broke through the barrier of the years, as she drowned in the depth of his shining eyes. Enough of the past ...unlocking of years now gone. Oh, schooling? With his educational background, there had been only seminary...work aboard ship accepted as internship...doctoral dissertation written as he recovered in the hospital. Nothing serious in a way that counted, just a game knee, fractured skull, impaired vision, *nothing serious.* What mattered was his clean bill of health *now.* He had his doctorate of divinity, might be called anywhere, anytime....But wives would be with husbands. He would remain in Reserves but not be recalled to active duty. Maybe a few scars were a blessing.

"We'll turn scars to stars," Titus said in boyish joy. "In the words of Sir Winston Churchill, 'Come then, let us go forward.'"

Marvel knew he was keeping a lot locked within him, as was she. But *nothing serious*—just the ecstasy of their prayed-for togetherness for now. God's smile reflected in the brilliance of afternoon sunlight spreading over their rediscovered world. The beautiful *heartland* was theirs.

Would she be an all-right wife? Titus' whoop of delight was his answer. The perfect wife, his Marvel: the writer, teacher, speaker—the *everything* wife! Titus told her as they strolled by a vendor whose wares included enormous red strawberries, paused to make a purchase, and then strolled on as, laughing as rapturously as two children, boy plopped berries into girl's mouth. Pearls were not for tears. She must tell Mr. Corey.

Marvel's inspired fingers typed a rhapsody that night. Near dawn she posted today's beautiful chapter. The editor would know only one remained.

In the immortalized words of Prime Minister Churchill: "I have nothing to offer but blood, toil, tears, and
sweat. *Come then, let us go forward together with our
united strength.*" His please might well have been that
of the Savior calling Titus Smith and Marvel Harrington to love's total commitment for "this was their
finest hour."

22

Honorable Intentions

Titus fit into the family beautifully. He was never a stranger at all. There are days, like places, that capture the very essence of one's heritage—places in the heart that whisper of God's presence, His world in harmony with nature. Today was such a day, handpainted in perfection, designed for foreverness—to transport those rejoicing in it back to the simpler, more gentle times. But Marvel was not rejoicing. Oh, if only she had remembered to tell Titus about the surgery—if only—

The oft-restored church held out its arms in welcome, the piano-violin duet echoed in sweetness like that of a giant, well-tuned music box, and the sermon by the visiting minister could not have been more appropriate. "Let us fear less threats of a third war than that depending not on control of land, sea, or air but within the souls of men. If we who love God fail, the whole world fails with us. *All* are united ... divided we fall...."

The scene, the service, and the warmth of it all prepared Titus well for the easy conversation to follow. And when his hand closed over Marvel's as the congregation joined in song, she wavered as before in the grave need to tell Titus what he must know—the vow she had made in showing his *Now, Once Upon a Time* books proudly at breakfast. Oh, the timing was all wrong! For words in his dedication sliced through her happiness: "... to leave the world a bit better ... *by a healthy child* ..."

"Titus," she whispered quickly, as they left the church, "don't go through the formalities today—asking Daddy. Let it wait— *please*."

That was their only moment. The hospitable Harringtons surrounded them. And suddenly they were home. Marvel felt both relieved and frightened. There must be no secret chambers. Yet it was sad, so sad that a storybook couple's love story should end in pain.

"Welcome inside!" Grandfather said with another hearty handshake. "Make yourself right at home. Ours is a family business." And the tone he used was that of a typical banker establishing an immediate kinship valuable to both parties. "We're not strangers, you know."

Grandmother flashed the two men a smile. "I should say not."

"I'm B.J.—remember? One of the last of the Harrington clan."

Titus extended his hand graciously. "I'm the *only* member of mine." Marvel turned away, concentrating on the vases of flowers Auntie Rae had scattered in just the right places. Titus might just as well have added, "until the next generation." The thought hurt.

When she turned back, the men were finding chairs, urging Titus to be seated, seeming comfortable and uninhibited with their guest. Daddy offered Titus his very favorite chair, an offer he declined in favor of a small settee. Grinning at B.J.'s saying, "That's reserved for lovers," Titus lightly patted one side invitingly to Marvel. But Mother's call interrupted. "Will you excuse us a moment—"

"If dinner's about ready," Daddy said, smiling. "We're starved."

"Oh, he's nice—" Mother said almost sadly to Marvel in the kitchen. "I want everything just right for you, like the home he never had. Is the table all right?"

The table was beautiful—and Titus told the ladies so. He won their hearts by praising their culinary talents (said never before had he bitten into such chicken, and which one of them baked this bread?).

"Marvel told me," he said in addressing Auntie Rae, "that you collect recipes—such valuable records of the past. I'm so glad (his voice softened wistfully) to have my late sister's—and would love to share if I may. We put them to use in the old Smith Hotel."

Auntie Rae beamed, and mention of the hotel drew Uncle Worth into the conversation...preservation of landmarks... bringing generations together...interesting guests...and rising costs. Finances led back to banking. And Grandfather was at his best. Of course, banking and land went together—and now there was oil.

"You're in all of this, aren't you, young man?" Alexander Jay Harrington made a point of withdrawing his trademark, the ornate gold watch. "And now turning out books. Right smart tyin' education and religion in with politics. And I understand now with all those years of service behind you—you (*ahem!*) are eye-deep in the Lord's service?"

There was a bad moment when the question hung there. Grandfather had no right, Marvel thought defensively, to treat Titus as if he were on trial. Automatically, her hand gripped his beneath the linen tablecloth.

A look of appreciation stretched over his weary face. Bolstered by her gesture, his gray eyes darkened with emotion, she saw, and felt the gossamer beauty of their love strengthen powerfully.

With a minimum of self-pity, Titus sketched the past with accuracy, minus the shattering heartbreak, the inevitable scars— except to say that sometimes he felt *old*. "Natural for my generation, I guess, sir. Older but richer for it—changed. God uses those experiences."

Grandmother tactfully suggested second helpings when Titus paused. "I guess we all know the rest," she said, lifting the lid from a silver tureen. "We attended the dedication ceremony, saw you in uniform, heard your testimonial. We'd talked by phone, but I didn't know—know that—"

Titus' face lighted with amusement. "That I was a chaplain?"

B.J. was enthralled. "A chaplain—and a football player! I get it—and so does my Uncle Dale. We're baseball players. He used to be big-league, but I guess football rules are kin folks. It all begins at home base. God coaches us from there. I write about that."

Talk turned to sports before homemade ice cream and angel food cake were served. Daddy's face was animated as Titus drew him out.

The harmonious hum of their voices drifted in and out of Marvel's divided consciousness as she felt a heightened awareness of the miracle of people's meeting for a first time and finding they were not meeting as strangers. Instead, the dearest people on earth to her found one another deeply absorbing. It was she who had brought them together. It was she who must break them apart. Another D day lay ahead.

Regretfully, they rose from the table. Grandfather glanced at his watch again—this time with greater significance. Marvel understood.

"Would you like to see the Harrington farm, d—" she began, then faked a cough to cover a slip of the tongue which would have tripped her into calling Titus *darling*. *(But he is, Lord. Oh, help me, he is!)*

"Of course he would!" Johanna Harrington said. "Right, Squire?"

The Squire rose without aid of his cane. "You took the words right out of my mouth. Now, we'll all pitch in on these dishes!"

Titus was first to arise. Rolling up the sleeves of his dress shirt, he leaned down and asked Marvel to loosen his tie. The nearness of him, scent of bay rum, and remembered gentle sweetness of his lips set her pulse racing. "You're too quiet," he whispered softly.

"I'm thinking," she said, longing to pull his head closer.

Dishes were done soon after. Packed into two cars, they left, pointing out landmarks to Titus on the way. Marvel's former gaiety returned at sight of her beloved home. "Oh, Mother— Daddy—look! Titus, *Titus*! Have I told you about the name?" With trembling fingers, she pointed to the newly painted signs the dubious architects had erected.

"Beulah Land!" Titus exclaimed. "How fitting, how right. You must have some imaginative architects—*married*, according to Isaiah."

"Good architects? The best that money can buy. Isaiah? Hmmm—maybe they're Jewish. Bad for banking, but good for merchants I guess, seeing that the Jews exchange gifts for eight days at Chanukah. Yep, serves well in stores."

"And the chaplain will serve them when there's a need, Father!" Daddy reminded him testily. "It was *our* architect who chose the name—our Marvel. Right, baby? Oh—there are the men now, so yesterday was—"

Their Sabbath. Probably, Marvel thought without concern, as Samuel and Herman Curtis appeared before Grandfather could finish his guess. "Sorry, folks," one of them explained self-consciously (it was hard telling which was which in their faded fatigues). "We—uh, observe our Sabbath differently, and took liberty with yours. Not meaning to offend—"

The spokesman stopped dead in his tracks and, looking flabbergasted, jabbed his partner in the ribs. Both dropped hammers and saluted smartly.

Titus returned the salute, although he had worn a dark suit and left his coat in the car. There followed a round of warm backslappings of reunion and a mingling of League-of-Nations voices which erased the builders' restraint. "It's all over, fellows. Drop the formalities," Titus said with an involuntary shudder. "We're home where we belong!"

"Over, Commander—*over*. God bless you! We' couldn't have made it alone. But past things don't matter, you told us out there. So come look!"

They all followed, discussing plans. B.J. was happy the crew had reserved space for the baseball field. Mother darted back and forth between the staked-off section for the house and the riot of color from the oversupply of bedding plants. She, Grand-mother, and Auntie Rae placed furniture—piano here, claw-footed table there, needlepoint drapes in the parlor (yes, Auntie Rae nodded, "like those I made for the church"). Titus praised it all and pleased Dale Harrington immensely when he hoped the pool in the far pasture would be seeded with fish—*loved* fishing, he said. The other pools were for the cattle, Grandfather ex-plained.

Marvel photographed it all in her mind. How deliriously happy they were. If the whole world were this happy, God would need to enlarge His footstool, else it would explode with joy!

True, with one exception. Titus suspected the turmoil inside her. She was too quiet, too withdrawn, try as she would to hide it. His anxious glances her direction registered concern. Marvel, avoiding his eyes, turned toward the persimmons—or where they used to be.

"They're gone, aren't they?" Titus, suddenly beside her, said softly.

Marvel nodded. "Gone—the persimmons and—my wonder-ful friends."

He grasped her hands and held them tenderly as if they were something very special and rare. "We can put them all back," he whispered. "Whatever it is you're wanting, we agree on. And when two are gathered together in His name, it will be granted. Christ doesn't break promises."

And I do, Marvel thought miserably. But she was unable to dismiss memories of the carmel-faced baby with that butterpat nose....

Back home, Titus said, "It has been one of the most wonderful days of my life. You're made me feel like family—the family I never had."

"Consider yourself one of the family," Grandfather boomed, obviously pleased with his position as patriarch and its privileges. "You are, you know—(ahem) seeing that Frederick Salsburg ties us all together in a roundabout kind of way. Marvel, I'm sure the chaplain here would appreciate seeing his—shall we say?—ancestor's grave?"

Titus glanced at Marvel and hesitated. "I shouldn't impose—"

"Impose, fiddlesticks!" Grandmother said quickly. "We have dinner at noon here—sandwiches for supper. You know how you liked that break hot, and it's lip-smackin' sliced cold. Now *shoo*! Out the both of you!"

Titus reached for Marvel's hand and tucked it possessively beneath his arm. Marvel felt his pulse pounding and smiled up at him, her heart in her eyes. "I'm glad you're staying," she whispered.

Little did she dream that walk would be her undoing....

Once they were alone in the fading twilight, Titus gathered her to him. "Oh darling," he said, feathering her brow with small kisses, "I adore your family," he said huskily, "but waiting drove me wild. Do you love me like this—and this—? Oh sweetheart, what is it? You're trembling. Are you cold?"

Cold? She was burning with fever—the fever of longing to respond.

"Oh Titus, I *do* love you, but they're waiting. Catch me if you can!" Marvel managed to laugh and then fled, his calls of "No fair!" at her heels.

The iron gate leading into the cemetery was lighted now by a bright-beamed streetlight. They stopped breathlessly before entering the quietude. The ancient cedars remained, their whispering branches showing signs of age. Picking her way past the simple headstones (heartbreakingly increased by the war), Marvel led Titus to the ornate statuary of angels marking her ancestors' graves. It was Titus who spotted the elaborate nameplate reading simply "Frederick Salsburg."

"It's strange," he said in near-reverence, "how people cross our paths briefly and change us completely—from here to eternity."

"Yes," she said, touched by his caring. "So much of me lies here. And there are so many memories." *Memories*. How strange that Archie had proposed here. That Elmer (she shuddered) had threatened her life here before being institutionalized until his demise. And now his father, Frederick Salsburg, who left a fortune to both her and Titus, was interred in the Harrington plot, while a Harrington was to be committed like Elmer. How strange, indeed, that life's drama unfolded in a cemetery—for now she stood here with the only man she had ever loved.

Breaking the silence, Marvel reached out to Titus, feeling so close to both life and death. "Oh, my darling," she whispered, ready to explain—and accept.

Marvel heard only his small gasp of joy before the familiar sound of B.J.'s voice split the moonless dark of the night air. "Marvel! *Mar-vel!* You'd better come," he panted. "It's Grandfather—"

Fearing the worst, the three rushed home to find Alexander Jay Harrington in a rage. Whatever set him off had done a thorough job. Grandmother tried to explain something about a telephone call. Mother and Auntie Rae attempted to behave normally as they prepared for supper.

Daddy and Uncle Worth were more forthright. "Make yourself right at home, Titus," Daddy smiled (addressing Titus by name for the first time). "Now, you'll meet the rest of us—the skeletons in the closet!"

Titus smiled in amusement before saying soberly that sometimes they were the easiest to understand. "Your father's open—no phony."

"You're right there!" Uncle Worth nodded. "Our father's makin' a mountain from a molehill—wanted his other sons here to meet you—"

Marvel could have hugged the men around her, and loved her grandfather for wanting the other members to join them. That meant he had welcomed Titus into the family circle. But one didn't say *no* to the Squire.

And nobody said *no* when his call to dinner interrupted Uncle Worth.

Grandfather's blessing was fervent, calling each person in the standing circle by name, mentioning the less fortunate, hungry, sick, and blind, and finally his "wayward sons not present." Then loudly he remembered Mary Ann and Jake. When at last he stopped, his bewildered captives sat down.

It was almost comical after the fright Marvel had felt so recently. But the older man's blood was still boiling when he picked up the breadknife and swung it across the loaf in the Sunday evening ritual. From beneath lowered lashes, Marvel caught Titus' eyes—and they twinkled.

She was totally unprepared for what happened next.

"Well, young man," Grandfather said masterfully, passing the silver tray of sliced bread with his left hand and brandishing the knife with his right, "you've met the Harrington family. Courtin's no substitute for marriage. It's high time you declared yourself."

Titus' reply was instantaneous. "Indeed, sir," he said.

"Then express yourself! Just what are your intentions regarding my granddaughter?"

"Strictly honorable, Mr. Harrington, Esquire!"

Then turning to Marvel's father, Titus solemnly went through the formalities of asking his daughter's hand. "I have the ring in my pocket," Titus concluded before hearing the surprised father's consent.

"The decision's up to Marvel," Daddy said uncertainly. "Baby?"

Up to Marvel. Of course, it was, she thought wildly, or should be. But hadn't life always been like this—Marvel's decision when decisions were already dictated by others or circumstances beyond her control?

"I'll be good to her," Titus promised, looking at Daddy. But it was Grandfather who responded. "You'd jolly well better!" he said.

In a dream, Marvel felt the ring Titus slipped on her finger, saw the lustrous sheen of the heirloom pearl tremble like a giant, unshed tears. And why not? Tears were falling like raindrops about them, mingling with laughter to form rainbows of promise. It was all so unreal, yet so real. Of course—like Mary Ann's wedding. Not the way the cousins had planned, but beautiful in a comical sort of way—like a pie-in-the-face slapstick wedged between acts of a tragic drama. *Oh, wait till I tell Mary Ann!*

"Now, chaplain—uh, Titus, it's all right to kiss your betrothed," Johanna Riley Harrington said. "Traditional in our family—"

"A beautiful one," he said, tilting his bride-to-be's chin....

23

For All the
Turtles in Heaven

Pink flares of morning brought sanity back. Tears were threatening again when Marvel appeared for breakfast. The big, airy kitchen was bustling with hurried footsteps and planning. Now, at last, a bride could descend that staircase. A wedding date must be set, but beforehand came the announcement party... unless Marvel preferred a statement in the newspaper instead. Flowers would be in full bloom throughout June, some in July, but the pair had been engaged for years...so why prolong matters? Last night had only "formalized" the issue.

Formalized? Yes, maybe—in a buffoonish, comic-strip sort of way. Let the talk go unnoticed. Marvel had determined before falling asleep, after apologizing for the shotgun-wedding tactics (how dare Titus laugh!), that nobody was taking charge of her life from here on. So she concentrated on Grandmother's "comfort food" of hot oatmeal liberally sprinkled with raisins, and let the older Mrs. Harrington talk on. No more cream, thank you—no matter that she was just "bones and a hank of hair" when brides must be at their most beautiful.

"She's too quiet," Grandmother grumbled in a little aside to Mother. "I'll get to the bottom of this even if it takes a swat there!"

"Give her time, Mother. It all came as a surprise to me— I mean, the way it happened. Give *me* time to get used to this, too."

"My stars, Snow White! It's not as if the child were swept off her feet by some foreigner—or control of her life were slippin' away.

He's one of us and good husband material. There's never been anyone else!"

✳ ✳ ✳

Titus called as Marvel was dressing to meet him. A change in plans, an orientation for making unscheduled calls in the new overcrowded, understaffed Culverville Hospital. Emergency, yes. ... these things happened—particularly when facilities remained under construction, some wings unopened until further funding could be found. Maybe he—she—they—

"The point is, my daring, I want you to come with me. It's unfair, but I need you. And this is what we'll be doing together. *Please!*"

The insistent voice brought him closer. "Of course I'll come with you. You don't have to beg! I know about first aid, both inside and out—agonies of waiting, hoping. Add those to my credentials."

"For being my wife?" Titus said humbly. "Oh, you have them all. You make me feel strong, excited. We can meet every challenge together—"

He may have said more. Yes, he did: words of regret for the necessary change of plans. Marvel remembered only that she felt grateful for the time to think through a logical approach to the problem within herself. She had all the credentials, she had boasted. He had agreed and added, when he should have subtracted. All the qualifications as a chaplain's wife, *Titus'* wife. The wife who could give him everything—except what a man wanted most: an heir to the dying Smith name.

Would her mind have reached back to recapture the vision unaided, or was it the soft strains of Mother's violin playing the same song, "The Waltz of the Flowers"? Marvel stood again in the world of long-stemmed flowers, seeming to sway to the music like ladies in gowns at a ball. All ladies—but for one. The only known "living half-woman," Portia Francisco, who was born without legs. Well, Ripley's Believe-It-or-Not collection could add another such "freak": Marvel Harrington, Half-Living (or half-woman). Then, in contradiction, Gabriel, Portia's giant outer-space husband loomed in her memory, his 8'–6" height bringing a wreath of smiles to his wife's face. He was her other half, Portia laughed merrily—made her life complete. That way nothing else mattered. Handicapped? *Hah!* Nothing could remove God's armor, Portia had declared with true courage. And together she and Gabe smiled....

Commander Smith looked boyishly vulnerable, rather than intimidating, in his braided white uniform, chest flashing with medals and pants pressed just so. Marvel had to restrain herself in the waiting room filled with anxious-looking people (some appearing too poor to afford a doctor), so deep was her longing to rush forward to Titus. But these people's needs must be met, their imploring glances said.

An understanding staff member handed her a white jacket when she brought Titus a list of patients. "Emergency, pre-op, post-op, pediatrics, counseling, the terminally ill," Titus said as professionally as a physician. Then with eyes lowered to the chart, he added to Marvel, "Just follow along like my nurse. And could you take my Bible while I struggle with this roster? I'll introduce you as we make the rounds."

A weary doctor, his rumpled shirt saying he'd been there all night, nodded a greeting. "Chaplain, Mrs. Smith, it's a blessing you've come. Folks who never darken a church door tend to get mighty religious in here."

The three were surrounded immediately by examples, gripping their hands and clinging. "Pray with us....Save our baby. ...*Why* does God allow this?"

As the doctor ducked out, Chaplain and "Mrs. Smith" made the rounds together, giving first priority to those without families for comfort, next, those without money to pay and frightened (there would be funds, Titus reassured them grimly)...the terrified pre-op, depressed post-op patients...the stoically resigned, convinced that "God doesn't care!"

The pace grew more hectic, as frenzied patients lashed out at their doctors, their pastors, mates, and then God. Titus was patient, said the right words to those struggling with disaster, pain, ultimate death. In the hall, he whispered to Marvel, "I feel so inadequate, so unworthy—in need of counsel myself. But the calling's like a magnet."

"We have no choice, my darling. We never did."

An elderly woman drew Titus aside, begging prayer, and Marvel moved on to peek into the crowded ward of newborns, distraught young mothers, and crippled children. The mothers rushed to her, said she understood, often then rushed out. Titus came in, bent to hear words or wipe tears of the older, and scooped the younger ones up in his arms *so* tenderly.

There was no time to be a spectator, however, for already the weak hand of a pale child whose chart read "cystic fibrosis" reached through the bars of her crib to tug on Marvel's jacket. In a voice little more than a sigh, the small patient coughed out her concern. "My f-friend—I l-lost 'im, w-will my—*pet* m-meet me—up there?" Marvel dropped to her knees, wiped away the weak tears, and silently prayed for guidance. It came.

"With God all things are possible, honey. You know the story of Creation, how it took seven days. But with His power, God could have done the job with a smile, then lifted His arms and put all kinds of animals in this world for us to love and care for. We know that the Lord loved them. Remember how He had Noah take them with him in the ark? Now, close your eyes and sleep for me, so I can tell you the rest." The child who had wheezed out that her name was Jody relaxed with a small smile. (In need of *counsel*? Marvel felt need for far more) Then she knew that she was not alone. God's presence was as real as the soundless tread of nurses' crepe-soled shoes. "It seems to me that God loved the birds' singing, puppies' barking, and kitties' purring on this earth, so why wouldn't He save them for the new earth of heaven? He loves us so much He wants to let us live forever, so we can pray that God prepared a room for our pets."

The little girl nodded with eyes still closed, although her voice was stronger, her smile still in place. "Thank You, God, for being kind and loving us. Bless You, bless everybody—and *all the turtles in heaven....*" The small voice drifted away in a slumber of peace.

The day ended with much unfinished: an alcoholic resisting restraint...a woman refusing to be reconciled with her estranged family but screaming, "Chaplain, pray for me tonight!" ...a suicide...and more.

"Oh Titus, we shouldn't have left," Marvel murmured as she collapsed in the car beside him. "I know your replacement came, but—"

"His response was to fold her to him in a new way of caring that both of them understood. They were in touch with God within those white walls. And, though footsore and weary, they were on a spiritual high.

"Still think you can hack it? You were wonderful, my Marvelous Marvel," Titus said, his voice tight with emotion. "But all your life, I mean? Don't answer. I'm too exhausted for a *no*. Just think."

"I don't have to think, darling. Today with you began our *someday*. It provoked my every emotion. I *hated* the sin we saw, but *loved* the sinners and saints alike. And I saw a new *you* I can't describe. Oh, patients loved you, made me love you more, the world more!" Her voice rose beyond her control. "When they call you again, take me with you! I'll read Jody stories from your *Now, Once Upon a Time* books!"

"Oh, little sweetheart," he groaned softly, "our Jody is dead."

The words were startling, heartbreaking. But Marvel reached for the God-given courage promised those who serve "the least of these."

"I was there for her. We touched each other and won over fear!"

"I've never loved you so much," Titus said thickly as he walked her to her front door. "Oh—I almost forgot this item. Read it—it's something you'll need to know." Handing her a folded paper, "Sweet dreams, *Mrs. Smith*," he said.

"Good night, my precious chaplain!" And with that, she stumbled inside.

* * *

Preoccupied, Marvel glanced at the newspaper article given her by Titus—at first. Romania could wait. Other matters were more vital. Or were they? Something disturbed a faint memory, so she scanned it again:

> *Familiar force stalks the Gypsies* (*Gypsies . . . Romania . . .* yes, she must read on). Someone falling asleep in 1938, now awakening, might find the war changed nothing. After rumors, the world found in '41 the Germans deported Gypsies. Nazis in their frenzied purge had no need for them. . . . "Heil, Hitler! Deport them as part of the Final Solution!" And the Gypsies, like the Jews, were marked for destruction. And 500,000 Gypsies perished in concentration camps. Survivors were sold into slavery. The few escapees must hide out, finding less refuge than persecution . . . scorned, spat upon, feared, these once-intelligent

and fun-loving people became forgotten victims of
the Holocaust. A beaten Germany offers no repara-
tions...no monument commemorates their tragedy,
and no state represents Romanian Gypsies at the
postwar United Nations. What happened to the high-
flown rhetoric that all men would be free? These are
real people, truly the "displaced"...forced to beg,
cheat, steal if you will, driven from place to place,
called vagabonds, turned away, judged guilty, and
stamped "dangerous" except by Soviet Russia which
swallows them up as if human exports. Romanian
Gypsies of today? How different are tactics behind the
scenes than when Goebbel's propaganda sheets were
distributed in the thirties? They are vandalized, beaten,
chased from one settlement to another...wanderers,
refugees seeking asylum. Can our country in its claims
of democracy, tolerance, and freedom turn our backs
on those we once wept for? Ask your God, ask yourself—and in the name of all that's holy, take note of
the historical parallel of the *then* and the *now*.

A note underneath identified Roma Nicoletta as the
author of *A Gypsy Incognito, A Lady in Exile, Living
Here with My Own Kind.*

Titus had given her this for some purpose. But could he know
the memories within her of flashing-eyed, dusky-skinned people
who befriended the Harringtons with "cat's-eye stew"? Another
example of persons brought together by strange circumstances
who could leave footprints on each others' hearts. So the book
must not end here, after all. There was more, she must tell Mr.
Corey—the Gypsies, and yes, the "freak" Portia and Gabe Francisco who knew the answers to life. Gypsies, like herself, had
asked questions: *What happens to me now?...Where is our
refuge?* The circus performers had peace from within. Now they
could care for God's creatures in Dallas, and pray for the turtles
above.

24

The Lost Chord

Alexander Jay Harrington, Esquire, had not forgotten the hem in his older sons' voices when invited to meet Titus Smith. Emory was giving him the dodge, no doubt about it, knowing how opposed Grandfather was to his son having his wife away without just cause. And Joseph—well, anybody'd know that harem of wife and daughters led him around by the nose. Their behavior was unpardonable, downright embarrassing to his favorite granddaughter's guest who now, thanks to his small push, was her betrothed. Well, he'd put his foot down in short order. They knew which side their bread was buttered on. So the matter was laid to rest.

Or so he thought, as did the rest of the family. In fact, the pace was so frenzied that Marvel wondered how she found time to write Mary Ann and Kate Lynn and post the Gypsy item to Editor Corey. There were quick notes of response, except for Mr. Corey, who called.

"Of course," he said without hesitation, "that belongs in the book. Matter of fact, the writer's publisher is the one pushin' for your conclusion. Stop draggin' your heels, you two. You both know the answers. Surely Titus let you in on how the Romanian piece ties in?"

"There's been no time for us to talk—really talk, sir—"

His sigh hummed through the lines. "He knows—well, never mind that. But *you* gotta remember Emerson's words, sure enough. "What lies behind you or what lies before you are tiny matters compared to what lies inside you!" And with that he hung up.

Titus was coming for supper and, remembering Portia, Marvel delighted B.J. with a suggestion that they have "groundnut gravy."

"Oh boy! There's a grind-your-own market here now. We're back in peanut country. Funny how many ways peanut butter can be used by us creative cooks! Oh, can Thomas come meet Titus? He's *nice!*"

Nice? Wonderful was more like it. Marvel wondered what prompted him to mention only casually that he would take care of some matters at the hospital, without asking her to come along. But aloud she said, "Of course, Thomas is welcome. And, by the way, he *may* come, not can."

"Right," he grinned winningly. "I know Grandfather'll be nice to Thomas. It's Uncle Emory who's got his nose out of joint. You'll see. Grandfather *thinks* it's all settled, but our uncle'll re-twist his shorts."

The day passed in a flurry of trips back and forth to the bank, to the farm, and to the telephone. Architects wondered about framing, needed more materials, and would the Harrington family want barn plans drawn for those "thousands of cattle" coming in like a stampede? B.J. wondered (from the market) if Marvel thought some "stolen chicken" would be fun in the groundnut gravy. Some fresh ones had come—not stolen, of course. Then the newspaper wondered if Miss Harrington and the commander had set a date for the wedding. And oh, should the title be commander or chaplain? Marvel wondered later if she made proper answers, considering the turmoil within herself. The builders' calls served as a reminder. Maybe Titus would like a small place of their own at Beulah Land. Both of them needed roots between the assignments he had alluded to. He loved fishing—and she loved the land. B.J.'s giggle over "stolen chicken" meant memory of the Gypsies, of course. Just what did Romania have to do with her and Titus, and how could Mr. Corey know? What truly bothered her, Marvel realized, were the words from Emerson. Yes, the problem lay within her. Until it was resolved, others had to stop pressing.

Meal preparations were in progress when the phone shrilled again. "I'll get it!" Grandfather said from the door. Moments later, the universe might well have exploded. He was shouting in fury and beating his cane at all objects in reach when Marvel saw Titus' car slow to a stop.

With a surge of her heart, she ran forward with both arms extended. Never mind what neighbors might think! "I want to hear all about your day. Oh, I sound like a wife greeting her husband," she murmured against the warmth of his chest. "There's so much to tell and to ask—"

"Never mind, Mrs. Smith!" Titus laughed down at her. "I'll go for that. Name the day—or we'll run away!" Then, comically, he dropped to his knees there on the walk. "Oh, Juliet, Juliet! Wilt thou be mine?"

"Oh Titus, be serious! You never jest about matters of the heart—remember saying that when we'd only first met? This is important!"

"So is this," he insisted when she tried to pull away. "No jest!"

"I—I'll marry you, Romeo, but not until after the murder. There's one about to take place inside. I—I came to warn you something's wrong!"

"The Squire again?" Titus guessed. "Your face looks as stricken as when he demanded to know my intentions. I understand you, read you like a book, just as I understand and love your family." He lifted her ring finger and touched the pearl as if to make sure it remained. "There are no secrets between us—just know that. Let's go calm our grandfather down. After all, we'd best reserve our energy for the funeral!"

"Uncle Emory's, I suspect. Aunt Eleanore, you know," she said sadly.

It was Uncle Emory—or had been. The brief conversation had ended, but Grandfather's fury had risen to a more feverish pitch. "The very idea, after all his raisin'. He knows every proverb, how a wise son hears his father's instruction, but a scorner hears not rebuke! A husband's commanded to cling to the wife of his youth. Marriage is honorable . . . instituted from the beginning. A man, a real God-fearin' *he-man*, forsakes all others, fulfills all obligations. Emory and Eleanore are of one flesh, I tell you!" He punctuated the statement with a jab of his cane and continued the dissertation without an intake of breath. "He's hard-hearted, bent on tempting God—and his earthly father as well. Tryin' to put her away without just cause. . . . There's no justification except for adultery. Bible makes no exception for a weakness of the mind. Let this be a lesson to y'all in this house! I'll cut him off at the ankles, disinherit him. I could cane him. Good thing he *didn't* show up. He's the one who's short on the smarts! He's not welcome in this house . . . not fit for the kingdom . . . couldn't have qualified for the ark either . . . entering like they did two-by-two."

The coffeepot boiled over, hissed angrily, and filled the parlor with smoke. *How appropriate*, Marvel thought, hardly knowing whether to weep at the sad situation or laugh at her grandfather's antics. Grandmother rushed to rescue the utensil, and the other Harrington women followed at her heels in thankful escape. Somehow Titus would manage to take over without appearing to do so at all, just as he'd done in the hospital. Time proved her right. Titus gave a miraculous report later.

Comforted by the lowering of the men's voices, Marvel listened as Grandfather's Duchess talked while refilling the coffeepot and nodding approval. Mother and Auntie Rae resumed work on a bouquet of roses, and Marvel chopped chicken for the bubbling kettle of groundnut gravy.

"No need explainin' the Squire of mine. You girls know him— more smoke than fire. But I wonder," she paused pink-cheeked, "if you know he and I go farther back, that you're seein' the end of a love story without its beginning. In between came—well, rambling, dishes, diapers, patent medicine in out-of-the-way places— *you*, my sweet Snow White. I was happy, while all the time wonderin' what happened to my first love, the love of my youth. But I wouldn't have deserted your father—and I think you know that. Things in life just fold together if we allow it, have patience, and know life's not perfect. Understand?"

"I do," Mother said softly. "You've told me about Father Harrington."

Auntie Rae pricked her finger with a thorn and quickly wiped the small stain from the tablecloth. "You're talking about Eleanore and Emory, aren't you, Mother Harrington—their not understanding?"

Well, yes, Grandmother acknowledged somewhat mindlessly, and then rambled on. A dedicated wife needn't spin flax and purple, but she should know the difference between true love and infatuation. There was joy in serving. She shouldn't expect all highs and no lows. The same man wore that black suit on Sunday who yelled when he couldn't find his pajamas . . . fussed when his hair dye bottle disappeared, while dripping toothpaste on the rug or (bending in laughter) running around in his summer shorts and swore he was freezing! "I wonder if Eleanore didn't concentrate too much on her children and leave Emory out—not that he was easy to live with, but life has to have balance. Am I scaring you, Marvel hon, seein' that you haven't tasted marriage yet?"

Marvel laughed. "Not a bit—and neither are you fooling us. We know what the Squire means in your life and what Daddy means to Mother and Uncle Worth means to Auntie Rae. Mary Ann and I are Harringtons!"

The women gathered to hug each other, understanding without further words. Auntie Rae said again how wonderful it was to have family. And they hugged closer, until Grandmother declared it was time to decide which their men preferred: biscuits, rice, potatoes, or some of everything over which to spoon Portia's magical gravy.

They were laughing and adding the final touches when Daddy called lightly, "Hey, you ladies! Just when do we feed my future son-in-law?"

Marvel had forgotten about Thomas. It was unsettling when he came in with the men. She hugged him in welcome, wondering if he overheard.

Grandfather's prayer was one of contrition. The storm was over.

Smiles traveled around the table and conversation turned light and airy. Wasn't the groundnut gravy just yummy, the biscuits light as a feather, and the coffee the all-perfect brew? Titus made mention of Auntie Rae's needlepoint draperies. Weren't they similar to those in Pleasant Knoll Church? It was her father-in-law who answered. His son's wife was the Michelangelo of muslin. There were talents among his family "too numerous to mention" (but he proceeded to name them one by one).

"I'll explain it all," Titus whispered, propelling Marvel from the confines of the table She nodded, watched the hearty handshakes among the men, pats on the heads of B.J. and Thomas, and the usual warm embraces between all men and their ladies. Did one really burst with pride? she wondered, when Titus thanked his hostesses, then brushed each glowing cheek with a light kiss. "You're an ideal family which, God willing, I'll be joining soon."

There followed jubilant reassurances and looks of gratitude for peace. Marvel heard little, as a usually reticent Thomas clasped her hand to say, "Oh, we patched everything! Why, I feel I could hit a homer, then hurdle the grandstand in one leap. I made B.J.'s team today—and Grandfather says the Baptist church'll sponsor me, Marvel!" Before she could utter congratulations, B.J burst out, "Oh, wait'll you hear it all—about the bank and stuff. My head feels like a hot-air balloon. *Titus*—"

Marvel felt their hero's hands gripping her shoulders. Willingly, their captive was marched into the darkness, where her Titus finished Billy Joe's sentence himself. It was incredible, unbelievable, a Shakespearean drama unpublished because the talented writer was unable to decide on an ending. His quill wavered between tragedy and comedy.

In the circle of Titus' arms, it seemed fitting that Mother should be playing Grandfather's favorite number, "The Lost Chord," on her beloved violin. The lost would be found soon, she knew.

"I'll recap for you, sweetheart, and then we'll talk about *us*."

Marvel hung on each word in amazement. Titus had seen the administrator at the Culverville Hospital, talked at length, found that with a loan, a few donations, and the long-promised funds from the state, the place would expand to accommodate needed doctors, nurses, and research. That called for volunteer chaplains. Well, she understood? The rest of the day he had spent in search of donors—yes, including those willing to give money, a necessary commodity, but those who would give of their services, as well. Response was good in Culverville, *excellent* in Pleasant Knoll. First to come through was none other than Harrington & Sons (son Emory serving as spokesman in the absence of his father who had gone to the farm) *Uncle Emory!* Had she gasped the words?

"None other!" Titus said with a low laugh, rich with joy. "The poor man wanted to tell your grandfather—*our* grandfather, Marvel—but was denied a hearing. Seems the institution had notified your uncle that room was available for his wife. And you know what happened next."

"Oh Titus, how wonderful! You and I—shouldn't we—*couldn't* we give, too? Wait—you made mention of that indirectly. Only I"m as guilty as Uncle Emory. I didn't listen, did I?"

"And you're not listening now!" Titus said, drawing her deliciously closer. "Just as you haven't before. So listen with your heart—"

Yes, yes, she must hear more. There was not a minute to lose.

Titus told her hurriedly. Back at the boardinghouse, things had fallen into place without effort, he said. Grandfather would see Uncle Emory tomorrow. Thomas, bolstered by need of B.J.'s team's confidence in his newfound skill, gave voice to interest in banking... first schooling, then on with the Harrington tradition. Uncle Emory, bursting with quiet pride, let his father claim credit. Having his own son draw close was enough. And Aunt Eleanore would know. Who knew what miracles the Lord would perform? Uncle Joseph was of like mind and, for the first time, took his wife Dorthea in tow. She was to help her sister-in-law, period! Daddy wished to contribute to the hospital's funding. Grandfather refused outright, preferring to restore the lands as the Almighty created them: a green-pastured Garden of Eden where living creatures could roam and eat daisies and wild eagles could soar without fear! But man must be practical, so there should be a cottage with roses clinging, like its newlywed inhabitants inside. It would be good, very good, just as God said.

"Oh Titus," Marvel breathed, snuggling closer, "it's perfect!"

"Well, almost. They've read our minds, I've read yours. Let's marry!"

Marvel withdrew slightly. "Oh darling, you promised not to press."

"Until we talked—and there's been too much talk already, too much waiting, longing. I don't understand. What have I done wrong?"

In the charmed circle of his arms, she felt the grueling frustration melting away. "It's not you, Titus. It's *my* battle within."

"Look here!" he said, taking her face between gentle hands. "No battle is won all alone. Husbands should be good for something. They're for a lifetime, you know. Oh," his voice became uncertain, "it's not—it can't be my choice of professions. I *can't* play deaf to God's call!"

"Oh no," Marvel cried. "I loved that. It's my calling, too! I want to be with you forever, no matter where life leads. Let me explain—"

"There's nothing to explain—nothing! I know every *page* of your life. Why wouldn't I? So we'll set a date when I get back."

Get back? "Where are you going that I can't go? Or is it secret?"

His embrace was so fierce Marvel was smothering—smothering in love, unable to think. "There *are* no more secrets between us! It's a three-day mission to Baylor regarding us both. So turn your prayers heavenward for me. We'll find that lost chord, Mrs. Smith!"

25

The Author and Finisher

Skies were cloudless, quiet-blue in their waiting as May's roses faded. June slipped in unnoticed by Marvel. Life kept her too busy for introspection, left time only for prayer—and phone calls which winged swift as homing pigeons between her and Titus in their three days apart. He had found both a doctor and a nurse, who in turn found three other such teams. Now Culverville Hospital could serve patients in a multitude of ways, one being a doctor well-versed in psychology who understood emotional instability. So Aunt Eleanore would have help. And his physical exam was completed. "In the pink," he said vaguely, "ready for the big assignment. Then 'We'll build a little nest, somewhere out in the West, and let the rest of the world go by'! Get your blood test, get ready...."

Dazed, Marvel could only murmur concerns. "I'm sorry, darling. I've been selfish, concentrating on *my* scars—forgetting *yours* are worse!"

Titus refused to listen. "Get that blood test, Mrs. Smith! You can't linger on the brink any longer. It's imperative *now*. Understand?"

No, she didn't. But yes, she would get the blood test—

With an "I love you, Marvelous!" Titus hung up, only to call back an hour later. "I've had a call from Mr. Corey." "Mr. Corey?" she parroted back as if she'd never heard of the name. Titus' laugh was low and intimate, but his words came through clear and strong. "Yes, our editor, Mr. A. Thomas Corey, our mentor. He

297

knows we're in touch about *The White Flags of Triumph*, our book—yours and mine together, you know!"

In a state of confusion, Marvel made good her promise concerning the blood test. Before she could change her mind, she checked the directory and with shaking fingers dialed the first doctor on the list—a Dr. Mason on the Culverville Hospital staff. She felt guilty, asking time for such a routine matter when seriously ill patients waited. The receptionist was enthusiastic. "Ooooh, a prenuptial exam! Oh yes," she breathed. "Doctor will see you this morning. We're getting more help—"

Once there, Marvel almost left but was called into a small room before there was time to attribute feelings to guilt or apprehension. The spectacled young practitioner drew blood samples and, in spite of her objections, insisted on doing a general check. "Too bad about the hysterectomy, but those things happen. Were there any lasting effects?"

And here she was again, pouring out her misgivings to a stranger. The doctor sat down beside her and said kindly, "I think you're making too much of this, Marvel—such a lovely name. This young man obviously loves you. So why do you punish yourself? Good heavens! Seeing all you've been through, it's understandable you'd suffer a delayed reaction. Why do I get the feeling that you know all these terms?"

"Oh, I do, I do!" Marvel said excitedly, as she rose to sit up. She told him all about her writing, the book-to-be, the perfect marriage ahead (stumbling only over her inability to conceive), and her and Titus' dreams for service—including Culverville Hospital.

The doctor became as excited as his patient. "So *you're* the ones in back of this. I thought I recognized the name. You two are godsends, dedicated, needed, and wise beyond your years. How good that life (although it seems unfair to our generation) taught us that 'wealth is in the heart, not the hand'! You have so much to live for. Consider all people your children, in need of your love." His optimism and enthusiasm were contagious, setting something in motion inside her—if only—if only—

"Belatedly, I tell you that I'm Dr. Mason and will be privileged to work with Chaplain and Mrs. Titus Smith. And, given my position, I shall counsel *you* here and now. First comes the indirect approach," he chuckled, "with which you are acquainted: the 'Baby Snooks' answering question with questions. Soooo, are you fretting over your condition or your future husband's reaction? I'll let you struggle with that while I go into my favorite act: the direct approach. 'Arise, take up your bed and walk'! I'll give you no seal of approval, regardless of how the blood work turns out, until you let this bugaboo out of hiding! *Now, do you tell Titus, young lady—or do I?*"

"I do, doctor!" Marvel sang out. He smiled and busied himself wiping imagined spots from his glasses. And she slipped out feeling buoyant. *Oh, dear God, thank You for sending me Dr. Mason. Oh, You knew he was just the right one!*

✳ ✳ ✳

At 16, how brave Marvel was, how courageous, how strong. She had known what was expected of her and did it. Then (quiveringly remembering), she had known what *she* wanted for herself and Titus and waited willingly with determination. All right, so life held hazardous detours. But wasn't God's purpose stronger than these? How fickle to fret over whims of fate! This plunge of despair was exactly what Dr. Mason called it: a bugaboo. So the older (but wiser?) girl within her willed Titus to call.

When the phone rang as expected, Marvel rushed with the answer he wanted to hear. But it wasn't Titus. It was a feverishly excited Mary Ann.

"Oh, I'm glad it's you, Marvel. I couldn't wait to write. Oh, isn't it wonderful, all of it—his bein' here. Titus, I mean? I'd have known him—and Jake did. They just took up where they left off—like we do. We're *all* cousins now! And—now don't interrupt me (*fat chance*, Marvel thought with a rush of affection)—I want you to know we'll be comin' since Grandfather hired Jake in the bank. Can't say for sure just when, but we'll stay. It's home to us. But I love school and *have* to finish now that there's a real purpose. And I still plan on teaching homemaking."

"Mary Ann, please take your time. I want to hear more, but you're talking in riddles—while I try to unriddle some problems here."

"There's no time—I'm meeting Jake. Titus can tell you everything. He's got it all written for that book of yours, anyway. Strange about the publisher being the one who did his children's books—and that woman's—what was her name? The Gypsy?"

Marvel caught her breath in surprise. "Why, it—it was Roma Nicoletta, *A Gypsy Incognito*—but what has the writer to do with us?"

"Don't be silly!" Mary Ann said impatiently. Then, "Oh, I'm sorry, cut my tongue out. I've gotta clean up my act—and you'll be there in the hospital to remind me. You knew my reading and research would get me ready for this. Oh, about the book—I remember now. The subtitle was *A Lady in Exile, Living Here with My Own Kind*. She is, too. Now, don't be coy with me. Titus has told you—and it'll fit into the book."

Mary Ann rushed on to other matters. . . . Oh, how wonderful Jake was. . . . They'd seen Kate Lynn, and soon they'd *all* be together just like they had planned. Auntie Rae had told her about the hubbub of Marvel's engagement (and her cousin bubbled with characteristic laughter, then paused).

"There's just one problem: the double-wedding we've dreamed about. My wedding wasn't exactly a young girl's dream, either! And our grandfather'll tolerate no more waiting—and neither will Titus! Fact is, you and Titus *have* to get married. Oh, I don't mean *that* way. It'll be because of this big assignment. I'm soooo thrilled. Oh, here's my husband!"

What was taking place? Dr. Mason was right—she must be suffering "delayed reaction." A part of her understood Mary Ann's run-on statement; another part did not. Mary Ann and Jake would return—as would Kate Lynn, who was now the wife and nurse of Dr. John Neal. Yes, that added up. Titus and John had become friends, so could it be that they were among those Dr. Mason mentioned? But the Gypsy piece mystified her. Well, Paul had the answer for women: "If they will learn any thing, let them ask their husbands. . . ." So let Chaplain Smith call home.

He did. "I'll be home tomorrow, my precious. News can wait!"

"But not my answer? I'm ready with questions, then saying *yes!*"

"Oh Marvel," he whispered, "ours is truly the *heartland* now!"

The family had gathered, each vying for attention, like thirsting flowers trying to absorb all the rain. Marvel wanted to hear every word, readying herself for Titus' return. But there was to be yet one more telephone call. To her surprise, it was Kate Lynn.

"Oh, Kate Lynn, your voice is music to my ears!" Marvel told her.

"More like music to my heart—after all these years! Just seeing Titus brought Bill back," she said with a catch in her voice. Then the lilt came back. "But I couldn't tell you before. You know Titus' love for surprise!"

Both Kate Lynn and John would join the Culverville staff—John as a surgeon, while she would continue in pediatrics. Of course, their duties would include counseling. And wow did they ever need help! Not exactly prestigious, but what "medical missionary" (and that was what the six of them would be: the Neals, Brothertons, and Smiths!) sought applause?

Kate Lynn bubbled on, repeating much of what Mary Ann had said, until the talk became more personal. "You're such a good listener—always were, Marvel, letting others impose. But that's why you're the just-right counselor, able to help in cases like your Aunt Eleanore's. But first me—I hope I've said the right things. It's John—he's sterile—uh—oh, not *impotent!*" (The embarrassed giggle of high school lightened her voice.) "But it's a flash in the pan as far as I'm concerned, honey. Who needs more babies when the world's bustin' with orphans to mother? It was the sloppy surgery—just a *hernia* for goodness sake! But I said to John, 'The Lord always has somethin' up His holy sleeve, and He's made you a more dedicated doctor for that.' Was I right?" Kate Lynn asked uncertainly. "Would it have altered your love for Titus?"

"Not a flash in the pan!" Marvel repeated, and they shared a laugh. "And you used somewhat the words I said to Titus—"

She bit the words in mid-sentence. Mercy! she shouldn't have said that. But Kate Lynn, reassured and happy, heard no slip of the tongue. "You see? That's why you're a wonderful counselor. You identify with what people say! *Now*, on to your aunt!"

Aunt Eleanore's problem was *delayed reaction* . . . not unusual in cases of shock. Just look at John (and *me*, wasn't that the phrase Dr. Mason had used?) . . . his, the atrocities of war added to messed-up surgery . . . hers, due to loss of a son. Kate Lynn suggested a program which might, just *might*, help Aunt Eleanore—one to which Marvel readily agreed.

"Except the time factor. Oh me! And Kate Lynn was gone.

* * *

Titus came home as scheduled, but their time alone was cut short. Both sensing that it would be, they huddled in the cocoon of darkness before reentering the front-yard gate. Marvel had rushed forward, Titus had rushed forward, and in unison cried, "Darling!" then laughed at colliding.

"Quick—they'll be here any minute, we both know that. So *when*?"

Shedding all reserve, Marvel Harrington clung tighter, feeling no embarrassment at all. "The sooner the quicker," she tried to tease, tiptoeing to kiss him instead. "But wait, there's something to tell you—"

"There's nothing I don't know. And nothing makes any difference!"

"You *know*? Who told you? I didn't write about my surgery."

"Of course you did—it's all in our book. Oh, I love *you*!"

It was hard to think, but she must. "But you haven't read it."

"Read every word. Our life's a corporate affair. Think I'm a copyboy only? Oh darling, what we have is too precious and permanent for anything so trivial to scissor apart! Ummm—" he murmured thickly, "your hair smells of lilacs. I'm an *aroma* being—should have a snoot for rooting out truffles!" The way he embraced her was no longer gentle, penetrating the depths of her soul. "We belong, oh, can't you see that?"

From the rapturous position against his chest, it was impossible to see anything else. "But Titus," she managed to whisper, "it was no trivial matter—when you—you thought you were flawed yourself."

"No," he said thoughtfully. "I was afraid it mattered to you—"

"*As you were, chaplain!*" she ordered. "So how does the book end?"

"Looking unto Jesus, the author and finisher of our faith..."

The intimate moment was broken by a subtle *ahem* from a most familiar throat. "Well," Titus sighed in mock surrender, "we might as well go up before Alexander Jay Harrington herds us upstairs with his cane!"

* * *

"The womenfolk here'll want to take over. You know how our Adam's rib ones are about weddings. They've been at it for months. But—*ahem*—first, more coffee, please, Duchess. I'll cover unfinished business. That's where we left off at our last general meeting!"

Grandfather's "unfinished business" followed proper parliamentary procedure, except that it never progressed to the "new": the *when* of the wedding date.

The two older sons had come to their senses. Emory would keep his wife, sticking by in "sickness and health." Joseph would see that *his* wife lent a hand. They'd resume duties as deacons—after all, they were ordained for life. There were times when a father just had to step in. And look what it had done for their children. Joseph's daughter, Erin, had discovered that one is an odd number, and divorce wasn't all it was cracked up to be. Thank God his younger sons and wives learned early, and Worth and Dale's children supported that claim. Well, Chaplain Smith seemed to agree about that. "So, Titus, we'll *praaaaay* I am right!"

"You are right, sir! I'll love and cherish our Marvel for life!"

26

Closer to Heaven

To Marvel's surprise, Aunt Dorthea answered when she called Aunt Eleanore's number. It was a greater surprise when Marvel was told that yes, her aunt would see her. "Just don't overstay," Uncle Joseph's wife whispered in caution when Marvel arrived.

"I'm expecting someone at my house soon—in fact, the man I'm engaged to marry," Marvel replied.

Piqued by curiosity, Aunt Dorthea ushered her inside the darkened hallway. Marvel groped her way forward in spite of her aunt's protests. "It's morning outside. You'll both go blind living holed up like moles."

"Wait! I need to hear more about this man. Wait, you *can't* go in!"

But Marvel was in already, thanks to her other aunt's call. "I knew your voice. But come closer and let me see you—my eyes are so weak." Daringly, Marvel opened the heavy drapes a fraction, enough to see Uncle Emory's wife in a tent-sized kimono, its floral material failing to conceal the voluptuous body underneath. "Oh, light's so unkind, so garish. I've gained pounds what with aging—and Duke." Her voice broke.

Marvel bent down and kissed her. "I understand. We've all suffered, lost so many dear ones. And we can't afford to lose *you*! We need you—especially now. You see, Aunt Eleanore, you're coming to my wedding!"

"Wedding? Whose wedding?" the weak voice asked vaguely. "I went somewhere else sometimes."

Oh, I *am* losing her, Marvel knew instinctively. So she rushed to tell all about Titus, her own fears, losses, and frustration—even concerning surgery—and then how love brought her through. Yes, she was young, but "so are you, not even 50 yet. So let's get those jewels from the vault, make ourselves beautiful for our men—young or mature!"

Oh, she *couldn't*, Aunt Eleanore murmured in sad protest . . . all that weight . . . her hair all a-frizzle. No wonder her husband never touched her! *Ugh!* she was all fat and horrible . . . her clothes hopelessly out of style. . . . But, well, there was Thomas—*he* loved her still.

She was weakening! "Oh, he's a wonderful boy, Aunt Eleanore—a son such as I'll never have. So," she said lightly, "now that you've posed some *fat* questions, let me help with *lean* answers for you!"

Aunt Dorthea gasped when her sister-in-law laughed.

Marvel talked quickly about eating wisely (food nutritious but short on pastries and fats) . . . exercising gently (stretching, then walking indoors before short walks in the cool of each evening—with Uncle Emory, of course!) . . . hair care (oh soft-water shampoos, lemon rinses at home—salons could come later). The prize? Why, her wedding, she said.

At the door, Aunt Dorthea said slyly she would take part in the program "just to lend moral support." Marvel refrained from smiling, promising copies of *Stretching to Survive*, instead.

The outside light was so blinding that she shielded her eyes with an uplifted hand. "Doing counseling, sweetheart? B.J. told me. He's my spy."

"Titus!" was all she could manage with her silly heart thrumming like a drumbeat at the sound of his voice. Titus, her man of surprises.

"Don't move. You're that picture I carried, the mascot that saw me through. Here's the car. Hop in. I'll allow two minutes for reports on the patients, then we have to *tell* the family—not *ask*. We have just one week before leaving. I have my orders, so yours are to plan!"

But she didn't know his plans, Marvel had gasped. Oh, she *would*, Titus told her masterfully, then said, "You have one minute left!" Breathlessly, she told of Aunt Eleanore, then listened in shock to his words. They struck in thunderbolt swiftness, taking her power of speech.

And then she was zany with joy. How mysteriously God made His moves! She and Titus had crossed that great gulf together, and the unicorns came back unafraid. Here, of all places, in the luminous warmth of bright sunshine, which promised summer eternal. Of course! They could serve their Creator's purpose anywhere *together*—even in California! It all came back in a twinkling, an ocean ruffled in dark blues and silver, white sailboats scissoring the waves. The trilogy of assignment would be deliciously demanding, impossible by human standards—made possible only through God. And there would be moments by His own arrangement when they could anchor their problems in the harbor down on the seashore alone, there to hear gulls calling above the sighs of the seas. Sometimes they would build sand castles, wade out in the surf at low tide, or lie counting the stars beneath the shelter of palms. When fog came, they'd roll in a blanket—*married*, in love!

Marvel stretched and leaned against Titus. "Mmmmm," she murmured, rubbing her cheek into his chest. He was right, nothing else mattered.

But something else did. "Marvel, there's just one question." His voice sounded tense and strained. "Will this remind you of Philip?"

"Oh, how can you wonder?" she asked in relief. "You've read it all in my book. You were declared dead—Philip was only your memory."

With a laugh of triumph, he drew her breathlessly closer. "Look!" he called loud enough for both aunts to hear. "The lady loves me!" And to Marvel he whispered, "I just needed to hear you say that in person." And lowering his voice even more, he said humbly, "Thank You, dear Lord in heaven, for this wonderful moment with the woman Thou gavest me."

Titus lived up to his promise. He handled revelation of their future plans with the precision and objectivity of a news briefing, allowing no time for questions. "Listen in later for full coverage," he might as well have said. Blood drained from the faces of listeners, but they did not panic as Marvel had thought they might. It was sudden. And *California*?

Commander Titus Lee Smith could have retired on a medical discharge but chose to remain as naval chaplain for special assignments. At present, maneuvers were in progress in preparation for leaving for an undisclosed destination—presumably in the area of Korea, where civil war was raging. Lest the southern sector be gobbled up by the north, the Allies would be entering the conflict. It was only a matter of when. The men would be in grave need of counsel. So, enter one Chaplain Smith. The *Iwa Jima* was docked-in-waiting, soon to be joined by crew, fighter planes, and run-silent-run-deep submarines. Yes, the vessel symbolized the agony of grinding battle, but spelled out in blood the triumph of faithful-to-the-death U.S. Marines. The college lad, in a glowing vision of peace, said cockily, "I can take it all in my stride," when tapped on the shoulder for the one-time assignment in Spain as a foreign reporters. Then he went back home to marry his sweetheart to live in a world gift-wrapped in the tissue of dreams. Only it had not happened that way. He'd seen it all. . . .

Commissioned, ordained, and experienced now, Chaplain Smith fit the order to report for the California assignment, prepared to serve Catholics, Protestants (of all order), Jews, and those of no faith at all. Each agreed that the church needed *changing*—differing on *how* from the start. When the vessels left on their mission, Chaplain Smith's mission shifted to Romanians seeking asylum, otherwise known as displaced Gypsies. This second assignment came from both government and the World Council of Churches—with a *third* job prompting him from the wings. Associated Press wanted on-the-scene reporters, as did Editor Corey, the churches, et al. In short, Chaplain and Mrs. Titus Lee Smith would be combining business with pleasure, honeymooning and serving—weaving the power of fact and the drama of fiction, in their eternal search for God's truth. . . .

"California!" Grandfather gasped. "The land of earthquakes!"

"When?" Grandmother asked almost simultaneously with Mother who whispered, "Where?" while Daddy said, "Just so our baby bear's happy."

"Oh, I *am* happy!" Marvel sang out like a song. "Everything's more wonderful than we ever dreamed. And please, Grandfather, don't worry. We survived and came back to you. It's God's will that we go away, but He's promised our safe return in three months. And Mother, you'll never believe this, but does Elm Street sound familiar? The Gypsies are there."

The faces of her beloved family melted in resignation at sight of their Marvel's luminous face and the shimmer of anticipation on that of the dedicated man gently holding her hand. One did not argue with God.

"Elm Street, Dale—imagine!" Mother exclaimed, caught up in excitement. He imagined. Then together they both imagined. Soon Uncle Worth, Auntie Rae, and B.J. joined them—and all commenced talking at once. "Elm Street...schools, churches, and hospitals...and, of course, the slums they had ventured into...the lives they had helped save in the quake."

Titus was laughing and kissing Marvel who, although near-blinded with happiness, was sure the elder Harringtons were smoothing away each other's tears. After all, they had a prior claim on this family. So didn't it stand to reason that they set the example of life's golden-age "bonus"? But, *ahem!* one must be practical, too.

"Attention!" Grandfather commanded, stabbing the floor with his seldom-used cane. "We still don't cotton to Gypsies—"

"Oh, I do, don't I, Dale darling? Where is my violin?" Mother cried.

Soft, sweet, and wild the music rang out, and the world did a fade-out in song....

* * *

There was a bustle of preparations. Grandmother Harrington (supposing herself unquestionably in charge) said the bridal gown—elaborate or simple—*must* be special. Touches of lace ...whispers of silk or elegant satin...a veil with train or without...high neckline, low, square-shape or V...off-the-shoulder or demure...long sleeves or short...

She fussed about, looking harried. "Oh, Marvel sweetheart, it's enough to send us rushing you to Reno!"

The needless frenzy had gone unnoticed by the bride-to-be until then. "Oh, Grandmother dear, let me set your mind at rest. You were the ideal conspirator in bringing Titus and me together for keeps. But there'll be no big wedding. There's no time or desire—that's *final!*"

Grandmother was unconvinced. She was not one to be won over easily but she had a special soft spot for her granddaughter Marvel, who was firm and resolute. What would become of trimmings already purchased? Use them on a gown for Aunt Eleanore, Marvel said (adding what a service that would be). And, as for the big ceremony, it would not be canceled, just postponed. By October, Mary Ann and Jake would be back to stay like they themselves would be—and they would have that long-planned double wedding.

Mother and Auntie Rae were ecstatic then. In October the mums would be blazing in bronze and gold, sweet gum leaves decked out in full glory. The cottage would be built according to plan, bulbs planted as well as hollyhock seeds—and there *must* be morning glories of heavenly blue in Beulah Land. A lilac bush for their unicorns? Oh yes, they agreed—with other surprises. An overwhelmed Marvel wondered just what else there could be as she left the scene to do her own planning.

Conversations with Titus were mostly by phone, as assignments demanded seminars, briefings, and documents galore. But love such as theirs required no "visible proof." Once he asked haltingly how she felt about planes, and she knew then they would be flying. "That they're here to stay!" she said, feeling no fear of the flight. And Titus said softly, "Oh, it's not exactly a stranger to *me*, Mrs. Smith. We're closer to heaven up there!"

The guest list would include only the family. And that was enough, goodness knows, Grandmother now agreed. As for the house, forget it! How thoughtful, how fitting, that Titus should prefer the Culverville Baptist Church. The hotel had a far different clientele, fewer guests since the veterans' facility neared completion and patients were transferred to the one finished wing. But there were—well, some surprises. And Aunt Eleanore did indeed respond to their offers of help.

"Mercy me!" Grandmother groaned, secretly pleased. "That woman leaves us no time to think." She, Mother, and Auntie Rae took turns seeing Uncle Worth's wife through exercises, shopping, and beauty parlor appointments—with a slimming-down Aunt Dorthea at their heels. Aunt Eleanore chose a bat-wing, long-sleeved pattern for the green miracle nylon fabric her mother-in-law "just happened" to have. "She'll be sporting that filigree triple-stand gold necklace—stupendous," Grandmother said in pride.

"She'll be stuffed on tranquilizing junk," Grandfather warned darkly.

"It's all right, Father Harrington," Auntie Rae said with a bright smile. "It's part of Eleanore's treatment. Mary Ann said Kate Lynn talked with Dr. Mason. It's his prescription, and she's getting better."

That was certainly true, they all agreed. Best be grateful for God's blessings instead of pining for what one couldn't have. Love made them richer than bankrolls, gave them faith to weather life's storms.

Mary Ann called with glowing best wishes, blissfully happy. Just recently she would have beaten her chest in remorse at being unable to stand up with Marvel. But life had found a new center. She was a rush of youth and energy, still wearing her honeymoon smile. Mary Ann and Jake redoubled their schedules ... went to school both night and day, so they could complete their studies before fall. *Then* they'd have that grand ceremony. Oh, there would be others before it: Jake's ordination as deacon (Yes, honest engine! she said)... and then graduation. All "dolled up" and ready for their new jobs ahead: bank, church, volunteer work at the hospital. But wait, there was more! Younger men where entering the Veterans' Administration facility, and Mary Ann had qualified under civil service for full-time teaching of reading as a part of the rehab program. "Oh Marvel, I used to think I could do nothin'. And this is not *nothin'* in God's eyes! And He's thrown love in to boot!"

"No, that's *not* nothing!" Marvel laughed, giddy with a love of her own.

B.J. was Marvel's shadow, reporting on family members (Grandfather was taken with Titus, just like Thomas—he knew so much about sports and was such a "good sport" on his own). Why, Grandfather would be the head cantor if Marvel asked him. He'd decided all churches had *some* "right teachin." ... "Which reminds me, you just have to see *this!*"

This was a paper B.J. had finished, based on materials Titus had sent. Marvel scanned her cousin's "In-depth Religion" piece quickly.

Now, once upon a time—a Roman Emperor named Constantine had a vision just before marching to war, he claimed. All men should become one, God had whispered. ...But words can win wars or can lose them. Constantine won in his new-formed councils. All yessed his decisions, and Christians were "unified." ... But were their hearts made more pure? The empire split like an atom. Converts? Maybe, but politics crept under the door, and the shine of imperial gold beckoned. Greek Orthodox pitched tents east, Roman Catholic west, in a Genesis sort of way (or, as the real victors might have snickered: "One flew east; one flew west. The rest flew over the cuckoo's nest!"). Unfamiliar with Christ's teachings and biblical accounts of organized church, leaders marched all through rivers by force in instant baptism. The ignorant, not daring dissent, were like rough boards sprayed with bright paint—with nothing changed underneath. Now, Constantine may have meant well, but his efforts all but wiped Christianity into oblivion. But God set His remnants to work....

"Oh honey!" Marvel told a glowing B.J., "we have something here!" For a quick glance had shown that his high-school term paper went on to the efforts of missionaries, Franciscans, Moravians, the Reformation ... quarrels, bribes, downright evils, and then their splintering results ... causes and effects ... and finally, each church spelled out in detail. "I have a heavenly plan—one I'll share with you later."

27

"Near You"

Although a revised ending had reached the editor, Marvel felt that once more it had to be changed. Not changed, she mused— just extended to include the demanding but wonderful life her two main characters would lead, fulfilling God's purpose together in their hoped-and-waited-for dream. The notes Titus sent B.J. pointed up the need for shedding all preconceived notions and showed why they must serve all.

Mr. Corey listened when Marvel called, then laughed with genuine pleasure. There would be millions of opportunities. "The sky's *not* the limit" for writers such as they, he said with conviction. More and more columns: "And try to keep 'em happy, honey. Readers all need it. We're facin' another war because this world hasn't learned how to live with peace!" Maybe best reach for the next generation . . . take the oodles of children's books she and Titus would write. The *Now, Once Upon a Time* series was under consideration for state textbook adoption. Oh, religion held all the answers, so the missionary work would "carve out readers in stone"!

"But it must wait, Marvel. *The White Flag of Triumph*'s finished. By now a literary review's out—winnin' us all prestige, you two as authors, and head-scratchin' good for me as your editor. Why, they're all lookin' at me like I was Columbus, sayin' I'd found a new world. Now, don't go sayin' you don't hanker to fortune and fame! Look at it this way: Reachin' out with feelin' makes readers listen about Christian faith!"

"But I told you there might be a last-minute change—"

"And there was—by your real-life Chaplain Smith! His account is congruent. Yep, you two are the *perfect match!*"

Marvel smiled through a mist of tears, understanding at last. That night in his bakers-dozenth of daily telephone calls, Titus listened to her report of the conversation. "'Perfect match'—but, of course, darling. The whole world will know tomorrow!"

Tomorrow. Then in unison they whispered their beloved John 21:25:

> And there are also many other things which Jesus did, the which if they should be written every one, I suppose that even the world itself could not contain the books that should be written. *Amen.*

* * *

Everyone said it was a lovely wedding. In a state of complexity, the Harrington women were undaunted—"feeling saintly," their men said. Why not? They reasoned. After all, God created order from chaos in the same number of days. He rolled back the darkness, lighted the face of the earth with constellations untold—He who could bind the sweet influences of Pleiades or loose the bands of Orion. Without rest, male and female He created and gave them dominion over animals of His garden. Surely it followed that He gave elders charge over their young. It was, therefore, their duty to arrange a simple wedding in the same number of days. Gifts? The long-delayed "big gift" of Christmas saved for a wedding gift would now be a housewarming gift. "No secret, that Cyclops!" the Squire said of the television set.

Marvel wore the heavenly blue morning glory dress to match the blue of her eyes—the dress Titus loved and remembered from his graduation here in the same church of high-arched ceilings and stained-glass windows. Incredible—a miracle of God's hand. The rafters echoed their soft-spoken vows, and the windows reflected their long-ago dreams. The radiant bride, feeling the poignant elegance of the single-strand pearl necklace against the hollow of her throat, glanced once at her ring finger. There the opulent beauty of the heirloom pearl whispered "Forever." Just a simple wedding? Oh, no—she was a princess in a fabulous gown giving her heart to her prince!

Year later, far removed form the simple scene at the altar, where the mellow drone of Honorable O. Marcus Bradford, retired chaplain, who—*God bless him!*—came back to officiate, the couple would remember and sing:

> If was just a wedding in June, but, oh, what
> it seemed to me!
> It was like a royal affair with everyone
> there, when you said "I do" to me.

He laid hands on the heads of the kneeling newlyweds and said in reverence: "I now ordain Chaplain and Mrs. Titus Lee Smith into God's service. 'And what God hath joined in holy matrimony, let no man put asunder. The Lord bless thee, and keep thee; the Lord lift up his countenance upon thee, and give thee peace'—and in peace, bring you safely back home." Guests managed to keep smiles in place until those words.

Control slipped away then. All burst into tears—including Aunt Eleanore (mascara no longer paramount in moments like this).

The Smith Hotel was emptied and waiting in hushed grandeur—until the backslapping, laughing wedding party arrived. The waiter looked puzzled, then took it in stride. The Harringtons pleased him as, diets forgotten, they ate something of everything—except the commander and his delicate, terribly frail bride. He took time to admire her long shaft of blonde hair that looked like a sheet of gold in the pale light. Well, after the honeymoon there would be banana splits topped off with chocolate—that is, unless another war engulfed them. Oh, those rations!

But now, in a flurry of footsteps, he got on with his business. Let them live on their island surrounded by borrowed mirth while there was yet peace.

Marvel and Titus, suspended, floating in wonder, would never recall one bite that they ate. They *belonged* to each other. At long last they did!

When Alexander Jay Harrington checked his gold watch, they knew time had come. Soon the newlywed couple—their Marvel—would go. Voices dropped and throats tightened in dreaded farewell. Except for B.J., whose pitch always rose when he was upset. "I know what *one* surprise is—persimmons! Imagine our grandfather who claims those trees are just pests! But he knows you like 'em. I'm a *pest*, too, Titus. You can ask Marvel. Oh, Thomas and I'll promise you one thing when the really big weddin' comes. We're gonna treat you to cat's-eye stew at the feast!"

Titus laughed, laid an arm on his young shoulder, and said in true-comrade manner, "Toss in anything, as long as it's not Spam!"

*　*　*

Marvel had changed quickly in the semidark powder room of the hotel. The "surprise"—an autumn-rose suit stitched by the creative fingers of her grandmother, mother, and aunt—was elegant, sleekly cut in the "new look" preceding the Korean War. And then the accessories—so glamourous they begged a long cry: a sky-blue lace jabot with matching gloves and a whimsical pillbox hat. Last came the traditional blue garter with an attached note that caused her to blush.

In the taxi Titus reached for his bride immediately. "This is the moment I've waited for all my life," he whispered humbly and proudly. Marvel could only nod as she surrendered herself completely to her husband's long-patient now impatient embrace. God had brought them together at last. Now nothing could draw them apart. "You were so marvelous, my Marvelous, my 'beautiful lady in blue,' I forgot my lines—and to give you your white Bible. And it has a pressed four-leaf clover on top!"

"Mmmm—I forgot everything, too." And when he gathered her closer, Marvel laughed, remembering the garter he was sure to tease her about.

All too quickly they were airborne. The giant naval transport plane circled in silver-winged flight, dipping once, Marvel suspected, above Beulah Land's emerald green. *Green*, she thought giddily: the signal for safety . . . the go-ahead sign for green pigments of summertime's leaves. Then would come cautious yellows of September, followed by fiery crimsons of October. Oh, the old hotel would be blazing with glory for the big day!

"A penny for your thoughts on your nuptial flight," Titus whispered.

When Marvel told him, Titus explained, "The brightness is always there, hidden by chlorophyll's green—life-sustaining, but masking the color until daylight strips masks it all away. A good analogy for life—"

"Oh, our tree!" Marvel remembered. "Even the trunk will be gone."

"Oh, trees have hearts—they remember," Titus said without sadness. "One log will light up our wedding. The others will wait at our corner of Beulah Land—'bank' on our grandfather's saw."

Marvel heard her own joyous laugh. "You handle everything so perfectly, bring together our past and our present—no detail overlooked."

"Your husband's a genius," he laughed with her. "At least, in the eyes of his wife's Marvelous eyes. Their editor's too—unless he assigns T. Lee to take a census of all the dogs in Monterey Peninsula—"

"He *what*?" She suddenly sat erect. "You have to be teasing."

"Well, the WPA put a young writer named John Steinbeck to sniff that out and keep his pen busy. But he sniffed out much more for his novel—that compelling account of migration in *The Grapes of Wrath*."

She nodded. "Yes, the novel. But I didn't know about dog counting—"

Titus pulled her head back to his shoulder. "Relax. You'll read all about it when our book wins the Nobel prize and the Pulitzer prize for fiction. Only we'll not tell them it's based on exhaustive research and living. That's *our* secret—and exhaustion? Forget it, and (he hummed) 'The toils of the road will seem nothing, when I get to the end of the way'! Lovely hymn. And how about 'L'Envoi'?"

"Rudyard Kipling's poem we had to memorize or fail senior English. I'm thankful for the discipline. It's comforting now."

"Let's try it together. Keep your eyes closed and just follow."

> When Earth's last picture is painted, and
>   the tubes are twisted and dried,
> When the oldest colors have faded, and the
>   youngest critic has died,
> We shall rest, and faith, we shall need it—
>   lie down for an eon or two,

Till the Master of All Good Workmen shall
    set us to work anew!

And those that were good shall be happy;
    they sit in a golden chair;
They shall splash at a ten-league canvas
    with brushes of comet's hair;
They shall find real saints to draw from—
    Magdalene, Peter, and Paul;
They shall work for an age at a sitting and
    never grow tired at all!

And only the Master shall praise us, and
    only the Master shall blame;
And no one shall work for money, and no
    one shall work for fame;
But each for the joy of the working, and
    each in his separate star
Shall draw the Thing as he sees It for the
    God of Things as they are!

They grew silent then. Contented and happy, Marvel snuggled
closer, her hand gripped closely in his. Feeling released from
earth's gravity, they soared on the wings of their love. Soon
enough they would be back to a far more complicated world in a
much less rarefied air. "Mendin' fences" together, their grandfather said.

And then above the drone of the airplane came a familiar
strain—one which forever after Chaplain and Mrs. Titus Smith
would remember as "our honeymoon song."

    If my life could be spent near you—
    I'd be more than content, near you—
    Dar-ling, make my life worthwhile,
    By tell-ing me that I'll—
    Spend the rest of my life—
    NEAR YOU.

Far below lay the restless blue of the ocean, spread white-capped and waiting. But above the sky was without clouds.

"I love you, I love you," they repeated in reverence—feeling near to the heart of God.

HARVEST HOUSE PUBLISHERS

For the Best in Inspirational Fiction

RUTH LIVINGSTON HILL CLASSICS

Bright Conquest
The Homecoming (mass paper)
The Jeweled Sword
The South Wind Blew Softly (mass paper)

June Masters Bacher
PIONEER ROMANCE NOVELS

Series 1

1 Love Is a Gentle
Stranger
2 Love's Silent Song
3 Diary of a Loving Heart

4 Love Leads Home
5 Love Follows the Heart
6 Love's Enduring Hope

Series 2

1 Journey to Love
2 Dreams Beyond
Tomorrow
3 Seasons of Love

4 My Heart's Desire
5 The Heart Remembers
6 From This Time Forth

Series 3

1 Love's Soft Whisper
2 Love's Beautiful Dream

3 When Hearts Awaken

4 Another Spring
5 When Morning Comes
Again
6 Gently Love Beckons

HEARTLAND HERITAGE SERIES

No Time for Tears
Songs in the Whirlwind
Where Lies Our Hope
Return to the Heartland

ROMANCE NOVELS

The Heart That Lingers, *Bacher*

Brenda Wilbee
SWEETBRIAR SERIES

> Sweetbriar
> The Sweetbriar Bride
> Sweetbriar Spring

CLASSIC WOMEN OF FAITH SERIES

> Shipwreck!
> Lady Rebel

Lori Wick
THE CAMERON ANNALS

> A Place Called Home
> A Song for Silas
> The Long Road Home
> A Gathering of Memories

THE CALIFORNIANS

> Whatever Tomorrow Brings
> As Time Goes By
> Sean Donovan

THE KENSINGTON CHRONICLES

> The Hawk and the Jewel

MaryAnn Minatra
THE ALCOTT LEGACY

> The Tapestry
> The Masterpiece (coming Winter 1994)

Ellen Traylor
BIBLICAL NOVELS

> Esther
> Joseph (mass paper)
> Moses
> Joshua

Available at Christian Bookstores